Fuse
Jackson Traine Book Three
Terry Hayman

Fiero Publishing

What came before

THIS IS JACKSON TRAINE: Book 3. If you haven't read Books 1 and 2 (and ideally the prequel novella, *Unglued*), you should do that now.

But if you're too eager to start at the beginning, or you read those earlier books some time ago and want a quick refresher, here it is.

Jackson Traine, a psychologist with a therapy practice and part-time teaching gig at the University of Washington, meets scientist Lena Cortland the same day a person from Jackson's past shows up and tries to kidnap them both.

It causes a lab accident which unleashes Jackson's ability to time travel back ten minutes when traumatized. He also learns the big brother he thought was dead is alive but apparently held captive. So, Jackson uses his newfound ability to go looking for him.

He fights gangsters, the CIA, and an evil doctor's private army to finally arrive at a SCIF (Sensitive Compartmented Information Facility) under the Capitol building in Washington, DC, where he is forced to offer his services to the doctor in order to save the people he loves.

Buckle up. Here we go...

1
Pieces of my heart

THIS WAS WHAT MY limited time travel ability had brought me to. While I waited to be marched out of the US Capitol basement, the four pieces of my heart who'd been held at gunpoint shakily exited the building and parted ways.

My sister, Kansas, called an Uber to get back to the apartment she'd been snatched from twelve days earlier.

My treacherous best friend, Jude Spiegelman, found his car and drove back to the George Bush Center for Intelligence, AKA CIA headquarters, across the river in Langley, Virginia.

The love of my life, Lena Cortland, let one of Bent's minions drive her to the airport for a flight back to Seattle. My office administrator, Megan, went with her.

Colonel Jian and the supposedly-shot-dead Wenling? I'll cover them later.

What's critical to understand at this point is that when psychiatrist Dr. Uwe Bent tricked the people I cared about most deeply into becoming pawns in his game, he exposed not only my vulnerability but his evil. It gave Lena, Kansas, Megan, and Jude a clear villain to fight.

If they chose to.

And because each one of their choices had a huge impact on how everything turned out, I'm breaking my convention of telling you only things I experienced directly. Instead, I'm mixing together things I learned after the fact with what I know of the key people involved to give their perspectives.

Their chapters are named after them.

All the other chapters are my personal experiences.

Clear?

Good. Because we're starting the big wrap-up of this saga with the non-me perspective of Dr. Lena Cortland.

You'll remember her as a beautiful, half-Persian doctor of theoretical physics, a professor at Berkley, and the researcher who was finally unraveling a quantum explanation of time travel. Not a woman to be cowed by Bent's power.

Also, she and I had pretty much owned each other's hearts from the first moment she sat in on one of my university lectures about PTSD last year.

If there was anyone who was going to fight for me, it was her.

2

Lena

On the rumbling plane back from DC, Lena sat in slowly fading shock beside Megan McKenna, Jackson's red-haired, freckle-faced office manager. Megan chattered on about how she administered psychological tests to Jackson't clients.

No, you used to *administer them,* Lena corrected her silently. *Before Jackson let himself get tangled up with Zhou Wenling's craziness. Physically as well as metaphorically.*

Yuck.

Even through the last shock of what had happened in the basement SCIF, the mental image of Jackson rolling around in bed with that Asian chameleon sent ice through Lena's veins. It made her want to curse and rage and spit into her plastic airline cup of Sprite. She should have asked for something harder.

At least Bent had shot Wenling dead in front of everyone. That should have horrified Lena but didn't. It felt like cosmic karma.

Though with Wenling dead, the funding for Lena's research was dead too. AS IF THAT MATTERED ANYMORE.

"Have you ever watched this?" Megan asked, leaning into Lena's left arm like she'd find comfort there.

That was seeking water from a dry well.

But for Jackson's sake, Lena turned her head and saw Megan held up her electronic tablet. The girl pointed to a movie that United Airlines had available via their Wi-Fi service. *Encanto.* Lena had read about it. A Disney movie about a teenage girl who's not magical, trying to love her family members who are.

Like Lena, a normal scientist, trying to love a man who can jump backward in time. *Please stick the knife in a little deeper, Megan.*

"Haven't watched it," Lena said.

"I've heard it's fantastic. Guy who wrote the songs did *Hamilton*, you know?"

"Really."

"Totally. But with more Spanish. He did *In the Heights*, too. And *Moana*?"

Lena ground her teeth. "Why aren't you more...?"

"Sad? Upset? Scared out of my mind? I am. Totally. But I figure if I can just not think too much about it..."

"So you watch happy stuff."

Megan beamed at her like her heart overflowed at being understood. "Yes!"

"Okay."

Lena turned away with her stomach roiling. Because Megan had a *right* to look away from everything that had happened. She was innocent. She hadn't caused it. While Lena, when you got right down to it, had. If she'd never sought out Jackson to ask him about his past-life regression work, he'd never have come to her lab, never been shocked by the super-collider, never learned he could time travel or that his supposedly dead brother was actually alive.

"I've been thinking," Megan said.

"About...?"

"Jackson's apartment. And his office."

The mundanity of it broke something inside Lena and she found her eyes suddenly watery. She turned away from Megan, grabbed the napkin from under her plastic cup, and pretended to blow her nose, while she furiously dabbed at her eyes and cheeks.

When she was done, she heard Megan murmur, "I'm sorry."

Lena turned back to see Megan's own eyes were brimming. The girl tried to wipe them, but it was no good. They spilled down her flushed cheeks and made Megan's freckles stand out even more than usual, making her look like a twenty-something Raggedy Ann doll.

Great. Now Lena was the monster who made Jackson's innocent young office administrator cry.

"I think it's good to cry," Lena offered. *Hypocrite!* She'd also tried to be compassionate and understanding with Jackson and his PTSD. How long had that lasted?

But Megan accepted it with a quavering smile and nodded hard. Then she spoke on, even as she located her own napkin and rubbed at the tears and the drip from her nose. "I think...you should move in there."

"What? I don't think—"

"Because he's going to be gone...a long time. Right? But when he comes back..." Megan let it trail off like she was hoping Lena would reassure her about an impossible-to-predict future.

Lena dropped her chin slightly, in what a hopeful person might take as a nod of agreement.

"When he comes back," Megan plowed on, "he'll need a place to live. And an office. And you know how hard it is to find good ones in Seattle?"

"How do you propose—"

"Oh, I've dealt with both landlords—the one for the office and the one for his apartment. They're both teddy bears. If I give each of them a note, signed by Jackson"—she looked around, then furtively pointed at her own chest—"they will totally let you look after the places until he's back."

The energy and right-on-the-surface hope of this Raggedy Ann office worker made Lena shut her mouth for a moment in perplexed awe. Because *of course* this was the sort of person Jackson would have recruited and won the undying loyalty of. Megan was, in her own way, a younger version of Jackson, minus the social anxiety, amazing memory, and ability to time travel. She was bold and open, loyal and smart. She led with her heart and didn't give up, even in the face of terrifying odds.

It finally made Lena, with her privileged upbringing, blush with acute embarrassment and grip the metal end of the armrest between them.

"Oh no," Megan gasped as she saw it. "What did I say wrong? Is it the money? Because Jackson got amazing deals on both places."

"I'm embarrassed by my lack of faith. And courage."

"Courage? You mean about the landlords?"

Lena shook her head, released her grip on the armrest, and held out her hand until Megan proffered hers. Lena took the proffered hand and held it with both of hers. She spoke very low, so the people in front and behind them on the plane wouldn't be able to hear. "You realize Jackson's not coming back here on his own?"

Megan's lips trembled, but she stuck out her lower lip as she matched Lena's near-whisper. "You don't know all the people who've tried to stop him before."

"But you saw what made him cave in and agree to go with that madman, right? Us. You, me, his sister, his university friend. He's not going anywhere if he thinks we're vulnerable."

Megan shook her head. "Maybe they'll just keep him for a while. He does what they want, and they let him go."

"The madman was ready to shoot all of us to make Jackson go with him. He's not letting him go. Ever."

Now Megan swallowed and started trembling again. "Then...what?"

"We have to get him out."

"What?"

"Before they do irreparable harm to his mind or body. You, me, his sister, a group of security experts I know—we have to find out where they're holding Jackson and get him out."

"The police?" Megan had dropped her voice to a whisper, like she feared others were listening.

"Maybe. And the FBI. But we don't have a lot to give them other than a missing person report."

Megan's eyes went wide. "What about what they did to us?"

"Who did? You got their names?"

"Samson? Simpson?" Megan screwed up her face. "It was Samson. The crazy doctor with the gun."

"He told me his name was Berkley."

"What?"

"He was messing with us."

"And in that room...?"

"His name never came up. He did the talking. One name he mentioned—the group or experiment or something he wanted Jackson to join."

"Scatter! Yes!" Megan looked around and lowered her voice. "I remember that."

Lena nodded. "It's a place to start. And I've got some other ideas."

"Like?"

Lena turned her face back to front and leaned her head back. I need to think them through."

"In Jackson's apartment? His office?"

"Yes."

She heard the audible sigh of contentment as Megan settled back into her own seat to watch her Disney movie. Her right arm pressed against Lena's like they were joined now. Comrades in arms. Them against the machine.

Except Lena had a gut feeling it wasn't truly a machine they were facing. It was one slightly unhinged, dangerous douchebag who was wielding a bunch of power. Even more, now that he had Jackson Traine and his time-traveling power.

What he couldn't know was how much Lena needed Jackson and how far she'd go to get him back.

Also, that she knew more about how Jackson's power worked than anyone else.

And, like the douchebag, had access to powerful allies.

In the same way she'd built her career one brilliant piece of research at a time, she would put together a rescue plan piece by piece. The first step was fully understanding what she was up against.

Lena rubbed her foot against the tan Everlane Weekender bag stuffed under the seat in front of her, where she'd found a quickly scrawled note. It had instruction on how to contact her most powerful ally. Her ace in the hole.

3

Kansas

Lena's ace in the hole, Kansas Traine, got out of her Uber ride in front of her "apartment building."

The two-story industrial building sat on the southwest end of a wooded, high-tech corridor. It was just northwest of Annapolis Junction and exactly 2.6 miles from the black-windowed NSA headquarters in Fort Meade.

Kansas wavered on the pavement in the dark sweater, jeans, and boots they'd pulled from her own cupboards to dress her for that show in the Capitol basement. Then she took a deep breath and marched for the front door like she did *not* feel she was being watched by Bent's goons from somewhere.

But on that twenty-foot walk over cracked concrete, her feet stuttered, and she almost tripped. Her gaze flicked about as she recovered. She took in the line of trees behind the building, the road that curved away on either side to other industrial buildings. There were windows. There were shadows in the trees. Most of all, there was the building itself. Her mind screamed that was danger incarnate. Her heart sped up to near bursting, wanting her to turn and run. But instead, she made herself keep walking until she reached the building's main entrance. She jammed her key into the door's keyhole.

This key they'd oh-so-graciously returned to her when they released her.

Like it was no big thing.

Like she'd been through nothing at all.

Like...

The lock wasn't *opening!*

As she struggled with it, her bloodless lips quivered, and she almost broke down in tears.

This, she thought furiously, must be what Jackson had been struggling with all these years. Visceral memories. The feel and smell of the thug who'd grabbed her out of her room in this building. And the noise of it! The crashing. The grunting. Even though she'd half-known it was coming, she'd exploded in terror and struggled like a wild animal until her abductor clobbered her on the side of her head, stunning her. Then he'd zip-tied her wrists and physically lifted her up over his shoulders. No small feat, given she was a big-boned five foot ten. But she was all brains, not brawn. Helpless in a physical encounter. Powerless then. Powerless later when they—

Click.

The lock turned, and Kansas pushed her way into the vestibule. She forced herself to stop quivering and breathe. But she couldn't. Blood pounded in her ears. She wanted to keel over on the faux marble floor.

Get it together!

One step more and she'd be able to look into the first of four main work areas in the building. The first, through a door to the right, held all the software engineers. They'd be pounding away at their computer keyboards or arguing about something with their fellow coders. She could hear the buzz of them now. Geek talk.

It should have been comforting. Something she was used to. A pale imitation of the intense hives in the NSA itself where she worked. Had worked. But everything around her now thrummed with danger and the unfamiliar. Did she even have a job in the NSA anymore, given how she'd just disappeared? Had forces inside the NSA somehow *approved* her capture? If not, why hadn't the organization rescued her? They were the frigging NSA. How could they not have found her? Or contacted the FBI or CIA to track her down? Even Jackson had managed to find her. True, he'd had the help of the treacherous Asian bitch who'd seduced Kansas three years ago as Elizabeth Chan, but still...

Elizabeth, dead.

Jackson, captured.

This. Was. Insane.

Kansas drew herself upright. Her mind, her reason, forced down her emotional reactions enough so she could walk down the hallway.

She got halfway to the stairs at the far end when she was hailed by the South Asian CEO who'd had this building constructed to house his growing defense software company. Kyle Gowda. Kansas had traded him some neat tricks on cheating web algorithms for her mostly hidden living quarters at one end of the building's second floor. Gowda had also let her plug into his company's T3 line. Not a direct connection to the NSA trunk, but pretty close.

He caught up to her and growled, "Where have you been?" with an odd mix of fatherly concern and landlord suspicion. His bushy gray mustache bristled.

Something in that—the confrontation?—made Kansas freeze. She literally could not move or speak.

Gowda must have seen it, for this face softened. He smiled and wobbled his head from side to side reassuringly. "I know. I know. The work you do. The people you deal with. I was only feeling worried for you. Raj and Suzanne, they said they were working late the Friday before last and..." He waved his hand in the air to signify whatever depravities his younger staff might be up to on a Friday night. "They heard bumping and cries from the second floor. But when they went up, your door was closed. There was no sound. They thought you were...exercising."

The last word was a question about her love life, Kansas realized, astounded she could figure out something so mundane when her mind was in such turmoil. Gowda, a stout widower at least fifteen years older than Kansas, had given her several hints over the last few months that he found her attractive.

And Kansas still could not speak.

Another head wobble as Gowda said, "Then, the next Tuesday, two men with government IDs attempted to come in and search your apartment. I asked for a warrant, and they went away. I knocked on your door, but you have not been here at all, I think, until now. And you look scared."

Kansas made herself consciously unclench and throw back her shoulders. She chewed her tongue to get her saliva flowing.

"I'm fine, Mr. Gowda. I've been away. It's nice to know you protected my place while I was gone."

Just to get him to leave, of course. Because whoever had come with government IDs could have just broken in later if they were from SCATTER. But why? By Tuesday, they'd already put her through sleep deprivation, extreme positions, withholding water, and simple indignities like slaps, pressure point pain, electric shocks, waterboarding. She was sure she'd babbled something. Maybe not enough?

"I will always look after you, Ms. Traine. And protect what is yours." Gowda bowed so deeply it would have been embarrassing if Kansas hadn't already been ready to pass out from anxiety.

"I'm under a bit of a deadline," she said in as much of a work voice as she could summon. "We'll catch up another time?"

Gowda nodded and bowed again.

Kansas turned awkwardly and continued down the hall to the staircase, certain that her would-be suitor was watching her walk away from him.

Upstairs at her door, she keyed in a long string of numbers into the lock that hadn't stopped SCATTER. The lock released.

She entered.

As expected, someone had clearly searched the place. Drawers lay open, their contents on the floor. Sliced pillows, batting spilled out. Her desktop computer was gone. As were all the backup drives from her NAS.

Oddly, it actually helped her get her bearings. These assholes weren't ghosts or all-powerful. They were just operatives. Or even common thieves. Sloppy ones.

The only painful loss was the micro-SD cards they'd yanked from her well-hidden surveillance cameras. It they hadn't, she could have taken the cards to the police or FBI. It reawakened the old debate she'd had with herself between backing everything up locally or using the cloud. She'd opted for local because she knew how easy it was for a good hacker to pull stuff from the cloud. This was one time it would have been a nice failsafe.

Dwelling on things lost helped nothing, though. After ensuring the blinds were closed on her one window to the outside world, she went straight to her oven range and pulled it out from the wall. Using a multi-tool from her kitchen junk drawer, she sliced down the faint line in the drywall where she'd created a hiding space between the joists. Her shaking hands made the cutting difficult, and she finally just kicked in the drywall with the sole of her boot.

Kansas reached in through the hole and pulled out a backpack that held her go gear.

She'd never been the sort of spy who'd needed to vanish on a moment's notice. Her work decrypting and analyzing signal intelligence (sigint) was a glorified desk job. The collection of human intelligence (humint) was the CIA's game. Which was also where the field agents and spies came in. *They* needed to be ready to bug out, get exfiltrated, or simply change their identities at the drop of a hat and disappear.

Then Jackson had called to tell her Kenny was alive, and Kansas had found the people holding him were talking with some covert government or military group. Not to mention that Jackson, and probably Kenny, were time travelers.

A go bag became a logical precaution.

Hers had fake identification documents, a clean laptop, a powerful and security-loaded prepaid phone, five-thousand dollars cash, and the key to a Wells Fargo safe deposit box she'd opened under her alternate identity. That box held more funds and a Walther Q5 Match Steel Frame 9mm pistol that was topped with Vortex Venon 6 MOA, a red dot site. It was the gun used by Venezuelan-born Gabby Franco now. Gabby had been a competitor at the 2000 Olympics and was Kansas' first celebrity crush. Owning the same gun Gabby shot with just felt...cool.

What she needed first was the phone.

She pulled it out and plugged it in. While it charged, she did a thorough tour of her living space, cleaning up and confirming that the search had been just that, not a "message" of wanton destruction. Her clothing and personal hygiene products had all been untouched. This included the hair scissors, hair dye, and very different wardrobe that she'd all used briefly to get her alternate identity documents.

Before using them, though, she had to check what her instincts were telling her.

The phone had 50% charge. Enough. And the security redirects she'd installed on it were still there. She dialed the private line of her directorate commander, Shane Garvey. Garvey's directorate was officially black letter, known only to those working inside the NSA HQ. His private line, requiring a string of numerical challenges, was known to a tiny subset of those.

Because of all that, he answered almost immediately.

"Don't know this number. Who is this?"

"Traine, sir. Kansas Traine."

There was the pause Kansas had been expecting. Then, "Where are you calling from?"

"Not relevant. Bent released me."

Another pause. A slight thickening of Garvey's breath. "Who's Bent?"

"I'm thinking you are. Sir. You didn't look for me when I went missing, did you. Told the rest of Epsilon I was taking stress leave? Vacation time?"

Garvey marshaled his energies and huffed into the phone. "It sounds like you should be on stress leave now, Traine. I don't know what you're talking about."

"I'm talking about the True Believers. Bent talked about them while he was torturing me. Might have even mentioned your name specifically."

There was a huff, then Garvey said simply, "Fuck."

"Yeah," Kansas said, her educated guess confirmed. "Herr Bent likes to talk when he thinks he has someone completely in his power who's never going to leave."

There was a long pause with a lot of heavy breathing from Garvey's end, until he asked, "What are you going to do?"

"Come on, Shane. I reported directly to you for five years. You've got to know exactly what I'm going to do now."

A laugh. "That's the thing about you, Traine. You're a weird bitch and I haven't the slightest clue wha—"

Kansas hung up on him.

And now the clock was ticking. She had to run.

4

Jude

By the time Jude reached his car in the lot at 101 Constitution Avenue, he felt lower than the bird sludge he'd picked up on his shoes walking through the Capitol grounds.

Vaguely suicidal, in fact, which was new to him.

He'd always had such a well-balanced view of life. From the Talmud, he'd known that success came from hard work, and action was the most important thing. Yet the very nature of the Talmud, the compilation of years of reflections and interpretations of the Torah so that it had become a book as revered in its own right, proved that deep thinking was also good.

Jude decided early on that these lessons blessed his fascination with the human mind. *Particularly when that fascination had a practical application.*

From that revelation and the full support of his loving parents, Jude had entered the field of psychology with such a sense of destiny that he would have been insufferably full of himself if he hadn't been working so hard to understand every person he met and how society guided, warped, empowered, or crushed them.

And then came Jackson Traine.

"Hey! You getting in? Or just going to stand there with your head up your ass?"

Jude turned to see he was blocking an angry-looking businesswoman, who'd *backed* her Smart Car in. She couldn't access her driver's door with Jude standing where he was.

"Well?"

"Sorry." Jude unlocked and climbed into his car. It was a five-year-old Audi that he'd bought used from a member of his synagogue who'd always seemed the epitome of success. Heated leather seats, retracting headlights, advanced navigation/audio console. They all said he too had "made it."

He started the Audi's engine and backed up as the older businesswoman grumped her way into her own little jellybean car. Five minutes later, he was in the afternoon rush of cars rumbling south and west on the 395 for Arlington.

His eyes were leaking. His sinuses felt so full they were going to explode.

Jackson.

Funny, shy, brilliant mind, uncanny memory, self-destructing from PTSD. Jackson had not only been Jude's roomie and best friend; he'd also been the ultimate example of untapped potential. Which is why Jude had understood when the CIA came for him. For both Jackson and Jude, actually. They'd offered to fast-track Jude into the CIA's applied psychology division if he'd look after Jackson Traine, keep them informed of his progress, and nudge him toward government service.

Jude's dream? Using psychology to change the world with his friend at his side.

Except Jackson didn't take the hints, so Jude finally went alone. Loved it. Met the legendary psychiatrist Uwe Bent and loved what he was doing. So much so that Jude became a kind of double agent—working enthusiastically for the Company but also for SCATTER. Because hey, both were trying to change the world for the better. Finally, Jude brought Jackson to Langley for a trial run that failed but seemed to prove something to Uwe, who'd been monitoring everything.

Everything.

It had led, Jude realized sickly as he crossed the Potomac and into the right lane to exit on Washington Boulevard, to what had just happened. Bent had lured all the key women in Jackson's life to that basement SCIF and threatened to shoot them if Jackson didn't join him.

And Jude could have prevented that!

Because just this morning, before anyone had gone to the SCIF, Jackson called Jude. He'd asked Jude to locate the legendary spy, Andre Poussaint at the CIA HQ and tell him about the meeting. Apparently, Poussaint's current job was to track down any remaining traces of SCATTER and obliterate them. So, if Jude alerted him, Poussaint could crash the party, capture Uwe Bent, rescue Jackson's brother, Kenny, and crush SCATTER.

But did Jude track down Poussaint and tell him?

No.

Jude had hung up the phone and called Bent.

He'd chosen Bent over Jackson.

Jude grabbed a tissue from the console between the front seats, wiped his eyes, and blew out a large wad of snot.

"Pimp!" he shouted at himself. "Jude-ass!"

And a Talmudic teaching his late father had tried to pass on came back to him: *Be wary of authorities who befriend a person for their own purposes. They appear loving when it is beneficial to them, but do not stand by the other person in his time of distress.*

Would that be Bent?

Or Jude?

Jude had turned off the highway at North Pershing and worked his way on automatic pilot to the front of his red brick townhouse.

He stopped the car in the driveway, turned off the engine, and just sat in the dead car for a long time as the chill from the cold January seeped in.

Did he just go back to work at CIA HQ tomorrow?

Was he still spying for Uwe there? Could he quit even if he wanted to?

He gulped.

He shouldn't *want* to quit anyway, should he?

But if he quit, he'd lose any chance of helping Jackson.

Maybe he should try to find the legendary Andre Poussaint after the fact? Tell him where SCATTER operated now?

Or...just do nothing. That would be easy. That would be the opposite of every ethic he'd lived by his entire life, and his mother and late father would both hang their heads in shame, but he could do it.

His stomach rumbled.

Maybe if he went in and had an early dinner, something would come to him.

He climbed out of the car.

5

I leave the Capitol

Finally, the specifics of how *I* left the US Capitol basement.

You'll remember the ass-kicking South Asian woman I'd dubbed Thing Two had used her boot to shove my face onto the SCIF tabletop where Zhou Wenling had fallen when shot. How my chin had slid through the bloody gore still pooled on that tabletop. You'll also recall that when I'd regained my feet and licked off some of the red mess on my face, it tasted like corn syrup.

That made my thoughts and feelings explode as Thing Two shoved me out of the SCIF.

First with a surprising surge of hope.

The blood tasting like corn syrup meant fake blood, which meant Wenling was probably alive. She and Bent must have staged the shooting for my benefit, to make me believe Bent was serious enough to shoot everyone I cared about. In exchange, I guessed, Bent had agreed to release Wenling's brother to her.

But I already knew this much from my dealings with Bent. He was cold enough to lie to Wenling's face, make her think they had a deal, go through with the act, then just blow her off. He's never give up Xiaobo.

Which was good! Because when Wenling realized she'd been betrayed, she'd want revenge. And since she'd had her creepy old doctor inject a transmitter into my lower belly, she could track down SCATTER by tracking me. She'd send in her troops. By then I'd have hopefully found Kenny and we could escape together!

Then I was stumbling out to the basement hallway outside the SCIF and I tumbled back to earth. Hard.

Why?

Because when we popped out, the last two people to exit, the same Capitol Police Officer who'd let me into this SCIF in five different timelines, barely looked at us. He just closed the door, locked it with a hard ka-thunk, and walked away. This despite having three civilians ushered in and out at gun-point and one woman apparently shot and carried out.

It meant that the guard, like Senator Jonquist and probably many, many others, were secretly in the employ or being paid off by SCATTER. So even if Wenling tracked me, she was up against hidden opposition everywhere. She'd accumulated great wealth using Xiaobo's ability to time travel, but she was up against power players trying to reshape the world.

Wasp meets Kong.

Put me in the same outmatched league. Forget being rescued, I'd fantasized that I could somehow give in to Bent, destroy SCATTER from the inside, and rescue Kenny. All the while keeping Lena, Kansas, and Megan safe.

But really, from the moment Bent had tagged me as a time traveler, I'd been his. It was give in or watch Bent kill Megan, then Kansas, then Lena.

No choice.

No power.

Well, shit.

"Faster!" ordered Thing Two and poked me with her baton.

So, I walked faster, vainly filing away the sight, smell, and sound of every door and overhead lightbulb, every intersecting hallway, every fire extin-guisher, every crack in the concrete floor. All useless now. I couldn't make a break for it. Megan, Kansas, and Lena remained hostages wherever they were.

And Kenny? Realistically, Bent would never let me get anywhere near Ken-ny. Kenny might not even be in America anymore.

So...I had to pull up my big boy pants and accept the choice I'd made.

I knew who I was, and why I'd chosen as I had. I'd protect those I loved.

And if there was truly no way out?

Then I'd adapt and survive. Survive and hope for...a miracle?

We finally caught up to Bent at the top of one of the many semi-hidden staircases and elevators that took you from the basement to the Capitol's main floor.

This one was a nondescript hallway that my sense of direction said was on the building's northeast side.

Bent's cadre had shrunk to just the ketamine twins, sweet-faced Natasha and big-bone Pasha. Thing One and Senator Jonquist were nowhere to be seen.

As Thing Two shoved me closer, Natasha stepped up to me with a smile, while Pasha stepped casually behind me and jabbed my neck with a needle.

For them, it was their first time injecting me. For me, the second go-round. I knew what was coming.

As Bent led us out a side door and around the building that suddenly looked ominously massive under the January overcast sky, reality went loopy.

"Why bother wihh?" I said lazily even as I hurried to keep up with Bent.

"The ketamine?" said Bent, not slowing his stride at all. "Precaution against you having second thoughts. Or seeing where we're taking you."

"Buh my mem'ry..."

"Everything you see, even half awake. Of course."

"Yeth..."

There was what sounded like a roaring squeal and a black limo pulled up at the curb. We were at a curb! The road past it was tumbling with cars that whizzed and spun and turned around on it like dancing puppets.

I leaned down to squint to see if Colonel Jian was driving, but it was Thing One!

Someone threw me into the back seat and yanked a black cloth over my head.

I woke in a zoo.

No bars or a tree to climb, but it felt like a zoo. A psychedelic one.

The pulsating ceiling and pastel walls—blue, yellow, and pink with framed seascapes and pastorals. Chunked out holes here and there said the walls were concrete.

Rolling my head left, I saw a galley kitchen with bubbling stainless-steel appliances and sink, a kitchen table, chairs, a couch, armchairs, a moving cart of books and magazines. A TV tilted off one wall. Rolled my head right and saw people. A ping-pong table swaying.

I blinked to stop everything from moving around. Why was I even awake, feeling like this?

And the overhead pot lights were so bright, like eyeball-scorching suns.

No windows.

One door. Locked?

And when I squinted hard against the sudden roll of nausea, I saw cameras looking looked in from each high corner of the room, their tiny green LEDs assuring me they were all on and letting whoever was on the other end of them watch me wake up.

Watch the animal.

Animals. Plural. The other people in the room.

The smells of old food and bodies and antiseptic cleaner made me want to puke. I kept my teeth clenched as I pushed myself up to sitting and realized, after a few slow breaths that forced my head to clear, this wasn't a zoo at all. It was a psych ward.

I quelled the sense of panic that induced by studying the proof of my instinctive understanding.

First, I was sitting in the middle of the room's scuffed vinyl floor like an overgrown child, clothed in institutional blue cotton scrubs. Tie up pants. Collarless short-sleeve matching shirt. Which meant that Bent, or whoever he'd assigned me to, had stripped off the suit I'd been wearing in the US Capitol SCIF and dressed me in clothes that were cheap and easy to wash.

Standing over me in a shuffling ring was a group of four disturbed-looking adults, all wearing the same blue scrubs.

Don't panic. Analyze. Focus on others, not your own terror.

Two men and two women.

One of the men looked my age. He was tall, wan, and skinny, with a bit of an overbite and a large, crooked nose. Mop of brown hair. When he blinked at me, his entire head jerked in some kind of neurological tic.

The other man was shorter and older, maybe fifty. He had terra-cotta skin, with a thick-boned head, chest, and wrists all shaved down to nubbly black bristles and large swaths of red and flaky eczema. His fierce glare said South American dictator to me. Drug lord maybe?

One of the two women rocked back and forth over by one wall. She was blocky, with short legs and a torso as wide as it was long. Her hair was blond, features pale and Slavic. Her eyes wouldn't meet mine.

The other woman was her opposite in both appearance and manner. Her skin was a rich black with large, sensuous lips most Hollywood actresses would die for. Long-limbed and clear-eyed. Late teens or early twenties. And as my eyes focused on her, she stepped in front of me and dropped to her knees, leaning forward and grinning aggressively as her gaping cotton top drew my eyes.

Oh please, no.

It reminded me too much of Ziggy's young niece, Chandice. But Chandice's come-ons had just been a game. There was something profoundly more disturbing at work here. Maybe because the muzziness in my brain was fading, and I was gathering who these patients had to be.

That CIA list Kansas had displayed briefly on my computer screen twelve or thirteen days ago—she'd known I would memorize it all in a glance and not forget a word. That and the research I'd done for each name…

Another wave of nausea and fear swept over me. I bent forward with a moan. Then I heard a sound of water flushing somewhere and wanted to run to it, lock myself, stay there until I got my bearings. But my limbs still weren't cooperating, so I just spread my hands on the vinyl flooring before me and tried to breathe.

The room's door banged open, and in walked mental patient number five. Or six, if you included me.

He was an overweight, messy man, who looked like he'd never had any part of his life under control. Happy though, in a simpler way than the aggressive Black girl in front of me.

"He's awake!" the man said. "Bet he hasn't talked yet."

"He wahz about to say someteen," the Black girl said in a musical contralto, "when you move yoh fatness in de room."

"Fuck you too, Ugly. Hey, you know who he looks like? Around the eyes?"

"We all see dat."

"Kansas," said the eczema drug lord, and his voice came out like the bottom of a big metal drum. As if I needed that to finally drive the icicle of my situation home.

Of course, Kansas had been here. Dressed in these same scrubs. Questioned. Experimented on. As I would be soon.

But at least I'd gotten her out. And protected Lena and Megan. That made it worth it.

"Hey there, guy," said the fat man. "You the crazy brother or the smart one? Betting on crazy."

"My name is Jackson Traine," I said, and a self-protection mechanism kicked in. I pointed at the girl still kneeling before me. "You're Sunday Salisu. Nigerian. Traffickers took you from your home when you were a child. They were going to ship you and fifteen other children to London to be sold. But you miraculously freed yourself and the other children."

The girl's dark cheeks reddened, but it was the reaction of the crooked nosed mop top that really popped.

"Aow," he said, eyes wide. "That bloody well's it, right?"

"Eet's not it!" Sunday shot back at him, jumping to her feet and pulling a fist at me like she wanted to punch me.

I pretended hard not to see that as I turned to the crooked nose guy. "You're a Brit. Norman Dankworth. Used to be part of the 'County Line.' I don't know what that means exactly, but you were a criminal. And then..." I paused as I saw his face twisting up horribly. It stopped me from revealing his (temporary?) gender dysmorphia that had gotten him raped. "You ended up helping the cops with a major drug bust. Miracle the rest of the gangs never found out it was you."

Dankworth's shoulders relaxed. "Yeh."

I turned to the bald terra-cotta man. "Columbian Police Chief Cruz Condore Quispe," I said, trying my best to get the soft Spanish lisp I assumed his last name would have. "You fought the drug trade down around Cali for almost twenty years. In Columbia, they called you 'indestructible' because you kept surviving attempts on your life that killed everyone around you."

I expected a challenge, but the fierce man just nodded.

I nodded back, then looked past him. "The young woman by the wall..."

"She don't speak English," Dankworth said.

"Her name is Zura Dobroshtan," I said. "In 2014, she persuaded her entire village in Crimea to evacuate the village a day before the Russians shelled it into rubble. Amazing. A miracle."

The woman didn't turn to look at me.

"I'm sorry for what your country went through back then. Even sorrier it looks like it's going to happen all over again. Worse."

This time, she turned with her eyes full of questions. Not so ignorant of English as she let on.

"Hey there!" said the fat man. "That's quite a trick. Now I know we never told Kansas or each other any personal stuff about ourselves. Kind of a rule. Because of..." He pointed to each of the four cameras.

"Seriously?" I carefully climbed to my feet. Everything was still swimmy. "You're here because of the miracles. They all made it into the news and are still there for anyone who searches your names. And you've been here how long?"

"Wheh did *you* get de names?" Sunday Salisu asked. Her balled fist said she still might punch me.

"From Kansas," I said.

"And *she* got 'em from…?" Dankworth asked, coming nearer in a way that suggested wanting to be closer to Sunday than me.

"Can't tell you that. Let's just say she's very smart."

"I bet she was a spy!" the fat man said, and my blood turned cold. "Pretended to be a prisoner here, but secretly worked for Dr. Bent. Every time she came in all tortured looking? Just an act to get us talking. You know what her tell was?"

"What?" I said, giving him such a cold stare that the entire room stilled.

I'm sure they could see the murder on my face, but the terrified looks on theirs said they bought the fat man's theory. Which meant they probably thought I worked for Bent too. It spoke volumes about how Bent exercised his power here. Not a kindly researcher.

And for Norman Dankworth, this would have been going on since 2010.

Twelve years!

For Zura and Sunday, eight years!

How were they not stark raving mad?

The one with the shortest stay here so far was Police Chief Quispe, tagged on the list as having been spotted in 2016. Half the time, twice as tough, but even he had apparently developed a healthy fear of Bent and company.

I looked from face to face, finishing on the fat man.

"Danny Reet," I said. "Should've just stayed quiet and I might have forgotten you. But you're good at self-sabotage, aren't you? Professional hustler out of Ohio. Used your apparent ability to see the future sometimes to cheat at cards, roulette, horse races, anything, anywhere. Talked too much about it. Made reckless bets. But you still got into the World Series of Poker 2016 in Vegas and almost knocked out the eventual winner, Qui Nguyen. Enough for a reporter to get you bragging. That's what landed you in the news and Bent's radar."

"Aow," said Dankworth from behind my left shoulder. "That bloody well's it, right?"

The others muttered among themselves as well, making me guess that Reet had hustled all of them on something.

Police Chief Quispe pointed a finger at Reet now. "Maybe *you* are the spy with the doctor."

Reet's face went red. "I'm not the spy!" He jabbed his own forefinger at me. "*He* is!"

"I'm not working for Dr. Bent!" I said and looked pointedly at the cameras. Spoke to them. "I'm only here because Bent threatened and continues to threaten the lives of some people I love. So, I'm going to cooperate with his research and *fully expect* him to treat me and everyone else here with dignity and respect from this moment on. Or he just might find out exactly how much power he has locked up in this facility."

All my fellow patients/subjects/prisoners stared at me with what I thought was shocked awe. Dankworth's lower jaw actually dropped, so I could see how badly he needed some dental work.

Then, like someone flicked a switch, they all laughed. Even Zura. Even Police Chief Quispe.

They slapped each other on the back, stopped to look at me, then laughed again. It triggered the social anxiety I thought I'd put behind me. My face flushed and my stomach churned. I broke out in a massive sweat. I wanted to hide.

Except here, of course, there was nowhere to hide.

The bathroom maybe?

I couldn't...take...

"STOP IT!" I shouted and, to my amazement, they did. Still afraid, maybe, that I secretly *was* with Bent. Or that I knew even more about each of them than I'd said and might shout it out right here and now.

Neither of those was the case. It was just that I was *so goddamned tired* of being afraid of people and myself and my past. Especially with this much bigger threat I'd have to deal with any day now. Any hour. Any minute.

Quispe, as the elder in the room, and the one bona fide badass in the room, stepped forward and clapped one of his thick hands on my shoulder. Even though I was a good six inches taller, I felt small.

"You know," he said in the Spanish-accented English Al Pacino had lapped up for his role in *Scarface*, "we do not laugh at you. We laugh at any of us telling Doctor Bent what he can or cannot do."

"You don't know, bruv," Dankworth's voice chimed in. "You don't know."

Sunday Salisu suddenly stepped in front of me. At that moment, her face didn't look like some child sex slave who freed herself and her fellow slaves from her slavers. Framed by her short, wild afro, her face looked both innocent and broken, her eyes too worn out to cry. She raised her hands up and put them on either side of my face, like I was the child here.

"Oh, Mistah Jackson Traine," she said. "He is the devil. You know what dat makes dis place?"

6

Summoned

I LOOKED INTO SUNDAY Salisu's spotted-brown eyes. "This is the anteroom of Hell."

Sunday pulled back her arms and Quispe's hand came off my shoulder. I saw they both wore the same look of confusion.

Dankworth spoke for them. "Why would an aunty stay 'ere, bruv?"

Reet started sniggering as he faded back towards the kitchen wall, probably to hide from further attacks and look for snacks.

"No, no. Not an 'aunty room,'" I said. "An an-tuh-room. It means a waiting room. If the place where Dr. Bent does bad things is Hell, this is where you wait to be called into Hell?"

"Aoh. Right," Dankworth said, rubbing his big, crooked nose. "And you fink you can bargain with him?"

"Maybe," I said.

From where he was leaning back against the sink with an open bag of chips, Reet called out, "I win *that* bet. He's cuckoo nuts."

I called back to him, "If you didn't talk about your pasts, why did Kansas talk about me?"

"Said you were going to save her." Reet stuffed his mouth with chips and talked through them. "I guess you did. Or she's dead."

"She's alive and free," I said.

"An' you came in her place," Sunday said and spat at my feet. "Stupid."

I nodded to her. "Thank you. Like you were stupid to free all your fellow trafficked children when you escaped."

Her face colored. "But I got *out!*"

"I will too," I said. "Maybe free you at the same time."

It sounded fake even to my ears. Sunday fluttered her lips, and everyone seemed suddenly done with me. Sunday walked to the wall to grab Zura like the older woman was her personal toy and made her pick up a paddle for a game of table tennis. Dankworth grabbed a magazine and flopped into an armchair that pointed toward their table so he could watch.

The Bolivian police chief grabbed a book and sat in a separate armchair to actually read. A glance at the cover told me the book was in Spanish.

The most basic part of me, the still needy child that was in all of us, felt rejected, ignored, cast out.

That left only Danny Reet and me. The two Americans.

I walked toward him.

He saw me coming and rolled his head back with a vast sigh, stuffing more chips in his mouth.

"Drug of choice to dull the pain?" I said, pointing to the crinkly bag of Doritos he'd just emptied.

"They don' give ush booze." Chip crumbs sprayed from his mouth and down his front. "Or knives or any food that needs them."

"Them?" I nodded toward the others.

"Sex. Sunday and the cop sometimes. Maybe the Ukrainian, too. The girls have crying jags. So does the Brit. I think Condor likes pretending to stab people and strangle snakes in his room."

"So, you all have your own rooms?"

Reet wiped his mouth and started looking for more snacks, opening every cupboard, so I felt like I'd seen the kitchen. "Own rooms. Share a bathroom. Separate showers, boys, and girls. Dorm life forever." He giggled a little but squeezed it off at the end like he was going to sob.

He didn't, though. Maybe this was like Zura Dobroshtan keeping her language ability from the other patients. Reet hid his suffering to feel he had something in reserve.

I was about to ask him about whether he'd ever met Kenny or Xiaobo, when a two-tone alarm of sorts went off in the room, followed by a computer-generated voice.

"JACKSON TRAINE, PREPARE FOR A TESTING SESSION IN…FIVE MINUTES. YOU WILL BE COLLECTED FROM THE…BLUE DOOR AT THE END OF…HALLWAY ONE."

Reet's face had gone pale, and I notice that the young women playing table tennis had let the ball bounce away across the floor as they looked up to the ceiling. The two men in armchairs didn't look up, but they'd obviously frozen. It looked like they were holding their breaths.

A couple of beats later, the table tennis and reading continued like nothing had happened. Even Reet was now standing with the fridge open, scanning everything inside.

On a hunch, I said, "They sometimes ask for more than one person."

Reet nodded without looking at me.

"The blue door?"

"Only one hallway," he said and pointed, clearly not willing to meet my eye.

"Thanks. And if I don't come back, it's been real."

Reet shot me a glance, but I didn't even bother holding it as I turned and went for my "testing."

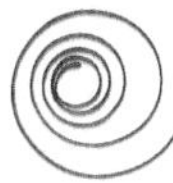

The blue door was at the end of a yellow hall. The doors along that hall, in their own pastel primaries, had name tags. "Washroom," "Men's Shower," "Ladies' Shower," and patient names had been written cheerily in blue marker on white cardstock and slid into a designated holding slot on each door.

Mine was at the very end, right beside the blue door at the end of the hallway. I guessed Bent wanted me close. I was his favorite new toy.

In the couple minutes I had, I tried the door of "my" room and found it and looked inside. The room was...efficient. Just enough room to sleep and breathe. Claustrophobic nausea swept over me, and I started to sweat. Panic rose in my chest.

The opening of the blue door startled me out of it.

A man stepped through. Unfamiliar. Medium height. Muscular. Square-jawed. Too-tight battle fatigues. Reminded me a little of Smiley, the Lead the Way former Ranger who'd trained me most of last year how to fight and keep my body in top shape.

That was probably what clicked my mind, which had slipped far from fighting shape, into an automatic battle readiness.

I scanned him for armor and weapons. He had none of the first but at least one pistol in a back-of-waist holder that he could draw quickly.

Not fast enough to stop a sudden attack from under ten feet, but why would he worry about that? Most of the patients he dealt with were drug frazzled, disoriented, or beaten into complacency, right?

I could take him.

Wasn't going to. But I could.

It gave me just enough of a boost that when the man gestured for me to head through the open door, I did so with my head high, shoulders back, and chest out.

The five-minute walk through some twisty halls had us occasionally ducking under or around protruding machinery like the building designer treated people as an afterthought. The walk ended at a sliding door that registered our presence and opened automatically.

I walked into what looked like a high-tech operating chamber.

Absolutely nothing about it was reassuring. Computer screens, desktops, keyboards, cameras, and entry pads clung to a u-shaped metal structure that took up one half of the room. Only two rolling chairs sat inside it, indicating at most two operators went in there even if all the screens and keyboards were active.

Displayed on those screens in various fashions, ranging from photographic to stripped-down-then-rebuilt CGI sequences, was something that looked like an operating bed that had inward curving sectional walls rising on either side.

When I looked at the real thing, which stood in the second half of the room, I saw buttons and dials and line-up tubes of liquid in the clear side panels. Pumps and IV lines ran up from them to join the many tubes, hoses, wired sensor that ran along the panels or hung just above the bed.

Those side panels looked only half-raised now. Fully raised, they'd make the bed an effective cage.

"It looks like fun, doesn't it?" said Bent.

My whole body nearly jumped out of its skin. He must have been in the shadows beside the door and stepped up like a ghost behind my right shoulder. I spun to face him, but he just stood there with such an open curiosity, that I lost all words. The fact he was wearing a white lab coat over a button-down shirt and tie made me feel like a lab rat. And those piercing blue eyes, they felt like they were slicing into my cerebral cortex, uncovering all my thoughts...

"The bed?" he pressed. "All it could tell us about happens when you jump?"

"You know what it reminds me of?" I shot back.

"What?"

"Third year university. I had to take an elective in either animal behavior or experimental neuroscience. The latter sounded more practical. I thought we'd get to see what was happening in rat brains when they were learning or remembering or experience intense drives and emotions."

Bent was nodding with a furrowed brow, like he was truly interested in what I'd experienced.

"You know what's coming. We weren't doing that back in 2008. We were just recreating brain dysfunctions like in rats that we experienced as humans. Parkinson's disease. The brain mapping and electronic stimulation and control didn't start happening until 2014, 2015."

Bent nodded. "And this reminds you of that how?"

"You don't know what you're doing. You're at the stage where you just kick the lab rat with chemicals and measure what happens."

"That's what you think we're doing here?"

"Sure looks like it. And I've already been there, done that."

"With Dr. Cortland. Yes. She had cruder ways to stimulate the time jump and cruder ways to track its occurrence, but yes."

"So, what's different here?"

Bent smiled, showing no insult taken. "Apart from our obviously wider pool of subject data, our experimental advantage is primarily containment and precision."

Containment. Meaning the bed *was* a prison. I had to admit it was a step above the way Lena had literally shackled me to a chair with the help of Irene Gopal, who I later found was a spy for Zhou Wenling.

As for *precision...*

"What do you hope to measure precisely?" I asked.

"Exactly what makes you time travel, beyond what you think makes you time travel. How that travel affects your physical environment. Whether it leaves traces. How you can better control its initiation and chronological distance traveled. Among other things."

"Like how each time jump destroys me physically and psychologically."

"That. Oh yes. Of course."

The smile as he said it—what was that all about? "I can tell you about the impact. It's bad. It leads to my psychological disintegration because of all the..." I didn't finish because I didn't really want to tell Bent exactly what triggered my time jumps.

He waved his hand dismissively. "Trauma. It's a common early cause of time travel among all our subjects. Though obviously, for talented jumpers, the trauma is no longer necessary."

"For who?" I asked, even as my less conscious brain gave up at least part of the answer.

"Zhou Xiaobo. Danny Reet. Your brother."

"My...brother."

"Yes."

"He's here? In this building?"

Bent gave me another smile, this one more unctuous. "He just might be. Not in the 'Pit' with the less talented folk where you are right now. No, Kentucky has proved himself worthy of special treatment. As I'm sure you will. And when you have..."

He let it trail off suggestively.

Asshole.

But despite that, despite everything, I couldn't stop the little flickering tingle that started deep in my belly. What was that?

Hope?

Seriously?

What happened to my big boy pants and being realistic?

The hope and questions must have shown on my face because when I looked at Bent again, he had an almost carnal glee in his quickly hidden smile. Like he knew exactly what he'd just done to me. The threat of hurting Lena, Kansas, and Megan were the sticks. The chance to see Kenny again, the carrot. And the carrot, of course, could also become the stick of *never* seeing Kenny again, or worse, making him pay if I didn't do what Bent wanted me to.

Holy *shit,* did I hate being manipulated.

The baldness of it was a mistake on Bent's part, though. If he'd been subtle, I might have believed Kenny was actually nearby. I might have worked towards the goal of seeing him and ended up as messed up as Xiaobo.

Instead, he'd prepped me for the long haul. Hunker down. Adapt. Survive. Give Bent only the minimum needed to keep my loved ones alive.

I gave an outsized yawn. "Are we done here?"

"We are not." Bent became all business and led me to the test bed. He pressed a button and the three segments of acrylic side wall on our side of the test bed lowered with a quiet hum. "Climb in."

"No strip down?"

"Not today."

He turned from me and walked to one of the two chairs in the monitoring consoles, ignoring me completely.

Deliberate temptation.

There was no one else here. The guard who'd led me to this lab had stayed outside, and the door was closed. I could attack Bent right here and now. He was as tall as me but showed no muscle. And he looked to be in his fifties—gray hair and wrinkles around the eyes and mouth. Unless he was secretly a martial artist, I could take him down without breaking a sweat.

Besides, if I risked it and got shot, or it became clear my actions set into motion some failsafe that was going to hurt or kill everyone I loved, I could jump back ten minutes in time and *not* attack Bent.

Simple, right?

So why had my hands and forehead broken into a clammy, cold sweat?

Because my body knew it wasn't simple at all.

First, when I jumped back to take over my body as it was ten minutes earlier, everything didn't just reset at that point. What Lena had established with her quantum entanglement was that when I jumped back, I created a new timeline, but the old timeline continued. In a parallel dimension, whatever. And in *that* one, I'd just gotten my loved ones hurt or killed, whether or not I saw it.

Second, my ability to time jump just wasn't reliable. It definitely kicked in when my brain felt overloaded by trauma or about to die, but without that kind of immediate, life-threatening trauma...

The Bent in this timeline, the one which was actually happening, swiveled his chair back so he could look at me. His elbows were on armrests, his fingers interlaced before him.

Pompous prick.

"You seem to have a bit of a Hamlet complex right now, Jackson. 'With this regard their currents turn awry, and lose the name of action.' That's not you, is it? Not with all the gangsters you fought, and my people in the Capitol."

Don't forget UFC fighter Rick Soder and Andre Poussainte's crew at the CIA headquarters in Langley. Oh, and Alvin Westor, leader of the Lead-the-Way crew who tried to prove Lena's claim I could time travel if I believed I was going to die. Every one of them was more badass than you, Bent.

Flushing in frustration and shame, I looked away from him to the mess of technology in the exposed ceiling—lights, tubes, and wires connecting the test bed subject to the monitors, cameras that would stream and record everything...

"Why didn't you kill me just now?" Bent continued. "Or disable me? Perhaps use me as a hostage?"

Real curiosity?

Possibly. Yes, he wanted to dominate and control me. But maybe he was feeling his way toward that end in the same way I was trying to figure out how to fight off that control. Both of us were taking risks to reach our goals.

I shrugged. "Why kill you now? The fun's just starting."

"Or you're afraid I have fail-safes in place that go off even if I'm incapacitated. I do. One puts your brother through considerable pain, though it won't kill him. He's still valuable. Your sister, though..."

"You're assuming I can't get around them."

Another disconcerting smile. "Oh, you'd try. Over and over. But do you think you could do that without actually *seeing* these people hurt? That doesn't fit Ms. Zhou's reports. Or your own statement that each jump 'destroys' you."

I bit my tongue. This was bad poker. I exposed some of my cards. He exposed some of his. But he'd exposed more, I thought. First, that Wenling had told him all about me, so I should assume anything she knew, he knew. Second, he still didn't know that jumping back in time didn't rewrite a timeline; it just created a new one. That meant he didn't have a close watch on Lena and her work.

I grunted like I'd absorbing his threats.

He showed his teeth. "Climb onto the bed and let's get started, shall we?"

After holding his gaze long enough to make him think I had a choice, I turned back to the bed and climbed onto it.

The surface was some kind of hard foam, warm enough to lie on but not somewhere you'd want to sleep. Quite apart from all the techno terrors hovering above me. There was a click and the side frame slid back up on my right side with its quiet hum. When it stopped, I turned my head to look through it.

Bent had risen from his chair and stood again beside the raised bed, looking down at me through the top curve of the plastic shield.

"You going to hook me up?" I said and looked up at the wires and tubes dangling overhead.

He smiled grimly. "Not yet. The road to your brother is long. You have to prove you can walk the path."

"Okay. Then..."

Bent reach to the lower half of the acrylic shield near his waist and pressed a button.

<h1 style="text-align:center">7</h1>

Real or not real

I HELD MY BREATH in the stillness.

And suddenly music started pouring out of speakers near my head somewhere.

What the—?

It took me a moment to realize Bent was giving me the cast recording of *Hamilton.*

With a sudden involuntary rush that made me wonder if Bent had slipped me some drug cocktail when I hadn't been looking, I was reliving my thirtieth birthday. Jude stood with me in the office I'd opened southwest of Chicago. My pudgy friend's lower lip actually trembled with anxiety as he pressed a sweaty hand against mine, and I realized he'd handed me a ticket. But not just any ticket. It was a front mezzanine seat to *Hamilton*, which was always sold out unless you went to scalpers or waited in line for weeks digitally or at the box office.

I could smell Jude's anxiety as he told me I didn't have to go if I didn't think I could handle it.

But I thanked him, hugged him, and booked my plane ticket that afternoon.

I thought the plane ride would kill me, but it didn't. The streets of New York, and especially the theater district on West 46th Street, scared me, but I managed them.

Then I got into the theater.

Those high-up mezzanines of the Richard Rodgers Theatre were built for people under five-ten. No empty seats. I felt trapped, hot, sweating, and about to panic. I thought I was going to have to run out, maybe trip over the front guard rail, and plunge to the orchestra.

But I stayed!

The music started.

The actors came out.

And it was so exciting. I wished Jude had been there with me with all his goodness and effusive spirit and...

I snapped back to the test bed with music still pumping in.

Jude was gone. Not just physically, but even the memory of him now. Because however clearly I remembered him, I'd never really seen what was going on in his head and heart. My eyes started filling over how much I'd lost with him, with Lena... And now to realize that Jude had told Uwe Bent about the Broadway tickets he'd given me, a gift I'd always considered private, sacred, transformative.

Did Bent know? Was this his fucked-up way of getting into my head, after all?

I involuntarily jerked and blinked angrily. I shook my head to clear it. It didn't help. He needed to *stop this damn music!*

"Bastard! Orphan! Son of a whore!" I shouted at Bent over the music.

"Pardon me?" He hit a button, muting the sound.

Breathing hard, I worked my jaw around and finally said with dripping scorn, "You've never even listened to the lyrics of *Hamilton,* have you?"

"Ah," he said. "I've always found musical theater rather trivial. Though their appeal to the mass psyche has always intrigued me. You enjoy them, do you?"

Fuck you! "What do *you* enjoy? Doja Cat?" I snapped out the singer's name as someone even less likely to be on Bent's radar than Manuel Lin Miranda.

Bent was way ahead of me. "Black rapper, singer, artist. She's half Ashkenazi Jewish. Did you know that?"

"Is that what you're into?"

"Are you asking about my sexual predilections now, or my musical ones?"

"Do you have either?"

"Touché. Does it feel good to snipe at me from such a position of helplessness?"

"Information gathering. While *your* behavior, abusing people from a position of strength, has various clinical names, sadism being one."

"You're suggesting I derive sexual satisfaction from inflicting pain on people?"

"Thank you!"

"I don't..." Bent let it die. I could almost see him reviewing our exchange in his head, trying to figure out if I'd maneuvered him into an apparent admission.

Of course, I hadn't, but I still I let myself revel in it as I tried to calm down. Tried to not let Bent see just how easily he'd gotten to me. If I made it too easy for him, he'd be traumatizing me over and over to make me time travel and my brain would turn to goo. Goo with electrodes strapped on and tubes up my butt.

Yeah, I feared him, okay? I feared this place and what could happen to me if I stayed here long enough. I said I'd just hunker down and survive, but if he learned how to dig up all my weak spots...

Then I blinked and had a second moment of intense frustration as I realized Bent had actually just pulled another trick on me, the same one he'd used back in the Capitol building SCIF. There he'd just talked and talked about his plans. Here, he'd maddened me with music that had painful associations, then blandly got me talking after I'd stopped the music with my insults.

In both cases, *he distracted me for more than ten minutes.*

He knew from Wenling, I realized, that my time jumps only went back ten minutes. He'd also know that if I did more than one in a row, I got increasingly disoriented. (At three jumps in a row, my heart sometimes stopped, and I could die.) All of which meant he'd just made it harder for me to time jump my way out of this without risking disorientation that he'd certainly pick up on and know immediately what I was doing.

I gnashed my teeth and realized he was staring at me. Maybe he had been for a while. Even though Bent showed no apparent special sensitivities, I had the uncomfortable feeling he was reading my mind, just as Lena and Wenling had done.

I was a goddamned open book of emotions for anyone who paid close enough attention, apparently.

"Ten minutes up yet?" I snapped.

Bent glanced down at his wristwatch. "Two minutes ago. Margin of error."

"Of course. So..."

"So do your thing. Ten minutes back in time. Whoopee. Or maybe drop the act and do something completely different."

"Pardon?"

He did his feral smile. "You convinced Dr. Cortland and Ms. Zhou that this was your limit, only achievable when you experience extreme trauma. That's probably how it started. But you and I both know those limits don't stick with people who have genuine talent. Xiaobo was past that in six months. Your brother? Well, his power is unique, but equally unrestrained. You, meanwhile, have all the talent and twice the mental stability of either of those two. It's why you're here. You're going to save the world from chaos. So shall we really explore, or would you rather keep bullshitting everyone?"

I looked at him through the clear acrylic shield, wanting to scream against his insanity even as a part of me wondered if it wasn't insane at all. It was just...false. But rather than give Bent that, the part of me that loathed him got creative. "My God," I said. "You're predictable. Just like in the SCIF."

He frowned.

I plowed on. "The last time, though, you gave me the save-the-world speech earlier. And it was Megan Thee Stallion I raised to check your sexual predilections. You knew a lot about her, too."

Bent's frown deepened. He stared, no...*glared* deep into my eyes like he could read my lies the way he could read my other emotions.

But I knew I'd guessed right about his familiarity with Megan Thee Stallion. He'd shown all the signs of being a polymath who followed at least science, Shakespeare, and popular culture. I'd hit him hard. Now I just let him stare while I vividly imagined my supposed "earlier" timeline in this room.

"You jumped without my help?" Bent asked. "Without trauma? What happened to, 'Each jump destroys me physically and psychologically'?"

"Oh, you helped. You just don't *remember* helping me because in this new timeline you haven't yet." I let some of my real anxiety and mental exhaustion crumple my face. "And you're wrong about my abilities. The destruction is real. My body gets battered by the process. My mind has to shift and strain to accept a reshaped reality."

Having worked with a lot of congenital and involuntarily habitual liars, I knew their best lies mixed bits of the truth into their stories. Those bits were often the ones their listeners already knew or believed or desperately wanted to believe were true. They'd nod their heads at the true bits and assume those proved the rest of it was true, too.

Here, the more Bent believed his fantasy that I was some super time-traveling hustler, the more he had to admit I *could* have time traveled without him knowing it. Without suffering or showing any disturbance.

Then he blew up these guesses about him.

"You don't look battered at all," he said. "Perhaps we can review the tapes and you can show me exactly where you jumped back to."

"Why? I thought you believed I was lying about the trauma involved."

"Even Xiaobo has visible signs when he lands in an earlier time frame. I said you were more stable, not better. I want you to show me the signs of the moment you arrived at the earlier time."

"Okay," I said easily. "Let me out of here and we'll do that."

"No need."

Bent walked out of eyesight past the head of my test bed and returned wheeling a gleaming metal cart with a dark video screen on top of it. He picked up a small remote controller from the car and used it to turn on the screen. He rewound the video recorded from one of the ceiling cameras that looked down on me, stopping at the moment I'd first laid down.

"Did you jump back to before you got onto the bed?" he asked.

Trick question. He'd implied I could jump back more than ten minutes, but if I picked a point before the bed, I'd be telling him he was right.

Resisting the urge to bite my lip, I shook my head, even as I reviewed, second by second, all that had happened from the moment I climbed onto this bed.

I found it.

I shook my head casually. "Play it."

He did. I lay on the bed. Asked if he was going to hook me up.

"Not yet," he said on the screen, made his little speech about seeing if I could walk the path, then pressed a button.

Hamilton began playing.

I could tell now from Bent's body language and expression on the monitor that he'd been completely aware of what he was doing to my emotional barriers. Music had a powerful way of bypassing logic centers and hitting emotions.

I glanced at the living Bent and saw only concentration.

Good. It would be more convincing if he spotted the apparent signs of a time jump himself.

And...there it was. The recorded me on camera jerked and blinked furiously, then shook my head like something was wrong. A beat later, my features cleared, and I shouted Lin Manuel Miranda's description of Alexander Hamilton at Bent, calling *him* a "bastard, orphan, son of a whore."

Bent hadn't stopped the tape or changed his expression.

I guffawed and rolled my eyes back. "It's gonna be like that?"

He stopped the recording and looked at me. "Like what?"

"Games," I said. "You try to psych me out, make me wonder what you did or didn't see, what you do or don't know, what you really think I can do, what you're going to do. It's an approach of sorts. Maybe a self-defense mechanism when dealing with time travelers who can see and do so much more than you." I shrugged and closed my eyes. "Let me know when you figure out how you want to play this."

A calculated gamble. Bent was obviously smart—Jude had called him brilliant—but just as obviously driven by an almost Trumpian need to be significant. He likely also had other things driving him I didn't understand yet. Maybe a raw need for political power. But alone in the room with me right now, he had to show that he was smarter. *He* was in control here.

So, I just waited, breathing deeply, trying not to let on how this simple act of vulnerability spun up in my mind every time I'd been insulted, strong-armed, kicked, stabbed, shot, strangled, punched, spat on. Perfect memory made them perfectly present.

Against my will, my heart rate shot up, and I broke out in a sweat.

That was apparently enough for Bent.

"I saw it," he said.

"Saw what?" The words came out in a crackly mess, but I kept my eyes closed, pretending not to care.

"Just before you shouted at me about being a bastard and the son of a whore. I gather those were lyrics from the musical."

"A description of the main character, yes."

"Hm."

"You should listen to it sometime. Learn some American history."

"I would rather make history than wallow in it," Bent said.

"What did you see?"

"You looked startled. Then disoriented."

"I did," I said. Totally true.

"Which means that everything that happened after that point the first time, only you know about."

"Pretty much," I lied.

"What was different?"

"Other than you confessing you have a deep and abiding passion for Megan Thee Stallion?"

His mouth didn't even twitch as he said, "Apart from that."

I yawned and tried to bring my arms up to stretch, but I found the clear acrylic walls were tight enough around me it was going to take more wriggling and contortions than I was ready to do. So gave a deep sigh and stopped struggling. "Let me out of here and I'll tell you."

Bent considered a moment, then hit a button and the acrylic wall hummed outwards and smoothly down.

I spun my legs sideways and down, then hopped off the raised bed until I was standing on the laboratory floor, hands on my lower back, cranking my hips around. That wasn't doing it, though, so I stopped, planted my feet just under shoulder width apart, and brought my arms down to my sides. I rotated my hands, so they floated out slightly from my body and forced my shoulders back.

A simple *tadasana*. Mountain pose.

Because trapped in the middle of a mad doctor's laboratory while said doctor was waiting for me to tell him about something that had never happened was the perfect time for yoga.

"You look foolish," Bent said.

"I feel wonderful."

"Good, then a recap, please."

I took one final calming breath, then gave him my imaginary other-timeline ten minutes. I told him how the music had made me first sad, then furious for exactly the reasons I knew Bent knew. So I'd attacked him for it, accusing him of destroying the friendship I'd shared with Jude. And he had struck back by telling me that Jude wasn't the main betrayer, that Zhou Wenling had been bargaining away my freedom for Xiaobo's almost from the moment Bent had confirmed that I was a true time traveler.

He'd dug at me repeatedly, rehashing my failures with Lena and my sister, how my own parents had effectively abandoned me shortly after I was born, how my PTSD made me a broken man, a useless thing, etc. He was good at hitting my sore points.

And I'd jumped.

Now I waited to see if he bought it.

He did. Mostly, I guessed, because of the implicit flattery he'd attacked my emotions so well. "Therefore, you can jump without physical trauma," he said.

"Have you ever had a clinical practice? No. If you had, you'd have seen, not just read about, how emotional experiences can be every bit as traumatic as physical ones."

"Still…"

"Yes?"

For a moment, I thought he was going to confess how all the other time travelers in the "Pit" where he'd housed me could not travel without physical trauma. And even then, not reliably. Bent had praised my mental stability, but I guessed what he really valued was my perceived consistency. Plus, of course, my perfect memory, which presumably would let me do the things Kenny did for him now—recognize when others were time jumping, and remembering what time was like before the time jumps.

At least, that's what I guessed he had Kenny doing for him.

It made me worry about what would happen to Kenny if I could do his job. I doubted he'd just let Kenny go. He let no one go. Even the members of the Pit, who seemed mostly devoid of power.

Why? What was he keeping them for? Did he think he could improve their skills? Were each of them somehow more talented than they appeared?

When Bent finally waved at me in dismissal, I left, determined to find out.

8

Uwe Bent

When Jackson Traine left, Bent carefully lifted the bundle of cords that connected the screen he'd used to play back Jackson's supposed time jump. He wheeled it back to its station beside the other monitoring equipment.

Then he walked around it to sit in his rolling chair and lifted a small earpiece off the console next to it. He put this into his ear, pressed its connect button, and said, "Did you get all that?"

Kentucky Traine's voice flicked up on the console's simple screen. He looked focused, more present than usual. Likely from the modafinil and piracetam cocktail he'd had Gordon inject him with fifteen minutes before Jackson had come into Bent's lab to see him.

"Well?"

Jackson's big brother managed to furrow his brow and speak. "Something happened."

"What?" Bent snapped. "If someone resets your world by time traveling with you watching, your reset self would remember the other time you lived."

"That...seems to happen."

"It does with Xiaobo. You said it's happened before with Jackson."

"Once."

"And this time?" Bent fought to keep his tone even. Pushing Kentucky's drug-and-time-travel-addled brain hard usually caused him to lose connection with the here and now. Not helpful.

"Not this time," Kentucky said slowly, his face breaking out in a hot sweat.

This could have been from the lack of circulation in his media cage, Bent thought. All the heat from the monitors and computer gear.

Or it could be this junkie-shit knew exactly how his words betrayed his brother and didn't like it. He couldn't not do it because his ball-sack was in Bent's drug-providing hands, but he didn't like it.

"What a punk," Bent said, referring to Jackson. Kentucky turned even sicker looking than usual. Bent cut off his feed.

Bent played the Jackson recording back again. When he was done, he shook his head and slumped back in his chair with a bemused smile on his face.

"A very talented, tricky punk. Likely a psychopath."

He said this with sincere admiration. The trick Jackson Traine had just pulled showed the young psychologist's mental quickness, emotional regulation, courage, and, of course, his uncanny memory. It was no doubt all these traits that had allowed Jackson, one of only five people Bent had found who could pass the "What's in the box?" test for time travel ability, to *not* deteriorate from the use of his power. Jackson's PTSD had definitely spiked after all the time travel experiences with the Demon Monks. But he'd worked his way out of that without apparent long-term pain.

Dr. Jude Spiegelman attributed it to his friend's incredible willpower and compassion for others, but Bent didn't see it that way. The willpower, yes. The compassion? Hardly. Simple observation proved social bonding and compassion interfered with achievement. Maslow got it wrong when he talked about man's social needs. Very smart people knew it was social *order*, not connection, that led to personal fulfillment. Particularly if you were in the class gifted with superior intelligence and therefore able to shape that order. This was the highest form of evolution.

Bent had attempted to prove this during his psychiatric residency in Johns Hopkins. Under the guise of regular psychotherapy, he'd pioneered a new treatment for patients who exhibited a mix of psychopathy and dissociative disorders. He'd encouraged their sense of superiority and privilege, that regular laws and rules need not apply to them *if they could rationally figure out ways to beat the system.* As these psychopathic thinking patterns strengthened, Bent found the patients became more grounded and connected with their immediate surroundings and desires.

To beat the system, they had to become focused and aware. Their dissociative symptoms effectively vanished.

Five of his patients were released from their long-term involuntary stays in the psychiatric ward during his residency. Two became criminals who ended up behind bars. One, who'd been a lawyer, returned to practicing law and eventually took over a successful firm of DC lobbyists. The other two entered business and rose quickly through the ranks. Both were CEOs the last time Bent checked.

One of the CEOs had married someone in the CIA. That someone spoke to the Director of the Office of Medical Services in the CIA about their husband's experience. The director approached Bent in person to invite him to join the CIA.

Which Bent did for the chance to study the psychopathy of professional killers. It was amusing, though not as enlightening as he'd thought it would be. He'd been planning to return to the private sector.

Then the war in Iraq brought him to Abu Ghraib and introduced him to an Iraqi interrogation subject who displayed a truly powerful and rare human ability...

"Now *he* was not a punk," Bent said to the screen where a frozen frame of Jackson Traine's face stared out at him. "But he also couldn't hack my training and died. How about you?"

Because what he'd said to Jackson about not needing extreme trauma to jump, about not being restricted to ten-minute travels? Bent believed it *could* be true. He'd certainly be testing Jackson in these areas. Pushing him. Seeing what it would take to break through the act, or the lies Jackson told himself. Either one.

Bent began planning exactly what Jackson would face on his next visit to this laboratory.

For one thing, Gordon would be here.

Jackson might like Gordon.

At first.

9

Learned helplessness

WHEN I RETURNED TO the Pit common room, I wasn't sure what I expected.

Not this, though. Not a total lack of attention, like no one noticed I'd been gone.

Police Captain Quispe was absent. I'd heard him in his room on my way here. Fine.

But Zura Dobroshtan? She sat on the ratty couch by herself, reading a book with pages that looked to be in Cyrillic. Okay. Interesting, I guess. This place was institutionally basic, but they provided books in Russian? Were there books in Spanish for the Captain? And in whatever was Sunday Salisu's preferred language? Assuming Sunday could read.

Sunday was playing a spirited game of ping-pong with Norman Dankworth. I had the distinct impression that Norman was letting her win. Not surprising, given his obvious crush on the girl. She apparently didn't see it, though. Her eyes shone brightly, and her laugh peeled out like deep wind chimes.

It had Danny Reet entranced. I don't think he was following the game play at all. He hunched in his armchair just to watch Sunday.

And like I said, no one even glanced my way. Except, I registered from the corner of my eye a glance from Zura. Was she curious about my experience? She'd been here eight years with Sunday and Norman, six with the others. What the fuck else was there to be curious about?

"Hey!" I called out.

Norman looked up from the ping-pong table and Sunday's ping-pong ball bounced past him. He pretended to be despairing and rubbed his big, crooked nose.

"Aaoh, bruv. Look what you done."

"I win!" Sunday called, raising both hands to the ceiling, her face flushed.

Norman looked at her, evidently took in the way her blue scrubs top stretched over her breasts, and blushed scarlet as she caught his eyes.

Danny Reet exploded in laughter and even Zura looked up briefly from her book.

"This way!" I called out impatiently. "No one's wondering what happened to me in the lab?"

A hush fell over the room so I could actually hear the breathing. Then some kind of fan cycled up somewhere, and that raised questions, too.

"Well?"

Norman, Sunday, and Danny looked back and forth between them. Finally, Norman said, "We don't talk about it, bruv."

Danny leaned forward and muttered at his legs, "We used to."

"Why no more?" I said.

"There ees no point to it," Sunday drawled out at me from the table like I was a simple child.

Norman nodded. "Don't change nuffing."

"Did he put your through tests?" I asked. "Did he try to control you? Did he hurt you? Did he make you play games? Did you time jump?"

"Some of doze," Sunday said. "I used to cry and cry. Now no more."

"Because..."

"I grew up."

I looked around at the others. "He make anyone else cry?"

Norman looked away, but subtly raised his hand.

Danny raised his with a smirk.

Zura, who'd seemed not to be listening, said quietly, "He kiss me sometime."

The others' mouths fell open, and they stared at her.

"On the forehead? Cheek? Hand?" I asked.

"On mouth," she said, working her way around the words. "And neck. And touch." She indicated her chest and groin.

There was a long silence in the room.

Suddenly, from the hallway, came the sound of footsteps pounding like someone was squashing small creatures as they came. Captain Quispe appeared in the entry to the room, the bottom of his scrubs poorly tied and slipping down. He grabbed them up as he looked at each of us wildly. "What is happening here?" he demanded. "I heard something."

Sunday and Norman looked at him with fear, but Danny said, "Zura, the Ukrainian. She spoke. In English."

That's what they took from this?

Then I rethought it. Of course, that was what they'd note. If she seriously hadn't spoken, at least not in English, since they'd known her...

"She says Dr. Bent kissed her on the mouth and neck," I said. "Did you know anything about that?"

Quispe looked at me as if, for a moment, he could not remember who I was. Then he nodded. "She told me this. Yes."

Norman stepped toward him. "You fawking knew? An' you didn't tell us?"

Quispe looked suddenly old. Tired. "It was, how you say, a confidence. But there was nothing I could do."

I turned to Zura again. She had turned away, but I knew she was aware of me. That she was listening. For some reason, I was the second person she'd confided in about what had happened to her. Another older male. And the need had been urgent enough that she'd blown her carefully protected fiction of being unable to speak English to do it.

Why now?

"Zura," I asked, "when was the first time Dr. Bent did this? And when was the last time?"

The room stilled again, waiting for her response. She finally turned and gave it. Just as Sunday seemed in her most vulnerable moments, Zura now looked far younger than her years. I'd seen this so often in clients I'd treated for early childhood trauma. Strip away our surface layer of adult competence and confidence, and we were all children. Always.

"First time," she said slowly, her mouth working hard just to make sounds, "I turn eighteen. He say happies birthday and kiss." She pointed to her lips. "Year and year and year, he do it. And neck. *This* year, he touch. He say is time. I scream. He say *next* time."

She had drawn her knees up to her chin as she spoke. She began to rock back and forth.

As a healer, I wanted to go to her, sit down near her, and talk her through this. Maybe have her work on some of the physical mindfulness exercises recommended by van der Kolk or Levine. But this wasn't the time or place.

Or maybe it was. Because no one talked about their pain. Or what they *should* talk about—their time travel ability and how to use it to escape. Something had them so bottled up that they could listen to a Pit mate tell them they'd been raped and…what? Sunday went hunting for the last ping-pong ball she'd shot across the net. Norman turned to help her look. Danny started humming to himself and looking at the ceiling like it was a clear blue sky. Quispe walked to the kitchen and filled a glass of water from the sink. Drank it. Left the glass in the sink and left the room.

Figuring my best bet at getting answers was my overweight fellow American, I walked to the armchair where Danny slouched and sat on one of the arms.

"Everyone here seems remarkably…accepting of how things are," I said to him, not lowering my voice, in case any of the others wanted to join in.

The *pe-tick! pe-tick! pe-tick!* of a new ping-pong game started, so apparently not.

"Combination of things," Danny said, not bothering to look at me.

"Like…?"

"Carefully managing how much pain each of us can handle."

"That's what Bent does?"

Danny grimaced and slouched down further in his armchair so that his belly was poking up almost as high as his nose. "Yup. He talks like he knows everything you're thinking. He's right most of the time. That's fucking scary. But it means he knows when you need a break, too. And when you need reassurance. To be told you're…okay. That this is your great proving ground, and you're going to come out a better man than when you came in. Almost a superman, because he's going to work with me to get control over my ability to time travel and see the future."

"So, you *can* time travel."

"Sure. But it's totally random. With Bent, I'm going to beat that 'sometimes yes, sometimes no.' When we finish working together, I'm going to be *sharp*." His eyes glittered with a feverish vision of this. He was breathing faster.

"Danny," I asked gently. "Do you know what year it is?"

He finally looked at me, took a deep breath, and one side of his mouth crooked up. "Not a lot to signal the days in here. Other than my work with Dr. Bent."

"You know when you came in?"

He concentrated hard. "Twenty…sixteen. 2016. Sure. Trump was running for office. Bent said he got elected."

"He did."

"Ha. Un-fucking-believable. Woulda lost that bet. How's he doing?"

"Just had one term. Impeached twice but not kicked out. Voted out."

"Wait. What?" Danny's face had gone pale. "What year *is* it now?"

"It's 2022. January."

"Holy..." Danny closed his mouth and swallowed down whatever had threatened to come up.

"Time has a way of slipping by, I guess. You ever think about trying to escape?"

He blinked furiously, like my words were triggering. "Used to. Tried. More than once. Fucking guards. Steel doors. Security cameras. Microphones everywhere."

"The others?"

"All of them tried. Different times. Different ways. Zura there... Wow."

"What about Salim Noor al-Rashid? You hear what happened to him?"

Reet shrugged. "Before my time. Before everyone here's time."

"And the Gonzalez brother and sister?"

"Fuck you."

"Didn't they—"

"You can't get out. You try and you pay. You lose your privileges. You go to the lab every fucking day. Gordo beats on you. The doc's mad at you. You get sick. Your mind goes...dark places. It's just...*not worth it!*"

The last assertion was so intense that the ping-pong game stopped. I could have turned to look, but I didn't. I knew everyone in the room was staring at me. In fact, I suspected every one of them had been listening in on this conversation. Feigning ignorance, pretending to be oblivious to it, to me, just as they pretended each day that this prison they were in was just how things were for now. However long "now" turned out to be.

Danny was speaking for all of them and knew it.

"Will you tell me what's been tried?" I asked.

"No."

"But—"

"You're not listening!" His gaze shot briefly to each of the security cameras in the corners of the room, then straight into my eyes. His face had none of his usual cockiness or cynicism when he said, "It's real simple, Jackson, brother of Kenny. You go along to get along. Get it?"

I nodded, and he jerked his gaze off mine and tilted his head back to look at the ceiling again.

"Don't mind me," he said, and started whistling. "Just got a few hours, days, and years to kill."

"Okay, then."

I touched my lower belly as something like a tiny electric shock tingled there. I knew, against all reasoning, it was the transmitter Wenling had ordered put in there. It had just gone off. Here in a concrete lined room that could be thirty feet underground. It felt like I had solid concrete and steel all around me.

Probably it had *not* gone off when I was being brought to this facility. Which meant Wenling, even if she was alive and angry that Bent hadn't released Xiaobo, wouldn't know where SCATTER was located.

I rubbed the spot where my implanted transmitter was presumably sending out little electronic chirps to bounce uselessly against the concrete walls and ceiling of the Pit.

Missed your chance, little buddy.

10

Go along to get along?

MY NEXT APPOINTMENT WITH Bent didn't come for a week. Almost like he wanted to give me time to think about my situation.

I had.

Over and over, I mentally told him to go fuck himself. Or I'd imaging knocking him out, finding Kenny, rescuing the other time travelers, escaping, and burning this place to the ground.

Then I'd come back to reality.

Forget that I, Kenny, Lena, Kansa, Megan, Jude, and everyone we loved would remain targets of the True Believers even if I burned this all down. The fact was, Bent had been dealing with time travelers for almost twenty years now. He'd apparently stopped every one of their escape attempts. Beaten them down. Killed some of them.

But the others were all hanging in there, right? I could adapt like them, bide my time, gather information, and keep looking for a way out.

Or not? A couple days later, Danny and Quispe both had sessions with Bent and came back seriously damaged.

Danny shuffled into the common room, hollow-eyed and nonresponsive. His scrubs reeked of sweat and urine like he'd pissed himself. He only stayed a minute before shuffling back to his private quarters. It confirmed that his way of dealing with trauma was suppression. When he came back closer to his baseline personality, I had to try some mindfulness yoga with him and the others, if they'd let me.

I needed them to survive both because it was the right thing to do, and because I knew I needed their help. Emotionally. Practically. I wasn't going to make it through without it.

But Quispe...

Before I proposed any mindfulness exercises, I'd have to figure out how to handle Police Chief Cruz Condore Quispe. He, too, came back from his lab session hollow-eyed and sweaty. But his reaction to anyone approaching him while he was in this state was to lash out violently. He literally threw Sunday—and I think Danny was right that she'd had sex with the man—against a wall, possibly giving her a concussion. She went as quiet as Danny and Quispe after that.

And finally, it was my turn to see Bent again.

Same notification over the concealed speakers. Same walk through the blue door at the end of hallway one. Same accompaniment by the muscly Smiley-lookalike. Same entry into Bent's laboratory.

A new person inside.

Bent was still there, of course, but now he gestured to a man on the far side of the test bed. The man reminded me of the risen dead in a comic book my big brother Kenny had given me to read when I was only nine. Deep-set eyes with dark rings around them. A small mouth in a taut, skeletal face. Skinny body, but ropy, powerful-looking forearms and hands like the roots of a tree. I imagined I could smell his dusty rot from across the room.

"This is Gordon Trench, Jackson," Bent said. "Former military. Spent time as a contracted interrogator in Abu Ghraib. If you know anything about the history of the place, you'll understand the haunted look he carries."

At that, the man named Gordon gave a pained smile. For just that moment I caught a glimmer of the happy, normal forty-something man he might have been in a different timeline, one where he hadn't seen and done all the things that had brought him here.

You would have thought that would activate my normally compassionate nature.

It did not.

Something in this man looked irremediably warped. It reminded me of the research I'd read into some of the nation's worst serial killers. When you probed what drove them into their psychopathic or sociopathic ways, the evidence suggested they were born without the affective part of empathy, along with narcissism, an urge to manipulate and exploit others, a lack of remorse. For some, these traits didn't emerge until triggered by life experiences, but once they did, they stuck. There was no real "cure" for the condition.

It let me see why Bent would have wanted Trench as an associate. They were outwardly different, but had some of the same cold rot inside.

"Many people find Gordon to be my better half, despite his appearance," Bent said. "Can you see that?"

I looked from Bent to Gordon and back again. "No," I said.

Bent raised his eyebrows. "Really? Why do you say that?"

"He lacks agency."

"Interesting. Continue."

"I believe that you, Uwe, are essentially broken, a psychopath. But with your training and intellect, at least you make your brokenness interesting. Gordon, on the other hand, looks like all the people who slavishly followed Hitler, Stalin, Mussolini, Idi Amin, Trump. Not full psychopaths, but willing to shut down their empathy and reason in order to follow a strong leader who urges them to indulge their reptile responses to things that scare them."

Gordon Trench's brow furrowed. It made the hollow pits that held his eyes even darker.

Bent laughed with delight. "So, I'm the prime evil and he's evil's acolyte!"

"Essentially."

"And you," Bent said with a considered amusement, "continue to surprise me, doctor. You're practically religious in a field that tries so hard to be scientific."

"Does it really? I'm here, the other people in the Pit are here, my brother and Xiaobo are here, because you're trying to wrest control of the movement of time, an elemental force in the universe, the fourth dimension in reality. If there was ever a time for a religious approach, this might be it."

Bent walked up to me so that we stood almost eye to eye. I could smell the peppermint candy he must have eaten earlier. "Do you believe in God, Jackson?"

"No."

"I didn't think so. Get on the test bed."

"Yes, *sir!*" I snapped and walked over to it, passing Gordon Trench en route. He did smell rank, but not from common body odor. It was more like the smell of fear and self-loathing leaked from his pores and turned into a kind of virulent hate. It poured off him in waves as I passed. Like he wanted to grab me. Suck me in.

I reached the test bed and climbed up onto it, waiting for either Bent or Trench to hit the button on the side of the bed that would raise the clear acrylic shields around me. The basic, scared animal inside me yearned for at least that much of a shield between me and these two creatures I was sure were going to do me harm.

Adapt. Survive.

Instead, Bent and Trench both walked to the test bed and positioned themselves—Trench was to my left, Bent to my right—and started pulling down the overhead gear.

Some of it was familiar. A neural headset. ECG pads.

And I wasn't particularly surprised when Bent and Trench suddenly held my arms down so that restraints that were built into the bed could shoot up over my wrists like fibrous steel weeds and trap me here.

I lifted my head to see exactly what had happened when Trench's palm slammed into my forehead, pushing my head flat against the bed so that a similar restraint could shoot up and around my neck.

Instant panic.

I struggled. My legs tried to kick. But I found my feet could only move maybe eight inches side to side, blocked there and above by something smooth and solid. I guessed wildly that the clear acrylic walls had risen and joined to coffin the lower half of my body. And hands—Gordon's I think—had pulled down the lower half of my blue scrubs to press sensors into my groin and around my penis. Or electric shock devices?

"NO!" I yelled. "I DO NOT CONSENT TO THIS! LET ME OUT!"

Before I could totally spiral, however, the cool touch of Bent's hand on my face shocked me out of it. Then his words came, calm like he was talking to a baby. "That's alright, Jackson. I know it's tough to feel restrained. But you're not, really. Not for long. It's just for a short while. To make sure you don't accidentally rip off your leads. We need to measure your brain patterns and other bodily functions. You understand, don't you?"

Who *was* this man?

Switched from pomposity and snark to empathic compassion? How *dare* he? How fucking *dare*—

"I can see your struggle, Jackson. You understand, but you're fighting your dislike of me, your fear, your need to be in control. It's alright. I can give you a sedative if that will make it easier for you."

The panic must have shown in my eyes, because my mouth had gone too dry to speak. I felt my neck restraint choking me, cutting off my air. The blood pressure in my temples, in my eyes and forehead, was building. Throbbing.

It only made Bent nod and smile with more gentleness. "That's okay. That's perfectly alright. Many people have fears about being drugged. Bad childhood experiences, their own or maybe...that of a loved one?"

Kenny. I pushed away the building stroke and worked up enough moisture into my mouth to say, "You know."

Bent nodded compassionately.

Compassionately? My blood started to pound in my head again. This demon would not—

"Unfortunately, we have to monitor your salivary response as well. I think you're probably familiar with this?"

He looked past me. I followed his gaze to see Gordon holding the oversized mouthguard with protruding tubes I was all too familiar with from my nightmare experiment with Lena. A day after I'd met her, I'd had my power to jump back in time shocked into existence. But she wanted experimental proof. So, she'd wired me up, jammed a saliva sensor into my mouth, talked to me for ten minutes, then shackled me to my chair and tried to suffocate me!

To make me jump.

It worked.

I was suddenly back in my earlier me's body with Lena talking and *BAM.* Sudden change in heart rate? Check. Blood pressure? Check. Saliva production? Oh yeah! Hating Lena for a time and planting in her the eventual seeds of our breakup? That too.

And here I was again.

Working up the little mouth moisture I had, I said, "Let's...not and pretend we—"

Trench's leather-tough fingers jammed into my mouth as I spoke and pried my jaw open. Could I have bitten down at that moment? Probably. But then the saliva sensor was in and secured with a strap.

Like the ball gags I knew some people used in S&M games. Why? Because they were freaking terrifying. And crippling. They took your voice. They stole your breath. I desperately flared my nose to get more air in, but it didn't help. I was suffocating and felt like I was going to choke on my spit, even with no spit there. Yet.

Though he was now outside my range of vision, I heard Bent say, "I think you're properly wired now, Jackson. I'm going to check that everything's live and we'll begin. Gordon, make sure he doesn't choke. Yet."

My head jerked his way. Had he read my mind somehow? Had he developed something to read minds now? Was that how they monitored the time jumps? Freaking telepathy? Which meant they'd know everything about me, about my intentions, my plans. What were my plans? Did I even know my name? My

God, I was panicking. My blood raced. My breath turned shallow and fast. I couldn't think straight. My internal triggers started tripping. All the calming work I'd done to shut down these PTSD... But they never went away, did they? Not for me. Not for the boy with the perfect memory. Hell, no! I get to be sick and tormented my WHOLE FUCKING LIFE!

"Better check his BPM, doc," said Trench in a normal voice. Just a dude trying to do his job.

"He's fine!" Bent called back, probably from that rolling chair in front of all the monitors. "I have baselines. So we just need to keep him amused for ten minutes or so! You know how that works, Jackson!"

"Want me to tell you a story?" Trench said, and I realized he'd repositioned himself again. He now stood beside my left shoulder. I could look straight into his eyes. And while the sockets might have been sunken into great black, ill-looking rings, the eyes themselves looked softly sad and pitying. Though it was self-pity, I thought, more than pity for me.

Without waiting for my assent, he began to talk.

I focused on him. Had to focus on something outside myself.

"There was this young guy named Salim Noor al-Rashid," he said. "Young guy. Early twenties. He was the very first time traveler we ever found, Doc and I. During the Iraq war. Difficult time."

He sidetracked to describe some things he'd seen during the war—the brutality of limbs being blown off, the hospitality of Iraqis who were living on next to nothing, how one Iraqi he'd caught trying to plant IEDs right outside the American compound south of Baghdad had yelled and spat at him so hard that the man's rotten tooth had flown out of his mouth in a spray of spittle and curses.

"Salim was cool, though," he said, swinging back to his main story. "He was Iraqi but in trouble there, under arrest, in a real bad spot. We got him out and brought him back to the States with us. Doc was still CIA at that point. Made things easier."

He paused then, as if waiting for me to ask a question. I obviously couldn't, but my breathing had slowed, and the look in my eyes must have finally shifted from panic and hatred to something like rabid curiosity. Because the name Salim Noor al-Rashid had been on the list Kansas had flashed on my screen to memorize before everything had started breaking open on SCAT-TER. And Wenling had told me about him. She'd said her investigator told her Salim was taken from Abu Ghraib prison because he "knew impossible things" about his torturers.

His torturers. Would that have included Uwe Bent? Or Gordon Trench? Was that how Trench and Bent had "found" him?

And why hadn't Bent ever mentioned him? Why wasn't Salim in the Pit with the others? Wenling had said some of SCATTER's captives had died. Specifically, the brother-sister team I concluded had to have been Sofia and Jose Gonzalez. They'd died while trying to escape. But had Salim perished, too? And if so, how? Trying to escape? From the trauma of his experiments here? From suicide?

"Anyway," Trench continued, "we brought him back here and tried to help him develop his time travel skills, you know? But he didn't pan out. Personally, I was never sure he *could* time travel, but Doc was convinced and he's usually right about these things. He keeps developing new tests and new ways to help you people time jump, you know? Innovating. Creative thinking. Like they pretended to teach us in the Military Police. Except with him, it's real."

Trench tapped his head to show exactly what part of his body Trench used for his innovative, creative thinking. It was so reassuring.

"That's ten-plus!" Bent called from his station. "Please proceed, Mr. Trench."

"Got it!" Trench called back. Then he looked down at me with what I think was meant to be a look of compassion. But he wasn't as good at faking it as Bent. Trench's eyes glittered and the corners of his mouth twitched.

Without warning, he reached out and pinched my nose closed.

The blood pressure shot up immediately. It was Lena's experiment all over again!

Which is probably why I instinctively willed my blood pressure down. The situation, the entire setup, *was* so similar to what Lena had done that a part of me had prepared by breathing deeper than normal.

Now I just stopped trying to breathe.

A healthy person should be able to stop breathing for a minute as long as they're relaxed and in decent physical condition. I, for all my anxiety issues, was in great shape from all the training I'd done over the last nine months with the Lead the Way Security team Lena had hired.

So, I looked calmly up into Trench's face even as I worked my lips and tongue around the saliva sensor apparatus Trench had earlier jammed into my mouth. Without being too obvious about it, I could suck in some air from around the device. It was difficult. It wasn't enough. But I figured that if somehow...

"Expected that one, hunh?" Trench said.

He let go of my nose and slapped me so hard on the side of my face and head that my ears rang. Then he yanked the saliva sensor out so roughly that it felt like he'd permanently loosened a couple of teeth.

"Always liked the old way better anyway," he said.

His face disappeared from my field of vision. Through the lingering ringing in my ears and the stinging pain of my face and mouth, I heard a gurgling sound.

Suddenly a thick wet cloth was slapped over my eyes, nose and mouth, followed by a glugging flow of water that hit the cloth and passed through it to fill my nose and mouth. Choking! Drowning!

I tried desperately shaking my head from side to side, but I couldn't shake free of it. Any breath in was water. Just water!

"Good," I heard an excited Bent saying somewhere.

As I fought to survive.

And *stay here.*

Can't.

Must.

I'm going to DIE!

Then maybe you should just—

"There was this young guy named Salim Noor al-Rashid," said a voice above me somewhere as I jerked my head about. "Young guy. Early twenties."

"Whuh?"

My head spun just a second longer before I realized I had the saliva reader back in my mouth, but my nose was clear! I wasn't drowning anymore. I could breathe! I could...

Oh. Right.

"Bingo!" called Bent from his chair in front of the screens that displayed. "Ridiculously easy. Set him up for another. Tell him the story of how we tested Xiaobo."

As much as I wanted to hear that story (Bent had figured out that much about me), the horror of what I'd let myself into with these two sadists overwhelmed my curiosity. It roared back into my chest, out through my tingling limbs, and up through my constrained neck into my gagging mouth.

I couldn't do this! Not again! Never again! I had to get out! Out of this place, this time, this freaking useless trapped shell of a body!

I COULD NOT DO THIS AGAIN! I COULD NOT—

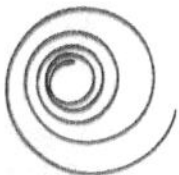

I was stumbling and grunting loudly, crashing into the side of some kind of raised bed that had a plastic shield running around it, covered in buttons and levers and...

Test bed? Yes.

Bent's lab?

Must have been walking.

I grabbed onto the edge of the bed to steady myself. Had to recenter myself. Be here. Be now.

I rolled around so my back was to the bed. There was Gordon Trench, looking at me curiously, deep-set eyes glittering like they wanted to tear me apart.

Just behind me stood the man from my nightmares, Uwe Bent. High forehead, thin-necked mad doctor. Genius psychiatrist, supposedly. Closet sadist who didn't work hard to keep it in the closet.

He stepped to my left now, while Trench edged over to my right, flanking me.

"Are you alright, Jackson?" said Bent in the same compassionate tone I remembered him using in the future of the timestream I'd jumped from. Right after he and Trench had wired me up, immobilized me completely, and jammed that goddamned saliva analysis device into my mouth.

"No, I'm not," I said. I shot a look of red-faced hatred at Trench that was only partly for show.

"You jumped," Bent guessed.

"Oh yeah."

"How far back? How many minutes?"

I almost screamed at him, *Ten! What do you think? I had to jump twice to get back here, out of your fucking restraints!* Except that truth was not something I wanted to give this son of Satan. Truth didn't help me. It helped him. It guided him. Let him know how to handle me. How to control me.

"Jackson?"

I blinked and shook my head in disbelief, like I was counting through the minutes myself. "Twenty? Twenty-five? That's not..."

Bent's eyes narrowed as he studied me. "Your time jump seemed significantly more...disturbed than the last one."

"My last one?"

"The one we had to check the camera footage to see. Your last trip here."

Something in his voice said he knew it hadn't been a real jump. How?

As if to answer, Bent stepped back to the bank of monitors and beckoned for me to follow. I didn't miss the look of disappointment that flashed across Trench's face.

At the monitoring station, Bent hit a key combination on one of the four keypads I could see. The screen immediately above it blinked and brought up an image of my brother.

The shock I felt wasn't on Kenny's face, though it was clear from the way his eyes moved he could see me. Playing along with Bent. Sure. It's why he had the dignity of real clothing. He wore a white, pinstriped, button-down shirt—a colleague, not a prisoner.

"Well?" Bent said to the monitor.

Kenny's drawn, hollow-looking face turned back toward Bent and he said simply, "He jumped. Things changed."

"What changed?"

Kenny's eyes went blank for a second, looking inside, I guessed, at the other timeline he'd seen. "You had him restrained. He yelled and struggled when Gordon put sensors on his penis. You calmed him down by touching his face and talking to him about his fear. Gordon put the salivation tool in Jackson's mouth, then started telling a story about Salim and your time in Iraq."

"And what caused the jump?" Bent asked.

"Fucking *waterboarding!*" I shouted before Kenny could come up blank. Could he remember through two timelines? Would he *see* them as two and reveal that? "Your fucking Igor here put a fucking cloth over my face to fucking *drown* me!"

Bent squinted at me, then turned back to Kenny's face on the monitor. "Is that what happened?"

Kenny's eyes went blank again for a second, then he nodded. His mouth sounded dry as he said, "Yes."

Something about it bothered Bent. He squinted at my big brother's cadaverous face and his voice dropped a couple of tones lower. "If I walk up to see you right now, Kentucky, are you going to tell me the same story?"

Kenny's eyes widened and blinked with horror. He licked his lips with a tongue dry as a lizard's. He nodded jerkily.

Bent held his gaze a moment longer, then smiled. "Thank you, Kentucky. Extra ration of Oxy for you tonight." He shut off the video connection.

Turning back to me, he said, "Twenty minutes? On your first real try here? Do you know what this means?"

"I..."

"Proof you've been bullshitting your earlier supporters."

"I don't—"

"Or else it was just the extremity of the encouragement Gordon supplied. Either way..." He began to list all the implications of my stretched time travel event, how it sped up his plans for me, and, in his pompous celebration of his amazing achievement, he completely missed what had to have shown on my face when he asked his question.

Did I know what this means?

Because, hell, yes, I did. If Bent could threaten to walk up and see Kentucky right now, Kentucky wasn't in some unknown, foreign location. He was alive and in this building.

Which meant all my earlier bullshit about just adapting, resisting, and enduring? That was done.

Somehow, I was going to rescue Kenny.

II

Lena

THE MORE TIME LENA spent with Megan, the more impressed she was.

Jackson's young psychometrist/office manager had indeed known the landlords of both Jackson's apartment and his office space. And her forged Jackson Traine signature, authorizing her to manage Jackson's office in his absence and sublet Jackson's apartment to Lena, were accepted without question.

She wisely kept Lena away from the apartment for a couple days so she could have some cleaners and restoration people clean up the mess made by the people from Scatter. Or was it an acronym? SCATTER?

But on this day, two weeks since they'd returned to Seattle, Megan had finally taken Lena to see Jackson's office because that restoration there was complete. Jackson had long ago set up automatic cloud backups for all patient and financial records, and entrusted Megan with the passwords to everything. That meant the IT people had no trouble rebooting the whole practice. And Megan said Jackson had ordered all the colors and replacement furniture before he'd vanished into the world of Wenling and then Scatter.

Of course, the only psychology that would continue here for now was Megan's psychometry. She had to call all of Jackson's clients to help each of them find a therapist until Jackson returned, if ever.

Lena noted that, for a young psychologist with PTSD, Jackson Traine had built up an incredible amount of goodwill among his colleagues in the Capitol Hill, Central, Madrona, and Washington Park areas of Seattle.

It reopened the ache in Lena's heart over everything that had happened between her and Jackson. For all their closeness, she'd barely scratched the surface of the full man he was. Blinded by the pain of losing her mother to COVID, she hadn't been able to handle Jackson's massive PTSD breakdown a couple weeks after the Demon Monks affair. She'd had no compassion, no patience, no time for him. Which had turned into no compassion, patience, or sympathy for herself. And the decision that she couldn't be with Jackson because *she* was deficient. Not him.

And all that stuff about soul mates? That was an unscientific joke created by hucksters were pushing greeting cards, chocolates, and rom-coms.

But then...time travel.

And Jackson.

The man literally seemed to move his soul between versions of his body, establishing the notion that there *was* something apart from one's active neurons that could move and bond across time and space.

Even the concept she'd explained to him in her first meeting about the "super-attraction" that existed between similar elemental particles and wave forms. Hadn't that been edging into the woo-woo of soul mates?

And you know who would actually be qualified to discuss this with some good research-backed analysis in the psychological realm?

Jackson.

Her maybe soul mate who'd given himself up to a madman, at least partly for her sake.

If that didn't deserve rescuing, nothing did.

"So, what do you think?" Megan said, appearing at Lena's elbow as she stood in the room where Jackson obviously did his counseling.

Lena unconsciously fingered the leather of the purse she carried over her shoulder. "It's very much him."

She knew this, even though his "identity" wasn't something he'd ever made much of. But when you got past the requisite overstuffed armchairs facing one another, you saw Jackson's soul. The repainted walls glowed like a warm, pinky beige sky. The accent pieces on shelves and paintings on the walls evoked fields, forests, and ocean of the Pacific Northwest. The strip flooring was the color of cedar woodchips.

Lena knew it didn't mean Jackson was a tree-hugger per se, maybe not even an outdoorsman, but he was acutely conscious of, and relished his human existence on, this beautiful planet. Ironic, given the anxiety he carried about with him everywhere.

"It's almost exactly like it was before the break-in," Megan said. "Except it's missing the extra chairs he always has for couples or family counseling. I figured we'd get them in if...when he comes back."

Lena nodded without comment.

The two women stood silently side by side for a moment. Megan finally turned to go.

"I called your policeman friend," Lena said.

Megan stopped and blushed so hard her face and neck were almost the color of her hair and her freckles all but vanished. "What did he say?"

"That nothing's showed up on any of the police lines about kidnappings or killings inside the Capitol building. He said they've opened a Missing Persons on Jackson, but that if Jackson was taken in DC, it's up to the DC police to investigate on their end. Or maybe the FBI. Neither one is doing anything."

"That's it?"

"No. We talked about getting together the people in town who care about finding Jackson and getting him back. We're going to meet at the office of someone called Ziggy Cheester tomorrow noon. I think Jackson mentioned him to me a few times. An artist. You said you were free then, right?"

"Yeah." Megan grinned at some secret joke. "Who else is going to be there?"

"You. Me. Bryan. Ziggy. My ex-Ranger guy, Alvin Westor, may attend by remote if he can. And, also remotely, Jackson's sister. You met her in that room in the SCIF. Kansas Traine. I've only talked to her briefly. She gave me the name of the mad doctor who took Jackson, by the way. Uwe Bent. Psychiatrist."

Megan nodded, but she'd grown serious again. "That's...great."

"What?"

"Jude."

"Jude. The guy who betrayed Jackson to Dr. Bent somehow. You saw that."

Megan nodded. "Which means he knows how to contact him again. May even know where he's holding Jackson."

Lena stared, appalled that her own loathing of the man who'd betrayed Jackson had kept her from seeing his obvious value. "What?" she said roughly. "You think he's just going to tell us?"

"I think... I think he made a mistake and knows it. We all do that."

This was even worse. Did Megan know just how badly Lena had treated Jackson? She did, didn't she? Of course she did. Lena felt stripped naked, suddenly, in front of a young woman whose respect and friendship she'd so quickly come to lean on.

None of that changed the truth of what Megan had just said about Jude.

Lena held out her hand. "You got his number?"

Megan nodded and held out her phone. "He called me once to pass on a message for Jackson. If he hasn't changed it."

Lena copied the number to her own phone and dialed. It rang four times, then went to voicemail. "Dr. Spiegelman," she said. "This is Dr. Lena Cortland. We've never met except briefly in that SCIF under the Capitol building. I'm the one with the darker skin and curly black hair. Jackson Traine's...girl friend. Please call me back."

She hung up and saw Megan had sucked in her lips. Her eyes brimmed with tears. In apparent appreciation of what Lena had just done. Which meant, despite all the ugliness Megan knew was in Lena, she still approved of her. And needed Lena as much as Lena needed her.

Lena nodded, firmly pushing down on her own surge of emotion.

"I'm going to have his apartment ready for you by next week!" Megan said. "Fingers crossed for Jude. And the IT guys says it looked like Jackson also backed up his home computer in the cloud, so...maybe something there, too?"

"Let's hope." Lena looked at her phone for the time and said, "Where would he normally enter his client records in this office? Is that computer all set up? Does it have a webcam?"

"Um, yes and yes. Room beside the front desk. Why?"

"I need to make an encrypted call."

The next day, Lena and Megan arrived outside the building where Ziggy was hosting the meeting for Jackson supporters. Lena swung the laptop shoulder bag further back under her arm and made Megan stop before they entered so they could admire the crazy mural that covered the front of the building. Bright, wild colors.

"Hunh," Megan drawled, and dropped her lips with exaggerated boredom. "Flaming SUV with cow on top? How passé."

Lena mimicked her. "And the monkey drinking the Eiffel Tower? So derivative."

Megan snorted and Lena flushed with a sense of accomplishment that she'd nailed the humor of her younger red-headed friend and ally.

"Shall we?" she said, and the two of them entered the building, and right into the din and heat of a humming enterprise that looked like it was pushing deadlines. It was all open concept, with high ceilings, metal rafters, wires, and lighting at all levels. Muffled dance music played from somewhere, but was mostly lost in the sound of people gulping coffee and guzzling chips as they banged away at computers. Some also stood sketching on large electronic art boards, talked on phones, or buzzed around the large-scale printers that made loud thwipping sounds as they churned out specialty product labels.

"Lakeview Design and Printing, ladies," said someone through the noise, and Lena turned with Megan to see a crisply dressed man in his forties.

"Um, Ziggy Cheester?" Lena said.

"The meeting. Few others are there already. Very back right corner. Follow the island music and find the 'door' in the plastic."

Then he moved on and Lena and Megan wove their way past everything else to reach the plastic, which looked backed by some kind of cotton or canvas sheeting. It was literally vibrating with the dance beat, louder now. Not music or rhythms Lena knew. They found the door and pushed their way in.

To find more of the bright art from the mural outside. Framed pieces hung on the vibrating canvas walls of what was obviously Ziggy Cheester's studio space. Unframed canvases sat propped up against the mostly paint-spattered tables and bookshelves that defined the outer boundaries of this studio. Others, in various stages of completion, sat on easels large and small near the wall opposite where Lena and Megan had entered.

At one side of the room, standing around a broad, simple table, stood a group of people, talking loudly over the music. The only one Lena recognized was Bryan Miller, the bluff, clean-cut young police officer (in uniform) who'd taken a bullet while trying to rescue Jackson and Lena from the Demon Monks last year. Now he was Megan's beau.

He was laughing at something said by an older black man with long hair and a beard both speckled with fluorescent paint. Lena guessed this was Ziggy Cheester. He fit the description Bryan had given her over the phone. He also had a strikingly beautiful young black woman who hung off his arm as she ate. Lover? Daughter? On Ziggy's other side was a slim, silver-haired older woman with a very straight posture and forceful presence. Maybe she was Ziggy's lover or wife? She and the girl—a Ziggy harem?

Her questions were over matched by the realization all these people were eating as they talked. Sandwiches! And the table held more on three large plates—thick bread holding cooked meat and grilled peppers. Pork? Smelled like fruity-spiced pork. Lena hadn't realized how starved she was. Other plates held pickles, olives, tomatoes, fresh fruit, baked desserts, napkins. There were plastic glasses, cans of pop (soda, her mother had called it), beer, and an open bottle of red wine.

"Oh my God, I'm so hungry," Megan said beside her.

They shared ravenous looks and headed for the table.

Before they could reach it, though, Bryan plopped down his sandwich and raced over to pull Megan into a hug so tight he lifted her off her feet. She beamed in delight.

At the same time, the older black man who had to be Ziggy Cheester ambled over and, after wiping his right hand on his pants, extended it to Lena.

She grasped it and felt comforted immediately by its large, gentle warmth. And Ziggy's toothy smile. Just as suddenly, a sense of profound loss flooded her whole being, and she had to blink hard to fight back the tears.

"You don't know how waan-derful it is to finally meet you!" Ziggy said over the music.

Lena cleared her throat. "The murals outside! They're all yours?"

"Oh, yeh! Hush now! Go eat."

He held her hand a second longer, like he was saying he understood. Then released her to the table, where Megan joined her. Lena stowed her laptop bag on a chair under the table, and she and Megan dug into the food.

When they'd had enough to feel rational again, Ziggy stepped up to Megan, put his hands on her shoulders, and said over the music, "Wah gwaan, sistren?"

"No-ting, bredren!" Megan said back. Then she smiled when she saw Lena's shocked expression. "Bryan's been teaching me!"

This made Bryan blush and Ziggy laugh. "Make him a yard man yet," the latter said. Then to Lena and Megan both: "Bring de food! Gwan introduce you to de two new!"

The first of the "two new" was the imposing silver-haired woman, who turned out to be a client of Jackson's named Hazel. She'd apparently pressed Megan for information about Jackson until Megan had given in and referred her to Ziggy. Because something had told Megan that what this woman need-ed more than anything else was a personal connection with someone who knew Jackson well and could help her deal with the loss of him. As odd as that sounded, the feeling Lena had gotten when Ziggy had welcomed her scant moments before made it completely understandable.

The woman was very tight-lipped, though, greeting her graciously, shaking her hand, but offering nothing more.

The second of the "two new" was the young black woman. She was Ziggy's niece, Chandice. Up close, she looked only seventeen or eighteen. But when Lena said hello, the girl gave her such an evil eye and up-and-down appraisal that Lena felt the unspoken, What you got that I ain't got?

In another time or place, Lena might have found that funny. In this moment, it seemed tragic.

Lena stepped back to the table and poured herself a glass of wine to drink with the remains of her sandwich.

When everyone had eaten and drunk their fill, Ziggy banged on the table for attention and pointed to Lena.

She lifted her hands and put a finger up to her ear. The music?

Ziggy shook his head and waved everyone to come in close so they were in a football huddle, head-to-head. Even with the music they could hear now when Ziggy spoke in almost a normal voice.

"Br-yan say we got to be careful no one listen in on what we be saying."

Bryan blushed at the call out, but he looked at Lena. "You told me it had to be a place they couldn't listen in somehow."

Lena shook her head with a tiny smile and nodded. "That's what Jackson's sister told me yesterday."

The others all looked back and forth, but it was Megan who finally said it. "You're in touch with Kansas? Is she...okay?"

Lena shook her head. "Not really. But she's going to speak to all of us here now."

Another buzz among the huddlers.

"Let's gather around the end of the table. And maybe turn the music down maybe twenty-five percent?"

Ziggy did that as Lena and the others gathered at one end of the table where Lena now pulled out her laptop computer, turned it on, and keyed in the URL and codes that Kansas had slipped into Lena's Everlane bag that day they left the Capitol together.

Jackson had described Kansas as the smartest person he knew. Her managing that information pass in the situation they'd been in had proved it for Lena. In fact, it had made Lena feel like all her theoretical physics were tortoise-like fumbling besides Kansas' quickness.

Kansas' note had also been what had given Lena enough hope to organize this group. Now she'd see if the people in this room would also—

Connection!

The laptop was using Lena's phone as a Wi-Fi hub as per Kansas' instructions, so the connection was a touch laggy, but the face that came up on the screen was clear.

The tired eyes of Kansas Traine looked out at the group gathered around, leaning in close to see and hear.

"I know Lena, Megan, Bryan, Ziggy," Kansas said on the screen. "Who are the other two? Full names. Address. Date of birth. Social security number of other government I.D. if not American."

Chandice and Hazel gave their information, though Chandice struggled with what matched the last criteria until Ziggy said he'd send along her passport number when they got home.

Of course, Kansas took no visible notes, Lena saw. Because she'd have the same Traine memory as Jackson and their brother, Kentucky.

"Can you all hear me clearly?" Kansas asked when the intros were done.

"Do I need to turn down the music more?" Lena asked.

"Not if all of you can hear me. Listen, I know you've already been sending questions to the police and FBI."

Lena looked puzzled.

"This was Megan and Bryan," Kansas clarified and added, "All those inquiries have to stop. They get funneled straight to Dr. Bent."

"Bent?" Bryan asked. "Is he the guy who took Jackson?"

"And physically tortured me, yes."

"He did what?"

Kansas opened her mouth, but her eyes went dark, and no words came out.

Lena said quickly, "Kansas told me more about him last night. His name is Dr. Uwe Bent. He's a psychiatrist who got his medical degree at Johns Hopkins. He made waves in his residency with a paper about treating people with multiple personality disorders and amnesia by reinforcing the psychopathic parts of their personality. Most did better. Some ended up in jail or dead."

Megan shook her head. "Why'd he kidnap Jackson?"

Lena knew Megan was asking her as much as Kansas. So did Kansas, as she looked at Lena to answer. This meant that for all Megan's seeming acceptance of Lena's pleas of ignorance, Megan hadn't believed them. She'd merely been waiting until Lena was ready to tell her what she knew.

And the others? Ziggy Cheester, she trusted implicitly even though she'd just met him.

Bryan Miller? He'd already gone out on a limb for Jackson more than once. Taken a bullet for Jackson and Lena. Risked getting in trouble with his bosses by using his work to contact the FBI about Jackson's kidnapping.

But Ziggy's niece? And Hazel, Jackson's former client? The people who'd brought them here, Ziggy and Megan, respectively, obviously trusted them to help Jackson. Did that mean Lena could trust them with the secret of what he could do?

If they couldn't, should they even be here?

It was Hazel who decided it for her. She gave a wry smile and said, "It's me and darling Chandice here you're worried about, isn't it? The only ones Jackson himself never really vouched for. Well, I'll tell you this. I'm sixty-six years old. Live alone. But I stable and train horses for about eight rich people at a time. They ever mistreat their animals or lie to me or try to get too friendly, they're gone. The people I trust enough to really talk to are few and far between, but Jackson was one of those. Because I saw right into him, the good of him, the very first time we talked. I got him. He got me. Called me Cassandra sometimes because I worried about things I saw coming and no one listened to me. But he listened, so...I want to help him now. I'm prepared to do whatever it takes, whatever the risks."

She turned to Chandice. "How about you, dear?"

Chandice blinked. Much like Lena herself, who guessed that this was the longest speech Hazel had given to anyone in years, other than to Jackson in therapy.

"Gway now," she said finally, her face flushed from all the sudden attention. "I would do anyting to save Jackson. He and me gwaan be married!"

Hazel held her eyes on Chandice until the girl finally turned back and met the look with an outthrust lower lip. "This woman"—Hazel gestured toward Lena—"needs to know if she can trust you to keep secrets even if Jackson doesn't feel like you want him to feel. Or even loves someone else. Is the only thing you got to offer your dream of being with him one day?"

Chandice glared back and forth between her and Lena, then to her uncle, who was watching her with a bemused question in his eyes.

Finally, the girl's lips quivered, and her eyes filled with tears. "Jackson is family wid my uncle. You don' give up family. Nevah."

Both Hazel and Ziggy nodded. Lena was less sure, but the fact all these people seemed ready to stake their very lives on invisible lines of connection with a man who had seemed incapable of making any close connections a year ago was a kind of wake-up call to Lena. Casual friendships had always come easy to her, but the deep connections she was seeing here were something else. As if the very difficulties Jackson had experienced in making friends meant that when he finally did, they came with a kind of magic glue.

He almost saw Jackson smiling at her when she finally nodded.

She glanced at Kansas, then back to the group. "Okay. We obviously don't know everything that's going on with Dr. Bent and Jackson, but we do know the main reason Bent took him. And while it's going to sound fantastical, I assure you it's not. I even have the scientific data to back it up."

She told them.

Everything.

12

Kansas

As Dr. Lena Cortland began the story about how she'd met Jackson and what they'd faced together when crooked Detective James Gillespie had come after them in Lena's lab, Kansas ran searches on Chandice Cheester and Hazel Cooperson on a second computer she'd set up. Much like a burner phone, she'd been using the second for more sensitive searches with the idea she'd scrub and dump it if she had to move on quickly.

It was bringing in a clean bill of health for Chandice and Hazel.

Good.

Kansas grabbed the box of sesame rice crackers she'd bought late last night and treated herself to some crunch and salt as she closed her eyes and half-listened to how expertly Lena was handling her new "team." She was fully engaging them in her narrative before hitting them with the hard parts. The woman was whip smart, beautiful, and balanced. An obvious catch.

It amazed Kansas that her sweet and sensitive baby brother had won this woman's heart. Jackson was smart but not brilliant, often reckless and emotional, and had lived through so much shit after Kansas left home. And still...Lena. And the loyalty of all these other people.

While Kansas had the loyalty of no one right now except Jackson.

There was a lesson in there that she'd have to unravel and study some day when she had time.

Wait! Lena had shifted gears. Kansas opened her eyes to watch her speak.

"...and Gillespie leaped at Jackson, who fell back onto the security cage around the active particle accelerator and ZZZZ-TT!"

She paused and Jackson's office assistant, Megan, stopped biting her fingers to ask, "He...died?"

Lena looked around at her people. Kansas knew that how the woman handled this next part would likely determine whether they all stuck together and grew even tighter in their possession of special knowledge, or folded and went their separate ways.

"I don't know what happened to him," Lena said to Megan. "This me has no recollection of the confrontation I just told you about. Or the two that followed it. None of Jackson's entrances into the lab any of those times, either."

"What?" Megan said, looking panicked. "But—"

Bryan Miller, the young policeman who stood behind her with his hands on her arms, leaned in and spoke in her ear. Then he drew her back against him, and she clearly drew strength from the way he wrapped his arms around her.

"The only thing I remember about Jackson entering my lab was him walking in and knowing exactly where I was working, out of sight, in what should have been a totally foreign, confusing environment for him. Then he told me all about my top-secret project and what I was discovering with it. Something that even the people I worked with didn't really know."

She paused.

Kansas could see Megan fighting hard to not jump in.

"Then he told me," Lena said, "that there was a man named Gillespie who was going to come into the room and try to kidnap or kill us, something Jackson had just lived through three times already, all with horrible outcomes."

Now the old Jamaican black man, Ziggy Cheester, was exchanging confused looks with Bryan, who was holding a pale-faced Megan tightly to him. The older woman in the back was looking to one side as if this resonated somehow with her, while Cheester's young niece was shaking her head and grinning like this was some sick dope shit or something.

"A time loop?" Bryan finally asked. "Like Groundhog Day?"

"No," said Lena calmly. "Not a loop. When he hit the particle accelerator the first time, it seemed to unlock a latent ability Jackson had to time travel short distances backward in time. Ironically, this was exactly what I had been studying and found evidence for in my experiments. With photons, of course. Not people. Jackson was the first person I had ever encountered personally who claimed this ability."

"And you believed him?" Bryan asked, clearly struggling at least as much as Megan, if not so dramatically.

"Gillespie showed up just like Jackson predicted. We escaped this time, though. And I designed a series of experiments to test what Jackson said he could do. They weren't pretty. His power isn't pretty. It's frightening and brutal in what it does to him. But I became convinced. Yes."

Lena turned back to look directly at Kansas' face through the screen, and Kansas startled a little, her mouth still full of rice crackers. She'd almost forgotten she was still visible to this group. Unsurprising, since she'd spent every hour since leaving her apartment doing her best to disappear. She was currently in a nondescript hotel in downtown DC with high-speed internet. She'd also moved all her money accounts and digital footprints to new aliases, changed every password, hacked into her old account in the NSA's Epsilon group and deleted every record.

Garvey could still find her if he used all the resources of Epsilon, but she figured she still had a day or two before she had to move again.

"Kansas?" Lena asked suspected was a repeated nudge.

Kansas reviewed the last few seconds while she'd been mentally woolgathering and found the question. How had she become convinced Jackson could time travel?

"Yes," Kansas said, reminding herself to keep it simple. "The CIA and other agencies in other governments have been keeping a close watch on Lena's experiments for a couple of years now. Once Jackson hinted to me what he was mixed up with, I dove deeper and found Uwe Bent's name associated with an operation called SCATTER. All capital letters, though it doesn't seem to be an acronym, just a testament to Bent's inflated sense of self-importance. Possibly drawn from the idea of scatter plots, which are gatherings of seemingly random occurrences or findings and putting them in one place to find how they're related."

"Or throwing out so much information yuh can't follow it!" Hazel called from where she stood behind the others.

"Possibly," Kansas said. "In any case, SCATTER was apparently set up back in 2004, specifically to find time travelers. This, after they believed they had found one. Since then, they've taken ten more into custody who they believe can time travel in some way. My brother, Jackson's older brother, Kenny, was one of those ten. Jackson was the most recent."

"What they be doing with them, mon?" Ziggy Cheester asked, casually signaling to the others it was time to stop questioning the time travel and focus on what was happening with Jackson. Kansas liked this man.

"We don't know, exactly," Kansas said. "Experimentation of some sort would be the beginning. This is likely what got Bent kicked out of the CIA. They've had past run-ins with House Oversight on human experimentation. But the online communications I've intercepted between Bent and numerous high-ranking officials, both appointed and elected, suggest Bent is involved in something political."

"Are you going to tell us who they are? The officials?" Bryan asked.

"After I get more confirming data and discuss it with Lena, probably. I will give you this much. They call themselves True Believers. I believe this speaks to a certain strain of fanaticism."

"No shit," Megan said, obviously needing the tighter squeeze that Bryan gave her.

"Just remember," Kansas said loudly, so they'd all pay attention, "you can't trust anyone in a position of power. The higher up, the more connected, the more righteous they appear, the more likely they or the people they report to are part of this."

"So where do we go?" Lena asked. "Who do we talk to?"

"Ideally? Only people you know and trust. People who don't care about political change or power."

"That leaves...you?"

"Don't rely on me. I'll keep looking, but my reach is shorter and dangerous now. Go through your networks. Take it slow. Someone somewhere knows something or someone that can help."

Lena and the others all looked thoughtful. Or crestfallen. Kansas couldn't be sure. Too bad. It was just the way things were.

She nodded at Lena and cut the connection.

Then Kansas sat back in the faux wood and cloth cushion hotel where she'd spent most of her time for the last three days cleaning her digital imprint and tracking Bent's, and she yawned and rubbed her eyes. It was mid-afternoon here to the lunch hour in Seattle. She wondered if she could afford the time to just close her eyes and—

Rap! Rap! Rap!

"Ms. Franco," whispered an urgent voice through the door, using the name she'd used when she'd checked in.

Kansas stumbled stiffly out of her chair and limped to the door. She was ninety percent sure the voice was that of little Salty Jones, the front desk clerk who had day duty, but her heart still pounded wildly. This PTSD nonsense. Instant recall of what it had been like for a stranger to break into her room and wrestle her to the floor. It was horrifying to have a perfect memory of such things.

There was also the fact that if it was Salty Jones, he was here because she'd paid him fifty dollars to keep an eye out for anyone who seemed to be looking for her.

"Salty?"

"Yeah," the voice whispered back.

Kansas unlocked the door. The Black kid from the front desk spilled in and stopped, kicking the door closed behind him. His thin mustache was shaking, and his eyes were wide as they saw her, like maybe he expected her to be packing a gun.

"Well?" Kansas asked.

"Two guys. 'Nother out the front door."

"Asking for me?"

"Say'n whah you look like. Like middle age, square face, no makeup, real smart. Like genius."

"Which had to mean me."

"The way you talk, girl. Said they traced some pee-eye here. No. No. Eye pee."

Her IP address. Not possible. But even saying it ID'd them. "What did you tell them?"

"That you was out. Comin' back rou' four. Don' think they leaving, though."

Kansas looked at the floor for a moment, weighing her best course of action.

"So, I get a tip?"

She looked up. "You get me out of here without any of these guys seeing, you'll get another fifty."

The boy's eyes lit up, and he nodded. "Two back doors. One, like never used. Through the laundry. I go first. Clean the way. Slick as shit."

Kansas nodded and did a quick circle of the room, pulling on her winter jacket and scooping the pared-down essentials of her life into her go bag as she went.

When she got back to the door, Salty Jones had his hand on the doorknob and was grinning at her from ear to ear.

She just hoped neither of them got shot in the next five minutes.

"Let's go."

13
Where did my friend go?

IT HAD BEEN THREE weeks since Bent had slipped up and shown me Kenny was in the same building I was. Three weeks of me trying to coax my fellow Pit mates into talking about their experiences, their powers, or how they'd tried to escape.

Because it occurred to me, from what Bent had said, that even Zhou Xiaobo's ability to jump back a full day might be only a hypothetical limit. That maybe there were time travelers out there who could jump faster and further than me, Xiaobo, or Kenny. Maybe they could even do that with no trauma at all.

That would by why SCATTER hadn't caught them. They'd be too powerful. You could trap them in one timeline, but they could always jump far enough back to start another where they weren't caught.

If they were selfish or evil and moderately intelligent, they could use their power to get fantastically rich and powerful, destroying all opposition.

If they were altruistic or empathetic, maybe they were already doing the work that Bent claimed he was doing. Because even one powerful time traveler, if they saw something horrible happen in the world, should be able to find a way, with enough tries, to make it not happen.

And the rest of us time travelers, we should be able to do something with our powers.

Like me saving Kenny.

I figured if I could at least get outside to the roof or somewhere at the right time—I'd been tracking when the little shock in my lower belly said my transmitter was on—Wenling might see where we were and come get us.

So...how to get outside. That was where the abortive escape experience of the other Pit residents should have come into play. I would learn from their small successes and from how they'd been caught.

Unfortunately, most of them wouldn't talk to me about it. And the one who now would, Zura, was only marginally helpful and kept introducing moral distractions.

She said her time travel gift was even more sporadic than Danny Reet's, but sometimes took her back in time almost forty-eight hours. One such jump, caused by Gordon tearing off two of her fingernails while she lay on Bent's test table, had made her wild enough to try an escape.

For the third time.

When she'd tried to explain how she'd almost succeeded, though, her rudimentary English made it so confusing that all I gathered was she'd know what the guard named Bobby would do, so she slipped by him. Beyond that, I wondered how much of her tale actually happened and how much was a memory her brain had played with so much the through-line had been lost.

She'd also said Chief Quispe was a rapist who'd had sex with her many times, but only rarely with her consent.

I asked her if Bent knew about that.

She said, "Camera all there. Yes? Maybe he like."

Meaning Bent liked to watch? Maybe he did. And this was where I was into the moral distractions. I couldn't just receive this information and do nothing about it. So, I assured her she could come to me if Quispe started bothering her again, but wasn't sure what to do beyond that. Confront Quispe? To what end? Validation for Zura? And what if, in these confined quarters, with possibly the ability to time travel his way out of it, Quispe then took revenge on the girl?

I finally spoke quietly with each of the other Pit mates, mentioning that Zura felt afraid of Quispe, so they might want to step in if he seemed to be crowding her.

They got the message and actually seemed to appreciate it. Especially Sunday Salisu, who nodded knowingly and set her jaw. Maybe about her own future interactions with Quispe as much as anything.

Quispe inevitably got wind I was talking about him and challenged me. When I deflected, he took a swing at me. I avoided the swing, grabbed his wrist, locked it, and stepped my leg around his to take him down and kneel on his thick chest. Hard.

After that, he grumbled and shot me dark looks, but didn't bother me. I noted a subtle shift in respect from my other Pit mates, too. Ah, violence. I still assigned part of my mind to keep track of where Quispe was always.

Somewhere in there, I also learned to play ping-pong, a skill that had eluded me in my childhood years. That got me bonding with Sunday and Norman.

This was good. Especially since I still believed my fellow Pit mates at least had the layout of this building in their collective experience. I'd need that to find Kenny and get the hell out of here.

Regularly interfering with my progress were my sessions with Bent, now coming once a week.

Most notable about those was how I fought with him enough over the sensing equipment that he eventually gave up on everything but the EEG electrodes. Of course, the price for this was I had to actually perform for him. That or face getting physically subdued repeatedly by Gordon and other guards, strapped in and brutalized. Until I time jumped, anyway.

I continued fighting however I could, though. It let me feel I was able to endure until I got enough information or a lucky break that would move me forward.

Then three weeks had passed and something momentous happened...

It came with the unfamiliar sound of the Pit's hallway door opening. I was playing ping-pong with Norman—he was whipping my ass—when we heard the ka-snick of the lock. The click of the latch followed, an almost imperceptible whoosh of air from the larger hallway outside, and the second click of the door closing.

The sound of footsteps.

Norman grabbed the flying ping-pong ball, and we all stopped what we were doing. No one was in their room. Guards never came into the Pit itself. The cleaning and food restocking always took place in the wee hours of the morning. I'd heard the rustling once or twice on nights I couldn't sleep, gone to my door, and found I couldn't unlock it.

Then the visitor entered the dayroom where we all held our breath, and I could almost hear the other six Pit residents all let go of their breaths at once in an, Oh, it's only...

I didn't.

Instead, my guts twisted up inside and I felt my head becoming hot, my hands going cold. It was some kind of fight-flight-freeze reaction. Total mind lock.

"Hello, everyone!" said Dr. Jude Spiegelman, looking around jovially, avoiding my eyes. "Monthly checkup!"

Without asking, Zura walked straight over to him. She didn't look at me as she passed to where Jude stood beside the kitchen table. She just pulled out a chair and sat, putting one arm up on the table for him to wrap a blood pressure cuff around it.

Total trust. She even gave him a little smile.

Of course, she did. Because Jude exuded goodness, didn't he? Kindness. Goodness. Soft in body and heart. Made you want to just snuggle in there and tell him all your troubles. Let him murmur them all away.

He put the pressure cuff around Zura's arm, with the disk of the stethoscope under the bottom of the cuff and the stethoscope earpieces in his ears. Then he pumped up the cuff before I finally broke out of my stasis and walked over. He was also wearing glasses. That was new.

"What's all this medical shit?" I said as I stopped beside him and Zura.

He held up a finger without answering as he released the cuff pressure and wrote on his clipboard, first Zura's systolic, then her diastolic pressure.

Zura ignored me as profoundly as Jude did while he removed the cuff and began taking Zura's pulse from her pale, thin wrist.

"You're not an MD," I said. "You're a psychologist. What are you doing?"

"I'll get to you, Jackson, but you have to wait your turn. Maybe over there." He pointed back at the ping-pong table. "You're making my patient uncomfortable."

"Am I?" I shot back. "Are you uncomfortable with me standing here, Zura?"

She looked up at me, curious. Then at Jude. "No."

Jude forced a smile, but his large cheeks quivered a little. "I still need some privacy for the next part of the exam."

"Which is what? Having her disrobe so you can check for welts or signs of self-harm?"

Zura frowned. I knew her English comprehension exceeded her ability to speak it, but it wasn't up to the task here.

Jude's face went pink. "No one has to disrobe. Ever. But I need to do an interview and for that, I need some privacy."

"In this place. Pagh! Good luck!"

I backed off across the room, anyway, surprised to hear gentle jazz music suddenly play over the loudspeaker. That hadn't happened once since I'd been here. They obviously meant it to protect the "interview" from both the inmates in the Pit and the listeners in the walls. Except I wagered Bent had software that filtered out the music, so the words remained clear to the listeners in the walls.

"Finish the game, bruv?" Norman asked me, holding up his own paddle.

I shook my head without looking at him. I couldn't take my eyes off Jude. Though it physically hurt to look at him as he sat down now, facing Zura, only a part of the table corner between them. My gut burned inside me. I felt a headache lance between my eyes.

How could he just be here? How could he bear it? He had to know what Bent did to every one of these inmates/patients. What he did to me. And he was blithely playing doctor?

Even from here, I could see Zura smiling, then she pointed to me. Jude followed the finger, saw my glare, and glanced back at Zura.

A few minutes later, he scribbled some notes, smiled Zura away and called for Quispe. It made me wonder whether Zura had told him about Quispe. I wanted to ask her now, but Zura walked right past me to her usual spot in the corner where she'd left her book. And when I looked back to Jude and Quispe, they were both laughing and having an animated discussion as Jude measured the older Bolivian's blood pressure. The unkillable Quispe indeed.

Jude saw all the others before finally calling my name.

By then, it had become clear to everyone in the Pit that I had some kind of major issue with this likeable psychologist who also pretended to be a medical doctor, so the others stared at me as I walked over to the kitchen table. I could feel their eyes on me. I could feel how intensely Jude was assiduously staring at his clipboard, like it had something important on it.

I reached the table and stopped.

He started to put the cuff around my arm, and I shook my head.

"I have to file a report," he said, still not meeting my eyes.

I sat down and waved him back into his chair so I wouldn't be towering over him. "Make it up. I'm in decent shape. No physical issues, even with all the ways Gordon Trench tries to torture and kill me."

That got him blinking, though still not looking. "Gordon Trench?"

"I'm sure Bent's introduced you at some point. Dark hollows around the eyes where he used to have a soul? Came back with Bent from Iraq with the first time traveler, Salim Noor al-Rashid, and managed to kill him here in the US. Maybe they just tortured him too much, and he died rather than jumping. Or maybe they intentionally killed him after he tried to escape, the way Bent did with Sofia Gomez Gonzalez and her brother Jose when they were eighteen and twenty, respectively. They'd been prisoners of SCATTER for six years by then."

"I...didn't know all that." More rapid eye blinks behind his new pieces of glass.

"You're a terrible liar. When'd you get the glasses?"

"Last week. Slight hyperopia."

"Can't see what's right in front of your face?"

"I just..." Jude's face had broken out in a sweat now. His entire head, in fact, glistened in the room lights like some kind of pale, mottled eggplant. "There were mistakes made."

"Mistakes?"

He forced his voice to be low and quiet. "When you're trying to change the world... When they're testing vaccines, for example."

"Don't," I cut him off, making no attempt to keep my volume down. "Don't you dare try to bullshit me with some kind of ends-and-means crap, Spiegelman. You had to know the nightmares going on in this place and you supported it. You willingly helped Bent force me in here."

"No!" He finally turned, pulled off his glasses, and met my eyes. His were red and full, and I almost caved. I'd never seen him like this. "That was never the plan. You were supposed to be a willing partner. And what you're describing in here? That's not what Bent told me goes on. He said they've found other ways to stimulate time travel. They abandoned the trauma-induction model ten years ago!"

I looked back over my shoulder at my Pit mates all watching us. "You didn't tell him?" I called to them.

They stared back at me with the same blank faces they gave me when asked about their attempts to escape.

I turned back to Jude. "Did they ever try?"

He was frowning furiously, searching for his glasses case in his pocket and sweating so hard now that his shirt had huge dark sweat stains around his pits and in the center of his chest. "They...might have tried. Once. Not...for a long time."

"Holy shit," I said. "What kind of psychologist are you that shuts down your clients?"

"I'm not a therapist!" he shot back, finding his case and jamming his glasses into it.

"Clearly."

"But I know where this is all going. Do you know where it's going? Why you're here? Why your brother's here? The Chinese kid? All these other amazing wonders of nature watching us now?"

"I don't. Tell me where it's going, Jude."

His lips suddenly pursed tightly together, and he looked up at the cameras in the corners. His face went beet red from the strain.

"Jude! Stop being a coward. Just tell me."

He broke, his body collapsing onto the table. His eyes leaked. His mouth drooled spit. Then he pulled himself together and faced me like he used to face me years ago, in that far-off time when I respected him, and we were still friends.

"Look," he whispered, unable to stop himself from leaning forward toward me like a stereotyped spiller of secrets, "I can't tell you if Dr. Bent hasn't told you yet. He'd kill me. Maybe kill you or any of these other patients if he thought they knew. But..." He looked around for a glass of water.

I waved a hand in front of his face. "But what?"

He nodded. "Okay. Okay. I can tell you this. The only way you're ever going to see Kenny again, in person at least, is if you're fully into the program. Fully cooperating. To where Dr. Bent trusts you."

"How do you know he even wants me fully in?"

"Don't be stupid. Why do you think you're here? You saw what he did in that basement room in the Capitol. That was all for you. He killed someone to persuade you."

I stared at him hard. "And you're okay with that?"

He gave a pathetic shrug. "Ends and means. This is big, Jackson."

I held his gaze for another long moment, then dropped mine. "Have you spoken to Lena or Kansas?" I saw him shake his head in my peripheral vision and snapped, "You little pissant."

"What?"

"You heard me." I looked him in the eyes. "Could you at least call them? Tell them I'm okay and they can't come for me?"

Jude licked his lips and again looked up at the corner cameras. Then he looked back at me and said, "I can do that. I will do that."

I nodded. "Thank you."

I pushed back my chair and stood. Jude did the same. I fought an overwhelming desire to hug him. And to punch him as hard as I could in his face. I finally just turned and walked back to the ping-pong table. There I very deliberately picked up my ping-pong paddle and looked over to where Norman was leaning against the wall, watching me with wide eyes.

He creaked his long neck back oddly, like a bird looking at something impossible. Then he bolted forward to the ping-pong table and picked up his paddle and the ball resting under it.

When I looked over to where Jude had been, he was gone.

And damn him if he hadn't just given me a surge of hope I never expected to feel in this place. Assuming Jude understood what I'd just asked him to do.

Norman served, and I smashed it back so hard the ball cracked.

14

Uwe Bent

BENT SAT IN THE shadows of his laboratory, the lights down low as he and Gordon watched the playback of the Spiegelman-Traine interaction. They watched it on repeat times without distraction.

Bent had enhanced the sound so that every word the two spoke to each other was clear. They dissected the emotive content and assigned grades of meaning with probabilities of alternate interpretations attached. So too the facial expressions, hand gestures and twitches, other physical tells, all equally dissected and put together to be weighed against the baseline behaviors Bent had observed in Jackson Traine both here in the laboratory and on tape for his interactions in the Pit.

Gordon was his final check. He was not highly educated, but he had marvelously canny instincts about people. It's why he was such an invaluable lab assistant. No one could get a person to break as consistently as Gordon Trench. He was the spiritual twin of the Grim Reaper, able to tell when a person's time had come and exactly what it would take to usher them across the great divide.

Bent stopped the video after its sixth playback and turned to Gordon. "What do you think?"

"Traine's too slippery for me to read, but Spiegelman? He's weak. He feels guilty for handing over his friend to you. I don't trust him."

Bent nodded. "My feelings exactly. His conflicted body language and half-hearted defense of the program. He's already a double agent. Inherently prone to deception. I want him followed. Contact our people inside the building to track him inside the building. Have Garvey and NSA follow his every move outside the building. I want to hear anything he says and does anywhere, even if he's all alone watching porn. Yes?"

Gordon nodded and Bent knew he'd follow through. He was a good soldier. He also, like his spiritual twin, the Reaper, scared the crap out of every normal person he talked to.

The True Believers would watch. If the once-enthusiastic Dr. Spiegelman was betraying SCATTER, there would be consequences.

15

Jude

JUDE LOOKED UP FROM his desk in the bowels of the CIA HQ in Langley, took off his reading glasses, and wondered if all the concrete around him on this level subtly reinforced feelings of being in the womb. Was that why he hadn't yet tackled the obligation Jackson had set on him four days ago?

He was safe here in his tiny, lemon-scented, security-protected set of testing rooms and offices. He had his drug cabinets and video recording facilities, talked to field operatives and stressed-out desk jockeys, recommended drugs he couldn't legally prescribe, ran experiments on how to counter sleep deprivation and mislead interrogators. It was not the exciting career the recruiters had implied he'd have when they approached him back at the University of Illinois, but it was safe.

Even his riskier work for Dr. Bent, being a spy for him within the CIA—that still asked little of him. It was make-believe fieldwork. It was literally just a once-a-month drive to the secret SCATTER headquarters. He'd have a sit down with Dr. Bent to talk about the Company, then a brief check on Kenny, Xiaobo, and the time travelers in the dayroom of what Dr. Bent called the Pit, and he was gone again.

It wasn't treason because he had nothing significant to tell Dr. Bent. All he knew about CIA operations were the garbled impressions he got from disturbed employees they sent down to him for examination. He often felt more like an outside contractor in Langley than a real member of the team.

And yet Jackson wanted him to...

He popped up from his chair, walked one full circle around his desk, then put his computer to sleep, called out to his assistant, Darryl, that he was going for a walk, and left the office.

If Jackson's request had just been what it seemed to be, a request for Jude to call Lena and Kansas to tell them he loved them, Jude would have done it already. Lena had been calling him regularly and leaving messages, which he'd guiltily ignored. But he could screw up enough courage to call her to tell her Jackson was okay and that he loved her. He could do that much.

Unfortunately, Jude knew that's not all that Jackson wanted from him. He knew how Jackson's mind worked.

He'd called Jude a "pissant." Why? Such a weird word. Not one Jackson ever used. No reason for it.

Except it sounded like Poussaint.

Meaning Andre Poussaint, the legendary, elusive CIA spy who'd apparently been assigned to rooting out any vestiges of SCATTER that remained anywhere. That was the guy Jackson had wanted Jude to contact back before the awful meeting in the Capitol basement SCIF. Jackson obviously still believed Poussaint had the clout to fix things somehow.

Except the somehow would probably include Jude getting fired, maybe tried for treason. Even if it wasn't treason.

"Really, dude?" he heard himself mutter and jerked his head up to see if anyone had heard him.

A dark-suited man and similarly attired woman were walking past him but didn't look up. Not surprising. He'd walked on automatic pilot to the main floor and was standing at one set of glass doors that led outside to one of the courtyards. Leaves still clung to the trees in the middle of winter because of the warm, wet fall that lasted all the way through January. It was just starting to freeze at night now, though, and all those clinging leaves who thought they'd had it easy were getting a rude wake-up call.

God, Jude knew what that felt like.

He couldn't bear it. He pushed his way outside, turned right, and found the walkway to the parking lot. He had to get out of here.

As he walked, then trotted along, he kept seeing the words of Rabbi Yahuda in his head: "The best of doctors is destined for hell." Elaborated on by the French Rabbi Rashi in the 12th century: "They do not fear sickness. They eat the food of the healthy, and they do not act humbly before God. Sometimes they kill."

But Jude was only a pretend doctor, right? Jackson had said so. And he feared every sickness and didn't eat well, so maybe...

As soon as he'd reached his car, he climbed into the driver's seat and pulled out his cell phone to call Lena. But then another wave of guilt hit him so hard he dropped the phone in his lap.

"Like I'm afraid she's going to shout at me? Expose me? What?"

Jude had never really grasped how someone as smart as Jackson could be so debilitated by his anxious fear of other people. He was starting to get an inkling.

He threw open his car door and climbed out. Pocketing his cell phone, he headed back to the newer section of the CIA HQ, the part that housed the psychology department.

He'd think about this tomorrow.

16
Planning for a raid

It had been five days since Jude had appeared and I'd given him his assignment: Get Poussaint to come and rescue me.

This assumed, of course, that he'd understood why I'd called him a "pissant" and to tell Lena that she and whoever she'd called on by now had to stand down and let Poussaint do the rescuing.

Possible, of course, that Jude still believed so fully in his ends justifying the means that he'd lied when he'd said he'd do what I asked, but I didn't think so. Jude had been fooled by Bent, but I'd given him the chance to see Bent's true colors. Jude wouldn't follow crazy or evil, and Bent was both.

Hopefully, that truth had also overcome any fear Jude had about Poussaint or the CIA going after him for being a double agent, because I needed Poussaint to come. He had the resources of the CIA, the world's most powerful intelligence gathering agency, behind him. They knew how to infiltrate, extract, kill, silence. And all those fears I'd had about True Believers blocking this kind of operation by Wenling, if she was indeed still alive, didn't apply to Poussaint. The old man I'd met in the CIA HQ was a politically savvy survivor. I was sure he could pull together an operation without the CIA's upper brass even knowing about it.

"Okay," Sunday Salisu said.

It jerked me back to the reality of the dayroom in the Pit. I'd persuaded Sunday to join me at the kitchen table to talk a little distance from the others. My modified pitch to her had been that I didn't need the details of her escape. I just needed to understand the layout of the building we were in.

"So glad you agreed to share!" I said and leaned forward to listen better.

She also shifted forward on her seat and squeezed her arms around and under her breasts, making them mound up under her scrubs top like they were really something.

I rolled my eyes and sat back again. "Sunday..."

"I jus' be checking." She widened her elbows and sat a little taller. Then she closed her eyes and spoke.

The Pit, she said, was one spoke on a set of halls that curved out from a central bank of elevators, with stairs in the middle and at either end of the spoke. We were maybe on the fourth floor? She remembered the elevator having twenty numbers on it. There was a second set of laboratories on the floor below us where they took you if Bent was testing more than one subject at a time. A lot more "smart boys" down there as well. I think she meant scientists or their assistants.

I could picture the lower floor clearly because I was pretty sure I'd been only there a few weeks ago when Bent's goons captured me before the SCIF meeting. It seemed like another time, though, because it was. A timeline I only hit once. And only Kenny would remember it, because it was his warning message to my earlier self that kept that abduction from happening again.

"Jackson!"

I snapped my attention back to the room to see Sunday glaring at me.

"I tell you all of this and you don' listen?"

"I heard everything. You described it all very well. You saw a lot."

That mollified her, and she went on. "I left thees place four times. Four times! Never got neah the front door."

I nodded, but inside wanted to tell her that she might soon lead all the others out through the hallways to find that front door. Just as soon as Poussaint's team came storming in.

I'd be heading down one floor to rescue Kenny.

The end was coming.

17

Lena

Per Kansas' admonition to explore the contacts they had who were not in any kind of elected office or arm of the government, Lena reached out to her university contacts to see if they'd been approached about the concept of time travel.

Some had, but not in any serious way that suggested someone was doing practical work in the area.

Alvin finally got back to her about her request for his backup on whatever rescue operation they planned. He and his Lead the Way team had been the critical calvary when both Lena and Jackson had been held hostage by the Demon Monks.

Alvin's voice on the phone was as steady as always, but the news wasn't good.

"You know we'll do whatever we can for both of you," he said, "but I don't know when. That shitstorm I thought we'd avoided with the Demon Monks fallout? It's coming back at us big time. Even with the body cam footage we had. Even with testimony from police on the scene and some of the surviving Demon Monks members."

"How? Why?"

"Take your pick. Mass shootings, Kyle Rittenhouse getting off with his claims of self-defense. There are a lot of people right now who don't like the idea of a highly trained security team using deadly force to rescue its clients. I think we freak them out more than the Proud Boys."

"You're being charged?"

Alvin actually chuckled on the phone, an indication of his high degree of stress. "No. We're not facing prison. We're being sued. By five surviving Demon Monks gang members. You'd like the suit being brought by the skinny leader we let live."

"Cutter."

"Right. Among other things, he's pleading unlawful interference with economic relations. Our gun battle apparently made some of his stock trading deals go sideways."

"That little—"

"Yes. The upshot is we have to lie low for a while. On advice of counsel, we're only taking gigs with a near-zero risk of anything over stage one violence."

"And you think a CIA program gone rogue and kidnapping civilians is above that?"

There was silence on the other end of the line.

"It was a joke, Alvin."

"Except it's not. I'm worried you're going to do something you're not prepared for before we can be there to pull you out."

"Maybe an arm's length consult when we figure out a plan of attack?"

"Of course."

When Lena hung up, she felt such a dark weight on her chest. She'd secretly been counting on Alvin and his team to be her ultimate execution team, she realized. Without them or the traditional authorities to call on, she hardly saw the point of figuring out where Jackson was. They'd have no physical way of getting to him, anyway.

Except Jude might.

She'd recently resumed calling Jackson's college buddy daily, leaving messages on his voicemail that urged him to respond. On Megan's urging, she'd tried to keep it positive, pointing out Jude's obvious sympathy for Jackson's plight and the deep friendship the two men had shared.

The result?

Nada. Zilch. No response. Not even a text.

Megan was wrong about him. Sometimes no answer was an answer.

She dialed Jude's number one more time anyway. Got his warm and funny request to leave a message. After the beep, she said, "Hello, Jude. You know who this is and why I'm calling. Up to now, I've given you the benefit of the doubt, thinking you had to work something through before you acted with love and honor. Time's up. If you don't call me back today, I'll be contacting your superiors and telling them what I know of your continued association with Dr. Uwe Bent, including your knowledge of Bent's illegal imprisonment of, and experimentation on, US citizens. And if that doesn't blow the lid off this thing, I already have information packets set to go out to every mainstream and crackpot media outlet I could find. Either way, get back to me or bend over real deep and kiss your ass goodbye."

She hung up, feeling vaguely queasy. Not because she'd threatened Jackson's friend, but because she knew she probably couldn't follow through on any part of that threat. Kansas had made it clear the CIA had at least some True Believers in its ranks. So, if they saw Lena coming after SCATTER, they were going to come after her. Hard. Ruin her life and that of all the people she'd recruited to help her find Jackson. Maybe just kill her and keep telling Jackson she was fine. How would he know?

She was so bad at this.

Jude's number came up on Lena's ringing cell phone. She let it ring twice more, her heart hammering, before she answered.

"Is this Lena?" a high, trembling version of Jude's answering machine voice said. "I mean Dr. Cortland."

"What did Jackson call me?"

"Um...Lena."

"That's it?"

There was a pause. She could almost hear his sweat drip as he tried, "The love of his life?"

"That's right. So don't fuck with me, Jude."

"I won't... I never meant to..."

"Do you know where they're keeping Jackson?"

A swallowing sound. "Yes."

"Where?"

"It doesn't... I can't tell you that."

"Yes, you can. Just do it."

"I think they're watching me."

Lena thought for a moment. "You're in the CIA, right?"

"Yes."

"And you're a psychologist?"

"Yes."

"So, you should have learned enough self-regulation to do what you have to do to figure this out. Find a way! My threat to you has been extended three days. Come Tuesday morning, if you haven't called me back by then..."

"Bend over real deep." He laughed, then choked over his call-back joke, and hung up.

Lena stared at her phone, wondering if she'd just killed him. And maybe herself and her team.

Theoretical physics was so much simpler.

18

Uwe Bent

BENT WAS STARING OUT the floor-to-ceiling window of his administrative office. The view was to the southwest, on the 24th floor, looking out across the Potomac. It afforded no sunrise views, but often displayed spectacular sunsets like the one happening right this moment.

It was doubly satisfying, knowing that those who had to work in the so-called power corridors of DC would never get such views. The entire town had a tiny-phallus fixation. It had ruled long ago that no one would build a skyscraper in the District that might outshine the Capitol and other houses of government.

Gordon Trench cleared his throat in Bent's office doorway.

Bent turned. "Yes, Gordon?"

"Did you see the report on Dr. Spiegelman?"

"I did."

"Do we kill him?"

Bent pursed his lips together. "I'll think about it."

"But—"

"He's not the only leak. One must be nimble."

"Site Two?"

Bent nodded.

Gordon gave a little bow and retreated from the room.

Bent took one last long, satisfying look at this view he enjoyed so much. It was hard saying goodbye, but he knew the views from his new office would be just as soul filling in their own way.

He walked back to his desk and began punching in the orders to evacuate.

19

Jude

Jude stood in front of the Ganouche Building on North Arlington Ridge Road and looked up its glassy façade to what he was pretty sure, squinting against the sun, were the four floors taken by SCATTER.

No signs of life up there.

Also, no one at SCATTER had answered his calls on the weekend.

It was odd enough that he'd wanted to drive right over to see what was up. But if Bent had put his number on some kind of do-not-answer list, did that mean he'd was in deep shit there? He didn't think his tiff with Jackson had that bad.

But if not that, then...

Jude felt an icy shiver travel down his scalp, into his spine and down, spreading around his chest, making his fingers tingle. Was it possible that...?

No. Not with the amount of equipment, the staff, the...patients.

Swallowing hard, Jude hurried up to the front glass doors and inside. At security, he gave his name and said Dr. Bent had called him in for an unscheduled appointment.

The guard gave him a once over, then checked his computer screen. "I don't have anything listed here, sir."

"I said it's unscheduled. Can you just call up?"

"Who'd you say again? A doctor someone?"

"Bent. Dr. Bent. Applied Science Connections."

The guard looked and shook his head. "No Dr. Bent here. No company by that name."

"Well, that's just..." Jude looked around desperately. The icy shiver had turned from earlier had become a great, yawning hole in the base of his stomach, sucking his heart and soul downward so hard he had to clench his teeth to hand on. He turned back to the guard. "Do you work here normally?"

"I'm new, sir. But I've got a full list of the companies in the building and..."

Jude didn't hear the rest because he was already staggering for the door.

They'd heard him call Lena. They'd probably heard all of her calls to him. They had been following him. What else had he done? What had he told Lena? Anything? But Uwe could have decided he'd shown disloyalty by just talking to Jackson's girlfriend.

Did disloyalty mean death?

His neck was on a swivel as he exited the building and paused on the sidewalk. He warily watched the cars roar by on North Arlington, and more cars just past the grass and bushed on Curtis Memorial Parkway. And the roar of still more past the trees on the Washington Memorial Parkway. All that din would easily cover the sound of a gunshot.

Would the bullet come from behind? From some window behind him? From one of these cars rushing past? Or would it be poison? Or an accident?

His heart thudded loudly in his ears now, each beat precious because each could be his last.

Trying hard to swallow, he hurried to the corner of the Ganouche Building and ducked down the alleyway that headed east toward where he'd parked his car.

As the click of his shoe soles echoed around him in time to his thudding heart, he fumbled out his cell phone and called Lena.

20

More drugs

THEY'D PULLED US OUT one by one from our rooms in the Pit before daybreak. I heard the others crying out and the sounds of scuffles, particularly from Señor Quispe. Our doors had locked electronically after lights out last night to avoid anything untidy.

You exit when we say.

For me, they hadn't even bothered asking nicely. One of the ketamine twins had been in the trio of muscle who grabbed me. He jabbed a syringe into my neck on the way out. By the time they put a black bag over my head, I was too loopy to resist, my body sensations too distorted to figure out anything about which direction they were taking us.

Now that we'd been here a couple of days, the eerie recreation of the Pit from our first SCATTER home is finally wearing off.

At first, I and my Pit mates kept wandering around the dayroom, the kitchen, the hallway, the bathroom, our private rooms. Everything was the same but different. Like maybe we were the ones who'd changed, not the habitat.

Now we all agreed it was the habitat.

The paint colors were just a little brighter. The main hallway was a step shorter. The taps and doorknobs, counters and floors—they were less worn. Almost new.

We'd been moved to a new location. SCATTER base 2.0.

To the others, with their carefully nurtured learned helplessness, this meant nothing. An experiment maybe. Or nothing to do with anything.

To me, it meant Bent had felt heat from somewhere and had bugged out to a fallback location. And what would have made him run? Jude contacting Poussaint.

I stopped against a wall near a new feature of our dayroom, a glass block rectangle at window height with changing light behind it that was probably meant to simulate a window. I leaned forward, pressing my head against the glass, forcing myself to accept the hard truths about what had just happened.

First, my play with Jude had failed.

Second, however SCATTER had transported me, it had been early enough in the day that the transmitter in my belly had not been active. Which meant my only other faint hope of rescue, Wenling, if she was out there and watching for a signal from me, saw nothing.

No one was coming to rescue us.

Why? Because nobody knew where we were, and the chance they ever would seemed remote.

Unless...

A very ugly plan took shape in my mind.

21

The bargain

"THAT'S WHAT I'M PREPARED to do for you, Uwe."

I was in Bent's new laboratory, which was, like the Pit, an uncanny copy that has just enough differences to make you keep asking where you were again? But my nemesis still faced me from his rolling armchair, wearing his oh-so-professional white lab coat. And now he considered my proposal with what I'm sure he considered a most professional scientific interest.

Except, of course, there was nothing even vaguely scientific in the bargain. I'd just offered my total cooperation with whatever he wanted to do with me—full monitoring of my bodily functions, torturing or trying to kill me, specific measures of how long I could jump down to the second, whatever. I would not resist. I would not argue. I would just perform.

Bent tilted his head in apparent amusement. "And in exchange?"

"After five such sessions, no longer than ninety minutes each, and assuming I'm still sane, you will let me see my brother and give us both twenty minutes of fresh air." Which, if Bent kept to his regular schedule with me, would put me in the open when the transmitter in my belly liked to go active.

"Hm."

"It can be in a high-walled compound out back. You can drive us in hoods to a place in the forest and keep armed guards on us. It can be in the middle of a rain or snowstorm. I don't care. But I want... I need to be outside of this place for a short time. Breathe some fresh air. And I need that for my brother, too."

"You assume Kentucky does not have outside privileges now."

I saw again the timeline Sunday had reminded me of, the one where I'd been abducted from the George hotel and taken her, where I'd seen Kenny before he'd jumped back and warned me about the abduction. The Kenny I'd seen in his full SCATTER environment had looked as confined as the group of test subjects strapped onto tables. There was no way they'd been letting him outside. Ever.

In this timeline, this here and now, I looked Bent in the eye. "I do assume that. But if you do, that should make my request easier."

Bent nodded, dipping his head with a slight smile. "I'll consider it."

"You do that."

He swiveled back toward the monitors and used the back of his hand to wave me toward the test bed where Gordon Trench waited to wire me up.

I didn't move.

Bent saw this, smiled again, and gestured to Trench, who came loping around the end of the test bed to grab me.

Except he missed.

He tried again, and I avoided his hands again.

Now, his face growing red, Trench pulled an extendable metal baton out of a holster he wore around his waist that I'd never seen him use. This kind of baton, though, I did have experience with. They'd been the favored compliance weapons of Thing One and Thing Two in the Capitol basement and had destroyed me. In my dreams and waking hours since then, however, I'd worked through exactly how to deal with them.

Trench came at me, swinging one handed. I folded with the swing and brought up my left arm to redirect it outward to expose Trench's lower torso. That let me snap a brutal kick into his belly. It folded him in half, making it relatively simple to swing myself behind him and put him in a choke hold. I tightened it until he dropped the baton, struggling to breathe.

Breathing hard myself, from adrenaline and the savage desire to kill Trench, I looked at Bent. He seemed to enjoy the show.

"Well?" I asked.

"This hardly feels like a good faith negotiation, Jackson."

"How about this? I'll let this asshole live, pretend he's not a psychopath and you're not a psychopath, and put myself entirely into your hands exactly as I promised. But only after you give me your word."

Trench's face was purple. He was almost out.

Bent raised his eyebrows. "You think you can trust my word, then?"

"Not sure. But you break it, I'm sure I'll kill you."

"Now that's an interesting psychological development, Jackson. Every other time you've killed someone, it's been in self-defense, hasn't it?"

"This would be, too."

"Ah."

"Few seconds the brain damage starts."

Bent nodded, smiling. I was uncomfortably sure he would have gotten a certain charge out of seeing Trench go that way.

After a beat, though, he raised both hands. "Terms acceptable."

I released Trench, and he slumped to the floor. Lay still. I had no idea if he was alive or dead. Then his chest heaved and sucked in a breath. Had brain damage happened? We'd have to wait until he was conscious to know.

Bent seemed to have reached the same conclusion and let Trench lie there. He was apparently more interested in me. "Impressive physicality, Jackson. Much better than your performance in the Capitol."

"Different stakes."

"Ah. I suppose so."

"Is this session one, then?"

Bent thought for a minute, then shook his head. "I think not. If I've only got your full consent for five sessions, I want them to count. And I'll need poor Gordon's assistance. So, you're free to go."

I turned and walked to the door.

As I opened it, he said lightly, "Next time you're called, Jackson, prepare for hell."

22

Hell

THROWN BACK INTO THE limbo of waiting to be summoned, I did something I'd never done before. I started pressing my fellow Pit mates to let me lead them through body awareness training.

From the time I was eleven and Kansas left home, I'd never asked anyone for anything. It made sense. If I asked my parents on the rare occasion they were at home, they ignored me. If I asked Kenny, he'd agree when he was in one of his expansive moods, then never follow through. If I asked schoolmates, I was shunned. If I asked teachers, they'd usually shame me for needing help.

Were these memories distorted? Possibly. My memories before I hit my teens have signs of emotional warping. I think because the brain I possessed at that age was different enough that things got encoded differently.

Regardless, by the time I hit my mid-teens, my burgeoning social anxiety was overriding any impulses to risk negative social responses.

So, other than that the request I made of my student Mikael when I was learning about my jumpback power, and the one I sent to Alvin and his team when I was running for my life in the basement of the Demon Monk head-quarters, I didn't ask for help. Ever.

I gave it when Kenny needed me. I gave it if a teacher or other person of authority asked. I gave it in grad school when Jude and others who knew of my abnormal memory needed help with their studies. And, ultimately, I gave it to my clients and students who had explicitly asked for my help by coming to see me or attend my classes.

But push my services on others? Pressure them to do what I said? The mere fact I was doing it now told me how much I my psyche was crying for support before it had to face Bent again.

It also signaled just how much I'd been changing over the past year. Not just dealing with my PTSD symptoms and anxiety, but actually fighting people who came at me, getting aggressive with others who threatened me or those I loved. And now I ignored clear signals of rejection from others and continued to push at them.

"You want to come out of this place a whole person?" I said to Norman and Sunday at the same time as they finished a game of ping-pong.

"Wotchew mean whole?" asked Norman.

"You tell me. What does Bent or Gordon do to make you time travel?"

"I ain't time traveled in...ages."

"Years?"

"Maybe."

"Do they still try to make you?"

Nods from both him and Sunday.

"What do they do?"

The two of them exchanged looks. Because they were standing so close together, Norman tilted his head down so his chin touched his chest. Sunday looked up so high it her face glittered in the light from the ceiling.

Finally, Sunday dropped her face to look at me and said, "He tickles my feet!"

"Is that an expression, or...?"

"I got sensitive feet and he be torturing them, Gordon do. And pinch. And reach up to my kootchy. Twisting. Aiyaaah!"

Not only Norman and I were staring at her now, but all the others in the dayroom. Danny Reet started laughing until Zura walked over and slapped him across the face. "He slap tits. You see!"

"I did not," Danny said. "But I wish I could."

Zura slapped him again, so hard his mouth trickled with blood. He just smiled at her until she walked away again.

Condore Quispe huffed and said, "Si. Gordon like twisting my testicles. Ees very painful."

"He is sick man. Sick!" Zura said.

And before I realized what she was doing, the broad-shouldered Ukrainian had lifted a kitchen chair high and run at the far kitchen corner to ram one raised chair leg into one of the ever-present glass video camera lenses.

The protective casing around the camera cracked and released its child, which tumbled down, severed wire flicking out behind it. It bounced on the vinyl floor maybe three times before it came to a stop.

"We is people!" Zura said and stomped her slipper hard down on it with all her might.

It splintered and cracked and looked thoroughly dead, but Zura kicked its pieces anyway and they scattered thither and yon around the kitchen end of the room.

"That," I said with an approving look and soft applause, "is a good first step in reclaiming yourselves. Now if any of you other inmates in this sanitorium would like—"

I was cut off by the blatting of the room speakers, a notably obnoxious electronic throat clearing before a familiar computerized voice said:

"JACKSON TRAINE, PREPARE FOR A TESTING SESSION IN...IMMEDIA TELY. YOU WILL BE COLLECTED FROM THE...BLUE DOOR AT THE END OF...HALLWAY ONE."

"Ha!" I said to the others. "They haven't even updated their systems. The door we've got now is green."

No one said anything as I headed for hell.

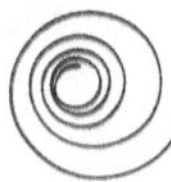

Roughly fifteen minutes later, Gordon strapped me down in a test bed that was so indistinguishable from the last one that I guessed it *was* the last one. They had to have hired trucks and movers to transport key pieces of equipment from the last location to this one. I wondered if Lena might pick up on that. If Jude gave her the old SCATTER address, that is. If he did, plus an estimate of when SCATTER moved from that address, maybe Lena could locate the moving company and track them to this location.

I didn't think so, though. It's why I'd made the deal I had.

Lots of maybes, but it was something to think about while Gordon Trench jammed in IV drips and saliva monitors. He clamped an erection meter around my penis.

I must have flinched on that last one because I saw a smile flicker over Trench's features in my peripheral vision.

Bent called over, "You think we're going to treat you like El Quispe? Not likely. He's a much tougher man than you. Less cerebral. With him, things had to be both basic and extreme."

I wanted to quip, *Like the things you do to me are subtle?* But I could only grunt around the saliva monitor strapped tightly into my mouth. I was finally realizing that its prime purpose wasn't to measure saliva; it was to gag its wearer. All these preparations also burned up time if you did them slowly, I realized. Which Trench was doing today. He readjusted, undid, refastened, repositioned. Perhaps he'd grown tired of trying to lull me through my ten-minute window so... Wait! Shouldn't Bent assume it was a twenty-minute window now?

Bent was on his feet, strolling over to the test bed as Trench finished hooking me up.

"You know what watching what comes next is like?" Bent asked, looking down into my secured and wired-up face.

I glared up at him. *Torture porn?*

"Torture porn," he said. He smiled. "Of course, it's all for legitimate research, seeing what types of stimuli are most effective at making you jump back in time and how far. But I confess to experiencing the occasional *frisson* of excitement over some of the experimental stimuli Gordon comes up with."

And here again, despite his care to be always in control, Bent had revealed another secret about himself. Maybe he didn't even consider it a secret. Maybe he assumed everyone in the Pit assumed the worst about him, so it made no difference.

But it did.

Sadism only sometimes linked to psychopathy, which I'd cautiously diagnosed in Bent. Psychopaths used aggression or violence as a means to an end, but rarely took pleasure in the violence itself. Sadists, on the other hand, took pleasure in the aggression or violence but then felt worse after the violence than they had before. This dip in affect implied a judgement of self, sensitivity to social norms, or a connection to the victim of the violence that you wouldn't expect from a psychopath.

Where did Bent fall in this range of traits?

Bent's voice cut into my desperate attempt to distract myself with analysis.

"I'm not going to be delving into your psyche this session, Jackson, so you can relax about that. This session is all about physical stimuli—fear and pain. You see, I don't believe you need these to time travel. And I think you know that. Your trauma-based narrative is just that—a story. I'm curious, therefore, what it will take to make you admit that to yourself. Or, if you actually do need trauma, must the trauma threaten your life or simply your bodily integrity? And to what degree? And must extreme pain be involved?"

I tried to retort, my words gargling around the saliva sensor.

"I suppose so," Bent said, pretending to have understood what I'd tried to say. Then he turned and walked back to his observation monitors. "You can proceed, Gordon!"

I looked to my left and realized that Gordon had not raised that side of the plastic screen between us. He'd also rolled up a medical crash cart that carried his "tools" for this part of the experiment. They included, in no particular order: a handheld circular saw with no guiding plate, curved bone clippers, a long silver pick and rubber mallet, and a set of surgical knives. All the cutting edges gleamed with a kind of living anticipation for the flesh or bone they were about to receive.

My stomach turned over and blood rushed from my head in a uselessly violent fight-or-flight response that made me grunt and twist back and forth.

Gordon smiled and picked up the clippers.

23

Lena

LENA SAT BACK FROM the computer she'd adopted in Jackson's office and ran her fingers forcefully back through her hair.

Too thick and tangled to work through.

Like the web of masks and lies between her and finding Jackson. They should have been resolving. Instead, they'd gotten murkier.

First, her experiments in the particle accelerator laboratory out in Redmond. The tricky exploration of quantum entanglement continued. Fine. But where was the money coming from to keep it going? Her grant money kept getting renewed. The site security, ZeroFail, kept getting paid.

So, follow the money, right?

The original checks and money transfers funding her research had come from Primary Logic, the shell company Zhou Wenling had first pretended was owned by Amazon. But the checks were signed with an unrecognizable scrawl, and the only contact Lena found for Primary Logic was a colorless voice on the phone named Edward, who refused to answer any questions not directly related to accounting issues.

And Zhou Wenling's death? No one anywhere was talking about it.

Nothing about her alias, Elizabeth Chan, either.

As for the older Chinese man who'd been so upset at Wenling's passing, her team had no name, no address, no clue.

But at least they now had Jude.

Sort of.

He'd clearly been reluctant to lay out everything he knew about SCATTER, other than to say it was not CIA anymore, though it had started as a CIA operation. Then he'd told her he'd tried to go to the building where SCATTER was located, and the entire operation had moved without telling him. No forwarding address.

Jude!

Lena had Megan trying to track down the moving or truck rental company that might have been involved, but so far, zilch.

And Kansas hadn't answered any of Lena's attempts at contact since that first team meeting. She could be dead or captured for all Lena knew.

There was a rap on the door and Megan entered, looking flushed, her orange hair frazzled and bouncing about her face. She started speaking before Lena could say hello.

"You know there's a tech team that's been making sure they brought back everything Jackson backed up to the cloud?"

Lena frowned. "I thought they'd finished with all that weeks ago."

"I did too! But apparently one of these guys—um, I'll call him Alan because that's his name—found a bunch of stuff Jackson had backed up from his home computer, except some of it's kind of, like...burned? No, wait, that's not what he said. But like, Jackson tried to erase it from his own hard drive and didn't do it well, so some of the...bits...got uploaded. Alan's been trying to put it together. He figured out it's an email that Jackson had tried to send! Guess who to."

Lena's mouth went suddenly dry. "Me?"

"Yes! And a bunch of other people. Like it was an insurance package, right? It looks like he wrote it right before his first trip to DC."

Lena worked her tongue around until she had enough moisture to speak again. "That's good. When does he think he'll have the whole email readable?"

Megan's face fell a little. "Soon. He thinks. He's not sure when, but I figured...hope?"

"Yes." Lena nodded. "It would be good to have something like that."

Megan tried to smile and turned to leave. Stopped. "Um..."

"What?"

"Maybe don't tell Bryan about this if you see him? He thinks Alan's been coming on to me and doesn't really want me talking to him."

"Overreacting?"

"Um...maybe?"

"Careful then, Megan. Don't risk losing something good. You never know if you'll ever get it back again."

After Megan sucked in her lips and left, Lena turned back to the computer and tried contacting Kansas again.

24

Jude

JUDE HAD PULLED OFF his glasses and was pacing about his basement office in the CIA's new building again. Drab white table and desk. Softly vomitous walls. Concrete floors with area carpets. A splash of color there and in the few hung paintings, all abstracts. Mechayeh!

And the heavy, heavy silence of a tomb. For this was the place where Jude spent days in clandestine research, then more days helping debrief operatives back from Ukraine. But all of it ended up hidden away, buried in the cozy hole he dug deeper and deeper for himself every day he worked here. Failing his country. Failing his best friend. Failing his best friend's girlfriend, who'd just wanted to know where to find the man she loved.

Just failing.

Until today.

Today, he was going to surprise everyone. Most of all, himself.

On his next pass around his desk, he scooped up his phone and slipped it into his suit coat pocket. Gray suit coat because he was a gray man. A man who looked competent but forgettable. It was how he'd been able to slip between the CIA and SCATTER for so long. He was just good enough at his job to draw neither criticism nor praise. He was just there.

Normally, this galled him. It was partly why, he supposed, he'd taken the risk of working for Uwe Bent when the CIA kicked him out. It made him feel important.

Now, though, he was counting on it to sell the story he was going to tell Andre Poussaint.

Jackson had told Jude in that phone call before the SCIF that Poussaint could be reached through Robert Wilson or Amit Dadashev. Jude had found Dadashev's number first and called him. Stuttering a little at Dadashev's Russian accent, he'd blathered something with "SCATTER" and "Andre Poussaint" in it.

An hour later, Dadashev had called back with directions to a third-floor office in the original headquarters building.

And here Jude was.

The office was fronted by an opaque green glass door over sound-deadening carpet. The door bore no badge or marking. Jude would never have dared to simply push his way in, except that Dadashev had told him that's what he had to do, so...

He entered to find only Dadashev, sitting in the one chair in the room, beside a side table just big enough to hold Dadashev's phone. The sharp-faced man looked up but did not rise. Only his upper lip did, a sneer clearly designed to frighten its recipient.

It worked. Jude's mouth went instantly dry and sticky.

He licked his lips and spoke anyway. "This is his office?"

"You see him here?" asked Dadashev.

The Russian accent made Jude's testicles retract. He looked around to avoid meeting the man's eyes, but there was nothing else to see except for the room other door, on the far side of the room. "Is that where...?" he indicated the door.

"No." Dadashev's word came out with such scorn that Jude blushed, suddenly knowing how all his Ashkenazi Jew ancestors must have felt at the end of the nineteenth century when Imperial Russia's White Army swept through them with pogroms again and again. They drove Jude's people from their homes, burned their possessions, destroyed their communities. Later, the Ukrainian units of the Red Army did the same thing in Poland. Then the Soviets.

"I told you why I needed to speak to him." Jude managed.

"SCATTER." Dadashev's face didn't twitch. "So?"

"Just tell him that. He'll see me."

Dadashev turned and spat on the floor. "I know what SCATTER was. We all know what SCATTER was. This is not some big secret. What do you know about SCATTER that we don't know about SCATTER?"

"That...it's still active."

"You know this how?"

"I…can't tell you."

"Really?"

Dadashev stood up slowly from his chair. As he did, Jude wished again he'd done this when Jackson first asked him to on the phone. Then he'd have had a time-sensitive location—the Capitol basement SCIF—to share and it would have been such good intel that…

The door on the far side of the room opened and Jude saw what looked like the most desiccated old white man he'd ever seen. Easily late eighties or nineties. Stooped. Frail. But with deep-set, sharp eyes and skin pulled taut over the bones of his face.

"Well, now, Mr. Dadashev," the man said in a drawl that Jude thought could have come straight off an Alabama cotton plantation. "I think I'll pick this up from hee-yah."

He waved Jude into the inner room.

Inside, Jude halted in surprise.

It wasn't from the extraordinary brightness of the office, with its wide windows looking out to the headquarters' well-treed grounds. It was the other visitor who had gotten here before him.

"You're the man who was with Zhou Wenling!" Jude said.

The man, Asian, possibly in his seventies or even eighties, but fit and ramrod straight, rose from his chair and bowed modestly at his waist to acknowledge Jude.

"Yeah-ump," said the crotchety southerner, who limped around the large glass desk that was clearly his. He dropped his skinny set of bones into the leather office chair there. "Doctor Spiegelman, this hee-yah is Colonel Fang Jian." He glanced at the Colonel. "I get that right?"

Colonel Fang nodded.

The southerner, who Jude was increasingly sure was the legendary Andre Poussaint, tapped his finger on the computer monitor on his desk and turned it sideways so Jude could see it. "We were watching you on my little screen hee-yah."

Jude looked and saw what was obviously the room he'd just come from. Amit Dadashev was still there, seated again, frightening even in this tiny digital version.

"Colonel Fang tells me you were working for Dr. Uwe Bent. That right?"

A shiver went through Jude. He had so carefully prepared his cover story about Jackson telling him about SCATTER, Jackson being his entire source of information. Now... "I was. Kind of."

"Kind of?" Poussaint smiled. It wasn't reassuring. "Kind of like independent contracting? Or like being a double agent and betraying your organization and country with a man who wants to destroy it?"

Jude frowned. "He doesn't want to..."

"Before he was kicked out of this organization, he proclaimed he was going to put together a team of time travelers who would correct all the horrible mistakes the US government had been making for decades. What do you call that?"

"Ambitious?"

It was a nervous joke, but Poussaint didn't take it that way. "Might call it treason. Which you have apparently been aiding and abetting."

Jude's blood ran cold. He wanted to deny it but knew without thinking that Poussaint would have little patience for that. "I...came here to help you stop him."

It was half true. Jude desperately wanted to stop Uwe's worst impulses. Specifically, the ones that made him torture the time travelers.

Poussaint was examining him now, but not in the way Jude would examine CIA officers to see if they were hiding things, emotional or otherwise. No, this felt more like an appraisal of Jude's most essential value. Was he worth listening to? Was he worth more alive than dead or incarcerated?

"I...uh...don't know where Dr. Bent is right now," Jude offered weakly. "But I can tell you where he was and when they likely moved out, give or take twenty-four hours. With that maybe..."

He gulped. He'd offered this much to Lena Cortland on the phone and felt her immense disappointment in him. Only a fraction of the disappointment he had in himself. And she'd still thanked him, welcomed him to the team of people trying to rescue Jackson, asked him to tell her if he came up with any new ideas.

But he hadn't told her he was going to do this.

Maybe he should have.

Maybe today was the day he became a vanished person.

Poussaint tapped one finger on his desktop. "Would you say you know Jackson Traine pretty good?"

Jude nodded hard.

"And if he had some kind of transmitter sewn into his belly, would he have told you that?"

Jude's mouth dropped open. He looked at Colonel Fang. "Did he ask for that?"

Fang's head twitched almost imperceptibly. No.

Jude looked back to Poussaint. "Never told me. No. But if he's got this tracker on him, who can track him?"

Fang and Poussaint looked at each other. Poussaint said, "We can. Now."

"Seems this tracker only comes on about two times a day. An hour each. Dr. Traine knows this." He looked for confirmation to Colonel Fang, who nodded. "But Colonel Fang hee-yah and ourselves have yet to pick up any signals. You think that's your friend's doing?"

"I d-don't..." Jude sputtered, then remembered Jackson's forceful coded request to get Poussaint to find him. He wouldn't have known that Wenling's henchman had told Poussaint about the transmitter, but he would have counted on it as some kind of backup. "No. Jackson wants to be found. Where they were keeping him was mostly concrete. The transmitter signal wouldn't have worked. That may be the same situation where he is now. How far is the range?"

Poussaint nodded at Fang, who said with a strong accent, "The transponder sends a signal to local cellular networks. Code tells it to pass the signal to communication satellites. They send it to our receivers."

"So as long as they're in a city..." Jude said.

"Your friend, Dr. Traine," Poussaint interrupted. "He gonna find a way to get that signal out?"

"Jackson's the most determined man I know."

"Well now, seems you and Colonel Fang agree on that much."

"So, when a signal comes through...?"

"We might just call on you then, Dr. Spiegelman. Meanwhile, we'll pick your brains to learn all we can about time travelers."

Jude felt a rush of hope. For himself. For Jackson.

"Of course. I'll cancel all my other plans and—"

Poussaint's chuckle stopped him cold. "Yes, you will," he said. He made a hand gesture

The door Jude had entered through now let in Amit Dadashev. The rangy brute jerked Jude's hands behind him, bound his wrists together with something, and marched him from the office.

25

Lena

Lena wondered if this was what a military general felt like.

At night, she was still sleeping at her aunt's house out in Redmond. Each morning saw her driving to the particle accelerator lab and touch base with her staff, review progress and brainstorm tweaks to the existing experiments. (Solid confirmation of cross-dimensional quantum entanglement was only months away. She was sure of it.)

Then she drove into Seattle to Jackson's office, where she was now. Here she sat at his desk and took over his computer and phones. She used these to cast research fishing lines into the great ocean of the internet and keep in close contact with the other members of her Jackson-retrieval team.

This was an intelligence war. Taking a chance, Lena was using the same procedures she and Kansas had used for their two video calls. Kansas had said it hid their calls under a cloak of redirects and bounced IP addresses. Lena hoped it would do the same thing for her online search for SCATTER and its True Believers.

Alvin Westor had tapped Kajika Bighouse to discretely help her. Kajika had directed her to a website maintained by a public nonprofit group called Open Secrets that listed all the financial disclosures of the sitting government officials in Washington, DC. Kajika had also shown her how to highlight anomalies. There were a lot.

It was a start, but how could she—

"Lena!"

Megan's frazzled orange hair and flushed face burst into the office, her knapsack purse swinging wildly around her torso.

The timing couldn't have been better. "Please tell me something new," Lena said.

"Two things." Megan brushed back her hair. She'd obviously run to get here because she hadn't been in the office this morning when Lena came in.

"First, Ziggy Cheester and his niece visited the East Precinct that Bryan works at and where Ziggy's done sketch artist stuff. He tossed around references to SCATTER and almost got arrested. Then Bryan stepped in—he's amazing! And Ziggy and Chandice came back with a list of three people who definitely know what SCATTER refers to."

"True Believers in the police force," Lena said. "You have the names?"

"Uh-hunh."

"Excellent! Second thing?"

"Allan, my computer guy,"—she blushed, but Lena said nothing, so she continued—"retrieved those emails Jackson deleted."

"Yes...?"

"Nothing really, beyond what you got from Jude and we already knew. It was back when Jackson thought SCATTER was run by the CIA."

"Then..."

"But while he was undeleting that," Megan said, "he found some contemporaneous notes about Jackson reading newspapers that changed in real time. Physical newspapers. He thought it was evidence of time travelers changing the timeline."

Lena frowned. "Or moving him from one timeline to a newly created one."

"What?"

"Does Allan have a copy of the notes?"

Megan dug into her purse and pulled out a folded set of papers. Handed them to Lena.

Lena unfolded them and began reading.

"It's weird, right?" Megan said. "Like, how could Jackson remember what the papers used to say? Shouldn't he have just seen the new headlines when the timeline became like that?"

"Yes," Lena mumbled, still reading.

"It's because he can time travel, isn't it? Or maybe just because he's got that memory thing. Can't be fooled by things changing. He remembers everything."

"Right." Lena was remembering Jackson's obsession with newspapers now as she read. It had started a few weeks after he and Lena had escaped from the Demon Monks, and he'd recovered in the hospital from being shot. He'd never told her what he was doing or why. Probably because she was already shutting him out by that point, and he'd known it. Had been afraid this would only drive her away faster. He'd probably been right.

"You know who else has that kind of memory?"

"What?" Lena's head shot up.

"His sister."

"Oh my God. Megan, you're a genius."

The girl beamed, her smile filling half her face as the color made her freckles pop. Raggedy Ann, the brilliant detective.

Because though Kansas had not answered any contact attempts since she'd helped Lena through that first meeting with the other Jackson friends, she might very well leap at this chance of tracking what SCATTER was up to.

Lena whirled back to Jackson's computer and started madly going through the communication protocols.

"Can I watch?" Megan asked quietly.

Lena stopped and turned. If anyone had earned the right, it was this young woman.

Lena nodded, then dove back into the process.

26

Hell X 4

It had been almost a month since I'd made my bargain with Bent.

I was in my fourth session of... How many had I promised him? Five. Right. I could bring that memory back with effort. But it was competing with SO MANY OTHER FUCKING HORRORS. And the coffee I'd managed to grab by pushing Quispe out of my way to get it just before the announcement calling me here? Had I drunk that? Had I gone somewhere?

"So, what are we going to try today, Jackson?"

"Where am I?"

I blinked and saw exactly where I was. The laboratory. Fourth session. Right. I wasn't blind, exactly. But there were so many VERY VISCERAL realities competing in my head at the moment. There was... No. Shut that out. And... That one too.

"You said we tried totally removing your sexual organs last time," Bent's voice said from somewhere, making me writhe and twist from the memory. I was on the test bed. Trench had raised the test bed restraints side around my legs, pinning them down. Now he was fastening my wrists and neck.

"No," I moaned. I saw my groin area, all intact down there. In this timeline. This one. Stick to this one. Until I looked at Bent and saw him waving the same scalpel Trench had used to cut off my penis and testicles. "Nooooo!"

"Or were you just making that up?" Bent said. "Like you made up how you jumped the first time in here when you didn't? Or how you jumped twenty minutes but somehow haven't been able to replicate that once?"

Bent sounded angry. Like maybe he really thought I had made up my post-jump report last time. I started shouting. Loudly. Maybe incoherently. It was so hard to separate what was happening from what had happened. But I caught words of it. Blood. Sliced. Spurting. Pain! HORRIFYING LOSS! BURNING! No, wait. The burns were another session. Acid and fire. My whole body...

"Jackson?"

"Shut my mouth! Shut my mouth!"

Wait! No saliva sensors in my mouth! Right. Right. Bent had ruled my being able to speak had more value than knowing how much spit my jumps generated.

A long silence filled the room. Had I gone deaf?

"Hello?"

Where was I again?

The Pit?

No. I walked free in the Pit. I bounced off walls in the Pit sometimes. Danny helped me. So did Sunday. After a couple of days, I'd come back to myself. Sort of.

Until I came back here, and EVERYTHING came RUSHING back in BRILLIANT, LURID, SENSORY, FUCKING DETAIL!

Still silence.

I swiveled my head back and forth. The laboratory lights seemed dimmer today, but I could see Trench standing to my left. Just standing there with his blank face and hollow eyes, watching me.

However much I swiveled my face to the right, I couldn't see Bent. He wasn't sitting in his usual monitoring chair. Had to be up and walking around, intentionally staying out of sight.

Was he even real? In this timeline, I mean. Had I killed him or something? There were so many realities and competing sensations—pain, more pain, panic, despair—coming between me and the here and now.

"I'm here, Jackson."

Bent's voice came soft and seductive from right behind the test bed, which meant above my head, the only place I couldn't look.

My body froze in fear. Tight. Vibrating.

"I have to say I'm disappointed in you," Bent said, still silky and seductive. "You said you'd give yourself unreservedly, but even with every opportunity I've given you, you've kept lying to us about what you can really do. Enough that I'm thinking you've programmed in those chains around your psyche."

"Chains?"

"Mental blocks. Controls. I'm not sure what you hope to accomplish through that. Such a pain-fraught plan must have enormous rewards."

"I don't...get it." But I was trying. I grit my teeth tightly and tried to focus on Bent's voice, what he was trying to tell me. Because if there was any way out of this state that had become my new normal, I really wanted to know. Focus. Listen. FOCUS.

"I know you've figured out that the trick of time traveling, at least for highly aware individuals such as yourself, involves giving up your ties to your current reality. Does it feel a little like death?"

I gagged in what might have been my body's attempt to laugh. "You've killed me how many times?"

"Now have we really? No, no, no. No need to answer. Just think about it. You say we killed you, Gordon and I. Did we? We hurt you. We scared you. We made you believe you were about to die, perhaps. But it was you, your will, your mind, involuntarily or not, that pulled the trigger and shot you out of one body into an earlier one. Is that death?"

"YES!"

"Yet here you are."

I squinched my eyes closed. He didn't understand. He still believed the bodies I jumped from, the ones he'd drowned, chopped body parts off of, burned to the bone, now simply never existed except in my memory. And I couldn't tell him that they did exist. Every time I jumped, I created a new timeline for myself and anyone my actions affected. Which meant one version of my self, my soul, jumped to an earlier body, but the me I jumped from also continued on, burned, drowned, maimed...

But I would not give Bent that knowledge. I'd keep that for myself to one day use against him. Even if he was sure I could do more. Even if he thought all he had to do was push harder, see just how much pain I could take.

Which meant what? Every sick thing he'd done to me, every awful trauma I'd experienced before Bent was in me. I could look away sometimes, but they never left. Real horror. Real pain. I could look at my arm and fucking vividly see, feel, hear, taste it getting hacked off and spurting blood. I could smell the cooking skin as Trench slid a glowing poker into my belly. I could—

"You've got to give it up, Jackson."

That voice. I wanted to choke the life out of that voice.

"The terrified grip you have on this reality—that's what makes each jump feel like death. You're habituated to the terrors that make you jump. Like a drug user, your tolerance increases, and we have to give you twice the dose to get the same effect."

"Not...true," I said.

"Really?" said Bent's voice, harder now. "Then prove it to me, Jackson. In five minutes, Gordon will begin to remove every piece of skin from your body. He'll start with your feet and work his way up, so you'll have lots of time to feel what's happening. A surgical flaying. Do you know that without skin, you lose most of your fluids and your other organs flop out all over the place?"

"Are you going to jerk off while that happens?"

"Jump back in time now. Tell me about this plan and I won't go through with it. Five minutes."

I started to wish hard. Focus hard. Had to... Had to...

"One minute left, Jackson," Bent called from his usual chair in front of his monitors. "Anything?"

Sweat ran in rivers from my face, into my ears, into my eyes. I blinked wildly and shook my head. My heart thudded so fast it sounded like a freight train in my ears.

"It's not that easy!" I shouted.

But it had been that easy at one point, hadn't it? When I was just a fragile, PTSD-ridden guy trying to please Lena but still reliving my teen traumas.

Now everything was so jumbled, I couldn't concentrate. I was so filled with terror of every timeline that jumping from one to another wasn't safety at all. I yelled at myself in my head, trying to find my failures and shame and need to escape, but it was like standing on a high board with snarling dogs behind me and an empty concrete pool down below.

Jump! Jump! Jump!

I can't!

"Twenty seconds," said Bent.

"I've got NOTHING!"

"That's too bad. Really sad."

"I can't...focus! This room. You. Gordon. This bed. Everything you've done. It's too much."

"Three...two...one."

I refused to look as I heard the wet sound of a knife slicing into flesh. Then the bolt of pressure and pain hit. I screamed and screamed and...

27

Kansas

KANSAS GAVE LENA VERY specific steps she had to take before meeting Kansas near Jackson's office.

The steps included: 1) finding an actress who could look like Lena to anyone who saw her through the office window, 2) having that actress enter Jackson's office building in a hooded raincoat, 3) swapping clothes with that person once she entered Jackson's office, and 4) leaving the way the woman had come in, carrying nothing of hers, no phone, no purse.

Kansas had tapped into the messaging system of the low-rent SCATTER agents surveilling Lena. She followed the chatter of the bored watchers as the hooded actress entered the building. Kept listening as Lena later left in that actress' clothes through the same exit. Their conversation confirmed they were locked onto trackers in Lena's clothing or personal items. Since those were still in Jackson's office, they assumed Lena was.

Five minutes later, Kansas drove her little rented Nissan to the place two blocks from Jackson's office. Lena stood waiting in the hooded raincoat, looking impossibly chic. At her feet was a stuffed daypack.

When Kansas opened the passenger door, Lena swung the pack into the back seat with a grunt. "The papers. No clothes. No personal items." She climbed in the front, unzipped the raincoat, and threw back the hood. So much hair. And a multicolored blouse that made everything about her pop.

Kansas nodded and drove them south, feeling hopelessly drab in her own brown sweater and slacks.

It was the first time the two women had been together in person since the SCIF in the Capitol basement. Kansas felt the silence growing awkwardly between them as she hunched over the steering wheel and drove south through dark drizzle and heavy traffic. But she had to concentrate, she told herself. Focus.

As they did the loop around to cross the Lacy Murrow bridge, the traffic bunched up and Lena finally asked, "Where are we going?"

"A place no one will look. No check ins. No records."

She could feel Lena's eyes studying her now and felt herself blushing. Jackson's woman was...hot. There was a physical presence to her that Kansas hadn't felt over their three video conversations. It was more than just the incredibly curly hair, dusky skin, strong cheekbones, and obvious intelligence. It was a way she had of moving, even now in her seat. Graceful and so sure of herself. Like she belonged wherever she was. And her gaze now burned almost as much as the touches that 'Lizbeth Chan AKA Zhou Wenling had given Kansas so long ago.

"Up close, I see the resemblance," Lena said. "You and Jackson. Same nose. Same eyes."

"Hunh."

"I miss his eyes."

The pain and longing in that one sentence brought Kansas back to solid reality. "We're heading down to Renton," she said. "Our childhood home. My parents still own it but are rarely there. The nanny we all had as kids is basically a permanent house sitter there now. I spoke to her. She knows we're coming."

"They weren't monitoring that?"

"Not since Jackson was taken. I've never gone back."

It was Lena's turn to say, "Hunh." Then, "Where've you been? I reached out ten or fifteen times."

"Florida. I'm being hunted."

"Explains the tan. The nervous eyes."

"The eyes are from driving in the rain. Haven't driven in years."

Even as she said it, some jackass in a Mercedes whipped in front of her and Kansas slammed on the brakes and swerved to the right to avoid getting rear-ended.

When she'd steadied out again, her hands white-knuckling the steering wheel, she looked to her right to see Lena's hands just as tight on the seat edge and grab bar. Their eyes met, and they both cracked up.

"That would be a way to go!" Lena said.

More cackling.

And just like that, Kansas suddenly felt like she'd found the sister she'd always wished she'd had growing up.

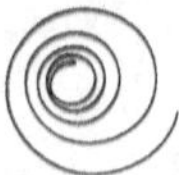

By the time they were creeping along 183rd, just above the parkland that surrounded Lake Youngs, Kansas' curiosity almost matched Lena's.

Kansas also felt guilt, of course. She'd left the place as soon as she was of age and never returned until Kenny went missing. And then, mostly just long enough to reconnect with Jackson. She'd apologized then for abandoning him, but hadn't really explained how, if she hadn't, she would have drowned in this place. Her mother's intense expectations had been like daily whippings from an absent goddess you could never please.

"That's the one," she said now, parked on the side of the road just past the driveway. Before getting out, she reached over in front of Lena, popped the glove compartment, and took out the gun she'd bought after her close call in DC.

When she drew back with it and snapped it into its holster by her appendix, Lena said tightly, "That's what I think it is?"

"Sig P365 with manual safety."

"You want to take that inside with you?"

"Not leaving it in the car."

She saw Lena think it through and nod, accepting it.

Lena grabbed her heavy daypack, and they both left the car.

Meeting Carmelita at the door and being enfolded by the woman's short, fleshy body felt surprisingly familiar. Enough so that Kansas hugged her back and actually shed a tear or two. Then Kansas introduced Lena and reminded Carmelita that they were mostly here for work. Private work.

Carmelita nodded. "I clean out the basement for you. Bought clothes for Ms. Lena. Fresh air. All good."

"Thank you, Nanny," Kansas said without thinking. She almost bit her tongue before she saw how much it made Carmelita grin from ear to ear.

Five minutes later, Kansas and Lena were in the basement study Kansas' father used to use as an office in the days before it all went mobile. The daypack's contents, twenty-two newspapers that included multiples of the Seattle Times, Epoch Times, and South China Daily News, were spread in piles on Kansas' father's old oak desk. Kansas and Lena sat on either side of it.

"Okay," Kansas said after she'd helped arrange the papers by date and mentally cataloged all the cover stories as they did so. "I know what you think Jackson did. What do you expect me to do?"

"The same thing." Lena explained Megan's theory of the Traine memory and her own understanding from Jackson of how it helped him time travel.

"I'm not Jackson. I'm not even Kentucky. I can't time travel. And if all it took was the Traine memory to see the changes time travelers make, why haven't I seen them before?"

Lena sighed and stared hard at the oak desk and spread-out papers. "I've been thinking it through. To start with, I established recently that time traveling photons don't change the timestream they jump back in. Once they 'land' at an earlier point in time, they create a new timestream that branches off and can be different. So, assuming the same process happens when humans time travel, they jump back and create a new timestream at some point. In that new timestream, different things happen, and the newspapers are different."

Kansas held up a hand. "Okay, let's say that happens. You're not the time traveler and you reach the point where the timelines split. You suddenly become two people. Version A keeps going on the original path with the original news stories. Version B is part of the new timeline where there are different news stories. Version A will only ever see the newspaper stories from the first timeline. Version B will only ever see stories in the second timeline. What am I missing?"

"Nothing," Lena said and grinned. "Except we know Jackson saw changes even when he wasn't the one jumping. He somehow saw both timelines."

"And? How?"

"Here's where we get into some exciting speculation. I established multiple timelines by showing a quantum entanglement between particles in one timeline and another. If the same thing happens between an individual existing in different timelines, I'm guessing the intense similarity between them, on some neural network level, actually shares experiences."

Kansas stared. Lena's cheeks had flushed, and her eyes sparkled. It reminded Kansas of her own inner excitement when she'd received a last bit of signals intel that had helped her put together a clear picture of what was happening inside a hostile foreign nation. Even so... "If we stay connected to our other-timeline selves, why aren't we aware of them or their lives?"

Another Lena grin. "I think we are. Sometimes. In dreams. In moments of déjà vu. Maybe in the visions some people claim to have. But the longer we're separated, and the more our different-timestream lives diverge, the more confusing it would be and the more we dismiss it as a weird memory artifact. Unless you have a very special kind of memory that knows exactly what happened at each moment of your life. Then maybe the shared memories would be so clear it would be like you'd lived both sets of experiences."

Kansas leaned back in her dad's old swiveling office chair. She felt a cold sweat on the back of her neck and wasn't sure why. Maybe it was the reminder that if she ever let her mind just drift, not focusing on the now, the vivid immediacy of the past could be overwhelming. "You realize that adding another whole set of memories to a person's life could drive them insane?"

Lena's face fell for a moment. She looked stricken with guilt.

Kansas waved it off. "But since you've got someone with that kind of memory here now, I'll tell you you're wrong. I don't have endless déjà vu experiences or double memories. I'd know."

Lena nodded. "Neither did Jackson before he started time traveling. I think the changes wrought by a time jump have to affect the world you see around you. And there may be a training period before you notice the discrepancies."

"Not counting his own time jumps, how long did it take Jackson to see changes? I'm assuming the newspapers were his training."

Lena had the grace to look crestfallen. "Months. It was a bit of an obsession."

"And we're here how long?"

"How long can you stay?"

Kansas held her eyes. "You want me to sleep here. With you."

Lena knit her brows, obviously feeling there was something she wasn't getting. "I figure you'll sleep in your old bed. I'll sleep in Jackson's bed."

Kansas put aside the foolish rush of disappointment and considered. "You arranged for your actress lookalike to stay in Jackson's office overnight?"

"One night. Two. Until I get back. I'm paying her well. I've spent days on end there without going out. It's not that strange."

"But expensive."

Lena shrugged.

"I can do two nights. Then I've got to move. Like I said, I'm being hunted."

Lena was suddenly all smiles and looked sixteen, not thir ty-seven. "We'll order in pizza!"

"We'll eat whatever Carmelita has in the kitchen."

"We'll laugh and tell each other secrets!"

"You don't sound like you're taking this very seriously. My brother…"

"…Is the most important thing in my life right now. And I am hanging on by my fingernails here, trying to cope. I thought maybe sharing some time and confidences with his brilliant sister while we unravel what the hell has happened to him might help. Is that alright?"

Kansas suddenly understood some of the manic energy in this woman. It wasn't Kansas' way, but she could see how it might help someone as emotionally labile as Lena. "It's alright. You really want pizza?"

"No." Lena turned to the newspapers. "I want you to scan through all of these once."

Kansas sighed and pulled her chair up in front of the first stack. "And what are you going to do while I do that?"

Lena smiled, stood, then said as she headed for the stairs. "I'm going to talk to Carmelita about food…and what you and Jackson were like as children."

Kansas wanted to feel grumpy but could only smile as she reached for the first newspapers. Emotional. Funny. Smart. To have her as a sister-in-law…

28

Chronodisruption

I'D AGREED TO FIVE sessions with Bent where I'd cooperate in whatever experiments he wanted to run on me. In return, he'd let me see Kenny. Outside.

It had been a bargain of cold-hearted desperation when I'd realized that other than Jude, no one who might want to rescue me knew where I was. And when we'd moved locations, even Jude wouldn't know. That left the little transmitter Wenling's doctor injected into my lower belly as my only hope. I felt it trigger regularly in what I thought was early afternoon. Also sometime past midnight. Maybe 2:00 a.m.?

So, if it lasted through five sessions, and if Bent kept his word and let me get outside at the right time, then Wenling or whoever monitored the signal could see it and come for me. And I'd had found out where they kept Kenny by that point. I'd rescue him, the others, bring down SCATTER.

I was so close, right?

But my fourth session, Trench flaying me alive, taught me I wasn't going to make it.

When I jumped back to my earlier body with my body intact, I kept screaming, over and over, unable to stop. I remembered my disorientation even as my brain recorded every moment, subjective and objective, in a crazy stew. Objectively, I jerked and twisted about on the test bed, the tug on my healthy legs telling my very unhealthy brain that the skin was gone from it, the blood and bones loose and bleeding out everywhere, that Gordon Trench was now slicing open my scrotum and perineum like the bottom of a bag of groceries, and...

Trench stepped closer to me in his pristine dove-gray set of pants and shirt. Maybe to hold me. Maybe to slap me.

I saw him covered in gore, head to toe. My gore. All over him.

I projectile-vomited at him, which set off a cackling nightmare of laughter from Bent, wherever he was.

My heart was pounding so hard it was going to burst out of my ears. My vision was shot with red and black, darker, taking away my world.

I passed out.

I woke up to find I'd been carried back to my room in the Pit. The change in location was enough to break the spinning horror that consciousness brought, but just barely.

I could still see, hear, smell, taste, feel everything.

All of it.

And again, not just the flaying, but the limb removal, the burning, the choking, the endless series of beatings and gunshots and knifings and falls, but all the way back to Dead Eyes nearly kicking me to death as a high schooler just trying to make his brother come home.

It was all there at once and equal in its pain and force, much more than before, because I was losing my ability to keep my then from my now.

"Fuck it," I breathed, fighting the panic. "You can. Get up."

I rolled out of bed and collapsed to my hands and knees on the floor, almost vomiting again.

"Get up."

Who said that? Me?

I pulled myself up and, foot by staggering foot, made it out to the dayroom, where the other pathetic inmates turned ghostly faces toward me.

"What?" I challenged them.

And collapsed.

A beat later, maybe an hour or three, I felt a hand on my shoulder. "Need a hand, bruv?"

I blinked open my eyes to see Norman's lanky, big-nosed form kneeling and leaning over me.

"Wh-when?" I asked.

"They brung you back three, four hours ago. Sunday thought you was dead."

"He look like what you pull out of dee ground," came Sunday's voice from somewhere.

"I feel that way," I said and was perversely gratified by her tittering laugh.

With Norman's help, I got my knees and hands under me. Then my feet. Finally rose to standing and pantomimed the wave of greeting a wounded soldier might give to his family when he returned home from the war.

As one, the entire crowd of them, other than Norman, who was holding me, returned the wave in ghostly silence.

There was a small squawk from our room speakers, like it was clearing its voice, and then it said in its usual robotic female voice,

"JACKSON TRAINE, PREPARE FOR A TESTING SESSION IN…FIVE MINUTES. YOU WILL BE COLLECTED FROM THE…BLUE DOOR AT THE END OF…HALLWAY ONE."

"Aaoh," said Norman from where he continued to support me under my right arm. "What the fug? Same day?"

Day? Was it still day? When had my last session been? Morning? Night? Bent had begun mixing up the times because he knew what it did to me.

"Chronodisruption," I muttered. "Thomas Erren and Russel Reiter. Also, sleep deprivation. Durmer and Dinges. Used in interrogations. Abu Ghraib. Guantanamo Bay. Mess up my cognition. What time is it?"

I looked at Norman, and he looked back at me. We both laughed. Because there were no clocks or watches in the Pit. Not even windows. Just lights on and lights off approximations.

"Think I could make five minutes be five hours?" I asked, and we laughed again.

I pushed him away and walked to the hallway.

29

Hell X 5

I ALMOST FELL A couple of times en route to the lab and my meathead escort had to catch me by the arm and support my walk.

It wasn't because I was weak or sick, though I was, but because I kept losing my sense of where I was and what I was doing. Was I walking? Standing? Sitting? Lying? Jumping from a roof? And suddenly my knees would give up and I'd fall.

The escort looked pissed by the time we reached the lab. Especially when I gave him a big, goofy grin, my current form of, "Fuck you very much." Just an attempt to feel something other than the terror that engulfed me as the lab door closed between me and Meathead, and I knew I had to turn and face Bent and Trench again.

"Jackson," Bent said behind me.

I didn't turn around.

"Jackson, this is the fifth session in our agreement. I need your full cooperation, or it's all been for nothing. Bargain canceled. What a waste."

I squinched my eyes and mouth tightly closed and turned around.

"Open your eyes."

I tried. It took fighting the little child in me that had come up from somewhere long buried deep in my subconscious. That little child had determined monsters only became real if you could see them. Ergo, the best way to fight them was to keep your eyes closed, so they did not become real.

"Jackson!" Right in front of me. I could smell the monster's breath!

My eyes flew open to see the watery form of Bent and his enormous forehead, long skinny neck, less than a foot away. I blinked and blinked and finally cleared the tears.

Bent studied my face. "Remarkable."

I swallowed hard, trying to find my voice, my courage, my sense of who the hell I was and where I was. Nothing came up.

"Don't you think it's remarkable, Gordon?" Bent called back over his shoulder.

Trench's sunken-eyed form grunted from his station on the far side of the test bed, the Satan bed, the restraining prison of the damned.

"Oh, it is," Bent insisted.

"Wh-why?" slipped out of my mouth. I had no idea what I was asking. Why was it remarkable? Why was I here? Why was I born? Why existence?

"Ha!" Bent laughed. "Even there. See? I think everyone who's ever known him has probably been impressed by his memory. This is understandable, of course. His memory is freakish. An absolute genetic anomaly. But it's unearned. Nature gifted it to him at birth. The time traveling is almost the same. The accidental application of a genetic gift. But compare him to his similarly gifted brother or sister. What do you see?"

I looked around me. What did I see?

"The brother, who, granted, has a predisposition to mental illness, cannot handle the drugs and traumas inflicted upon him and his mind becomes silly putty. The sister takes all those traumas and analyzes them into the ground. Her brain would rather disintegrate the irrational than use it. But this sibling...oh, he has fought hard to function despite his trauma, to find meaning and control without denying its existence!"

I was gritting my teeth now, struggling to process Bent's rant because it might tell me what was coming next. But all I'd managed was, "I...fight."

"Yes, you do, Jackson. Even though I've done my best to drive you past that to where you need to go to become truly effective, you just refuse to go. Your mind will jump from mortal peril, perceived or actual. But you never embrace the act. You keep returning to your rational world, your principled, limited self. Very disappointing. But fascinating."

I stared at him, open-mouthed. I had no clue what he meant. Though, to be fair, I was having trouble putting together who he was and why I was here. The facts were there, but the meaning of it all eluded me.

"You know what we're going to do here today, Jackson?"

My gaze shot involuntarily to the testing bed.

"No. Not that. Today, I'm giving you a free pass on your fifth session, because I think how you experience your reward will tell me more than anything I'd get from hurting you in this laboratory."

"Reward," I said. I was pretty much down to one-word summations.

"As agreed to," Bent said and signaled to Trench.

Trench walked around the test bed and straight to me. I saw he had something dark in his hands. He raised the dark, floppy thing as he approached, and only at the last second did I see it was a thick black bag. Maybe the same one they'd pulled over my head when they'd driven me from SCATTER HQ1 to HQ2.

On it went.

The sudden blackness threw me into instant panic, all my realities rushing in to fill the void. I flailed about and my knees gave out, but someone had me around my chest. A great iron vise around my chest. Squeezing me. Killing me!

"I got ya, doc. Calm down."

A rough voice. A tortured voice. Trench's voice. Like he wanted to soothe, but that part of him was long dead and the words came out like cudgels.

It made me stop struggling, though, and just sagged in his arms, breathing hard. The physical restraint and awful voice had reminded me of where I was. Giving me a modicum of control. Barely there, but there.

"Maybe today is not the best day to meet your brother, after all?" Bent's voice said.

"N-no! I mean yes. Today!" It came out thick and a little garbled. Like my brain at the moment, fighting hard to hold on to myself. This self.

"Very well, then. Gordon, take him upstairs."

"Is that...?" I struggled to put my thoughts in order. "Is that...?"

"Where Kentucky is waiting for you? It is. We've cordoned off a section of the roof where you two can chat, or babble and grunt, to one another in the fresh air. Twenty minutes, as per our agreement."

"Wh-why?"

"Because we don't have time for your nonsense anymore. Do you understand? Things are accelerating and I need someone reliable on my team."

I wanted to call out something brilliant like, Oh, then I'm obviously your guy! But even turning my head to where I thought Bent stood made me so dizzy, I had to stop and breathe deeply. I was really not in good shape. It was all in my head, of course, but even as I struggled to cling to the now, all the wounds and beatings of my body kept resonating inside me, roiling my stomach and making it hard to believe I could stand and breathe and walk.

When Trench released my chest and shoved me toward what I assumed was the door leading out, I stumbled and stopped. Something had just twinged in my belly. The transmitter!

"Time?" I called out.

"It's still light outside. You won't be in the dark," Bent replied from some-where.

"Time!" I insisted and felt my stomach roil again. Was that all the twinge had been?

"Time is our line of work," he said carefully. "Isn't it?"

He must have signaled because Trench shoved me again, and we were out in the hallway. I heard the change of the echoes, the thump of our feet, Trench's and mine, turning corners, walking through different soundscapes than I'd heard before. Typing. Buzzing. Blowing air. Conversation. I get lighter and more focused the further I get from Bent's lab, even with the smell of Trench beside me.

I heard an elevator door slide open. We went in and it closed. Buttons clicked. We rose upwards like soundless spirits.

Trench spoke en route, so quietly I almost couldn't hear him. "Sorry," he said. "The flaying. Acid. Limbing. I don't remember doing any of it, of course. But I've done worse. Necessary."

"Am I going to die?"

"I don't think so. Why?"

"Why are you apologizing?"

Trench didn't answer for a moment, and I started to think we'd reach our floor before he did. But then he said, "I just... If anyone could understand, I figured it'd be you."

What did that mean?

Before I could ask, we'd reached our floor and the elevator door dinged open. Trench marched me out and down another set of halls. Then he stopped without explanation.

I swallowed and reached out with my non-visual senses. There was some thing...familiar about the air. A smell? An electrical feeling?

I lifted my hands, unbound, since Bent assumed I'd cooperate to get to see Kenny. He wasn't wrong. But now I asked, "Can I take off my hood?"

From maybe a couple of feet away, a voice as familiar to me as my own rasped, "Jacky?"

My heart flipped over, and I went to tear off my hood, only to have both my hands caught by others that were hard as steel.

"Don't," Trench growled in my ear.

"Kenny," I said. "It's me."

"They told me I was going to see you." His voice sounded exhausted and lost.

"You will. He will, right?"

"Outside," Trench said.

"Okay," called another voice from somewhere further down the hall.

Trench shoved me and I heard a stumbling sound and other footsteps like Kenny's minder had shoved him along, too.

A couple of minutes later, we'd gone through a door into a room that smelled of gasoline and grease, climbed some metal stairs, and pushed through a creaking metal door. Wind blew into my clothes, cold but not icy. Almost like it carried a hint of spring and the sound of distant traffic. Once upon a time, I could have gone back through every day I'd experienced in this place, counted them up, and known exactly what date it was. But my time with Bent had mangled that, mushing my timelines together in an unholy, unruly jumble.

I was just glad I could stand up and connect with where I was right now. Especially where I was right now.

I felt Trench's rough hand on my head and the thick bag that covered it suddenly shot upward.

Brilliant light hit me in the face, and I shut my eyes tight. Then opened them just a slit, squinting and shielding even that with my right hand.

And there beside me, almost comically mirroring my moves, was a face I'd seen on screens over the last year, and before that way back as a teen. And the face that time was getting dragged away, beaten and bloody. Weeping.

Now it squinted at me, hand at its tired golden brow for shade, gradually opening its eyes wider and wider until the person was fully revealed. A person who, despite the hollowed-out sallow skin, too many wrinkles around the eyes and forehead, and a look of vague bewilderment, was someone I knew and loved.

"Kenny," I whispered.

"Jacky," he responded. "I didn't believe them."

"I know. I wouldn't have either."

"I didn't see this."

"Because you haven't been through this timeline before," I said.

"I didn't see it."

"You didn't live it."

He didn't speak for a minute, apparently trying to figure out what I meant. Like maybe he believed he'd been seeing the future? Could be. But I'd long ago concluded it was more likely he did some version of what I did, living one timeline, then jumping back to an earlier point in that timeline with a memory of the first timeline's future. If he was still being fed narcotics, stimulants, or psychedelics, he'd find it awfully hard to get it all straight in his head.

Witness my own struggles today. No drugs involved.

At least I had finally had enough clarity to take in the view—a harbor, tall buildings of a downtown area across the water from the flat concrete rooftop we stood on. I didn't recognize the downtown or harbor, but something was pinging in the back of my mind. It would find a match later. Also, Trench. He still stood there, barely a foot away, listening in.

"You mind?" I said to him.

"I don't mind, but I gotta watch."

"In case what? We plan our escape? Jump off the building?"

We had to be at least twenty stories up, and the idea of planning anything with my muddled-brain brother...who'd time traveled to save me from being snatched back in DC! Who (despite Lena's explanations) helped get me and Lena out of the Demon Monks' HQ back in Seattle!

"Don't be a wise-ass, Traine," Trench said and glanced at his watch. "Sixteen more minutes."

It was the shortness of time that turned me around. Why had I only asked for twenty minutes? Why had I offered five full sessions of hell? Didn't matter. It was what it was. And I couldn't feel the tingle in my belly that I sometimes felt when the transmitter was on down there, which made me think my earlier feeling had been wishful thinking.

Besides, the sky was still bright, but the sun was way back to our left. How late in the day? And did we have to be in DC for Wenling or her watchers to pick up the signal? This was definitely not DC.

What I should be focused on was my brother. Here. Now. This brief time we had.

I turned back to Kenny, who was looking at me with big, watery eyes that were going to make me cry, too, if I didn't find a better direction to take this.

"You know where we are?" I asked him. He wore a vee-neck sweater and khakis like a real person, so maybe?

"Baltimore. Yes. Xiaobo says it's one of the worst cities in the country to find a girl. He liked DC much better." It was like he wanted to say how much he loved me and had missed me and how miserable his life had been, but he knew he couldn't speak about anything directly.

"They let Xiaobo out? He can come and go as he wants?"

Kenny's head bobbed. "Long as he comes when he's called. Long as he tells them the truth."

"And you. Do you ever get to go out?"

"I don't want to go out."

"Even like this? Fresh air?"

"I've got important stuff to do."

"Like what?"

"Like checking on Xiaobo. And you."

"Checking how?"

Kenny's eyes wandered like he couldn't bear this anymore. His lips started making sounds like he was a bass guitar. "Bum bum, ba-bum bum bum, bum bum. Back up. Watch traffic..."

"Kenny..."

"Xiaobo's finished his operation. He's going out."

"What?" Kenny had developed ESP now?

"The motorcycle sound down front. Xiaobo rides a Triumph Street Triple RS motorbike now. Very loud. I follow him on video sometimes. SCATTER-follow did a whole night surveillance last week."

"Really?" That sounded pretty Orwellian, but maybe it helped explain why Kenny didn't feel the need to leave the SCATTER nest. Ever.

"He's not leaving. Whatever he did... He doesn't know where to go now."

"I thought he was a loyal foot soldier."

"He used to be," Kenny said. "Until you talked to him..."

It looked like was about to say more, but Trench suddenly stepped forward and clapped a hand on Kenny's shoulder. "That's enough."

Kenny swiveled his head to look down at him. "I didn't say..." He stopped and raised his eyes from Trench's face to the distant sky. "What's that?"

I looked where Kenny was looking and saw an array of three dots against the pale gray horizon, evenly spaced out. They seemed to be getting bigger and bigger.

Then I heard the sounds.

The roar of jet engines sounded farther away than the growing dots, but maybe that was because those dots had already broken the sound barrier and were getting here faster than their sounds.

Up the Maryland coast? From where? Why? Going where?

"Fuck me," said Trench behind me. "They're coming straight at us."

They did look like they'd ducked down slightly and changed course. We saw only their noses now, getting bigger fast. Grey bodies. Windshields. Stubby wings with downward bristles. "I don't see how you can..." I began.

Trench grabbed my arm and Kenny's. "Come on!"

I shook him off. "We've still got time! You can't just..."

Then I stopped as two of the bristles under the lead jet's wings dropped and shot straight for us. Mesmerized by the approaching rockets, I almost missed how that jet pulled up while the second and third planes kept coming.

I saw Trench running for the door going down, and I finally grabbed Kenny to run after him.

We got five steps before the first missiles hit, and the world exploded.

30

Killer jump

Things got confusing.

My training under Bent had dulled my body's automatic time jump reactions, so I didn't jump until the missile had hit and sent its explosive force and chunks of concrete tearing through my body.

Then my mind finally said, I'm out of here!

But even as I found myself standing dizzily on the rooftop again, the bag coming off my head, something suddenly ripped me from that body, too.

I was back in my room in the Pit. My head spun harder. I felt nauseous.

But when?

And...how?

The smell and feel of my body, warmth of my bed. Beginning of my day? How could I be here?

Xiaobo!

Except, how did I even know I'd been yanked back? The other times he'd jumped me, I didn't feel it. I was just back in time, not knowing it was different until something didn't fit my unconscious memories of the previous timeline.

But this time, I knew instantly. Why? Because I'd been jumping at the same time as Xiaobo? Or I'd been sensitized by all the stuff Bent had been doing to me? I didn't know. I was stupid. Couldn't think straight.

All I knew was seeing Kenny and running from rockets had gotten me yanked back here. Different timeline. Different possibilities. And...and...right! I was out of that memory vortex thing I'd been swimming in. I think my brain was too dull to be there now. Or fighting too hard to figure things out.

Go with it.

Okay. The jets. They'd come for me, hadn't they? Homed in on the signaling device in my belly and...tried to kill me. Us. Everyone.

Shit. So much for a rescue.

I wanted to vomit again.

Or at least drink some coffee.

I stumbled from my room and down the hall to the dayroom. Quispe was standing with his big brown face and stolid build right in front of the coffee machine, sipping from a mug. Without even meeting his eyes, I pushed him to one side, grabbed an empty mug, and poured myself a cup. Dark black. No cream or sugar. Never even used to drink the stuff before coming to the Pit, but now...

Of course, the second the hot bitterness hit my lips, I remembered doing exactly this in the other timeline. Which meant I was about to hear the call for me to come for my fourth session of hell with Bent and Trench.

"JACKSON TRAINE, PREPARE FOR A TESTING SESSION IN...FIVE MIN-UTES. YOU WILL BE COLLECTED FROM THE...BLUE DOOR AT THE END OF...HALLWAY ONE."

I looked up and just grinned stupidly at the other members of the Pit. They were all watching me. Because of how I'd been acting with them, the state I'd been in the last time I'd drunk this coffee, heard that announcement. That time, I'd tossed my coffee mug into the sink and staggered from the room like a suffering drunk. I'd gotten lost going down our single corridor. Worse, I'd found the exit door anyway and waited there for Mr. Studly Guard to collect me and take me to where I got skinned alive and...

Yeah, no. Fuck that. Sorry, Kenny. Can't.

I leaned my bum back against the kitchen countertop and sipped my coffee with trembling lips. Pretended I didn't have a care in the world.

The others in the Pit started whispering among themselves. Quispe, who still stood near me, my shove having only moved him over a foot, quirked his head slightly at me, his mouth twisting up in a knowing smile.

"You had enough, yes?" he said.

I looked into my cup. "The coffee? It's really bad."

"Not Starbucks."

I squinted. "You've had Starbucks?"

"Oh yes. I always get *Manjar Blanco*, Grande. You don't have it in America."

"Wouldn't know. Coffee's not my thing."

"But here."

"Yeah."

He sipped his coffee.

I sipped mine.

"You know," Quispe mumbled into his coffee cup, so that even I, right beside him, could hardly hear, "when a man has had enough, and the other side does not know this..." He shrugged and threw the rest of his coffee into the sink.

I blinked at him. Even freed from my vortex, I felt like my brain was operating at half speed. Too much trauma. Too much stress. But I got he was trying to tell me something that no one else could hear, not the listening microphones or anyone who could read lips.

When the other side, Bent, doesn't know...

I got that.

Throw out the coffee?

I looked into Quispe's eyes and saw the hardness there that no doubt came from confronting death over and over again, but not crumbling like I'd been crumbling. Maybe because, unlike me, he'd been raised and trained to fight bad men. Arrest them or...kill them?

"They're going to come get you soon," he said and walked away from me.

Yeah. Shit.

Caught up in the dread inevitability of it, I stumbled down the hallway to the blue door after all, staring dazedly at my feet, only half acting. The door opened as I arrived and I looked up in surprise at the Mr. Studly, Mr. Macho man, Mr. Get-a-bigger-uniform-that-actually-fits-you-dude Guard who was there to collect me.

He looked pissed when I didn't just step through and start walking. His square jaw clenched and unclenched. Finally, he grabbed my shoulder and dragged me into the corridor, then shoved me in the direction we usually walked.

I recalled stumbling a few times in the last try at this timeline and repeated those.

The guard grabbed me and moved me along.

Until I entered the laboratory and fell into such strong PTSD panicking that I almost lost myself.

Almost.

The last time, I'd been so overloaded by my memory vortex, I'd gone into some kind of fugue state. So bad I had no memory of the time between when I reached the lab and when I was strapped down onto the test bed.

This time, I was dull but aware. I took in Bent standing beside a crash cart of surgical knives like he wanted me to see them and freak out.

Don't catch his eyes!

Don't show him you know!

I rolled my eyes and staggered a bit, running blind because I truly had no memory of what I'd done last time between this moment and being strapped down on the bed.

Quispe, I knew, would just grab one of those surgical knives and kill Bent right now. But I couldn't do that, could I? Yes, it would end Bent only in this timeline, but this me would go forward forever (assuming Trench didn't kill me) knowing I'd murdered someone.

Or would it be murder? Couldn't it be self-defense? A jury of my time-traveling peers would certainly recognize that.

Or would they? Was killing a man who killed other versions of you warranted? How about killing a man who planted in your mind and body memory after memory of terrifying, soul-destroying pain?

"Come here, Jackson," Bent said.

I staggered his way, looking everywhere but at him, shaking my head like I couldn't fix my focus on any one point.

In my peripheral vision, I saw him raise the scalpel and my stomach turned over. "See these knives?" he said. "You told me that this one was used to cut off your penis last time."

He put it down. Lifted another one. "Gordon will use this one today to cut around the top and bottom of your leg. Then he will slice longitudinally down from the inner thigh to the ankle bone and peel back your flesh like it was—"

I launched myself at Bent's neck first, driving a fist into it the way Alvin had made me practice on a freestanding training dummy over and over. The fact Bent's neck was long, and he had a habit of raising his chin to look down on me, made the target that much easier.

My fist connected with his trachea with a satisfying crunch that might, by itself, have been enough to kill him. But as he went down, I pivoted to the surgical crash cart, grabbed the heftiest scalpel I could see, and followed Bent to the floor, slicing him deeply on both sides of his neck until the blood started pumping. Then I struck him across the temple hard so he couldn't try to save himself.

In the four seconds it took to do that, Trench had ducked around the test bed to come at me, his truncheon out and swinging.

As I dove and rolled away from him, I saw an impossible person in the doorway—

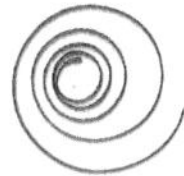

I was standing in a claustrophobic darkness, my heart racing hard, brain clearing fast.

Blind?

No. I felt a cold wind. Heard traffic. Scritching feet beside me.

I knew exactly where I was. But it made no sense. I never got here in the timeline I'd just been in. I'd killed Bent. Trench wouldn't be taking me up to the roof. It was like I'd somehow been jumped back to before I'd killed Bent and had a memory loss starting from before waking up and needing coffee to being here, or...what?

Even as my mind boggled, a hand pulled off my hood.

I was at least prepared for the light this time, shooting a hand up to shield my squinting eyes. Then I turned, desperately seeking the impossible person I'd seen a moment before in the doorway of Bent's laboratory.

He was there—Kenny in his vee-neck sweater, shading his eyes like I was. His awareness of me was in them.

My heart dropped into my gut. "No."

"Yes," he said.

"He's still alive then." I turned to see Trench, with his dark, sunken eyes, lackey of the devil himself whom I'd tried so hard to kill. "Fuck."

"We have to get off the roof," Kenny said.

"I killed him. You understand? I ended it. And then... Did you do this?"

Kenny frowned hard, bringing his blond eyebrows down and together, his hollowed out, wrinkled cheeks sagging like an old man's. "I don't think so? I saw myself run down to the experiments floor where I saw you in the room standing over his body. You must not kill him."

And so you jumped me ACROSS TIME STREAMS? Panic rushed into my head again.

Fuck! Focus.

"Why can't I kill him?" I asked.

"He's important."

"Why?" My voice rose in pitch. "What is he doing? He's fondling his female inmates! He's cutting off my limbs and skinning me alive! Is that what you want him to do?"

I was yelling by this time, so loudly maybe Trench thought people on other floors of the building or down below might hear me. He stepped forward with his hands out.

I whipped a spinning back kick into his chest that was hard enough to drop him to the rooftop, stunned.

"How do the jets know?" Kenny asked me, his eyes wide in what seemed like honest confusion.

"How did you do it—jump into the middle of a different timeline? Which would split it again. Three times we get bombed."

"What?" Totally confused now. Well, so was I. This was insane.

"Where were you before here?" I asked.

"I...saw...starting a day. Then I got called by Uwe to watch the lab because you were coming in. And you attacked him. Killed him. You can't do that. I'll have to warn him."

"In this timeline when I didn't attack him?"

"I don't understand."

"You can't warn him about something that's never going to happen now! That time's gone! That timeline's gone! What the fuck do you think is going on here, Kenny?"

He just stared at me stupidly, even as Trench, groaning, finally picked himself up and pulled out his truncheon. I just shook my head at him with a face that obviously had enough of my rage in it to make him think twice. He walked back to guard the door to the stairs and pulled out his cell phone. No doubt to call Bent for directions.

While I looked back at my hopeless brother and realized he really didn't have a clue what he'd done, how it worked, any of it. Still lost in his drug-ad-dled brain. I figured he really thought he was only seeing visions of the futures he jumped back from. Which, again, I got. It was so easy to lose track of where and when you were.

But to jump from earlier to now?

I know Lena and I had wondered about jumping to timelines I'd left before. I never wanted to. They were usually too horrible to return to. So why did Kenny? No grip on reality? Lack of judgment? Masochism?

I was almost about to attack him again before remembering this was the sibling I'd spent eighteen years missing, sure he was dead. The sibling I'd let down and so badly wanted to save. And here he was. Here I was. What the hell was I doing?

"Kenny, look," I said quietly so Trench couldn't hear. "You hear Xiaobo leaving the building this time around?"

Kenny visibly listened, then shook his head.

"How does he remember?" I said and swore. "Okay, he's probably long gone, then. Won't jump us back. So, when the jets show up any minute now, we've got to be off the roof, like you said. And we'll use the distraction to escape."

Kenny frowned. "No."

"To what part?"

"No escape. Uwe needs us."

"For the cause."

"Yes."

"Which is?"

Kenny pointed over my shoulder. "Planes."

I turned, saw the approaching speck in the sky, and grabbed his skinny arm, dragging him with me toward Trench and the door going down.

Trench pocketed his phone call as we approached, and he held up his hand and truncheon. "He said I gotta keep you up here for the agreed upon time. Beat you if I have to."

I shook my head with a cold laugh. "You want to be up here where the roof blows up?" I pointed back at the approaching jets, bigger now.

He looked, then furrowed his brow at me. "You've been here before?" He looked at Kenny. "You both been here before?"

Kenny nodded.

"Everything blows up?"

"All of us," I said.

Kenny nodded again.

"I guess we leave," Trench said. "Hoods."

I shook my head. "We have to get down at least three flights of stairs in the next twenty seconds."

I shoved past him, dragging Kenny with me. Trench didn't stop me.

We went through the door and barreled down into the dank machine room I remembered smelling the first time. There we came to a stop, unsure of which way to go.

Trench clattered down the stairs behind us and ran ahead, straight for what I now saw was the door out. We followed and burst out into the top office floor corridor I remembered from the smell. Trench was running for what looked like the fire escape stairwell. I grabbed Kenny's arm, and we sprinted after him, ignoring the surprised, doomed faces who looked out their office doors as we raced past.

Were they SCATTER? Or did SCATTER just rent out a bunch of floors of a normal office building and control the world right under the feet of tooth-paste marketers?

We were two floors down the concrete, closed-wall stairwell, the three of us within ten stairs of each other, when a massive double BOOM shook the walls and stairs under us. Loud cracks and the screech of twisting metal followed. Then a torrent of concrete chunks, dust, smoke, and blistering heat battered down on us and filled the stairwell.

Kenny had tumbled just below me to the next landing down, his back to the door, choking on the debris and heat.

I ran down to pull him back to his feet.

"We've got to keep going!" I yelled. "More missiles incom—"

The sound of a distant boom cut my words off. It hit somewhere on the far side of the landing door we stood beside. It shook our stairwell, but the way down looked stable. Trench had paused just down from us, looking up with a look of feral desperation on his face. Now he turned and began going down again.

"Let's go!" I shouted and pulled Kenny with me to race after Trench just as a massive explosion blew out most of the stairwell below us.

It disintegrated Trench and sent up a shrieking geyser of burning smoke and flame that hit me like a giant fist from hell, slamming me into the door. My head hit like a bouncing coconut, cutting off my scream.

I grabbed for Kenny as I collapsed on top of him. The stairs below us were dropping into nothing. The platform we lay on rumbled and tilted crazily down toward the billowing nightmare below.

"Grab onto something!" I yelled, though I couldn't see anything that wasn't plunging.

"Jacky!" Kenny yelled and reached out to grab my shirt...

31

Moooo

I FELL ONTO THE grass. It was deep and cool, but summer above.

I picked my nose and looked around. Where—?

A field. Did I know it? The sky was big and blue up there with bits of cloud. I heard water and saw a shiny, winky stream down a little hill. A big tree and a bunch of cows over there, too. A fence with that nasty prickly wire. Flies buzzed some place. I heard a bell that cows wear.

"Moooo!" I called out.

Someone laughed. I turned my head and saw Kenny sitting. The sun was behind him, so his hair looked like gold. He was chewing a long piece of grass.

"Kenny?" I asked. My voice sounded funny.

So did Kenny's voice when he answered, "Yehh-up."

Then I shaded my eyes, squinted at him, and got real scared. My big brother looked six or seven years old.

"It's okay, Jacky," he said, his voice still high like a kid's, but sharper than I'd heard him sound in forever. "Yeah," he said. "Mind's clearer here. Drug free. Brain's not fully developed, I figure, so abstract thinking's harder. But my adult mind's been kind of loose like a kid's for years now, really free, so..."

"Wh-where are we?" I said in my own high voice. I looked at my hands and they were all smooth and pudgy. "What, what, what day?"

"July 1999. Dad's checking out a possible franchise in Olympia. We made a day trip out of it. Stopped along this random little stream for a picnic. Best family trip we ever did."

1999. I was three. I couldn't speak or think right. I didn't remember stuff.

"I go here whenever things get too much," Kenny said. "My quiet place."

That scary'd me and I cried. "Where's Mommy?"

"She and Dad and Kansas went to buy some food. I always leave before they come back. You know. Too confusing." He frowned so hard his entire six-year-old face screwed up. "I don't wanna get stuck."

"Yeah!" I said. I didn't want it.

"But I think sometimes, you know, maybe staying, starting all over, you know. Maybe that wouldn't be so bad?"

Really scary'd now. I didn't want it. Didn't! Too much stuff to do twice! "Can we go?" I whined. I rolled over in the grass to hide my face.

Kenny touched my shoulder. "Sure, Jacky. I just needed a moment."

And...

32

28 home runs

Everything was suddenly dark. Not hood dark, but dark because it was nighttime. And I knew exactly where I was. But when? Warm. Smell of new growth. Spring?

I sat up straight in my childhood bed and ran my hands quickly over my body. My face had a lot of acne, so I was in my teens, still in high school. My face had mostly cleared by the time I left for university.

I clicked on my bedside lamp and looked around. The Marion Jones poster wasn't on my wall. That put me before my senior year, when I'd developed a very late-in-the-game crush on the American sprinter.

A sound made me spin to the door, and I saw Kenny standing there, tall and healthy, All-American looking. He had a scuffed baseball in his hand, turning it over and over. "You remember this?" he asked.

"Or course," I answered, now knowing the approximate date. My freshman year. Fourteen years old. "But it's not signed."

"I sign it and give it to you tomorrow. I hung onto that one night after winning it just to, you know, soak it in. Last thing I did I remember being proud of."

"Twenty-eight home runs in one season!"

"School record."

He held it up to his face and sniffed it. Ran it over his cheek. His fingers quivered. I wondered if his high school senior body he'd jumped back into, dragging me along, had sniffed or injected something before bed and was still feeling some of its effects. I wracked my memories but only came up with seeing him right after the game, then the next morning when, like he said, he gave me that baseball, signed.

"Why don't I remember this conversation?" I asked.

Kenny shrugged and sat down on my bed beside me, making it creak. "I'm living in my SCATTER office. Just...seeing this, and you."

"Talking with me," I said.

But what I wanted to do was shake him and tell him, No, Kenny. You're not just seeing this. You're living it. You jumped us here and made a new timeline where the teenage you and I have grown-up minds and knowledge of so many things in the outside world. Just like there are now multiple timelines, apparently, with six-year-old you's with older minds inside them. Holy Hell! If those kids continue in those timelines when you jump out of them, what will their lives be like?

And this life here, when Kenny jumped me out of it, would this changed version of my teen self continue on with its older mind, just as crazy as all the other older-mind Kennys?

Kenny nudged me with his shoulder. "I need to tell you why you can't run away from Uwe. He needs you to help him save the world."

"From what?" I asked sourly. "Armageddon?"

Kenny finally frowned at me, something he'd rarely done for as long as I'd known him. "I saw what happened three years after you killed Uwe. You and I were out of SCATTER. Xiaobo went rogue, no surprise. When Russia started losing the war in Ukraine, China released a bad virus in the US, Japan, and Europe that... COVID times a thousand. Then they hit Taiwan. Everyone got involved. Russia and China launched coordinated nuclear strikes on the West and its allies."

"Nonsense," I said, but wondered if he actually had lived that time. If there was anyone who could and come back here to tell me about it, it was obviously Kenny.

"I don't think anyone really believed they'd do it. It wiped out most major cities of Europe. Russian and Chinese cities, too, in retaliation. North Korea and Iran got involved. Billions dead. The Mediterranean Sea poisoned for generations. Most of our west coast. Washington, DC. Chicago. New York. Vancouver. Japan. I saw another year to see if they figured out exactly who did what when, but the skies all got...dark."

I stared at him. In the dim light thrown from my bedside lamp, the way he was curling over and into himself made him look cadaverous. I reassessed my earlier impression of his health.

All I could manage was, "Lena? Kansas? Where are we all living?"

"You and I were in Canada."

"Lena?"

"I don't know. After we escaped, you weren't able to find her."

"SCATTER took her?"

"I don't know."

"And Kansas?"

Kenny shook his head. "We never found her, either."

"They might have survived."

"Maybe?"

I hopped off my bed and paced around my small childhood room, banging walls as I went. When I got to the window, I stopped and looked out at the dark streets of our suburb, the trees all so healthy and lush. Couldn't help imagining them shredded or burned by a nuclear blast.

"How do you know it changes if Bent lives and I stay with him?" I asked.

"SCATTER weakens Putin. Saves Volodymyr Zelensky from assassination. Twice. Makes China change course. But then you... I help you on your first mission. You direct raids on different Chinese factories suspected of producing the aerosol Ebola they developed to cripple the US."

"Delightful."

"Your first eight attempts fail, but you get it right on try number nine."

"What happened with the first eight timelines?"

Kenny shook his head. "It doesn't matter. You get it right the ninth time."

"Holy shit." I stared at him, instinctively trying to add together in my head all the billions of people who died in each timeline where I failed. I...couldn't. My brain skipped away, wanting to ask if Kenny had also known about the jets attacking the SCATTER building ahead of time. Or was the future I'd lived helping Bent one where he'd somehow kept me from ever going up onto the roof so the jets had never come? "Did you see what happened next? I stop the biological war and they still turn to nukes?"

"I don't know. I don't think so. I think Xi died? I think... I think..."

"Yes?"

"I saw what happened when you killed Dr. Bent."

"You told me."

Kenny's whole body was trembling now. "I saw f-four years..."

"It's a lot," I said, starting to shake as well as I really pictured everything he'd lived through, all the consequences of my bad choices.

I sat back on my bed beside Kenny and took a long series of deep breaths to get myself out of this future guilt. But the familiarity of that maneuver had the counter-positive effect this time. Rather than calming me, it flooded my currently teenaged mind with all the timeline horrors I'd lived before my wild sidetracking with Kenny. I gritted my teeth and growled at them to go away, to let me be for just long enough to clear my head and weigh the consequences of everything I'd just heard.

Except how was I supposed to weigh my definition of reasonable against the apocalyptic visions of a junkie brother who'd actually lived through the things he'd just described to me?

I reached over and gripped his thigh.

"You know if I go back," I said, "it's to a man who's delighted in having me beaten, burned with acid, literally cut into pieces, and flayed. You know what flaying is? It's when Trench cuts off my skin, my guts plop out, and I either go into septic shock or bleed out. Now that I made jets attack SCATTER, what do you think he'd do?"

"I've been thinking about that," said Kenny. His body still trembled, but his thoughts seemed to have focused, engaged in planning. Was that where I learned it from? "I think it matters what point in time you go back to."

I stared at him, intrigued. Kenny's suggestion that I could choose where to reenter a timeline suggested he thought I actually jumped through time, even if he did not. It made no sense, of course, given that my ten-minute jumpbacks couldn't accomplish what Kenny was suggesting, but drug addicts were notoriously good at rationalizing incompatible realities.

It also stuck a quiet, subtle, and terrifying needle of doubt into my understanding of how limited time travel had to be.

I mentally drew out and threw away that needle before I waved at Kenny. "Explain," I said.

He did.

Then he had me walk with him to his childhood room and watch him return his championship baseball to a place of honor beside his bed. He lay down on the bed itself and had me sit beside him.

He took my hand, smiled, and...

33

Lost sheep

THE STAIRWELL LANDING! CONCRETE pebbles pelted my shoulders. Dust and hot smoke blew into my lungs. I felt pain from the places this body had been hit. A trickling sensation on my forehead. Blood, probably.

BOOM!

It hit somewhere on the other side of the door we stood beside.

Kenny blinked rapidly, ghostly with dust and bits of concrete, bleeding from somewhere behind his right ear. Trench crouched ten or twelve steps below us, glaring up at us with his teeth bared, face running with sweat.

"Door!" Kenny grunted.

I nodded and grabbed the handle, twisting and yanking it hard. It scraped and stuck! Kenny's hands went around mine and we roughly dragged it open together.

Trench called out, "Wait!" and started up the stairs.

Fuck no. Kenny and I dove through the door, landing in the chaos of an office floor that had people running in every direction.

And suddenly even that went to hell as a missile took out the far wall of the stairwell where we'd been. The concussive force of it hit us and those near us like a giant fist. It literally rolled me and Kenny over each other and into nameless office workers who tumbled over or around us.

Muffled screams and wailing rose from somewhere, everywhere, trying to work its way through my shell-shocked ears and brain. I blinked at the wall beside us where a woman now hung on a jutting piece of wood like a coat. Her face and torso were bloody. She was staring at a red stump that used to be her arm.

I struggled up and toward her, but Kenny grabbed me from behind and yelled something that sounded like a muted trumpet.

He pointed.

We ran.

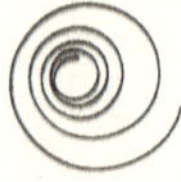

Two more rockets had hit the building by the time we made it down to the ground floor lobby. We ran through the lobby to an electronically locked door off on a side wall. Kenny somehow had the combination code to it.

Scared people ran by us as Kenny laboriously punched it in, throwing us looks like we were insane. Or maybe somehow part of this attack. Their clothes and faces were just as torn, bloody, and caked in rubble and dust as Kenny's and mine, but they were smart enough to be heading outside, away from this nightmare.

I secretly agreed with them that maybe, yes, we were likely insane. The sounds of cracks, thumps, and booms from above didn't sound good. We should have been running for the street like everyone else.

Kenny got the door open and dragged me inside, shutting the door behind us.

Another stairwell. Seriously?

I wanted to just stop for a second, catch my breath, and process. Fuck all this running and survival bullshit. I'd been in at least two different timelines of my youth, two stories my perfect memory hadn't recorded. The three-year-old failure I understood, but I would have remembered the teenage me. Ergo, Kenny had definitely jumped us into those earlier bodies, started up two new timelines, then jumped us back to a timeline in which those visits had never happened. Cross dimensional shit. I'd speculated it was true before, but this confirmed it.

And fuck it. Fuck it! How many versions of me and my fucked-up life were running parallel to this one now?

"Come on!" Kenny insisted and started hurrying down.

And I did, too mentally compromised to do anything but revert to my childhood instinct of just running after him wherever he led. So many shit shows had come of that. But here I was running back toward the madman who stroked my head before having his goon cut off my skin. All so we could save the world. Or one version of it.

What could possibly go wrong?

Maybe forty stairs down, though, we reached a well-lit tunnel with an honest-to-god private subway like the ones that ran to the Capitol basement in DC. But here there were no trains in sight, and Kenny was already walking his emaciated body purposefully along the sidewalk that bounded the tracks. However jagged and hitched his steps were.

I followed, caught up to him, matched his pace, and asked, "Where are we going?"

"Site Three," he said.

34

Kansas and Lena

"WELL, THAT'S DIFFERENT," KANSAS murmured at the newspaper open before her on her dad's old oak desk.

"What is it?" Lena said, instantly at her elbow. She'd rarely been more than a couple feet away since they'd come down here. It was their third day in the Traine basement.

"You brought me these papers just after lunch. Did you read what was on every single front page?"

Lena frowned. "What do you mean? They're all different."

"Really?" Kansas moved the newspapers to one side and covered them with her arm. "What did they have?"

"The American ones—the Seattle Times, USA Today, and Renton Reporter—talked about inflation, mask mandates on airplanes, Russia and Ukraine peace talks. The Chinese one had something about South Korea testing a ballistic missile?"

Kansas looked at her closely. "Nothing else?"

Lena shrugged, eyes wide.

"You don't remember, two hours ago, bringing in the newspapers with tears in your eyes because of how horrible they all were. All the same story."

Lena perked up and slid into a chair beside Kansas, pulling the newspapers out from under her arm. She scanned them quickly. "There's nothing here that I'd call...horrible."

"There was this morning. On all the electronic outlets, too."

Lena looked at Kansas expectantly and Kansas, looking back into those large, deep hazelnut eyes, again felt a little flutter in her heart and nether regions. Yes, their relationship had become very sibling-like, wonderfully so, but...

Lena cleared her throat and Kansas pulled herself out of the might-have-beens to speak. "Zelensky was assassinated. Blown up. Russia denied responsibility, despite the strong evidence, then did a major push into Mariupol, blew up the Azovstal Iron and Steel Works, and slaughtered every remaining Ukrainian man, woman, and child in the city."

Lena's breath caught. Her face became red, and tears formed in her eyes. She wiped them forcefully away. "The headlines changed, then. Completely. From this morning to now. Same newspapers."

Kansas nodded. "And I understand why Jackson wanted physical newspapers. If it had just been electronic, I would have just assumed the early reports jumped the gun and got corrected."

Lena was nodding hard, working it through. "So...when you read it this morning, Zelensky was dead. But somehow, between then and now, someone jumped back in time and changed that. I don't see a change because the me in this changed timeline never saw the earlier headline. But this you, somehow, 'remembers' what the you in that other timeline read. How does that feel?"

"Knowing there's suddenly another me in another timeline? Or that I have some of her memories?"

"Either."

Kansas frowned and looked inside herself, remembering other things that had happened after she'd read about Zelensky's assassination. How Lena had hung over her shoulder, wiping her eyes and sniffing, while Kansas had read the story. How Lena's closeness and her distress had made Kansas want to turn, stand, and take her in her arms. But she hadn't. She'd let Lena pull herself together, and they'd continued working.

Then—when exactly had that happened?—Lena had seemed happy again, like the tragedy hadn't even happened. Because for this Lena, intently studying Kansas now, it hadn't.

"It's disconcerting," Kansas said. "Doesn't feel like a dream. More like a second set of memories. I remember you bringing in the paper with tears in your eyes and I remember you coming in with them humming some melody I didn't recognize."

Lena thought, then blushed. "Stupid earworm." Then, more seriously, "You're describing the two sets of memories you said could make someone crazy. Jackson presumably has a lot of those."

"Uh-hunh."

"And another thing out of this."

"Bent."

"Yes! We're assuming it was one of his time travelers who changed Zelensky getting killed, right? Does that mean he's a good guy after all?"

Kansas curled her lips back.

"He's a narcissistic psychopath who treats people like chess pieces. Could he have been responsible for saving Zelensky? Maybe. Also possible that he started the war in the first place and saved Zelensky to keep it going."

"Because?"

"It drives up the price of oil. Disrupts the usual supply chains. Causes massive inflation and a global recession. I don't know. Maybe it's part of his war against China."

"You mean from Jackson's observations of what happened in Taiwan."

"Yes."

Lena considered it. "Have you been checking for changes online?"

"I will now."

She pulled her laptop closer, tapped it on, and opened one of a dozen live newsfeeds she'd been following earlier in the day.

Her blood ran cold.

She felt Lena at her shoulder and heard her intake of breath.

Kansas flipped through news feed after newsfeed to confirm this story that wouldn't be in the physical papers yet. Finally brought up a female talking head on CNN.

"The Pentagon confirms that the three jets which destroyed a Baltimore office building this afternoon with laser-guided missiles were scrambled from Andrews Air Force Base. They have not said for what purpose, but unnamed sources describe the building as a headquarters for a terrorist Al-Qaeda cell which moved in multiple truckloads of scientific equipment and security a month ago and was planning an imminent terrorist attack. As firefighters and medics pick through the rubble, and casualty estimates range from seventy to several hundred. The President himself has called for immediate answers for this unprecedented use of military jets against a domestic target."

The talking head's male counterpart jumped in with details of the hunt for the three pilots involved and the stonewalling around who gave the order for the attack.

Kansas closed the CNN window and sat back, a dull throbbing starting in the back of her head.

At her left arm, Lena looked like she was vibrating with fear and anger. "Is that them?" she demanded. "Did SCATTER do that? Or cause that? Some kind of domestic terrorist attack? Is that different from what the reports were a minute ago?"

"It's breaking news," Kansas said. "There's… I would have no way of knowing anything changed unless I'd been watching a live report about that specific part of Baltimore just before this report came out. And to answer your question—no, I was not researching Baltimore just before this report."

"But…SCATTER? Do you think they did it? True believers in the Pentagon? Or just on the air base?"

"Because why?" Kansas said, the throbbing getting worse.

"Because…this man, Dr. Uwe Bent, he's crazy enough to attack his own people. And he's a megalomaniac, right? Maybe he wants to start a civil war to bring down the government. Install an autocrat. Maybe himself."

"Maybe." Kansas squeezed her eyes closed tightly.

"What?" Lena's voice pressed. "You're thinking something else. What?"

Kansas didn't want to speak because she hadn't put together all the pieces that had led her rabbit brain, what others would call intuition, to a very different conclusion than what Lena was suggesting.

"Please," Lena's voice said by her ear, quieter, pleading.

"I think," Kansas said, "that it wasn't Uwe Bent who ordered the attack. I think he was the 'terrorist group' that moved in their scientific equipment a month ago. Which means there's another power player we haven't identified who wants Bent dead even more than me."

"Who?"

"I…don't know yet. But you remember I said after Bent found his first time traveler, he formed SCATTER and abducted nine more possible time travelers before reaching me and Jackson? I've got a gut sense that whoever's after Bent now is tied to someone on that list."

"You going to give me that list?"

Kansas pulled open two drawers of her father's oak desk and pulled out a legal pad and some pens. She wrote the names. The two women stared at them together.

Lena seemed to see the same thing that had been shifting around faintly in the back of Kansas' mind until this explosion in Baltimore.

"Number ten. Zhou Xiaobo," Lena said. "That's…"

"Wenling's brother."

"But Wenling is dead."

"It sure looked like that," Kansas said. "Very dramatic and all. Have you been able to find any reports of her death or even of a female corpse found in the Capitol basement?"

Lena shook her head. "Nothing about who's running her company now, either, though I keep getting monthly deposits for my research."

"Which Wenling had been funding?"

"Yes. You know she convinced me for a year that she was Elizabeth Chan, an assistant to Jeff Bezos?"

Kansas nodded. "She made me fall in love with her under that name. Two of the happiest months of my life. Happy ignorance."

The two women looked into each other's eyes. Lena laid it out first. "She made a deal with Bent. She'd help convince Jackson to go with him if Bent returned her brother to her."

"But Bent never returned her brother," Kansas theorized.

"Because why would he? She's a multi-billionaire, but he's got money plus the True Believers."

Kansas nodded. "He would also assume that once SCATTER moved locations, Wenling couldn't find them."

She saw Lena shut her mouth, having finally caught up with the implications of Kansas' theory. "If Wenling thought SCATTER was in that building," Lena said, "and she blew it up..."

Kansas shook her head. She'd already considered what Lena was implying, and it felt wrong. "She wouldn't have blown up her own brother."

"Unless she somehow got him out first, then killed everyone else."

"No. Because even with all her money, I find it unlikely Wenling would have been able to take control of enough people at Andrew Air Force Base to pull something off something like this. There's something else at play."

"And Jackson's dead."

"No," Kansas snapped. Then she read the agony behind Lena's huge, deep brown eyes and forced herself to soften. Lena might be a scientist, but she wasn't heartless like the people Kansas was used to breaking things down with. "Okay, it's possible. But we don't have enough intel to even know for sure they were targeting SCATTER or that they hit the right building if they were. And..." Kansas hesitated to reveal the very illogical feelings she was processing right now. But she knew intellectually that sometimes sharing illogic was critical for fieldwork, which this was.

"What?" Lena demanded, the word thick.

"I don't feel that Jackson is dead. Do you?"

Lena pursed her lips and shook her head.

"Okay then. I'm going to find Wenling. Because if she's actually alive, she may know more than we do about everything."

Lena nodded. "And I can look at the other names on the list. There must be other families. Maybe one of them knows something."

"Good." Kansas began packing up her laptop and looking about for any other personal items she'd brought. Avoiding Lena's eyes.

"We're done here?" Lena's eyes were welling up in a show of emotion Kansas suspected the scientist had given few people. It warmed Kansas' heart.

"We confirmed your theory about my ability, determined SCATTER is messing with the war in Ukraine, and discovered there's another player in this game that may be trying to destroy SCATTER. I'd say we have a serious push ahead if we're going to save my brother, your lover."

Kansas could see Lena wanted to hug her. But Kansas knew that if she did, Kansas might not let go. She gave Lena a grimace of a smile, finished packing, and headed up the basement stairs.

35

Everything's different

The long underground walk with Kenny away from the destroyed building where SCATTER had been should have been a good time to talk to Kenny. I could have quizzed him about Bent and SCATTER. Could have learned more about his powers. Told him that I loved him and was sorry I hadn't been able to save him as a teen, that I'd never forgotten him.

But our minds and bodies were both worn out. And while our respective head wounds had stopped bleeding, mine seemed to have made me paranoid. I kept thinking someone was following us in the tunnel. There was no evidence of it when I stopped, listened, looked, but the feeling was strong. We had a ghost following us. Maybe one of the poor souls who didn't make it out after the bombs hit.

Some thirty minutes along, there was a muted boom from behind us in the tunnel. I turned to feel a tremor run under our feet and a push of hot air around my face.

"The building coming down?" I asked.

Kenny had also stopped and shook his head. He spoke with some difficulty. "Someone blew the tunnel entrance. Didn't want rescue crews to find it."

"So, if we'd been too slow getting down here…"

Kenny made his eyes bug out and his fingers splay apart from each other with a whoosh. It was almost like I remembered him, that sense of humor. But he didn't hold on to it. He turned and started shambling faster. Probably reminded that we'd already missed the train and couldn't afford to miss the bus, too.

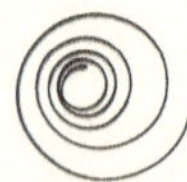

One of the SCATTER functionaries left inside the tunnel's boarded-over street-level exit to collect any straggler was none other than Mr. Studly, the square-jawed guard who had always walked me from the Pit to Bent's laboratory. In the smoky beams of sunlight that made it through the boarded-over entrance, he looked only minorly scuffed up, but majorly pissed. Like he'd had to wait here just for the two of us.

"Where's Major Trench?" he asked.

Kenny shook his head.

"Dead," I said.

"Fuck. Anyone else?"

"No one else," I said.

"Well, I'm not fucking staying around here another fucking minute!"

I opened my mouth to say something, but Kenny shook his head at me, and I shut it.

Studly made a phone call with an apparently unscratched phone and shouted at whoever was on the other end that we needed evac now!

I sidled up to the boards and looked out through a crack at some random city sidewalk. Gray winter sunlight. Lots of pedestrians. It struck me this was my last chance to change my mind. I could take out Mr. Studly, slip through what looked like the one movable part of the boards near where he was currently standing, and just join the crowd. Disappear. With one hand firmly dragging Kenny behind me, of course.

Except he wouldn't come, would he? He had to save the world or something. Wanted me to help him do it. All I needed to do was to truly give myself over to a psychopathic sadist who would probably figure out I'd somehow signaled SCATTER's location. He'd locate the transmitter in my belly and extract it with the maximum amount of pain.

That and other thoughts of all the nice things Bent would do to me now, even with Trench out of the picture, danced through my head in ever-increasing ferocity. I finally had to shut my eyes and breathe harder and faster than I had in a very long time to refocus back on the present.

Twenty minutes later, a panel delivery van with Fresh Host Farms! and a scene of cows, chickens, eggs, and a sad-looking sunrise on its sides skidded to a stop at the curb. The ketamine twins from the SCIF adventure jumped out. They walked casually to the side of the boarded-up entrance. Studly saw them and let them in.

"Seriously, guys?" I said at Natasha, while Pasha slid up to me and jabbed a needle in. I looked at Kenny. "Don't let them do anything nasty to me while I'm out, okay?"

By the time we were out of the boarded subway entrance and crammed into the back of the van, I was having a fine old time.

When I woke up this time, my head swam, and my tongue moved in my mouth like a log in dry sand that smelled bad. Sour. Rank. I lay on a bed in a small, dark room, lit softly by moonlight through an actual window on the wall to my right.

The room was empty other than the bed, a wooden bedside table and chair, a low two-drawer dresser, and me. No cameras I could see.

Hunh. Okay. A chance to catch my bearings unobserved.

Come on. You can...

I rolled unevenly off the bed and stumbled to the tall window in my sock feet. Five steps on warm vinyl. The glass or plexiglass looked like it opened, so I grabbed the bottom and pulled up hard, expecting resistance. Instead, it just flew up smoothly and stopped, leaving me gaping. Then I gasped as a breath of cold night air rushed in at me. Cold, not freezing. No snow on the ground. We hadn't traveled to Canada then.

Metal window bars covered the opening in a crosshatch arrangement that only a very skinny kid would have been able to crawl through. But the fresh air! The smell of budding things! The brief times I'd spent on the roof with Kenny, then in our childhood field, then my bedroom in Renton, they'd reminded me how much that meant. A connection to nature. To the world.

And the season? From this second-floor viewpoint, I saw lots of bare trees, but my nose smelled the emerging green. It had to be spring, or almost spring.

The building exterior, as far as I could tell, was brick, with a pillared entrance like something built early in the last century. Craning my neck to look up, I saw what looked like another two floors above the one I was on.

The scritch of the room's door opening made me spin around and the lingering effects of ketamine made me almost lose my balance. But I didn't fall.

I just blinked my eyes, then squinted as my room's intruder did something that made the room's light turn on.

Uwe Bent.

"You're up," he said. "Good. We have things to discuss."

I grunted. For all that had passed between the last time I'd seen him and now, my body still wanted a PTSD terror state every time he got near me. And this was near. The large window made the room seem big enough for one person. With two, it seemed tiny. Claustrophobic.

Except, I reminded myself, we weren't in a laboratory right now. Bent no longer had Gordon Trench to call on. And I'd proved I could PUT BENT DOWN anytime I wanted to.

Okay, scaredy cat?

Okay.

And I knew he was really a good guy now, right? Because Kenny said so. And I had to trust Kenny.

"It's very confusing, I know," Bent said, slipping into that voice of understanding and reassurance he'd used on me just before he's ordered Trench to start cutting off all my skin.

"Not really," I lied.

Bent smiled and nodded. "You know where we are now?"

I said nothing.

"Massachusetts. A little town called Belmont. It's like a western suburb of Boston. Do you know why I brought SCATTER here?"

"You clearly want to tell me."

"I do," Bent said, walking into the room and within a breath of me to reach the window I'd opened before turning back to me. "We're on the campus of the best psychiatric hospital in the United States, though Johns Hopkins, where I did my residency, might say second best."

I instinctively backed up as my mind flicked through the boatload of psychology-related articles I'd read over the years and came up with the name. "McLean Hospital."

Bent clapped ironically.

"How?" I asked. "Aren't you a psychiatric pariah after the CIA kicked you out? All it takes is one set of loose lips, right? Whoever sent those jets after you…"

"Don't play stupid, Jackson. It doesn't suit you. Given the jets arrived during your rooftop excursion, I had your body scanned and we removed the little location transmitter you had inside you. It's currently on its way to Texas."

My hand went to my belly, felt the stitches there, and was surprised by the relief that flooded through me.

Bent caught it and nodded. "Exactly. Ms. Zhou was both trickier and more vindictive than I gave her credit for."

"But she wouldn't..." I let it trail off.

"Yes?"

"If she was still..."

"Alive? You spent enough time with her to know how her mind works. It was why you bargained for time outside, wasn't it? Though I am curious how you figured out our little ruse with the gun."

Confirmation. Thank you. "I licked the 'blood' she left on the table."

Bent raised an eyebrow at me. "Fascinating. Daring, really."

"She wouldn't have attacked the building she thought her brother was in."

"You don't think so? I actually agree. I think she teamed up with someone even colder and more psychopathic that she is. For which I respect her enormously."

I frowned. "Andre Poussaint."

He stared at me, and I could almost see his brain clicking. "'Pissant.' Ha! Yes. An obsessed individual. I met him when I worked at the CIA. He was already old then. Must be in his nineties now. I suppose, at that age, sending guided missiles to a domestic target doesn't seem such a big deal. But can you imagine how many safeguards he bypassed to accomplish that? And the quick planning! Two of the pilots landed their F-16's on the Carrol County Regional Country airport runway, which should not have been possible, even with no remaining payload. The third pilot actually landed on Highway 97. It ran beside the same airport and had been mysteriously blocked to traffic for the fifteen minutes before the landing. The pilots vanished, of course, leaving their aircraft behind. There are no reports of them being apprehended."

I shook my head. "How many died?"

Bent shrugged. "Other than Gordon, I don't really care. My people did not have the top three floors, so we mostly made it out unscathed. All the key ones are with us here. The rest will have their contracts paid out."

"The other time travelers?"

"All safe. All part of this exciting new phase of our project where I am known as Dr. Poli Andros, from the University of Zurich." He let his usual precise diction slide into a German accent. Or Switzer-Deutsch? "I am recommended by Harvard and funded this one-hundred-and-eighty-million-dollar new center, the Andros Building. It was custom-built to complement McLean Hospital's current work on neurological-psychiatric research and the treatment of PTSD." He dropped the Nazi scientist vibe and resumed the more familiar one of a strangely needy egomaniac. "You like the décor?"

He waved a hand around the room at what I finally registered as having a modern, light wood aesthetic, with indirect lighting and a deep burgundy accent wall behind the twin bed I'd woken up in.

But it didn't take my attention off Bent. He'd swept his hair further back from his tall forehead today. That look, his blue eyes, and his primly smiling small mouth made him look like a priest who'd just announced the Rapture had occurred and I was lucky enough to be among the Saved.

"Why?" I asked.

"Well, that's what we're going to discuss now, Jackson. You see, until you met with Kentucky and listened to what he had to say about what we are doing here, I truly believed you were a classically disguised psychopath who was playing an elaborate game with me and the world. You couldn't hide your ability to jump back in time from the woman you were falling in love with, but you knew the sheer scope of your power would terrify anyone with half a brain. Being able to jump back and rewrite reality—well, that's playing God, isn't it? It's certainly what we're after here at SCATTER. With the goal of world stability, of course."

Inside my head, my brain pinged little warnings at me. "You said you 'used to' believe I was just pretending."

"Yes. After listening to Kentucky's story—the most rational he's been in months—I realize your power is actually as pathetically limited as you claim."

"Well, hallelujah."

"But it needn't stay that way."

The pings rolled into a massive iron ball that dropped into my belly. "So. ..new location, same torture porn?" I found myself inching around the room, keeping the door in sight for a quick escape.

Bent raised his eyebrows at me. "Why would we do that? The trauma induction clearly reinforces your attachment to the status quo."

"It literally kicks me *out* of the status quo."

"Yes! They make it so costly, so terrible, they reinforce just how precious it is to stay, how you can only go when it's clear there's no other choice!"

"But..."

"If you could simply leave this reality—"

"What?"

"—to go to a better one, no stress or pain required, then holding on to this one would feel foolish, wouldn't it?"

"I..." I thought through his proposition. Would it?

"Or if you decided no existence holds more value than any other, you could just jump around between them however you like."

"Which would be nihilism. No values. No rules. No meaning."

Bent laughed. "Now that is more your sister speaking. Seeking a rational understanding of the ineffable. There is a psychiatric term for that."

"Obsessive compulsive? Hyperrational?"

"The delusion of meaning."

"You made that up."

"Did I?"

I glared at him. "You make it very hard to like you."

He shook his head and ambled forward. "If you think that's important, Jackson, then you've totally missed the point of everything. It might be a good place to start with Dr. Sauveterre when you meet her in a few days."

"Who?"

He walked past me to the door, then stopped and turned, smiling broadly. "Oh, you will like her, Jackson. And she will like you because she likes winners. And you, my boy, are at last on track to become one. You are about to grow into your destiny."

"Wait! What am I..."

Bent slipped out before I could finish.

36

Jude

THE ONE GOOD THING about being a prisoner, Jude thought as he marked off another day on the wall of his cell, was the enforced diet. It was also the worst thing.

Not because he missed his favorite foods, which he did. It was because he recognized that a part of him had always equated his big, soft body with a love of life and a connection to his humanity. It had also been both an armor against the insistent dogma of his parents—*May God keep and protect my mother. God, full of mercy, provide a sure rest to the soul of my father.*—even as Jude felt his oversized body contained their oversized love within it.

Which meant now, five weeks into one meal a day of fish, rice, peas, and carrots, sometimes pieces of beef in soup, sometimes pieces of chicken, when the fat had shrunk so much from his chest, belly, arms, thighs, and butt that he had loose folds where there had once been pillows, he felt as cut off from the world in his spirit as he was in the physical world.

Dadashev had walked him down here with a blindfold on. That was funny because Jude had such a bad spatial sense that he wouldn't have known where they were going if they'd drawn him a map.

The joke had continued when Dadashev turned his nose up at the layer of dust over everything down here. Because Jude had grown up with dust—dusty books, dusty relatives. He'd just been glad the place had a working toilet and sink.

And a nightlight.

Jude had always been afraid of the dark.

Of things that came to bite you in the dark.

The room's main light was on some kind of timer that he was pretty sure ran on a 24-hour day. Messing with a prisoner's internal clock was a tried-and-true way of disrupting their sense of reality, but he didn't think Poussaint cared about breaking him. The four times Poussaint interrogated him (so far!) Jude had told him everything he knew about Uwe and SCATTER. It turned out to be pathetically little. And even that much Poussaint sneered at like he thought Jude was some deluded cult member.

After that, Poussaint stopped coming.

Then it was only surly Amit Dadashev, resenting his new chore of feeding Jude daily.

"We should just kill you and melt your body," he said one time in the second week, after entering the locked room to deliver Jude his food.

"There's a lot of me to melt," Jude replied, though he'd already felt his belly shrinking by then and it freaked him out. Hence the humor.

Dadashev did not laugh. Instead, Jude's joke brought out the man's cruel streak. From then on, every time he arrived with Jude's daily meal, he made Jude run laps around the small room and do pushups and sit-ups. After three days, he would increase the number. Soon, Jude could only eat after doing twenty pushups and thirty sit-ups, or ten burpees. Burpees made him want to cry.

Sometimes Dadashev would inspire him with stories about killers known for melting their victims with acid.

"John Haigh," he said in the Russian accent that seemed twice as thick now, like he was using it to intimidate Jude. "You hear of him? English man in the 1940s. He killed at least six people. Each time, he stuffed them in an oil drum filled with sulfuric acid. But it only half worked, yes? When they caught him, the rubble pile outside his workshop where he poured the remains? It had twenty-eight pounds of human body fat, gallstones, a piece of foot, and a denture from someone's mouth. Alright, you're done. Eat!"

Another time, Dadashev explained that a much more effective way to melt a human body was to use alkaline hydrolysis, a base versus an acid. But because it had to be done at about 300°F, you'd probably have to chop the body into small pieces and use a pressure cooker.

"And even then, it won't get all the bones. Eat! This is more than my brave countrymen in Mariupol are eating today."

Jude would eat. Dadashev would collect his dishes and utensils and leave again, locking the door behind him.

That was the golden time of day when Jude's belly felt almost full. He would daydream about his times back in the apartment he shared with Jackson back in uni, eating a huge lunch, then listening to his best friend describing one of the thousands of research studies he could recite at the drop of a hat.

One of the only ones Jude remembered now was the lifespan research done by a group of US and Chinese scientists working with rats. Basic finding: consistently feed a mature rat thirty percent less food than it normally ate, and its tissues and cells started looking like those of a much younger rat. In other words, they not only lived longer, but healthier! More vibrant!

Screw that, he thought now, five weeks less a day from the time he'd been locked up down here. The rat would be hungry. All. The. Damn. Time.

And less spiritual. Less loving. Less filled with the love of the people who mattered. People who, for all Jude knew, were frantic from worry over not hearing from him. He normally spoke to his mother once a week. Would she have called the police to break into his townhome? Would someone have gone to his workplace and confirmed that he hadn't been in there for the last month? Would they search for him? Would they have concluded, finding no evidence of foul play, that he'd had some kind of early midlife crisis and just...left?

Jude suddenly trembled with such anxiety that he mimicked what he'd seen Jackson do when his PTSD overwhelmed him. He dropped to the ground and did some pushups. Then some situps. Then eleven burpees that left him sweating and curling up into himself on the concrete floor he'd worked so hard to keep clean. There he cried and shook until the anxiety got tired of him and left.

Finally, he just lay there and thought in a way he'd never forced himself to do before.

About escape.

How he might do that.

37

I am made ready

FROM MY EXPLORATIONS ON my first full day there, I gathered I had the run of this floor of the Andros Building, AKA Bent Manor. The floor held my sleeping room, seven empty rooms like it, a common area with a kitchen, a library, and a washroom with four sinks, four showers, and four toilets. The toilets and showers had privacy barriers. They'd left full sets of eating utensils in the kitchen, with prepared foods and raw ingredients in the fridge and freezer. In the common room, I learned to operate the large flat-screen TV that had a movie channel. Maybe best of all, the dresser in my room had multiple clothing options. I'd graduated from scrubs!

There were still surveillance cameras, but they seemed limited to the building exteriors and stairwells, neither of which I could access.

Oh, and I was the only resident on the floor.

This, even though Bent had said all the other time travelers got out. Which meant Xiaobo along with the members of the Pit.

So why wasn't I with my former Pit mates or with Xiaobo and Kenny?

I brooded over that for the four days before concluding that Bent hadn't separated me so I wouldn't corrupt the other time travelers. No, he'd separated me so they wouldn't corrupt *me*.

And maybe to prep me emotionally for working with this Dr. Sauveterre. Getting me to value my current reality less by making it one of isolation and loneliness.

But four days? C'mon!

By the end of my fourth day, I was beyond ready. I wolfed down a Greek yogurt snack in the kitchen, then rambled restlessly through my floor's dark rooms and hallway with the lights switched off. Who needed light when there were no people? No freedom? No purpose?

As I rounded the corner to my room, led by the moonlight through the southeast windows, a rush of dizzy euphoria hit my brain and I felt the mental barriers I'd erected to keep me from thinking of Lena crumble like sand against an incoming tide.

Whoa.

From seeing this happen to others many times during my summer working in a psych ward, I diagnosed a stealth delivery of drugs. Probably in the Greek vanilla yogurt.

Delicious. Eat your benzodiazepines.

I staggered to a halt just outside my assigned room and grabbed the doorframe to keep from falling. My concern about the drugs was gone, though, swept aside by a memory of Lena mouthing, *I love you,* in the Capitol basement SCIF before being dragged out with Megan, Kansas, and Jude. Her words. All the meaning in them. While I... I...

Was lying to myself!

I pushed myself back from the doorframe and shook my head to clear it.

Yes. I *was* lying to myself.

Astounding.

Because drugs or no, I could still go back and review all the moments in the SCIF clearly, particularly those at the end. They proved that Lena said nothing to me there. The person who'd spoken about love had been Bent. He'd said it had been easy to make Lena come to DC because, "Love makes people very easy to manipulate."

To which I'd said, "Love?" and turned to look at Lena.

And I'd read the tears in her eyes as the answer I wanted.

Damn it.

Damn it, focus.

Maybe this was the real reason I'd shut off thinking about her for so long. It was better to have the impression she loved me frozen inside than to review what she'd actually said. Had she cried because she loved me or because she no longer did? Had she only come to the Capitol out of guilt or sympathy?

"God*damn it.*"

Now I was cycling through the whole list of betrayals. Lena, Wenling, Jude, my brother. And the frigging NSA who'd let Kansas get kidnaped and tortured. Her eyes had been so haunted.

It set my already-free-flowing brain flipping through moment after moment that proved each element of my world, faster and faster until I felt again like I was living everything at once simultaneously. Forget holding onto just one reality; every single moment of just this timeline was so intense and *real*. I didn't know where to look, what to breathe, what to hear, to feel, to taste...

I tried to enter my room, banged into the shadowed doorframe, cursed, and stumbled past it to my bed. I stripped naked and threw myself violently under the covers, squeezed my eyes, dragged the covers over my head.

I huffed. I yelled. I sobbed and thrashed around. Sweated through my sheets. Wallowed in my stink. I moaned and tortured myself mentally worse than anything Bent had ever come up with.

"*Why!*" I roared under my sheets. About the drugs. About my life.

Until whatever I'd ingested finally carried me, bumping and moaning, from my hallucinatory conscious state into an unconscious one with extravagant dreams.

In these dreams, my stinking bed was flooded with a powerful perfume, like all the lilacs whose scent sometimes blew in through my window were trying to overwhelm me.

I fought my dream self free of my dream sheets only to see a dim vision of Lena in a diaphanous gown, climbing up on top of me, her breasts larger than I remembered, swinging pendulously, her hips and belly softer, her hair shorter, bouncing softly around her head in the moon-streaked shadows.

She pushed me back flat on the bed, sliding over me until my sex responded. Then she slid it into her and rode me with an undulating rhythm that rocked and grew along with my passion. I thought I heard the wind whuffing through my open window. My nose filled with the lilac perfume that Lena never wore in conscious life, but swam in now.

She rocked and rode me until my dreaming self finally thrust into her as furiously as she thrust into me, and we found a delirious, desperate beat of friction and rushing blood. It filled my head and chest as my body caught fire, building in pressure around my middle.

Building.

More.

Now.

Now.

NOW!!!

Uhhhhhh!

Uhhh...

I fell into blackness.

38

Ocean, save the Earth

NEXT MORNING, THE SUN rose before I did.

The drugs, obviously.

The sheets and my own body smelled...clean, like they'd taken me out of my bed while I slept, washed both me and my bedding, then plopped us both back here like we'd never left.

Crazy.

And someone sat in the bedside chair!

Lines of gray streaked her mousy brown hair, but her friendly face said mid-forties. Pleasant looking if a little plump. Big busted. Wearing light-purple cat-eye glasses and a doctor's coat that told me she was likely Dr. Sauveterre. I guessed she'd finally reached me on her list of priorities.

I rolled half up to sitting when I recalled I was naked and quickly pulled my sheets around me.

Sauveterre gave me an apple dumpling smile and tossed me the boxer shorts, tee-shirt, and jeans I'd stripped off and left on the floor by my bed the night before. "You can grab a shower and fresh clothes after our talk," she said with a French accent that slid like fingers over satin. "This is just a preliminary meeting. A quick introduction of each of us to the other."

"Except you have a file on me already, don't you?" I'd pulled my boxers under my sheet and struggled into them before casting the sheet off to don the shirt and jeans. I felt her eyes raking over my body as I did so. What was she looking for? She didn't hold a clipboard or voice recorder—no visible way of taking notes. Unless she had my kind of memory? What were the chances?

"You had a private practice, Dr. Traine," she purred. "You know how little someone's file tells you about a person."

"Do I?"

She gave me the smile again. "Of course, there *is* Dr. Bent's assessment of you as well. How accurate do you think it is?"

Mostly dressed at last, I jumped off the bed and walked away from her in my bare feet, establishing my freedom and ownership of the room.

But when I turned to gauge her reaction to that, Sauveterre hadn't stirred from her chair.

"What's your first name?" I asked.

"Océane."

"Meaning ocean. So, your full name is Ocean Save-the-Earth. *Sauve-terre.*"

"You speak French?"

"Enough for that. Your parents?"

"My father is French. He met my mother when she went to Paris to study. She was a tree-hugging hippy from Sausalito. I think she liked my father as much for his last name as anything."

"Hunh."

"I think she hoped I'd become a marine biologist and save the coral reefs."

"And instead, you're what? A psychologist? Psychiatrist?"

"The latter."

"You responsible for the drugs in my yogurt last night?"

That finally put a hiccup in her smile, and she adjusted her glasses with a frown. "Drugs?"

I stared at her, tempted to give her my guesses of the exact drug and doses based on my reactions, but it felt too much like a smartass kind of knowledge waving. Besides, her look said she'd deny everything. Why go there?

Bad way to start a therapeutic relationship, though.

Was that what this was going to be?

If you really want to work your way into Bent's plans and save the world.

But did I? Really?

The lingering internal struggle on that score kept me staring way past a comfortable pause, but Sauveterre waited me out, face still gentle, if more serious now.

"You know about SCATTER," I said.

"Not every detail, but its objectives, yes." She waited, then her lips formed an oh. "The time travel, of course. Is that why you were wondering? The extent of your abilities, your experiences with Dr. Bent, as much as he could know, of course—they're all in your file."

"And...you believe it."

She must have picked up the need in my voice. Maybe a bit of a whine, an unspoken cry that if she knew who I was and what I could do and how my entire understanding of my life was trying to rearrange itself, why had she left me alone for so long? What could have been more important than—

"I've been working intensively with your brother and Zhou Xiaobo for the last four days," Sauveterre said. "They've both been decompensating in major ways, and I couldn't leave them. It was actually them that Uwe called me in so desperately for. He's a brilliant researcher but—how would you say it?—a shit therapist. A deconstructive analyst. Not very good at putting his subjects back together after taking them apart."

I considered her. She still hadn't moved from the chair beside my now-empty bed. I hadn't moved from the middle of the floor where I stood barefooted, my arms folded over my chest.

Sauveterre raised an eyebrow. "So, what do you think?"

"About?"

"Us."

For just a second, I had an odd flash from my dream of Lena.

The psychiatrist must have seen something on my face and laughed. "That bad?"

"What?"

"The two of us working together, Dr. Traine. Can I call you Jackson?"

"I'm not decompensating."

"You don't appear to be. True. Which is remarkable, considering."

"Considering Bent's deconstruction."

She nodded. "Among other things."

"I've worked with other therapists."

"Did they help?"

"Some. A little. No one since I learned how to…" I waved my hands around.

"There aren't many of us experienced in this area."

"You work here? The McLean Hospital?"

Sauveterre gave a little chuckle. "No, of course not. They wouldn't have me any more than they'd have Uwe if they knew who he was. I was with him in SCATTER back when it was CIA. And however secret the operation, our 'release' from the Agency was still somehow leaked to all the main power brokers in the AMA and APA. Uwe went completely off the radar so he could continue his work. I set up a kind of life-coaching institute informed by things I'd learned working with time travelers in SCATTER. Uwe loaned me some of the seed money in exchange for my as-needed help with key operatives."

"Why don't you work with him full time?"

She stood and walked up to stand directly in front of me, close enough that I could smell her scent, which was…nothing. Maybe the slightest whiff of vanilla or sandalwood—a basic soap smell. "I suspect you know the answer to that," she said, looking up through her glasses at my face. "One can believe in the goals of a project and still be uncomfortable with how they're achieved."

She turned. Walked to the door.

I called out, "Océane!"

She looked back, one eyebrow raised.

"How *do* you work with traumatized time travelers?"

"With you, Jackson, very gently, I think."

"But—"

"Tomorrow," she said and was gone.

I wasn't sure whether I was looking forward to our next meeting or scared shitless.

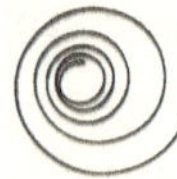

Turned out it was both.

The next morning, after I'd showered and eaten, I donned track pants and tee shirt and sat on the warm vinyl floor of my room in a relaxed Sukhasana pose, knees out to the side and ankles crossed. I closed my eyes to review my life and wait for Dr. Sauveterre.

Ujjayi breath took me down and deep into stillness before unleashing my memory review, breathing through it to accept the avalanche, the crazy-making everywhere/everywhen. And I almost found a flow of understanding before my heart rate ticked up and my breath rose to shallow puffs of panic.

Shit. Calm down.

Calm!

I heard a rumbling sound and thought I might have finally pushed myself into a stroke…

Shit!

…until it turned into a knock on my half-open door.

My eyes flew open to see Dr. Sauveterre standing there, hand still raised in a fist, blinking at me through her periwinkle glasses. Her other hand held the top of a wheeled office chair she'd obviously just rumbled through the halls up to my door.

No stroke, then. Good. Catch your breath.

She'd ditched the doctor's coat to wear a simple, covered-shoulder V-neck dress in a black-and-white houndstooth check. It fell to below-the knee and had a simple belt around the middle, all form fitting enough to emphasize her large bust and make her waist seem small by comparison.

My penis swelled up.

Stupid. Stop that.

"Special chair?" I asked.

"It is comfortable. Would you like to do this here or in the common area where there are a couch and tables?" The French accent, too. Seductive.

I said stop.

"Here's fine." As soon as I said it, I realized that left me only the uncomfortable straight-back bedside chair or my continued floor seat where I'd be looking up at Sauveterre's legs and whatever.

I was about to change my mind, but Sauveterre had already rolled her chair into the room and stopped it a couple of feet in front of me, near the foot of my bed. She sat and opened her satchel on her lap.

With a smile, she said, "I have a gift for you," and pulled out a brown moleskin journal and a pen. She held them out to me.

I rolled up to my feet before her, realizing belatedly that this put her hands reaching toward my crotch and my eyes looking down her cleavage.

Really?

I backed up quickly, faking a need to shake out my legs and arms, before turning back to her.

"What's the point of that?" I said.

"You write your thoughts and feelings after our sessions. I find it helps my patients sort through what was said, what they thought about it, how it made them feel."

"You said you read my file. You know I don't need to write anything down to sort it out. I can review any item at any time."

Sauveterre smiled and sat back a little in her chair, pulling out her own moleskin journal and what looked like a very nibbled-on pen. "Of course, *I* need to write things down. I don't believe in video or audio recordings of my patients unless there are security or legal concerns. They get in the way of honest sharing."

I nodded. Good.

"But I'm sure you've also read the research that shows writing things down improves our comprehension and analysis of them, not just our memory."

I shrugged and opened my mouth, but she wasn't done.

"It also reduces stress. Writing your feelings isn't about memory at all, but about understanding yourself. And for you... Well."

"For me, what?"

"Your file says a perfect memory. Every moment. Every smell, taste, or other perception."

"Yes."

"In most people, the most powerful and meaningful things that happen, they are what we remember."

"Incorrectly."

"Perhaps."

"Not perhaps. You want me to cite the research?"

She held up her hands in mock surrender. "Still, for most of the world, our brains give us cues about what things are important in our lives because we remember these best. Yes?"

I shook my head. "Even *if* that were true, do you really think my brain doesn't trick me into dwelling on the things that hurt or terrified or made me..." I stopped. My heart was pounding already. It took so little now to set me off.

Sauveterre, to her credit, read that correctly. She dropped her pitch and volume to ask softly, "Yet there have been times, your file says, where you can't seem to sort out what was from what is. And not like your brother, who often can't keep track of what year it is. No, you seem to remember things so intensely that they seem like they are happening as you remember them. More real perhaps than what is happening to you in the moment you remember them."

My lips felt like rough paper as I licked them. "Tell me about Kenny," I said.

"Kentucky? No. This time is about you."

I planted my feet. "Tell me about him, how he's doing, what you did to work with him. Convince me you know how to help people like us, and maybe I'll listen to you."

Sauveterre considered that for a moment, casually brushing back a wispy lock of mousy hair that kept falling in front of her eyes. She finally nodded and set her satchel on the floor beside her chair. She laid the moleskin and pen she'd offered to me on top of it. Her own moleskin notebook and pen stayed on her lap.

"*D'accord*," she said. "However, I will start with Zhou Xiaobo first. The problems he has are different from those of your brother and you, but still the same."

She began to talk.

I had to walk around the room as she spoke, because the crashing combination of excitement and dread took hold of me again. This time because I was finally about to get some *answers* about time travel, after all this time, from someone other than myself and Lena. And the two of us had such a small data set to extrapolate from, even with my adventures and her experiments.

For instance, all the bullshit I'd told Wenling about oceans and one person's time travel only affecting small parts of it so that those outside the effective radius wouldn't even know it happened, that... Well, actually, that might have been a brilliant guess. At least it still seemed to hold through my experiences of getting jerked about in time first with Xiaobo and then Kenny.

But the triggering HOW of time travel, beyond Lena's vague theory of superattraction of near-perfect replicas through the energy of space-time...

Dr. Sauveterre's discussion of Xiaobo's now didn't answer it either. But it helped.

She told me that Xiaobo always leaped back to the beginning of his day because that was the one moment he always captured with a meditation practice he'd started when he was nine years old. It had helped him deal with an abusive father, then an abusive sister, then Uwe Bent.

I raised my hand. "That explains the *when* he goes to but not the *how* of his jump. I jump when I'm about to die, physically or emotionally. That seems to release my mind or spiritual essence from the grip of the reality that's killing it. But Xiaobo—it seems like he can do it whenever he likes. No biggie. No trauma."

Sauveterre raised her eyebrows at me, apparently struck speechless. But only for a moment. "Did you say, 'No trauma?'"

I felt like I'd just been called stupid and flushed in embarrassment. "No apparent trauma."

Sauveterre took a deep breath and muttered, "So young." She opened her notebook, jotted something in it, then looked at me. "Zhou Xiaobo is nothing *but* trauma. It's not always shaking and sweating, stomach cramps and headaches, is it?"

I finally understood what I'd missed. "Dissociation," I muttered.

"Exactly. His way of coping is, and has been for almost two decades, to separate himself from the world. The world is a filthy, painful thing for him, so he barely acknowledges its reality."

"The only real parts being…"

"His morning ritual. They are what he calls a 'spawn point' in the video game that is his life. He has missions. He wins points and levels up. He considers himself a genius player who is toying with the 'newbies.'"

"Like me."

Sauveterre looked at me. "Back in January, Uwe says, Xiaobo started to change. He started to not listen. To not do what he was told to do. This was when you were invited to join SCATTER. Do you know what happened?"

I shook my head, even as I recalled telling him how he was being used like a chess pawn to make his sister offer me to Bent. And how I convinced him he was the one with all the power in the situation.

"This made Uwe give him harder work and interrogate him more. Push him more. Demand more."

"To prove he did *not* have power."

"It helped save Ukraine. The various democracies sent weapons. SCATTER sent Xiaobo."

"To do what, exactly?"

"Various things. All from a safe remove, of course. God only knows what would happen if he was allowed into the conflict area itself."

"Because…?"

Sauveterre's eyes looked far off into some ugly place. She blinked, looked back at him, and spun her pen around in her fingers. "Let us say his actions could become highly unpredictable. Even under Uwe's supervision, the increased stress almost severed his attachment to any consistent reality."

"And you knew this how?"

"He was fading into a catatonic state. When I arrived, the EEGs showed almost no brain activity. Then…none. Brain death. Randomly, he would return. He would talk to me."

"Has he done this before?" *Say no*, I mentally urged her. Lena's work had shown that photons which had created new timelines interacted with at a quantum level with the timelines they left, most probably the earlier versions of themselves. Which suggested those earlier, original photons didn't vanish when a version of them left their timestream. I'd concluded for my peace of mind that this meant when *I* jumped back in time and created a new time stream, a copy of my brain or spirit continued on in the timestream I left. But what if it didn't? What if every time Xiaobo or Kenny or I jumped back, the body we jumped from in the timeline we left just...died, emptied of mind and spirit? My God, like the guilt over the messes I caused with every jump could get any worse. The thought of the pain my sister or Lena or some innocent bystander would feel to find my brain-dead body...

Sauveterre was watching me closely. "Has he done what before?" she asked.

"Gone catatonic. Left his body."

"I don't think that's what is—"

"Isn't it? You said it yourself. It's how he time travels. He dissociates from the present reality and jumps back to the beginning of his day. What happens to the body he leaves?"

Sauveterre furrowed her brows, her study of me even more intense. "It does not matter?" she said uncertainly.

I stomped toward her. "How can you say that?"

She didn't flinch. "Who he was before he time traveled back to the beginning of his day, it is rewritten. It no longer exists. There's now only this new Xiaobo, perhaps remembering the old Xiaobo, but only as a part of his history, some hours of which *only* he will remember."

I glared at her until I realized she was only thinking like I had before Lena proved each jump created a new timestream. And of all the things to get wrapped up in, the state of the body I left behind might be one of the smaller ones. Impossible to know, anyway. You couldn't jump across time streams to see.

At least *I* couldn't.

"How does Kenny...do his thing?" I'd been about to say "jump," but I didn't know how Sauveterre or Bent viewed what Kenny could do. Kenny himself hadn't seemed to think he was time traveling so much as visiting places in his memory or seeing the future.

Sauveterre didn't blink at my sudden change in direction. She made another note in her book, nodded, and brushed back her rebellious lock of silver hair like she was stroking my hand in sympathy.

"Your brother is a special case. You know this?"

I nodded.

"His ability to see the future is already a different kind of time travel than every other time traveler SCATTER has studied."

"Because he's traveling forward in time, not back?"

"At first, Uwe thought he *was* just jumping back in time to tell us what he saw. But Kentucky does not speak of 'traveling' from one time to another. It is as if only his mind jumps to places and returns. And I have seen Uwe test him, giving him a future time to jump to. Kentucky will close his eyes, exhibit obvious REM beneath his lids, then reopen them and relate the future he has seen. He can travel forward months or even years and speak of what he has seen."

I shook my head furiously as she finished. This was idiotic. All Kenny had to do was live beyond this time. *Four years,* he told me in his childhood bedroom. Then he jumps back far into the past. Maybe five years. At some point Bent asks him, in this new timeline Kenny's living in now, to jump to the future. Kenny closes his eyes, remembers what he lived through, opens them, and tells Bent.

Sauveterre obviously understood nothing about Kenny's power. Nor did Bent.

"Jackson?" Sauveterre asked calmly.

"What happened to Kenny? Why did Bent have you see him?"

She considered just a moment before saying, "Kentucky became...lost. He had mind traveled so far, so often, many times under the influence of drugs, that he could no longer tell in which reality his real self was based. To see reality change so dramatically before his eyes again and again, it is a wonder he has not given up on the concept of any objective reality long before now."

That might have been, sadly, exactly what happened. But she was also missing a big part of the why. And only I could fill that in for her.

I swallowed and turned on my heel, walking away from her until I was over by my window, as far from her as I could get in this room.

"When I jump into an earlier version of myself," I said, "it's like I've tricked my earlier mind to accept me. It *thinks* I'm just like it, a near perfect copy that just took a walk or something. But then I'm *in,* and it freaks out at the sudden flood of all these new experiences, sights, sounds, feelings, tastes, smells, and thoughts! I shake and my head spins. But then, you know, I *adapt.* And I'm really in. There. Back in time."

I turned my head to see Sauveterre nodding excitedly, jotting notes. When she looked up, her eyes sparkled. It made my stomach turn over. Bent didn't know this stuff. Xiaobo's experience would be different. But Kenny had my type of brain, or I had his. The Traine memory. Sauveterre had to understand it if was to have any hope of really helping him. And me.

"It's like astral projection!" she said now.

"No," I said. "You're missing the point. What I described is when I'm only jumping ten minutes back in time. When I do a double jump, my brain freaks out twice as much and I want to puke. When I jump back three times in a row, I risk having a heart attack and dying. That's thirty minutes! I think Xiaobo jumps back up to twenty-four hours because he's probably only storing bits and pieces of what he sees in his memory, but Kenny has visions that seem to encompass *years*."

"Yes," Sauveterre said, "but—"

"He's got the Traine memory. Every sight, sound, smell, touch, and taste. Why doesn't it *kill him?*"

Sauveterre bit her lips, jotted a note, then waited for me to calm down, motioning subtly to me to breathe.

When I'd calmed myself, I realized I literally backed myself into a corner of the room. My loss of control around this calm, quiet woman troubled me. Was it some kind of learned response to therapy? I'd certainly poured my guts out in my early PTSD therapy sessions during my university days.

Or was it just being in the presence of a knowledgeable woman who truly seemed able to understand and handle my storms of emotion? Like Lena had done once upon a time.

Sauveterre stood up from her chair and, leaving her notebook on the seat, stepped to my bed, pulling up its sheet and bedspread, straightening them and centering the pillow before smoothing them all out with her hands.

Then she patted the bedspread and called softly to me. "Come sit, Jackson. Let me tell you about your brother."

39

The story of my brother

"First," Sauveterre said, "I want you to think back to your childhood. Your times at home with Kenny. The times you saw him at school."

I sat in a relaxed cross-legged Sukhasana pose on top of the bedspread now, my hands loosely together in my lap. The taupe-colored, stitched quilt bedspread felt rough under the sides and tops of my bare feet. I consciously breathed in the scent of the early spring that drifted in through the window.

Sauveterre had returned to her rolling office chair and notebook and crossed her legs. Her dress rode up above her knees, showing smooth, shaved legs. Maybe it was her French side. Comfortable with her body. Able to be a desirable woman and a professional at the same time.

But these were all only my objective notes, because my little head was no longer engaged here. The turmoil in my head and guts, my need to maybe finally *understand* what had happened to Kenny all those years ago, kept me focused mostly on Océane Sauveterre's lips. As if reading her lips while hearing her words ensured I wouldn't miss a thing.

"Do you remember?" she asked.

"Everything."

"Do you recall when he first started losing control of his emotional states?"

"He never completely lost control," I said.

"Of course not, but—"

"But he struggled. Almost more with the ups than the downs because he *knew* what was happening inside him. He was always very self-aware back before that was a thing."

"Did your parents have him diagnosed?"

"My parents didn't really raise us."

"I read you had a nanny."

"When we were all little, yeah. But as soon as my big sister turned sixteen, my parents let Carmelita go. So, it was just the three kids. Kansas, my sister, was boss. She was...a good mom. But then she headed off for college and it was just me and Kenny. And he was a good big brother, handling things, for about a year or two. Then his bipolar swings took all his attention and..."

The emotional overwhelm took me by surprise. Shame for Kenny's weakness flooded me...My face burned. My throat tightened. It was foolishness from a clinical point of view. Even calling what Kenny had a "weakness." Mental illness wasn't shameful or a weakness to be hidden away, camouflaged, and not talked about. It no more belonged in the closet than cancer or drug addiction.

But what I felt wasn't my adult understanding. It was my teenage experience, riddled with fear and anger over my brother's increasing spells of depression or mania. They disrupted the delicate home/school picture we'd created together for the world. We were outsiders working hard to fit in. Come on!

"What happened?" Sauveterre asked gently.

"He started self-medicating. Just weed and caffeine at first. Then he played hero to save a girl he saw getting beaten, only to find that she and her boyfriend were members of a local street gang."

"This was the gang Kenny became part of?"

"The Demon Monks. Yeah. They ran drugs. They got Kenny hooked."

"Do you know what drugs?"

"Both uppers and downers. I'm guessing heroin and coke. But could have been meth. Opium. He definitely had track marks and stashes of pills and powders."

Tears coursed down my cheeks now, but I still spoke with a fairly even, professional voice. Sauveterre took notes. I was reliving each discovery of Kenny's downward spiral. Even before all the gang stuff took hold, I'd broken out in panic and fear for what would happen to me, to Kenny, to us. There'd been so much anti-drug hysteria back then that Kenny's addiction felt like a maelstrom sweeping up both of us.

Sauveterre's gentle voice cut into that again. "Did he talk about it with you? Did he describe what he was going through?"

Part of me wanted to snap, *No! That was the end of things, okay?* But the part of my mind that recorded everything offered conversation after conversation that I'd had with Kenny in those years. "Yes," I said. "Friendly fog. Clarity. Looking for the balance. Trying to be there for me." I shook my head. "Really, the only thing that made what he was going through any different from classic substance abuse with underlying bipolar disorder was the fact he never lost track of who he'd been and who he was from day to day."

"The Traine memory," Sauveterre suggested.

"The Traine fucking memory."

She gave me a sad smile. "And you believe he still has that?"

"You ever hear him give Dr. Bent a report?"

"No. I—"

"You said he was 'lost.' Like how? He was tired and confused when he brought me here, but he'd been very with it right up to when we escaped the bombed building."

Sauveterre pushed back her rebellious lock of hair and stood, leaving her notebook on the seat. She drifted to the window. Given her calm demeanor up to that point, this was the equivalent of wildly waving her arms in distress. I closely watched the sunlit profile as she spoke.

"Your brother is...conscious and seemingly aware of his surroundings. But only on a superficial level. While Xiaobo routinely rejects the *importance* of reality, so it mostly functions as a kind of playing board he can dip in and out of as it suits him, he's very clear about which environment he's in at any moment in time. Kentucky is not."

She frowned. "There's a part of him, I believe, that thinks he's back in high school with you, and everything that's happened since then is some kind of lucid dream. All of SCATTER, reporting to Uwe, seeing the world half-destroyed by nuclear war—yes, he shared some of that with me—are all part of the dream. Of course, they feel very real to him, but the out-of-order nature of his experience seems to have convinced his drug-loosened brain that he cannot actually be *living* through any of it."

I studied her, wondering if some part of her felt the truth of that statement. That the consistency of Kenny's existence in one place might somehow be as loose in reality as it was in his own mind.

"So, how did you help him? And Xiaobo?"

"Much like this," Sauveterre said. She sauntered to the left side of my bed and gracefully sat on the mattress so that the vibrations and depression of it reached where I sat, unsettling me. Then she reached out to take one of my hands to hold between both of hers. The warmth and softness of her skin, the intimacy of the move, broke me down more.

"That's..."

"Surprising? Yes. But immediate, too. Look at my hands, follow my arms up to my eyes,"—God, she had beautiful deep green eyes—"then look around the room. Breathe deeply as you do it. In to a count of four. Hold for a count of four. Release for a count of four. Hold again…two…three…four. Breathe in…two…three…four…"

She kept going, directing my gaze, making me focus on the feeling of her hand, being aware of each part of my body, then the smells of the room, the temperature, the sounds.

Even with the distraction of her sexual energy, I settled into this quickly. It was so close to my usual yoga and centering practice. And I guessed that having someone as present as Océane Sauveterre lead Xiaobo and Kenny into it could be incredibly powerful, giving them a way to find their missing connection to the body and reality they were in.

"Okay," I muttered after a dozen breathing cycles, "can I have my hand back now?"

Sauveterre smiled and released it but didn't move from where she sat. That presence! It was her age. Her sexual energy. Her calm acceptance of what you were and could become.

"How did they react? Xiaobo and Kenny?"

"At first, not at all. But each day a little more."

"Are they back now?"

"As much as any time in the last few years, I think. This is why I could finally come and see you."

"To send me in the opposite direction."

"Pardon?"

I smiled bitterly. "Bent thinks I hold on to each reality I'm in too tightly. That's why it's so hard for me to time travel and why I jump back only about ten minutes each time."

Sauveterre crossed her hands in her lap. With her feet just slightly to one side on the floor and her knees together, her back straight, she looked the model of simple propriety. But there was nothing simple about the intensity of her focus on me. I wanted to squirm away or reach out to touch her just to see if her whole body was as real as her hands had been.

She shook her head at me with a considered smile. "You are not Xiaobo, and you are not your brother. They have abandoned a firm grip on the now out of a kind of hatred or confusion. With you, the trick will be getting you very comfortable with who you are and what you can do. Then you can loosen your grip, knowing you won't lose anything *unless it is something you want to give up.*"

With that, Sauveterre pushed herself up off the bed and turned to collect her notebook from the rolling chair she'd clearly decided to leave with me.

She walked to the door, smiled, and left.

The chill that ran through my body told me it somehow understood and feared her last words more than my mind.

It was terrified.

40

Kansas

KANSAS KNEW SHE'D BEEN pushing it when she snuck back into DC on a Greyhound bus. But when she came out of the Weekenders internet café near the Mayflower Hotel and spotted a tail trying to look nonchalant, she didn't freak. Too many good moves were paying off to run away now.

The main good move had been tracing the "Primary Logic" electronic deposits that had been funding Lena's research to a Miami bank account. That account was funded by a small Texas corporation that was a shell corporation for a Maryland operation named LWQi. And LWQi showed an active guest account with the Mayflower on Connecticut Avenue NW, Washington, DC.

The fact Kansas was being tailed here meant she was getting close.

She chuckled as she adjusted her ripstop carry bag more securely over the shoulder of her pale-blue raincoat and hurried east through the drizzle on L, then south on 7th. She hadn't done a bait and grab since a CIA agent she'd dated took her on a Company games picnic.

Ducking around the corner at K, she sprinted to the Farragut North subway station and hurried down the escalator to wait around the corner at the bottom. It was a perfect grab point in the middle of the loud, overripe afternoon crowds who streamed by her to get tickets or rush to the second escalator down to the tracks.

Twelve seconds later, her tail, dressed in a damp, orangey-tan suit that was too big for his skinny young body—a new recruit or reassigned computer jockey—came rushing from the stairs to stand just ahead of her. He scanned the station desperately, looking for her.

And here the smart move might have been to slip by him and back up the stairs. Or at least draw the gun she now carried in the waistband near the small of her back. But there was something about the lost-lamb look of her pursuer that emboldened Kansas to try something new.

She slipped a pen out of her shoulder bag, stepped up behind the kid, and jammed the pen's tip into the fleshy small of his back.

"Don't move, yell, or look uncomfortable," she said. "This syringe contains two milligrams of fentanyl in a citrate and sodium chloride solution. Do you know what that means?"

"I...get high?"

"At two milligrams, you die, kid."

The kid—he looked barely twenty—gave a strained laugh. "You know, most people fake a gun when they shove something in your back."

"Your call. You believe me and tell me how you marked me and the contact protocol with Garvey, or you don't."

"And then...?"

"I don't need you, kid. And the world won't give a shit."

Kansas heard the kid's breathing speed up, and she tensed for a fight. Then it settled and where she had contact with the small of his back, she felt a shudder run through him.

He'd given up.

"I was just supposed to watch the Wallflower for a...person of interest."

"Me?"

"No. Just...someone who's been visiting Langley. He's stayed there before."

"Why the interest?"

The kid broke out in a fresh sweat and stopped breathing, clearly wondering how much more he could reveal and not get fired, or withhold and not get stuck with the hypodermic.

Kansas took a shot in the dark. "Person was involved in the attack on the Baltimore building that killed four-hundred and twenty-seven people, yes or no?"

The kid started breathing again. "Yes. But it was four-hundred and twenty-five."

"Two more confirmed yesterday."

"Shit."

"Who's the shitbag you're looking for?"

Another held breath.

"Kid, just tell me. You're almost out of this."

A hard swallow. "Former Chinese military. Colonel Fang Jian."

Kansas blinked. Couldn't be. "Give me your phone."

The kid froze.

Kansas pressed the point of the pen hard enough that the kid cried out. Kansas laughed and leaned into his neck to cover it for the one or two people walking past who'd noticed. "I just have to press the plunger. The phone."

The kid fumbled a hand into his breast pocket and came out with a cell phone.

"Unlock it. Show me a picture of Colonel Fang."

He did.

The picture was not a great angle, but everything about the man—his posture, his careful way of speaking when he drove her and Elizabeth AKA Wenling out to dinner or a show, the way he'd roared out his pain when he thought Wenling had been shot dead in that Capitol basement SCIF—was unforgettable.

Kansas took the phone from him. "A Boeing Black. Very special. Blackberry lives on."

She saw the red flush run down the back of his sweaty neck. "Can I...have it back?"

"Tell you what, kid. I could destroy this phone and get you into a deep, stinking pile of excrement with your boss. *Or* you walk ahead to the ticket gate and wait there for ten minutes. I go back up these stairs, drop your phone in the trash can up top, and leave town. You collect your phone, forget you ever saw me, and no one'll ever know how you fucked up. Choose."

Fifteen minutes later, Kansas had, of course, *not* left town. She'd instead walked quickly to the Mayflower front desk, flashed her credentials at the desk clerk, and collected a confirmation that Colonel Fang had a standing order for stays at the Mayflower per the Maryland corporation LWQi, but no specific dates booked.

That meant he could show up tomorrow, two weeks from now, or never again. Ridiculous for Kansas to stay here, so close to Garvey's seat of power and all his minions who were scouring the country to find her. But she'd gotten a strong vibe that the kid who'd spotted her wasn't going to report it. And a hunch that with all the shit going down about the Baltimore air bombing, Fang was going to come around again.

He obviously still served Wenling. Whether he helped arrange the attack in Baltimore or not, he'd still be Wenling's eyes, ears, and hands in the real world so she could stay dead.

The question was why? Now that Kansas finally understood the depths of Wenling's deceptions and narcissism, she didn't see how a man as seemingly honor-based as Fang gave her his loyalty.

It might be the first thing Kansas asked when she finally followed Fang back to the witch's lair.

She wasn't going to ask nicely.

41

Jude

Clonk! Clonk! Clonk!

"Hey! HEYYY!"

Jude threw the metal cup and pitcher he'd been striking the door with back at the bolted down cot where he slept. They clattered and bounced across the concrete until they came to rest in the scary shadows below the bed.

Jude looked up at the small surveillance camera Dadashev had installed some weeks ago in the left corner of the room near the door. He began jumping up and down in front of it, waving his arms out from his sides like a madman. Then he planted his feet, pointed at his temple, and smiled broadly like he'd remembered something! Palms out. Utter joy! He danced around and looked back at the camera.

Then more jumping jacks to catch the attention of whoever monitored this feed. More charades. *Think! Idea! You have an idea? Yes! A wonderful idea! You want to give it away? You want to* share *it. Yes! Yes!*

Then a third and fourth and fifth time, with increasing desperation. Until his clothes stank with his sweat.

His clothes. The one now-baggy-all-over set with the pants held on by a belt he'd had to punch new holes in, that he washed out in the sink piece by piece over a few days once a week and hung on the corner of his bedframe. Those. The ones he'd washed and dried enough times that all the pieces had developed holes and rips. They now stank like boiled cabbage. Even more than when Dadashev visited every few days and had him run laps around the room and do burpees and pushups.

Jude staggered to a halt, staring slack-jawed up at the little round surveillance camera.

He listened for the sound of steps running to see if he'd gone mad.

Silence.

Nothing.

Dadashev's visits were only once a week now. Jude's food came in the night, in the dark, delivered by someone unknown. The door opened with a barely audible groan that still woke him up every other time. The empty bowl and pitcher were to be left by the door for pick up the next night. If they weren't, there was no delivery.

Jude still hadn't decided whether this brutal system was some kind of calculated cruelty meant to break any remaining resistance he had in him—silly since he'd had none to begin with—or just done to minimize the inconvenience of illegally detaining him in the bowels of building he used to work in.

Maybe, Jude thought again, no one was actually monitoring the camera at all. Maybe the camera with the tiny red light was not connected to anything beyond this room. It was just a small plastic and glass doodad that you put up in a conspicuous place to make would-be robbers *think* they were being watched and recorded.

And wouldn't that, as his childhood rabbi used to say when Jude wondered if God found our suffering funny, *be the shiksa?*

Which Jude had never understood because a *shiksa* was a gentile female. Until he got older and realized his rabbi was both a bigot and a misogynist. But when things went really sideways for Jude as an adult in ways that seemed perverse and cruel, the expression still came to mind.

Maybe this was why he hadn't found a wife.

Have to get the cup and bowl.

Yes, he did. Even though he hated the shadowed underside of his bed. When he bought a bed for his first apartment, he'd made sure it didn't *have* a space underneath it. It was a captain's bed with stuffed drawers that went all the way around it. No place for estries or mazzikin or gentile boogeymen of any sort.

The bowl.

Jude giggled and wiped his mouth. Yet another way he was becoming more like Jackson. Talking to himself. He knew Jackson did it all the time. Except Jackson's was always critical. He called it his anxiety demon. Jude's was commanding but good natured. Kind of like he used to be when he had more fat than muscle and considered himself a soft, comfy, *intelligent* vehicle of God's love in the world.

Now he could just drop to the floor like a badass—*Ha!*—shake sweat from this face and hair like a Hollywood action hero—*Looking* good!—scootch forward, reach in, and swipe that cup out from under—*Yunh-hunh!*—then grab the pitcher and—

Rattle, clank!

Jude scuttled backwards on his hands, knees, and toes. He banged his head on the bedframe but thankfully kept hold of the pitcher.

He jumped up and spun around as Dadashev stepped into the room.

"You came!" Jude rasped, his voice cracking. He'd finished all his water early today and his tongue and mouth felt like rough cardboard.

"What are you dancing about like an idiot?"

"Dancing... Yes! I remembered something!" He did his charades again, pointing at his temple. Then thrust his open hands at Dadashev. "I want to share it with you!"

"What?"

Jude worked his tongue around in his mouth to get some moisture and used that time to quickly organize again in his mind, the plan that he'd come up with a couple of hours ago and thought through carefully.

"Well?" Dadashev looked about to turn and leave.

"First, you know that one of the time travelers that Dr. Bent is studying is Zura Dobroshtan?"

Dadashev frowned and looked down like he might have heard the name, but—

"2014. She was the hero of Prudke. At fifteen years old, when Russia was taking over Crimea, she warned her village about an approaching team of secret Russian Spetsnaz troops who were killing and raping Ukrainian nationalists. Zura persuaded the entire town to evacuate and hide in the Crimean mountains until the troops left, then returned them to the town."

Dadashev nodded. "I remember this. Then the Russians took over all of Crimea, shipped out the Ukrainians who loved Ukraine, and brought in Russians, like maggots, like reproducing flies and maggots feeding on the shit that was left."

Jude swallowed and nodded. "Um. Yes. I guess. The thing is, I gathered from a comment you made last week that you all thought you'd found SCATTER and...destroyed it."

Dadashev shot him a murderous look.

"You didn't say it directly," Jude said quickly. "It was a comment about time travelers being, well, maggots, who should have died. In context, I gathered you meant an attempt had been made, but it failed."

"This is why you called me down here?" Dadashev said, moving closer to Jude. "To tell me we almost killed a Ukrainian hero?"

"No no no. Well, yes. But because if I tell you where I think SCATTER is now, I need to know you're not going to just go in and shoot everyone."

"Like a Ukrainian hero I should care about. Because you think I didn't know she was there last time or I would have stopped it. I would have told the Director of Special Missions Poussaint that he should not do what he was about to do." The sarcasm dripped from his mouth in a way only a thick Russian accent could carry off.

"Did you know? About Zura Dobroshtan?"

Dadashev held his sneer for a full five seconds before he said, "No."

"And now that you know, can you stop DSM Poussaint from killing them all?"

"Like your friend."

"Yes."

Dadashev kept his eyes on Jude so fiercely Jude felt himself melting. But then the Ukrainian-American CIA agent nodded. "Tell me."

"I don't know the exact building, but I've been thinking about it. And from things he said to me once, I'm pretty sure I know where Dr. Bent's next fallback for SCATTER is. There's this particular medical campus where they have a psychiatric department that specializes in treating trauma victims..."

42

Lena

Lena jerked up straight at her desk in Jackson's restored office.

Someone there? In the lobby?

She strained to hear, even stilling her breathing as her whole body tensed. But not to grab something to defend herself. It wanted to run into the lobby to see if he could really be...

Don't go there.

There was no sound, anyway. Nothing beyond the nearly-inaudible hum of the computer she'd been working at. Through the closed windows and blinds, a rumble of the Saturday afternoon traffic outside.

Megan was off today.

Lena was here alone.

She shut off the computer and stood, gathering up the few charts and summaries she'd printed from yesterday's accelerator runs. Everything was accessible in a highly encrypted vault online, but these days she felt she needed to feel the paper and trace the figures with her fingers. They sometimes changed in importance and structure depending on how she held the paper, just like the phenomenon they were studying. And they were so close. Quantum entanglement between parallel dimensions! Salazar had found a change in the particle signatures of newly created photons related to the energy applied to pre-replacement photons that was showing promise of mathematical consistency. If they could predict the effect of vanished photons on their replacements, they could track the duration and degree of the entanglement. Possibly even see secondary vanishment, suggesting the creation of yet more dimensions. It was all here in these few papers of data.

But even as Lena saw visions of space-time splitting over and over, her awareness kept jerking back to the feeling she'd just had of Jackson's presence. Like his consciousness had somehow become quantumly entangled with hers.

No crazier than time travel.

Except there were simpler explanations. All that time she'd spent in Jackson's childhood home with his sister, seeing his eyes in hers every time she looked, hearing his vocal inflections every time she and Kansas talked. Yeah, Lena's subconscious was primed. Then she'd gone back to her research at the accelerator lab but left each night to sleep in Jackson's restored apartment. And when she wasn't at the lab or his apartment, she was here in Jackson's office. His style and presence was in every touch of the restoration. Like *he* was here.

"But he's not," she growled at the room and started stuffing her papers and binders into her briefcase. "Could be dead. Could have joined with the enemy. Already know he'll abandon everything to chase a pretty piece of rich, beautiful ass. Don't we?"

It didn't matter that Lena had *told* him to go. Or that Zhou Wenling had saved him, at first, from the people stalking him. It was still a betrayal. And stupid! Look where it had gotten him.

And Wenling.

Unless Wenling was really alive.

But then what?

Despite Kansas' intuition, Lena believed Wenling would readily have sent planes to bomb her brother and Jackson if she'd had the connections.

Just like Jackson's parents had left Jackson's upbringing to someone else.

And the Demon Monks tried to kill him.

And his best friend, Jude, betrayed him.

But the very worst of all? The real love of his life, the person he defended with his life over and over, gave his body and secrets to, and swore his love and fealty to, *gave him up*. It was her who'd sent him into Wenling's arms, which led to him ending up as a prisoner of SCATTER, where he might very well die or lose his mind.

"I'm so sorry," she whispered to the spirit she still felt around her. "Just... that."

Lena finished packing up, kicked the office chair back into place, stubbing her toe. She hopped, cursing, out of the office, locking up behind her.

When she exited the back of the building, the sun was ironically bright and beautiful. At Jackson's little blue Chevy Bolt hatchback, she threw in her briefcase of reports, slid into the driver's seat, and pulled out her phone.

On it was the list of twelve names Kansas had written out for her. She'd found stuff on most of them from some intensive internet searches and Bryan's help. The only one that was almost a complete black hole was the very first one on the list.

Throwing politeness to the wind, she dialed Megan. When the young office assistant answered, all out of breath, Lena cut her off before she could even say what she'd been doing.

"Tell me you spoke to some of these people. Or found someone who knows Salim Noor al-Rashid."

"Are you okay? Is it..."

"I don't have time to chat. Just...data. Anything? Any fucking thing at all?"

There was a silence on the phone and Lena realized she'd been barking like a feral dog. Before she could apologize, Megan spoke so softly that Lena had to still her breathing and rage just to make out the words. Clever girl.

"Repeat that, please," she said quietly when Megan was done.

"The list is wrong," Megan said.

"You're saying SCATTER never took al-Rashid?"

"I think they thought they did. I found a story buried in the Washington Post from November 2004. Some worker at the CIA headquarters named Salim Rashid suffered a heart attack. They posted a grainy photo that looked like it had been taken for a passport."

She paused dramatically.

Lena didn't have the patience. She squinted out at the sunshine, breathing heavily.

"I copied that news story and photo," Megan said quickly. "We sent it to all the Al-Rashids I could find. Which is a lot. You know there's an Al Rashid in Canada? The name's got all this historical significance because Haroun al-Rashid was this caliph who ruled Islam at the turn of the seventh to eighth century. In Baghdad. *The Thousand and One Nights*, AKA *The Arabian Nights*? That took place in his court. And the name itself means something like 'One who is directed to the right path to obtain their objectives in the right way.'"

Another pause. This time, Lena snapped, "So? Did you get a response?"

"*We* did. Me, Bryan, Ziggy, Chandice, and Hazel. We worked it all together. It was actually Chandice who got the first email back."

"Which was?"

I heard Megan work her tongue around in her mouth and swallow. She was breathing quickly. But she spoke slowly and clearly as she said, "That wasn't

Salim Noor al-Rashid. It was someone called Haval Barzani. He was a Kurd who served as a translator during the Iraq war. Went by the name of Benny. The Al-Rashid guy who recognized him confirmed it with Benny's brother, who said the last time he saw him, Benny was working with the interrogators in the Abu Ghraib prison, just southwest of Baghdad."

"What is that all—"

Megan jumped back in. "It gets better. The Al-Rashid guy who recognized Benny says he himself was a cousin of Salim's. Not close. Hadn't seen him since Salim's mother died just before the Americans invaded. But he'd heard that Salim got arrested and thrown into Abu Ghraib. Vanished there."

Lena was too dumbfounded to reply, so she just sat there, with Megan on the other end of the line. A little bird nearly fluttered as it nearly struck the windshield of the Bolt. It landed awkwardly on the hood right by the window, its tiny three little toes on each foot curved over the lip behind the windshield wipers and it cocked its tiny head at Lena inquisitively. Lena thought, *You and me both, bird.*

"You still there?" Megan asked quietly.

"How long were you going to wait to tell me?"

"Monday, we figured. You've been...pretty stressed. Thought you might be taking a day off."

"Ha!" It exploded out of Lena before she knew to keep it in. She wiped her eyes. Stressed was one way to describe it. "So, what do you and the others think it means?"

There was the shuffling sound of the phone being handed to the next person. This woman spoke with a lower voice. Almost a drawl. Hazel, their horsewoman. "Hey, boss girl. How're you doing?"

Lena smiled despite herself. "I don't feel like much of a girl these days."

"From where I'm standing..."

"Okay. Megan handed the phone to you because she thinks you've got a theory?"

"Yup. Switcheroony."

"Meaning?"

"Salim al-Rashid gets thrown into Abu Ghraib, right? Benny Barzani's working there as a translator. They both vanish. Benny turns up later, supposedly working for the CIA as Salim Rashid. Switched places with him. Question is why? And what happened to the real Salim?"

Lena was fully focused now. "What do you think happened?"

"Oh, I got all kinds of crazy ideas. Don't matter, though. Real question is whether the real Salim could time travel and where he is now."

"You think he's still alive."

"Don't know. But I dated a guy worked at Abu Ghraib long time ago. Real haunted. Said there were prisoners got shipped in there that the CIA kept off the records while they questioned them. 'Ghost' detainees who sometimes 'disappeared.' But Megan found a list of detainees checked in. Salim was on there. Just never showed up as one of the detainees they finally released."

"If he switched places with Benny, he could have just walked out."

"That's what I'm thinking."

Lena was frowning and breathing heavily, leaning forward in her car seat.

"What are you thinking?" Hazel asked.

Lena sat up and took a deep breath. Her pulse was racing now. "That there's a time traveler out there who managed to escape his CIA captors and has probably been watching what's going on since when?"

"2004."

"Nineteen years. We've got to find him."

"Figured you'd say that. Texting you the name and number of the cousin now."

43

Something's coming

In the five days since Dr. Sauveterre had told me we'd be exploring who I was and how I'd become something more, three amazing things had happened with improbable speed.

First, I'd given up the professional distance thing with her, in both my mind and body. To me she was now only Océane. In an extreme case of therapeutic transference, she'd quickly become my Lena, my Kansas, my Jude, my big brother all rolled into one. Her words were my emotional law. I'd become ridiculously attached to needing her praise.

Thankfully, she'd given me a lot of that praise. In fact, she'd spent so much time admiring my resilient and balanced soul that I was actually starting to believe her more than my anxiety demon who'd spent most of my life tearing me down. That was the second thing.

And why did these both happen so fast? I think because everything I'd gone through with Lena and the Demon Monks, then fighting my way through Wenling's traps, and finally facing my worst nightmares over and over again with Bent had overloaded my internal trauma registry. I was so broken down inside that I would have taken almost anything to get whole again.

Océane gave me that.

"All this trauma, the things that happened to you," she said, "they are all bullshit. Most of this world is bullshit. The only thing that is always not bullshit, is you. The only thing that needs to be fixed is your too-tight attachment to this world."

As nihilistic as it sounded, the aggressive form of mindfulness training we'd begun together—a traditional meditation and breathing, extended discussions of Buddhism and astral projections, rhythmic chanting, ice packs, hot pads, tea, and gongs on a face-sized gong Océane used often—were making it real.

I hoped this was good, because the third thing that had happened was, I lost my ability to jump back in time.

Now maybe trying to kill me could have triggered it.

Maybe a carefully timed evocation of my worst memories.

Or just the appearance of Bent's terrifying presence.

But short these, I was stuck like glue to where I was. It was just me and Océane talking, then sitting to hum, focus, defocus, float in the nothingness...

I was almost...happy.

Then, on a morning which Océane said was the second Tuesday in April, a feeling shot through me that something in the physical world around us was very wrong.

We were in my room in McClean Hospital's Bent Wing, meditating together on the floor, both of us cross-legged. Océane stayed shallower than me so she could also play the gong, a regular reminder to shift my focus out of myself, out of the boundaries of our environment.

Océane described this as being mindful of infinite space, of the weightless, totally intangible essence of our minds and spirits.

Except my ears caught sounds coming in through the open window. And smells. Movements in the air. Something powerful was moving aggressively towards our building.

44

Jude

JUDE JOGGED ALONG IN a state of happy surprise that they'd included him in this raid.

It had been so long since he'd been outside, and to find the drizzly winter turned into sunshine and 73 degrees! He wanted to run even faster than they were going. Or just throw himself down on the hospital campus grass they crossed. He'd roll under a tree and smell the earth. He could do that now! Not only free of his cell, but free of all the extra physical weight he'd put on and carried about him as an emotional shield since his father died. Sure, the way he'd lost it was a little sick...

"Don't smile," growled Dadashev at his shoulder.

They were way back in this trotting strike team of about fifteen men in body armor and rifles. Since the CIA was supposed to be an intelligence gathering team that did not do domestic ops, the strike team all had FBI badging on their combat vests.

Jude, of course, did not. Instead, Poussaint had graciously loaned him a fresh suit and tie that fit his new weight but was getting damp with sweat in this weather and approach. Beside him, Dadashev, in his own plain brown business suit with body armor underneath, kept Jude moving at the strike team's pace.

"When we enter take the building," he growled at Jude, "you will point out Zura Dobroshtan."

"Yes," Jude said. And the other SCATTER members. To make sure the CIA took them hostage, not...something else.

The team rounded a corner and jogged along the side of the perimeter buildings, heading for the imposing, multi-storied building that Jude figured intel had pegged as the most likely place for SCATTER headquarters.

Hand signals from the strike-team leader flashed in the sun and groups of three peeled off in either direction to flank the building or cover the front door breach.

A second signal from the team leader and the strike team ran, boots clumping hard. Dadashev was right with them, which meant Jude was, too. Excited.

We're coming for you, Jackson!

45
Strike!

Whatever it was, it was here!

I jumped to my feet and ran to the window. I'd left it open to let in the April breeze, but as I reached it, the breeze roared suddenly into a squall of icy rain that slapped my face. Take *that!*

"Jackson? What are you doing?" Océane called softly from her cross-legged place on the floor.

I pulled the sliding casement window down to shut out the rain and turned back to her, dripping wet. "Nothing. I...thought I heard something rushing the building."

"The rain?"

"Maybe."

"Or your perceptions were opened up to other times or places?"

I was about to scoff, but the feeling I'd had of something approaching hadn't felt like the air pressure of rain. It hadn't been any kind of physical sensation at all, really. More like...the edge of a memory? An artifact of a timeline being altered that had only now showed its differences? Like the changed newspaper stories. Like a different word from Bent. Ripples in an ocean.

Or maybe it was Océane herself who was different? Or my changed feelings toward her? The sexual dreams I'd been having definitely weren't about Lena. They were about Océane. It shouldn't have been surprising, given the intensity of the time we were spending together and the doubts I'd had that Lena really cared for me. But it still made me uneasy.

It was all part of the change. I was changing. That was scary.

"Just a glitch," I said and sat back into my meditation pose, determined to bear down and wait for Océane to ring her little gong to help me back in.

46

Jude

Terrified nurses let the strike enter and search the first floor, but Jude knew, long before the team moved up to the second floor, that he'd made a terrible mistake.

He was flushing all shades of purple by the time they'd disturbed the patients and staff of a clearly busy psychiatric hospital on the second through fifth floors.

The team leader called it, and they exited quickly out the back before the local authorities arrived on the scene.

Dadashev grilled him as they retreated, accusing him of every kind of base treachery in both English and Russian.

All that Jude could mumble was, "Not Johns Hopkins. I was wrong. Not his *alma mater.*"

He wondered if they'd let him keep this new suit or just toss him back in his cell wearing nothing at all.

47

Letting go

Paradoxically, all the meditation I'd been doing to loosen my attachment to the world seemed to have increased my sensitivity to its ebbs and flows.

Over the next two weeks, as I continued chasing the ineffable with Océane, I sensed a tension in the building. I began to notice that when I was silent at night, I could hear thumps and bumps and even muted screams so dim I first thought they were mice squeaking in the walls. Then quiet. Then slammed doors.

The feeling of things coming at the building itself was borne out by an increased number of trucks and visitors arriving. They drove to the side of the building, a likely service entrance, not visible from my barred window.

Finally, there was Océane herself.

As a practiced and very skilled therapist, she had learned to always exude calm in my presence, to be focused on me, her client, rather than herself.

But as someone now enthralled by her every motion and sound, I could see the tension she now carried in her neck and the fine lines around her eyes. I also heard when she struck the gong just a shade too hard. Or when her brittleness leaked into her questions and assurances.

Whatever was going on in Bent Manor generally, I could only imagine that my lack of progress put twice the pressure on her.

I had to get it all out in the open before it broke her, which would also break me.

So, one day, as we were shifting back and forth on our bare feet, settling into our bodies. She was in a tight pink onesie with yoga pants below, smiling and looking delicious as she said how the warm breeze from the window tasted like buttercups—*Vraiment*. Truly. And how the changing of seasons presented the greatest metaphor a person could have for finding renewal in themselves, and how my own journey was like that.

I said, "Kenny and Xiaobo aren't out of the woods yet, are they?"

Her chin jerked just a little in what looked like fear before she calmed herself and smiled. Breathed in the spring air. "They're coming along. Just as you are."

"But not working. Not saving the world."

"You really think that's what they do here?"

"I think *they* think that, or they'd have escaped long ago."

She looked at me pointedly. "Like you did?"

"I have a fraction of their abilities. You know that."

"No. I do not." This time she let deep frustration squeeze her face. I wondered whether it was a reflection of how much Bent was squeezing her. She had to heal his two psychically wounded superstars and develop his chronic underachiever, me.

Océane suddenly put her gong and mallet to one side and shuffled to me on her knees. When she put her hands on my bare forearm—both of us had taken to wearing tee-shirts and track pants for these sessions—she gripped me firmly enough that her fingernails dug into my extensor digitorum muscle. (Or maybe my extensor digiti minimi. The picture I'd seen of the muscles in a human forearm didn't seem to show a clear delineation between the two.)

"I want you to try something for me," she said and shook my arm for emphasis.

I licked my lips and nodded. I'd trained myself to not look away from her eyes during training. It was too easy to be distracted by the lock of silver hair that threatened always to fall out of place, or the rising and falling of her chest.

"While I hold your arm, I want you to go into the deepest, clearest meditation you know how to do."

"With no gong?"

"We both know you don't need it. We both know you've been riding the line between gross matter and the spirit for four or five days now."

It was true. I don't know how she knew, but she did.

"You ride that umbilical cord, that thin ligament of attachment between this you"—she squeezed my forearm—"and the deeper, lighter, quicker you that's excited by the freedom but scared to let go."

I swallowed and nodded, caught by her eyes, her certainty.

She leaned closer. "When I say go, I want you to go deep and wide as fast as you can. Let yourself rocket to the end of that tether. And when you get there, when you feel it barely holds your soul, I want you to send a signal back through that tether to make your physical self give a single nod for me. And listen for the message I send. Do you understand?"

"Yes." I could hardly breathe, the excitement was already building inside me, like the *me* me was already fighting to get free.

"Then *go.*"

I shut my eyes, though I could meditate now with my eyes open, all while tossing off a series of pushups, making my bed, or turning in circles.

My thoughts, my self, coalesced into a point of concentration as pure and insubstantial as light but focused as a laser, as a moving thing, a stream, a point, a waveform. Until I was, as Océane had predicted, literally hanging off the end of a stretching magnet, a fine wire that barely held me to this reality. No reason why. No logical argument. Just...held me.

And the purity of myself reached down through that wire and through the body on the other end of it, the head, the neck, the muscles thereof, and made it nod.

Then listened. Every part of it.

A pressure that I recognized as Océane's grip pulsed on my forearm, and her voice somewhere out there said, "Let. Go."

And...

I opened my eyes to see Océane shifting her weight back and forth on her bare feet in front of me and smiling with delight. And the pink, skintight top she wore over her yoga pants looked like it might explode from the movement of her bosom. Her nostrils flared to receive the warm breeze from the window.

"It tastes like buttercups," she said. "*Vraiment.*"

I just stared at her, blinking blissfully.

She colored. "Something on my face? Or..." She looked down her front, then back at me. "Jackson?"

"Next, we talked about changing seasons and the healing metaphor they present. You pointed out how that renewal showed up in my own recent story."

Her embarrassed smile dropped from her face as she processed it. "Past tense. You...jumped?"

"Trauma free."

"You... How did you...? How far back?"

I looked around the room, finally. Everything was just as it was. Except that, for me, about fifteen seconds ago, I'd been sitting cross-legged four feet away, with Océane on her knees beside me, gripping my forearm. I touched where she had grabbed it in the last timeline. "You squeezed my arm. You said, 'Let go.' I did. And...poof!"

"How far back?" Her eyes were shining now, welling up with tears. Her entire body was trembling as if hijacked by joy.

"Just ten minutes, I think. I guess it's a hard limit that—"

"No! The only thing holding you back now is habit!" She leaped through the two feet of space between us, half tripping over the gong she'd left at her feet as she did. It fell and clattered as I caught Océane in my arms.

"You okay?"

She wrapped her arms tightly around my torso and squeezed herself into me, her face grinding down into my chest. "It's a breakthrough, Jackson," she murmured there, her shoulders shaking. "I believed. I knew you could. I knew..."

"Yeah. Um. Okay." Now I was turning red with embarrassment at the way my body was responding to her physical attention. *We did not touch!* Yet here she was, all her soft and warm curves mashed against me. And I was growing as hard as the first time I'd seen Lena naked. So hard I'd taken Lena straight down to the bed and rolled around with her and furiously entered her despite all the social anxieties that should have made me shrink and run away. Because with Lena, everything I was meant to be had been made manifest in our joining. I knew it then, instinctively. I should have told her. I should have kept telling her over and over and...

"NO!"

I twisted myself in Océane's grasp and pushed her back from me, fighting to make it firm, not a shove that would send her stumbling back.

"Jackson? What is...?"

But I'd turned from her by then and walked away. Created space.

Océane's face had gone scarlet. "I'm sorry if I... I was just so..."

"It's fine. I get it. It's fine." I stared down at my groin where my erection had finally gotten the message and was drawing back into its flaccid shape. *Hey, no problem, dude. I can wait.* But it wasn't only what my little head wanted that was the problem.

"Yes." Océane regained her earlier composure and injected her practiced warmth and certainty into her voice. "Yes, it is fine. Very fine. And I would like to hear more about it, maybe tomorrow, and discuss how you can jump farther and farther, more than Xiaobo, more than anyone."

I shook my head hard and turned to look back at her. "I can't. I won't. You don't understand what that *means*. I'm not going to jump so far away that I can't come back to you. You like this."

Her practiced smile dropped, and a look of strained horror crossed her face. "We'll talk about this tomorrow," she said and hurried out.

48

Uwe Bent

DOWN IN THE BASEMENT laboratory far below Jackson's feet, Bent finished removing his blood-covered latex gloves with a snap. He disposed of them in the medical waste container at the foot of the test bed where Norman Dankworth lay strapped in, now passed out. Dankworth wore only his shorts. His thighs were a mess, like he was some teenage girl who'd gone wild with her self-stimulative cutting. Though the cuts Bent had made were purposely deeper for dramatic effect.

No time jump, though. The skinny Brit had simply screamed for a while before being overcome. Nurse Adelaide Cochrane, a reliable woman in her fifties, was mopping him up and applying stitches as needed.

"Do you see?" Bent snapped at Dr. Sauveterre as she walked into the basement lab. "This subject has time traveled exactly six times in the last twelve years. Yet he questions my use of pain and terror."

"Is this what you're using on all of them now?" Sauveterre asked him, her face pale as she watched Nurse Cochrane's clean up.

"Cutting? Of course not. Pain and terror, yes. At least until you can prove to me someone other than Xiaobo can jump without it. Jackson?"

Sauveterre froze with her pale face turned towards his. Bent felt his interest officially piqued.

He stepped closer to his miracle worker and took her soft, weak hands in his own. "He jumped without trauma?" he asked softly.

Sauveterre nodded. "Yes."

"Reliably?"

"I believe so. I won't be sure until I do more tests, but—"

"It is about *time!*" Bent cried at the ceiling. "Meaning, as I'm sure you can deduce, doctor, that this should have happened sooner. His brother saw it happening sooner in his recollections. Which means we are behind schedule! And also meaning that if we do not use Jackson Traine's ability to move through time *on time*, we will have run out of time, and for millions of Americans and others in this world, this will be the end of time."

"There's...more," Sauveterre said.

"Will it stop him from ordering strikes on different Chinese virus laboratories and jumping back with each negative strike until we find the right one?"

Sauveterre licked her lips. Bent supposed he would have found that a sexy movement if his sexual interests leaned towards fleshy women past their prime. He had been both surprised and amused by the recordings that showed Jackson himself was not so picky.

"Speak," he said when it was clear his miracle worker was again lip locked.

"Jackson said he could not jump back past his ten-minute mark because of me."

Bent raised his eyebrows at her.

"I gather because he can give up his current reality to jump, but not so far back that he changes things in a way I might not be there."

Bent grimaced. "*Mein Gott*, as my father would say. The solution?"

"It's a little extreme..."

"Then I'm sure I will love it. We'll try it *after* he saves the world, yes?"

"But the ten-minute limit..."

"If he can do it reliably, we can work with that."

He turned to where Nurse Cochrane was efficiently stitching up a cut on Norman's inner thigh that Bent had made so long and deep. It had been a game to see how far he could go without striking the femoral artery. "Ms. Cochrane, my dear, could you please go to the operations room and tell Mr. Zungu to put our hit teams in China on alert and prepare the order delivery and response system?"

Cochrane nodded without looking up from what admittedly looked like a complicated stitch. "Soon as I finish this."

For a couple of seconds, Bent let himself savor the glandular flood of adrenaline and cortisol rage that shot through his system. Then he said calmly but firmly, "Ms. Cochrane, I need you to go immediately."

"But—"

"LET THE MAN BLEED!"

The woman spastically dropped the needle and thread from her fingers, spun around, and ran from the room.

Bent looked from where she'd run out, back to Norman's half-cleaned and stitched-up cuts, and finally to Sauveterre. "Do you think she'll remember to send someone else up here to finish?"

Sauveterre gave him a look of incredulity.

Disappointing.

Bent sighed. "I miss Gordon."

49

The mission

WHEN BENT SHOWED UP in my room with Océane the next morning, I wasn't surprised. I'd finally learned the trick of easy time travel, after all. Trauma free. I'd proved it to myself with three more jumps last night. Still had the ten-minute time limit, some disorientation, and physical distress when I jumped too many times in a row, but I'd flipped the switch.

All it took was seeing the temporary, *small* nature of any given now. It made everything clearer.

I understood Océane's stony face and refusal to meet my eyes. It meant I'd achieved a critical facility, so it was time to use me.

Bent confirmed this even in his dress. He had ditched his usual medical coat for a three-piece velvet suit in a deep midnight blue, satin button-down shirt, a sparkling red tie, and oxblood Oxfords with pointy toes that somehow suited him. It screamed Eurotrash scion of generational wealth who was dressed for some kind of triumph. Presumably one that I would deliver to him.

He stared at me now, his eyes bright with fascination. "Do you know why I'm here today, Jackson?"

"I'm guessing…a picnic?"

He ran a hand back over his hair. "Of a sort. We're going down to the operations room. It's mostly computer screens and communication equipment. Xiaobo knows it well. As does your brother, though not for the same purposes."

"I want Kenny down there with me."

Océane shot a look at Bent, who shook his head at her without fully acknowledging whatever it was she was trying to say. "That won't be possible," he said.

I looked back and forth between the two of them. "Because he's still sick. He hasn't recovered in all this time? What's happening with him?"

Océane started to speak but again Bent cut her off. "If we could use your brother and Xiaobo right now, they would be with us. Since we can't, you get to finally do what you signed up for when you came back to me. To do what Kenny promised you would do."

I grimaced. "I'm supposed to order raids on suspected Chinese virology laboratories. Stop them from shipping a deadly created virus intended for the United States. Did he tell you how many tries it took?"

Bent blinked placidly. "Nine."

Océane gasped.

I nodded. "She gets it. Nine jumps in fairly rapid succession. Because I'm guessing there's a deadline on this, isn't there? Kenny didn't tell *me*, but I'm betting—"

"Our intelligence says the Chinese are planning to ship out their bioweapon in three days," Bent said. "But the date Kentucky said you directed the teams is today. And who are we to mess with success?"

Now Océane was looking furiously at her feet, like she couldn't believe what she was hearing. But I believed it. It only amazed me that it wasn't until I had learned to jump without trauma that the implications of what this mission could still do to me became clear.

"It's why I need Kenny," I said.

"I already told you—"

"I don't need him to read the future or hold my hand. I just need him to remember what he saw me do before, so I don't make stupid mistakes. So I can either duplicate it or jump straight to the good part."

For the first time since entering, Bent fully closed his mouth and grew thoughtful. Then he turned to Océane. "Is he lucid enough to follow this kind of operation?"

She answered quietly, but I caught the one word I'd expected: medication.

"Even on drugs," I said, "his memory will work just fine."

"But he may not know where he is," Océane said. "Or who you are, what you are trying to do."

Her concern almost reached into my fear center, but that center seemed harder to reach the morning after I'd seen the physical world for what it was. Besides, this was my moment. This was what, despite the seeming chaos of the long road that had taken me here, I was meant to do. SAVE THE WORLD.

Or some version of it. Some timeline.

"I've been with Kenny when he's been strung out before," I said. "He always knew more than you thought he did."

Bent snapped a pointed glance at his watch and said to Océane, "Oshee, would you please go to Kentucky Traine and bring him down to Operations? Jackson and I will be there, reviewing the plans and preparing to begin at zero-ten-hundred. Don't be late."

He turned to leave, and both Océane and I hurried after him. Océane muttered under her breath. I, even in my Zen state, was excited to be leaving this damn floor at last.

The operations room was in the basement, which appeared, from the length of the halls I saw, to be larger than the building that was visible above ground. The ceilings were actually higher, too.

But when Bent ushered me into the operations room, that all changed.

The room was like a high-tech submarine command center—wall-to-wall tech with blinking lights and computer screens. Focused young men and women controlled most of the seat-level screens. One conspicuously empty seat faced a bank of four large monitors. Each monitor displayed a high-definition image of dimly lit men and possibly women, sitting on two facing benches in what looked like the back of a delivery van. They all wore attack gear, solid black. That included gloves, rifles, and helmets that had attached eye gear and headsets.

Breathing.

Waiting.

I looked from those scenes to the room's "captain," a man whose skin was even blacker than Ziggy Cheester's but shaved clean from his bull neck up. His skin gleaned in the room's low light. His bulk consumed most of the center O that ran around a waist-high hub of controls. I suspected only the captain touched the hub.

He offered Bent a curt nod.

Bent smiled back and said, "Mr. Zungu, may I address your crew?"

Zungu nodded and Bent began.

"Some of you have worked with us on numerous missions. We've foiled assassinations and helped freedom fighters stave off government coups. Today's mission, however, is the most critical one we've undertaken to date. In China one month ago..."

He gestured at the four-screen setup and the pictures of the strike team members slipped to a map of China that filled the four screens.

"...the People's Liberation Army, under orders from Xi Jinping, moved as much as five percent of their force from backing up local officials in COVID lockdowns to protecting various sites believed to be virology labs."

He paused as a series of red points began appearing on the map of China. I counted twelve before the crowd of points in Wuhan and Beijing became too many to distinguish.

"In one or more of these, according to Taiwanese and American intelligence, Chinese scientists have been working throughout the pandemic to develop a biological weapon. This weapon is a custom-designed strain of Ebola with a delayed symptom onset and aerosol transmission. Experts believe it could cripple the already-weakened government and social fabric of the United States and other nations. If not stopped, China will send it out by sea, air, and overland through Russia and Europe in a matter of days. China will then seal its borders to protect itself until the virus has burned itself out by consuming all available hosts. At which point the virus will have wiped out a few cities, a region, half the country, or half the world. We don't know. We don't believe the Chinese leadership knows. And we hope we will never find out, since our mission is to find this bioweapon and destroy it and all research used to develop it, so it never leaves China."

"Destroy it how?" I interjected. Kenny hadn't told me that part of the story.

"Not your concern," Bent said.

"So, I'm just going—"

Bent jerked up a hand. "Autoclaving. Every one of their labs will have a machine that can superheat any of their samples and kill them."

Kenny couldn't have told me that? "What about the records? All their research notes."

"We'll leave that to the soldiers you get into the labs, shall we?"

He turned back to the rest of the room.

"Alpha One, whom many of you have worked with, isn't available for this mission. However, we are fortunate enough to have a second Alpha with us this morning." He turned to me. "Alpha Two, why don't you say hello?"

I gave him a lopsided smile, then turned and waved at the room.

Xiaobo was obviously Alpha One, their main boy, their power piece who came to this room and remotely reshaped history with a series of operational orders that ultimately won SCATTER's objective for that day.

Of course, the team that witnessed success with Xiaobo would see him order only one strike or maneuver and think him a genius. The Teams stuck in all the timelines where his orders didn't succeed? Not so much.

It made me wonder, especially given Xiaobo's current state, if I was in a timeline that had ended on success or one where he'd failed.

"I'm assuming you know where your seat is, Alpha Two," Bent said.

I looked over at the four-monitor station and the empty chair in front of it. The screens had pictures of the different strike-teams-in-waiting on them. "I see it. I don't see the other person you agreed would be here."

"Yes, the Seer," Bent said with a smile. He paused and let the news circulate in the room. It told me 1) they'd heard about Kenny's power to "see" the future, and 2) it was a rare or never occasion for him to appear down here. "He'll be here shortly."

As the rustle of excitement grew, Mr. Zungu smacked the back of one tech. The room quieted.

"Now, shall we?" said Bent, pointing me to my chair. "I need to run through how you'll give the GO, and when you'll hit RESTART."

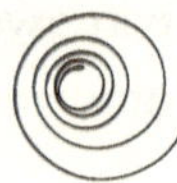

Before Bent was fully done, a dull-eyed Kenny took a seat in the chair that appeared by my right arm. Océane hovered a couple steps behind him, looking worried. But to me, Kenny was no worse than the drugged-out older brother I recalled from my last high school days. That was a relief. The rational brother whom I'd met on the roof and gone time tripping through our childhood was actually far less familiar than the one now beside me.

It also struck me, though, that I wasn't getting any memories of having been here before, even though Kenny said I'd done this. Did that mean I was exactly on track with what I'd done in the timeline Kenny had already seen, and this *was* the timeline he'd seen? Or...

The suddenly oppressive silence in the room made me look around the room. Most of Zungu's "crew" had turned in their chairs and were blatantly staring. At Kenny, I assumed. The Seer.

The young South Asian woman to my left tried hard not to, but her eyes kept darting over.

Bent refocused everyone by clapping his hands once. "It's 10 a.m. our time, 10 p.m. in Beijing and Wuhan. The night shift is on in most of the labs, but the outside security shift changes in one hour. The time to strike is now. Mr. Zungu, open comms to Strike Team One."

The top left screen at my workstation flashed and over the image of the designated team, their location flashed. The Wuhan Institute of Virology. Biggest biosafety level 4 (BSL-4) laboratory in the world. Where the COVID19 virus might have escaped from. Intentionally, if you believed conspiracy theorists. After all, they'd supposedly been conducting gain-of-function research with dangerous viruses to study them, understand their transmissibility and effects on humans, and develop vaccines. Why not just release the worst virus you found and infect your enemies?

Except it was Wuhan itself, and now most of China, that had suffered the most with what happened. Oops!

So, either the CCP learned from that fiasco and were upping their game, or they were just *inspired* by all the havoc they accidentally wreaked on themselves and the rest of the world. They just had to be more careful this time to shut the damn borders once the virus was carried past them.

"Alpha Two, you're up."

I turned and looked up at Bent. *Really? We're sticking with Alpha Two?*

He gave me a supercilious grin in return.

I turned back and looked at my brother, who was now staring at the screen, apparently mesmerized. "You with me, Kenny?" I asked.

No response. Not even an eye flicker. Because he'd seen it happen before and didn't want to change anything? But why? Didn't we know the endgame? Did it really require we get there by the same tortuous route I'd supposedly followed before?

Shaking my head at the pointless nature of that, I readjusted my headset and microphone and touched the button Bent had shown me earlier.

"Commander," I said, per Bent's instructions, "this is Alpha Two. Confirm."

There was a slight pause for the transmission delay, then I heard the voice of the man I could see on screen one talking into his own headset microphone. "Confirmed, Alpha Two."

"You are a go," I said, mimicking the command voice used in every military movie I'd ever seen. "Report status at nine minutes."

"Roger, Alpha Two."

The man on the screen gestured. The back wall I could now see was the rear of their truck or van split wide open to an only slightly brighter night—*10 a. m. here, 10 p.m. there, yes*—and the entire team poured out with such precision it was like they were making a training video.

The camera feed switched to a helmet cam worn by someone near the back of the team. Some impressive in-body-stabilization in the cam made the next nine minutes bouncy but watchable.

They stormed the structure, their leader giving quiet commands through their headsets which also played through the speakers on the console before me so everyone in the room could follow it. My understanding from something I'd read once was that these military communication systems were close-range only, which meant they had to be getting funneled to us through a repeater. Probably the vehicle all these guys had streamed out of.

"Forward, spread out."

"Marcy, Richman, Jovi, Burton to the door. Others, cover."

"Take out the lights and cameras, right, left."

When they shot out the perimeter lights and cameras, the five guards those shots alerted streamed out. Our guys shot them. The four members who'd launched an assault on what appeared to be the main front door—solid steel surrounded by what looked like dark metal cladding of the building. The other four members, meanwhile, followed orders to split and circle the building in opposing directions for other entry points.

I mentally tuned out the chatter as I glimpsed an adjoining building. Maybe the BSL-2 or BSL-3 research was done? I assumed preliminary scouting or intel had identified the most likely place we'd find the plague that was going to kill the world. If it was in this city at all.

The cameraman focused on his three teammates packing what plastic explosive around the door handle and lock, then looked up as the team retreated for the boom.

Four stories high, the place looked solidly built, like a square, flat mountain in the night. Lights shone out of a couple of fourth-floor windows.

Boom!

As the team rushed forward and entered, the video I watched became a disorienting run through hallways and stairs. The leader's orders suggested intel and schematics, but the actual visuals suggested they were running blind. The place was enormous, with biohazard signs and bins and freezers and screened-off security areas everywhere, but the team leader was clearly heading for the fourth floor.

I felt the clock in my head counting the seconds and minutes as they slowed their approach near the fourth floor.

At the top of the stairs, they reached another area screened off by floor-to-ceiling reinforced plexiglass panels covered with obvious warning labels in yellow and red. Behind the barrier the camera could see a multitude of tables and lab equipment, more freezers, and microscopes, and biohazard bins, and one frightened Chinese scientist in jeans and a tee-shirt, holding what looked like two glass slides, one in either hand. He looked under forty. His eyes stared at us wide-eyed from behind his glasses. No biohazard suit, I noted. That didn't say deadly virus area to me.

The team leader still ordered one of his team to the closed door that led through the barrier. The man tried the door and shook his head. The leader pointed his assault rifle slowly at the door, then at the man on the other side of the glass.

The scientist carefully put his two slides down on a worktable and hurried to the door. He pressed in a code that disengaged the lock and pulled the door open.

The strike team poured in, with the leader backing the scientist up against a table with his rifle, pinning him there and shouting at him in Chinese.

To which the young scientist babbled back passionately, trying to sound calm, but losing control of his pitch as he spoke.

The South Asian girl to my left muttered the translation: "'I'm just doing genome sequencing, guys. I like calm and quiet.'"

I turned to her. "Do you speak Mandarin? Is that actually what he said?"

She blushed. "I majored in Eastern languages. Yes, that's what he said. Approximately."

The strike team leader, who also evidently spoke Mandarin, nodded his head but just yelled louder at the man. Then he grabbed him by the back of his shirt and marched him over to one of the freezers. There he shook him back and forth, yelling into the back of his head as the scientist burst out repeatedly with cries and strings of incomprehensible dialogue.

I looked over at the South Asian operator near me and she whispered, "He doesn't know anything."

Yuh. Kinda figured that.

The time had crested eight minutes. I spoke into my headset. "Commander." Then louder, "*Commander,* this is Alpha Two."

The team leader stopped shaking the scientist and threw him at the freezer in disgust. Maybe knocking over a few bottles of anthrax? Good *job.* "Your time is up. Do you have a positive finding or other discoveries to report?"

There was a moment where I could almost hear the helmeted man swearing without opening his hard-set mouth. Finally, he said, "No."

"Your mission is done. I recommend you withdraw to safety."

"Roger that, Alpha Two," he said.

But I barely heard his last response because I had dialed down the audio, stepped out of my chair, and sat on the floor beside it with my eyes closed. I saw only my brother, who slid from his chair to join me on the floor. Blindly taking his hand, I slipped easily into my familiar state of altered consciousness. But this time, I knew exactly where to go and how to get there without Océane's help. Just needed to step away from this wretched reality where I'd indirectly killed a host of Chinese guards and terrorized a young scientist for no reason at all.

Pointless.

Just...let go...

I was in my command seat again, not on the floor. Kenny sat to my right with a wondering look in his eyes.

I could work with that.

Behind me, Bent said, "Alpha Two, you're up."

I didn't look back at him. Instead, I turned to Kenny. It was time to get him to earn his presence here.

50

Kansas

At the same 10 a.m. in Washington, DC, Kansas sat back in the metal café chair behind her wobbly outside table at Gregory's Coffee. The Mayflower Hotel's main entrance was about one-hundred yards northwest of her, with good sightlines.

Kansas had cut her hair in a short men's fade and wore clear glasses above a man's navy suit and tie. She'd wrapped her breasts flat under the button-down shirt. With a café au lait in one hand and a partially raised front section of the Washington Post in the other, she casually studied each person who approached the Mayflower entrance by foot or vehicle. She also snuck the occasional glance at the third-floor office of the Bender building across the street. That held the third set of NSA operatives who'd replaced the kid she'd scared in the subway station. They'd all had binoculars and electronic monitoring equipment, but none of them had her patience.

She'd been waiting twenty goddamn days.

The other thing she had over them was movement. She'd be sometimes here, sometimes there. Across the street. A rooftop. She donned polo shirts and khakis under raincoats. Sunglasses. Hats. Umbrellas. Canes for the vision impaired. Today it was the suit, glasses, and newspaper.

And while she didn't have the wiretaps like the Garvey team, she had an alert hack planted inside the Mayflower registration system that would tell her if Fang signed in. She'd gotten the password by shoulder surfing the front desk clerk when she first logged in to look up Fang's name for Kansas.

Twenty days ago!

She took a sip of her coffee and grimaced. It had grown cold. End of April. Too many days of drizzle and wind and seeing nothing.

While Jackson was being broken. He could have spilled his guts to Bent by now. Could be working for him. Or Bent might have lost patience with Jackson's limitations and shot him. All likely scenarios.

The thing that really killed Kansas, though, was that even if she managed to tag Colonel Fang before Garvey's men and follow him back to Zhou Wenling, and even if the bitch admitted to triggering the Baltimore Harbor craziness, Wenling might have no clue where Jackson was now.

While the rest of Lena's team stayed obsessed with finding Salim Noor al-Rashid, who might or might not still be alive.

Kansas angrily slapped down the newspaper. Putin was crowing about taking Mariupol, Le Pen's far-right party was poised to take control of France, and the US midterms were threatening to drown the country in MAGA red. This didn't help. Kansas could feel time running out like sand trickling down inside her legs and out through her toes. When it was all gone, what would—

"May I sit down here?" said a familiar, Chinese-accented voice at her left shoulder.

Kansas spun that way in horror to see Colonel Fang himself.

He was dressed more casually than she'd ever seen him, in a gray button-down shirt covered by a featureless tan raincoat. His head sported a brown checked flat cap that somehow disguised the ramrod posture that was as distinctive as his impassive face.

Kansas saw no weapon or threat, but he'd obviously spotted her, snuck up on her, ambushed her...

He sat down in the chair to her left before she could object. She noted he kept his back to the Bender building and face down.

"Hello, Colonel. You know about the NSA team watching for you?" she asked.

He nodded and spoke with slow, accented consideration. "Across from the hotel, I am guessing."

"Because..."

"When I was in the army, we had a saying: If you kill their children, they will hunt for you."

"How did you recognize me?"

He finally raised his eyes to meet hers. "You look different than I remember, but you and a friend of mine—same eyes."

Kansas felt a surprising rush of emotion. "A friend."

"Yes."

"That your boss betrayed and gave to Uwe Bent."

"Yes."

"That you and Wenling sent jets to blow up."

His eyes closed in visible shame. "Not us. I made a mistake to trust a man older than me who said he would *free* the time travelers."

"Name?"

His eyes opened but did not meet hers. "Andre Poussaint. CIA."

"You trusted him like my brother trusted you. And your boss."

Fang's mouth tightened, the lips stretching thin and exposing the ravages of time that his posture and self-possession otherwise hid so well. "Ms. Zhou was wrong to do what she did. With you, many years ago. With your brother, this year. Worse, she was unwise. She trusted Uwe Bent to return what he took from her."

Kansas noted the wording. Fang wasn't pretending that Wenling cared about her brother. More that she'd wanted her *property* back, her little time-traveling fortune teller. Fang knew what his master was and judged her for it. But still... "You cried out in anguish when you thought she'd been shot. And you went back to serve her even after you found out she'd tricked you along with all of us."

Fang sighed and let his old body lose some of its tightness. "Yes."

"Why?"

He looked into Kansas' eyes again, considering, then finally licked his lips and said, "I met Zhou Lok at Peking University. He studied engineering like me. We became...good friends. Then the Great Revolution closed the university. They put me in the army and sent Lok south to be a cement worker. There he met Chan Bi. She was also from Beijing. They married. She gave birth to Wenling, then died. Lok sent me letters, asking for my help. But I was too busy. Fighting in Vietnam. Fighting the Soviet Union. Fighting inside China with the Red Army. I had no time for my friend. Only many years later, when I left the army and went to find him, I find out he had changed. He *hurt* Wenling. Then he married again to a woman who gave him Xiaobo. He beat his new wife and his children so much they killed him and ran away."

Kansas shook her head. "You chased them?"

"I was filled with shame. I never found Lok's second wife. But I tracked his children and found they had gone to America. So, I came to America. I found Ms. Zhou and offered myself as a friend of the family."

Kansas felt her mouth had gone dry. Something didn't add up in Fang's story. "You 'offered' yourself. Out of guilt?"

Fang avoided her eyes again as he nodded.

"And she just accepted? Did she know you knew what she'd done?"

"She never asked."

"What about your life? Did you ever have a wife? Did you ever look?"

"I...cannot marry."

"Because...?"

"Like you."

"Too busy? Too... Oh." She stopped and fingered her men's clothing. "Zhou Lok."

For just a second, the man's impassive face that looked like it could face Hell itself and not show concern flushed red, and his eyes narrowed like they might cry. Then it passed, and he simply nodded. "Yes."

Kansas slumped fully back in her chair and studied this walking contradiction. "Thank you for telling me."

Fang straightened himself on his seat so much that Kansas worried if either of Garvey's men glanced this way, they'd know just from the man's posture that they'd found their target. She was about to tell him to relax when he suddenly stood up completely and looked down at her gravely. "I can take you to Ms. Zhou if we leave now."

Life could turn your way just like that, Kansas thought. She tucked a ten-dollar bill under her coffee cup, stood, straightened her tie and suit coat, and followed Fang.

51

Changing the series

"Kenny," I said.

No response.

"I've got something I need to ask you."

Still no response. Even with the rest of the operations room now so still, I could hear them breathing. Uwe Bent's shuffled his feet impatiently behind me.

Kenny just stared at me with wide vacant eyes like he was trying to prove he wasn't completely riding the Océane-supplied drug train for all it was worth.

But I knew his secret.

I knew that even when he was buzzed or stoned or tripping, that same Traine mind that let him, me, and Kansas remember everything we experienced in indelible detail let him process the world in ways most people never could.

"Okay, just nod for now," I said. "You see the map of China in front of me? On the screens?"

I'd flipped a toggle Bent had shown me earlier to wipe out the live video feed of the Wuhan target I was supposed to be giving the Go signal to (for the second time, for me). The flip had brought up the map to fill all four screens again. The different known or probably viral laboratories still stood out as dots of red with small black labels.

Even tripping as Kenny was now, he turned his face directly at the screens and nodded.

"Good. And all the dots showing where different virology labs are?"

Another nod.

"Do you remember being here with me in this room before? Looking at this map? Watching me give orders to strike team after strike team until we finally hit the lab that was producing this bioweapon we're looking for?"

This last one was a gamble. Kenny had never said he'd been with me in the room when I'd done that. But I figured I would have asked for him to be there if he was around. The question was whether Bent would have let him when—

"Nine times," Kenny mumbled.

Yes. "That's right. You told me I went through eight wrong choices before hitting the right one. And I started with the main Wuhan lab just as I did this time, right?"

"Wuhan," Kenny confirmed.

"What were the next eight labs we tried?"

Kenny listed them all. His Chinese accent was no better than mine, but obviously clear enough because some signal from Bent made a list of Chinese labs appear on the top left screen in front of me, numbered as Kenny had said. The numbers also showed up on the corresponding points on the map.

"The last one. Harbin. That's where we found the weaponized Ebola virus last time, right?"

Kenny blinked and nodded.

"What happened in that raid? How did we find it? Did we autoclave it? Did we wipe all their records? Kill their scientists? What?"

Kenny opened his mouth, but he couldn't seem to engage his tongue.

From behind me, Bent said, "The Seer gave you the final target, Alpha Two. Do you need him to hold your hand as you give the order?"

I didn't look back at him. He obviously saw how going after Harbin now would diverge from the future Kenny saw, but that didn't matter to him because, in his understanding of time travel, we'd just be doing what we'd done "before" in a more efficient way. For me, it was going into a different timeline. And if I didn't suddenly recall all the other timelines Kenny had described...

Either way, Kenny had given me a target and couldn't or wouldn't give me a reason not to hit it. So, I simply clicked on Harbin and brought up that location's attack squad on the screen.

Another dim truck interior. Another team of trained killers with guns.

I gave the Go order and the reminder they had nine minutes.

I watched them storm the five-story facility that was one of only three BSL-4 labs on the list, along with the ones in Wuhan and Kunming. Kunming had been number three on Kenny's list. Why had Harbin been number nine?

From the speakers on my console came quiet commands, one after another, an elegant play-by-play. The guy leading this team was good.

It also helped that this facility seemed to be in its own compound in the middle of a city block. It apparently kept a few exterior lights shining on the laboratory building's front entrance. Lights also shone in various rooms inside the building itself. It made it easier to follow the firefight with a few guards outside and five guards inside the building, plus the kamikaze search that finally zeroed in on the fourth floor. (Again!)

The final lab held two women. They wore blue nitrile gloves and ballooned-out, positive-pressure biohazard suits being pumped regularly with oxygen that was brought down from valves in the ceiling through long, curled blue hoses. It presumably kept positive pressure in their masks and full head covering, too.

The team leader got them to shut off and unplug the hoses. He tore their masks off them and started roaring questions over their frantic babbling.

"Do either of them know anything?" I asked the South Asian girl to my left.

"Doesn't sound like it," she said. "The tall one says she's the chief scientist, Dr. Yīng Fāng Lì. Worried about getting infected."

"By what?"

My translator blanched. "Deadly. Smallpox, I think?"

From somewhere else in the room, a tenor male voice called, "We have PLA troops from the guard block coming in fast. They know we're there!"

A second one chimed in. "Chatter from Beijing. Mentioning Harbin. They were warned."

"Almost out of time," I said to the room. Into my headset microphone, I said, "Team Leader, time is up. Army troops are incoming. Abort mission."

But Bent's voice cut into the same comm line I was on. "Belay that order, Team Leader. This is Alpha Prime. Proceed as planned."

I turned around to give Bent a WTF look. "If I don't jump back now, there is no way to cleanly try again, or have a clean slate if there's ultimately nothing there."

There was a pause. Then Bent said, "Alright, jump."

"But—"

"The time," Bent reminded me.

I slid from my chair with Kenny doing the same, closed my eyes, and...

"The Seer gave you the final target, Alpha Two. Do you need him to hold your hand as you give the order?"

I was back sitting in the command chair. Of course, I was. On the screens in front of me was the map of China with the list of Chinese labs that the me in the timeline *that I didn't remember* had ordered raids on, one at a time.

Something wasn't adding up here.

A hand touched my shoulder, and I almost jumped from my chair. The hand's owner, Uwe Bent, leaned down to speak clearly, not quietly, by my right ear. "Alpha Two," he said, "it's time to give the order."

I nodded, though my mind also consciously processed another thing that hadn't made sense before—me giving the orders. There was no absolute need for it. Bent could give the orders, I could watch and just jump us all back when he indicated we needed to reset.

But Bent was first and foremost a mind manipulator. I think he figured if I gave the orders, I'd feel responsible for what happened and invested in getting it right.

It worked.

Even as my detachment from this world continued to grow entropically inside me, my moral sense of responsibility compelled me to send in these strike teams to save the world, abort the mission when it failed, and jump back in time to properly try again.

Except that last strike.

Bent hadn't let me abort the mission, just jump out of it.

That meant that some ten minutes from now, in the timeline I'd jumped from, the Harbin strike team was still questioning those two scientists as they all got infected by whatever was loose in that lab, while People's Liberation Army troops arrived and likely slaughtered them or took them hostage.

That couldn't happen this time.

"Alpha Two…"

I hit the button that opened my link to the Harbin strike team, gave the order, and watched them pile out of the back of the truck.

This time, though, I also fed them a stream of warnings as they approached the building that harbored the BSL-4 laboratory. That building sat inside what looked like a ten-foot concrete wall that ran around most of the compound. In the southwest and southeast lay two blacked-out smaller buildings that held at least a dozen guards. Security cameras on those buildings monitored everything, especially the street access from the west.

"Roger that, Alpha T—"

The thwack of the bullet that entered his face and exploded the back of his skull.

It rattled mine, too.

I jerked back in my seat and gasped even as I registered the rest of the nightmare. It wasn't twelve sleepy guards streaming out of the blacked-out security posts. It was dozens of PLA guards in their own black camo gear running out of the blaze of spotlights shooting out from the southeast building. They'd flooded the entire approach. Half of the SCATTER soldiers were mowed down instantly, their screams cutting intermittently into the comm feed. The second half, including the cameraman providing the coverage, sprinted for cover around the east side of the lab building, shouting commands to each other. But they were pinned there as they watched their delivery vehicle, a cube truck, take an incoming rocket. It exploded in a greasy black and orange fireball.

That rocked my headset, too. I wanted to yank the damn thing off my head. Except I could still hear orders being shouted. The strike team must have had a backup comms repeater somewhere. A second truck?

Instead, I spoke loudly and clearly in my microphone. "Abort mission. Acknowledge! Abort!"

Except the remaining team members were too busy fighting for their lives to respond.

I slid off my chair to the ground, pulling Kenny down with me. I sat. He sprawled. I closed my eyes, saw this reality for the shit show it was, and...

I was in my chair, my right hand pulling on a toggle switch.

Suddenly all four of the screens in front of me again showed the map of China with the list of known or probable viral laboratories indicated by dots of red with small black labels.

Kenny turned his stoned face to me and smiled weakly.

What?

Oh. Right.

"Never mind, Kenny," I said. "We get back on the horse?"

He nodded.

"What do you—?" asked Bent from behind me. Then... "Oh. What happened?"

I shook my head. "Unexpected resistance. Doesn't matter. We know which direction they came from. Let's do this again."

I pressed my comms button, automatically bringing up the view of the Harbin attack team sitting on facing benches in the back of the silent, undamaged truck. The round-faced team leader and front half of the team looked good for men I'd seen torn apart by PLA bullets a few moments ago.

"Team Leader, this is Alpha Two. We are a go at my signal, but *not,* I repeat *not* as per the planned frontal attack. There is an overwhelming force guarding the front of the building. You will need to approach from the rear, avoiding security cameras close to the building. Copy."

A slight delay, then, "Copy that."

"Vehicle operator," I continued. "Do you hear me?"

A crackle, then, "I hear you."

"Rocket launchers are trained on your current location, so you will reverse out of the area the second your team exits. Copy."

"Roger that, Alpha Two."

"Good. Team Leader, GO!"

And they were out the door, splitting to either side of the exit door and reuniting in a mad, silent, dark dash for the rear of their target as their truck immediately reversed in a skidding turn and roared away from the building.

I followed the loping rush of the strike team as they skirted the perimeter of the lab building to approach from the rear. Muttering updates on the comm as they went. The team leader split them up before they rushed for two promising entry points, likely anticipating more cameras and more troops they'd have to take out.

They encountered nothing.

They entered, and I reworked in my head what I'd seen of the layout of the place during the first assault. I passed on my directions and interior guard locations, hoping that if the team avoided heavy firefights and dead-end searches, they might have enough time to properly don a biohazard suit or two and "persuade" the two female scientists to show them what we were looking for.

The five interior guards were where I remembered them. Located. Shot.

When they found the two female scientists, they walked in and grabbed them without bothering to follow any safety procedures. But the two scientists didn't babble like last time. They seemed almost...calm. Especially the taller one. Ying.

I leaned left toward my South Asian translator. "What's your name?"

"Sita Joshi, sir." She brushed back a few stray hairs self-consciously.

"What are they saying, Sita?"

"Um...not much. Just...we work with many viruses, yes...No weapons...You're welcome to see. We'll show you."

And then the two scientists did exactly that. The team leader and his lieutenant, now wearing a biohazard suit, motioned to the one other strike team member in a suit to go with the women. That team member presumably had some idea how to recognize whether the women were bullshitting him.

The women were in no hurry. They opened the freezers the lieutenant wanted opened. Took out whatever samples he wanted to see. Walked them to the computers to show them the records.

They were expecting this visit.

I shook my head, told the team leader to abort, and signed off even as Bent objected behind me.

"I'll tell you why ten minutes ago," I told him and slipped to the floor with Kenny...

52
The great multiplying me

THIS TIME I GOT back just before Bent was about to ask me if I needed him to hold my hand as I gave the order.

I preempted that by jumping to my feet, grabbing Kenny, and telling both Bent and Océane that we needed to talk in a private room.

Bent pursed his lips but nodded and led us two rooms down the hall and into what might have been his office. Desk, couch, sideboard, computer, the smell of greasy sausage and salsa.

The minute he closed the door with all four of us inside, I turned to my brother to ask him which timelines he remembered living. Caught myself and rephrased it. "Kenny, you...saw a future where I killed Dr. Bent and no one stopped the virus from being released to America, and then we had a nuclear Armageddon, right?"

Kenny nodded.

Océane gaped. Bent gave a surprised huff, then looked at me keenly. Kenny had obviously not told *them* this version. For obvious reasons.

"And you also saw," I pressed before his focus could wander, "a future where I decided to work *with* Dr. Bent. In that one, we sent strike teams into nine different Chinese virology labs until we finally hit the one in Harbin where we found the bioweapon, right?"

Another nod from Kenny.

"But you never saw *this* scenario, did you? The one we're in now, the one where we jumped straight to Harbin and could not find a bioweapon there. Did you ever see that?"

He blinked at me dully. Finally shook his head.

I squeezed my eyes shut to hide the rush of intellectual celebration I felt.

This was how the order of Kenny's journeys and warnings all came together. But more, it answered that gnawing question I'd thought unanswerable from the time Lena had confirmed we were creating new timelines when we jumped, not rewriting existing ones.

What about the bodies we jump from? I'd wanted to ask her. *Do they continue or just fall over, mindless, soulless?*

Now I had the answer.

Kenny had lived two different timelines I had no memory of. One went to shortly after my nine raids on the virology labs and one went four years further out.

In the first, he'd seen "me" cooperate with Bent and find that bioweapon so it didn't decimate the US. But somehow Kenny's jump back to report on that to Bent had started the timeline where another "me" killed the mad Dr. Bent, let the virus escape and cripple America, and started a chain of events that resulted in Armageddon. Four years out from today.

In that one, I guessed I'd convinced Kenny not to jump back right away, so we'd all lived four years out and saw both the viral nightmare from China and the nuclear apocalypse.

And only *then* did Kenny do the longest jump he'd ever done—*Four years!*—to show up at the door of the testing laboratory where I'd killed Bent. There he jumped me back to a place in his past that was also in mine, even though it was in the future chronologically—us wearing black hoods on the roof of the Baltimore harbor building with Bent still alive in the building below us. Then the jumps to our childhood, our teen years, then back to the exploding building, eventually bringing us here.

Everything after Kenny's four-year jump back was with this me *who'd never commanded those first attacks on the Chinese bio labs, nor the four years that led to Armageddon!*

I could never see the future in timelines I jumped back or got pulled back from, but KENNY HAD.

It proved that when we jumped in time, creating new timelines, the Jacksons and Kennys in the old timeline kept going too.

It meant—*Holy shit*—that every time I jumped, I didn't just create a new timeline, I multiplied myself.

The great multiplying me.

That had...potential?

"Jackson?" Ocean's voice. "Dr. Traine?" Bent's slyly insinuating voice.

I opened my eyes. "You know what this means, of course."

"Enlighten us," said Bent.

"We're not repeating. We're writing new. Anything can happen. And I think there's another time traveler, someone on the ground in Harbin, who's messing with us."

"What?" Bent said. "Explain."

"We took three runs at Harbin," I said, looking at Kenny, who nodded. "The first time we were too slow and jumped back. The second, we were met with overwhelming force. The third, there was almost no resistance but also no bioweapon."

"I don't understand," Océane said.

Bent frowned. "Someone knew you were coming the second and third times."

"Maybe even the first time. They changed what we encountered."

Bent drew himself up tall and began pacing the room. I'd never seen him so thrown. Well, hey, welcome to the confusion, doc. You ain't the only player in this game after all.

He spun back to face me. "You're looking far too collected. You have an idea on how to counter it."

"I need to go there."

"No."

"If I go there, I'll be in the middle of the change when it happens. I'll be sucked into it. I'll have time to see what's happening. I can find the other time traveler and stop them."

Bent curled back his upper lip. "For the sake of argument, let's *assume* that I could summon enormous favors to somehow get you into a country that's almost hermetically sealed with COVID lockdowns. It would take at least a day to get you there. And they ship out the weapon in two."

"So?"

"What if the time traveler helping them is better at it than you?"

"Better at..."

"Perhaps they can jump back more than ten minutes. If they're able to arrange such different and elaborate changes involving the government, the army, their scientists, don't you think they might be jumping back days or more at a time? What if they just change the schedule and ship the bioweapon out early, or from another location? Perhaps they've done so already."

I stared at him, his long hard face and high forehead, his piercing blue eyes. And for just a second, I felt a tremble of the old PTSD I'd associated with him rumble around in my gut and threaten to climb up my chest to my face to screw up my breathing and make me break out in a sweat.

Except...fuck it. He was just a part of this particular timeline. Not even the smartest part. Certainly not the best.

Also, there was something about the pattern of the two counterstrategies my time-traveling nemesis in Harbin had employed. Extreme force, then pretending the bioweapon was never even there. What was it? It was almost as if...

"They can't move it early," I said. "They can't move it to another facility."

"Explain," Bent said.

"It's a gut feeling. There's a certain...disorganized element to the way they're responding to our assaults."

Bent scoffed. "Based on what?"

"The way China has locked down its country. They've poured everything into it. One hundred percent. But with *this,* the most aggressive international attack they've ever made, they're using a time traveler to send a few extra troops to stop us? Or hide the bioweapon from us?"

"What are you suggesting?"

"I don't think it's the government."

Bent frowned again. It reminded me of our earliest mental jousting matches. Before he started in with the torture.

"I think it's a rogue time traveler," I said, "or maybe the Chinese equivalent of SCATTER. I think they're calling in warnings to make the government respond. But the government will only do so much. They have a plan, a production and shipment schedule. And the CCP is a big, lumbering autocratic entity. I don't think they listen well or change easily."

"And if you're wrong?" Bent asked. "If they've already changed where the bioweapon is held and when or how it will be sent here?"

"Then I guess I'd just as soon be in China."

I meant it as a joke. No one smiled.

After a moment, Bent said. "I'll see what I can do."

Océane sucked in a breath and touched my arm. She had tears in her eyes. I turned from her back to Bent. "One more thing. You're right about my limitations. If this has any chance of success, I need someone who's better at time traveling to come with me."

"Kentucky?" Bent scoffed.

"No," I said. "Xiaobo."

53

Kansas

Riding in a Cadillac that was humming south on the I-95 under a clearing sky, Kansas could easily have let herself fall into a stupor. All those endless forests of ash and hemlock, spruce, whatever. The comforting calm precision with which Colonel Fang Jian drove. And that plush rear rider's compartment? Incredible. Way nicer than she remembered from her time dating Elizabeth/Wenling.

Kansas didn't like stupors, though. Nor would she ever have let someone trap her in a cushy box behind the driver. That's why she now rode in the front passenger seat beside Fang, something she'd *never* done when she'd been dating his boss.

She also needed to gather intel about the situation she was approaching. Fang probably knew the real Zhou Wenling better than anyone. And he was taking her there with murky motivations.

So, she'd asked him questions about himself, his life, and especially his life working for Zhou Wenling. He'd answered tersely but had told her Wenling was at her favorite home, a thoroughbred horse farm. She did not know Fang was bringing Kansas there.

It was a start, and she had a feeling she was wearing him down. If she could just—

A distinct ring tone cut off the thought. Kansas had been ignoring that ring tone of late, but not because she didn't want to talk to the caller. In fact, she probably wanted to talk to her too much. But talking with Lena could get her so emotionally worked up that her concentration suffered. And she hadn't been able to afford that with Garvey's people looking to tag her.

But now that was done. And since she still had half of what Fang said was a two-hour drive ahead of them...

She clicked the answer button, then OK to run the decryption protocol associated with this number, and Lena's voice came on, speaking quietly but sounding both tired and wired.

"You're there? Well, that's just... You actually deigned to take one of my calls?"

A little pissed, too, apparently. "Hello, Lena."

"Yes. That's good. 'Hello, Lena.' I would have liked to have heard a lot more of that over the last couple of weeks."

"I've been busy."

"Have you? Wonderful." Heavy on the sarcasm. "Looking for Wenling? Find anything?"

"I'm currently in a limousine driven by her driver, Colonel Fang Jian. He's taking me to see her."

There was silence on the other end of the line. Listening closely, Kansas thought she could hear Lena breathing. She could certainly picture it. Lena's dark, dark hair. Her glowing dusky skin. Her chest rising and falling... Then Kansas heard a jerking intake of breath and exhale that made her own throat tighten immediately.

"Lena...?"

"I'm... I'm just scared for Jackson. Lost my mom and now I don't know if I've lost him, too. For good."

Kansas took a deep breath, letting herself be aware of the same worry and pain in her own chest. Her baby brother... Something made her look to her left, and she saw Colonel Fang frowning and nodding slowly as he drove. That he understood made her pain worse.

She shoved it down and said evenly into her phone, "Where are you now?"

A sniff. Lena obviously pulling herself together. "I'm in the spare bedroom of a scientist and his family in northeast China. They're all asleep. It's almost midnight here. A city called Harbin. I got a visa by having that scientist swear to the scientific necessity of my visit. Had to quarantine for three days at a designated hotel by the airport, then another three at his place. This is my last day."

"Why on earth did—?"

"Salim Noor al-Rashid."

"The first time traveler."

"First one SCATTER found, anyway. I found his cousin. Worked my way through his other relatives and friends until I found his wife in Baghdad. She told me he'd come here. Wouldn't say why, but she gave me an address. He doesn't use a phone. So, I came here. I'm going to see him tomorrow."

It was Kansas's turn to be silent, thinking it through. Then, "You think he'll tell you something about Uwe Bent we don't know?"

"He was the only one who ever tricked him and got away."

Kansas chewed on that, seeing possibilities.

"What are you going to do when you see Wenling?"

"Like you, I think. Gather information. Hope something helps."

She saw Colonel Fang's head moving again in her peripheral vision, shaking from side to side.

"Or maybe I'll punish her for what she did. Make her see the error of her ways."

A quick glance at Fang revealed the slightest flash of a smile.

Lena said in her ear, "I'll contact you tomorrow or the next day to let you know what I've discovered. You can tell me then what you've found out, too."

Kansas smiled. Now there was the take-charge woman who'd stolen her heart and might be her sister-in-law one day.

She confirmed Lena's plan, they wished each other luck, and Kansas ended the phone connection.

The second hour of the car trip flew by so fast she could have sworn Colonel Fang sensed her anxiety and pressed his foot harder on the gas pedal until they were almost flying. Then, suddenly, they were off the I-95 and only fifteen minutes to the horse farm Wenling loved so much.

Against all odds, and even after the gratifying conversation she'd had with Lena, Kansas found her heart squeezing and aching at the thought of seeing her old lover again. Her hands got sweaty. Her fingers flew up past her long square face to see if there was any way she could grow back her hair or make it...prettier.

Not that her appearance had ever been what Wenling, as Elizabeth Chan, had ever loved about her. It had been her *mind,* she'd said. Kansas' intelligence and rapier wit. And when they'd shared their bodies with each other, the intimacy had been so deep that every scar on Elizabeth's back, Kansas had felt on her own. Along with the thrills of joy, of laughter. Kansas couldn't remember a time past the age of seven when she had laughed like that with anyone. Especially that one time when Elizabeth had come up from licking her to orgasm, made a joke about lesbians that made Kansas howl, then ducked back down to keep her lover's wild release going so long that Kansas saw Heaven and love and shooting stars and so many things she'd never believed were real.

And of course, they weren't.

"What am I supposed to say to her?" she murmured at the windshield, but really to Colonel Fang.

"You tell her the truth," he said evenly, his eyes never leaving the road that had turned to a narrow two-lane, slower stretch bounded by plowed farmer's fields, spring-green trees, and horse pastures.

"What truth?"

"About what she did. How it made you feel."

"She'll just laugh."

"Maybe. Maybe not. You...made her happy."

Kansas turned her head to stare at him. "I don't..."

"She used you. She did not see. With you, for a time, she was happy."

Kansas turned her face back to the fields and pastures that rolled by. When she spoke again, she almost didn't recognize her own voice. It sounded so childlike and lost. "And I'm supposed to punish her?"

"I think only you can. She needs...direction."

Kansas could almost hear the grunt of effort it took for Fang to say those words. Like they were a betrayal of his oath to help and protect his ex-lover's child. Or just the hard consequences of it?

They drove in silence through the greening beauty of the Virginia spring until Fang said. "This one ahead on the right. Slide down in your seat. There are cameras at the gate."

Kansas unbuckled quickly and slid as best she could below the front dash, but not before she saw the archway over the broad metal gate ahead. As Fang slowed the limo and turned right, she asked from her cramped hiding spot, "Eastern Lightning Stables. Really fast horses?"

"Yes."

She caught the undertone of disgust in his voice. "What?"

"The name is a—What is the phrase? Dog whistle?—to other Chinese in the horse racing community. Eastern Lightning is a banned religious group in China. They believe Jesus has returned and is living as a Chinese woman."

"Her?"

"She wants other people to wonder."

"Ah. Of course, she does. Power."

"Fear," said Fang.

"Which is a kind of power."

"Yes. Come up now. Someone else is here."

Kansas surfaced to see that the long drive in from the gate was through mostly open fields—pasture land, training areas, barns, stables, work quarters. Fifteen or twenty horses were grazing under the bright blue sky. They watched the limousine slowly drive in toward the house that looked like something from another era—Greek Revival in white wood lap, crisp black shutters lining each window, and four round columns extending ground to roofline across the front.

Kansas saw what had caught Fang's eye. The driveway approached the house head-on, then swung right to curve around the back where there was presumably a garage or parking area. But someone had parked their car just off the drive, directly opposite the front door.

As they got closer, she snorted and leaned forward in her seat so she could reach around to her belt band just to the right of the small of her back. Yes, the Sig P365 was still there. "I know the car."

The putty gray BMW sports car still screamed male midlife crisis and a distinct lack of taste.

"Not a friend?" said Fang.

"My old boss, Shane Garvey. Controlled by SCATTER. He wants me dead or captured."

"He might not know you are here. I did not know you would be until I saw you at the café."

"And it looks like he came alone. Would Lizbeth, I mean Wenling, have called him?"

"Why would she do that?"

"She's got sources. Maybe someone told her Garvey was working with SCATTER."

"That is possible."

They had passed the car and were swinging past the front of the house. Kansas sank down low again in case anyone was watching from inside. "Which way do you normally go in, the front or back?"

"There is a rear entrance to the house and my quarters. Ms. Zhou will be expecting me."

"Is there another way I can get in?"

"Are you a good climber?"

Kansas blew out in disgust. "Do I look like I am?"

"No." They had reached the separate three-car garage that stood behind the house. Fang pressed the same clicker he'd used for the front gate and the rightmost door swung up.

"So...the front door?"

He shook his head as he drove in slowly. "Better behind me."

"If he shoots you..."

"Then you shoot him." Fang stopped the car and killed the motor.

Kansas looked down at her hands. They trembled. "You know I'm an analyst, not a field agent, right? Got certified on my target shooting, but I've never used a gun on a person."

"Jackson never used a gun before he had to."

"And I'm the big sister."

"Yes."

"Oh, shit. Okay. Let's go."

Fang opened his door, climbed out, and exited through a door at the back of the garage. Kansas pulled out her gun, thumbed off the safety, and hurried after him, swearing under her breath. She caught up with him as he reached the back door of the house. A kitchen was visible through a window to the right. Kansas faded in behind Fang, slouching down so she no longer stood taller than him.

Fang opened the door and stepped in.

Kansas followed on his heels.

They entered a mudroom with coat hooks and boots racks. The kitchen was through a doorless arch to the right. A narrow staircase went up on the left. Ahead, an open door revealed what looked like the main entry hall of the house, wide and gracious, all polished wood and wainscoted walls, lit from the large windows above the entryway. It smelled of old money and the same Guangdong cooking of scallions, ginger, and garlic, maybe some pork, a dash of fish sauce, that Elizabeth— *Wenling!*—had delighted sharing with Kansas in the two months they'd been together.

"Colonel Jian!" called out Wenling's voice from somewhere. Then she was there in the hallway, facing them. She wore riding boots, jodhpurs, and a white shirt buttoned to her neck, her glossy hair in a plaited ponytail behind her. Her face registered surprise, then annoyance, as she saw Kansas peeking out from behind him. "And Kansas. You have stupid timing."

All the sharp wit Kansas remembered flowing out of her during her time with Elizabeth Chan completely abandoned her now. She just stared at this incarnation of the woman she'd loved so deeply.

"Actually, it's fucking amazing timing," said Garvey's voice as he stepped into the hallway behind Wenling and pulled a pistol from inside his gray suit coat. "The elusive Ms. Zhou here calls me out of the blue, saves us the hassle of finding her in case *you're* looking for her too, and voila!"

Garvey was in his fifties. His voice was irritating, high and nasal. His squashed nose and wobbly jowls cheeks were pug like. And he'd rarely understood any of the reports Kansas had given him until she'd simplified them to fifth grade level. And while Kansas might have risked her heart in loving Wenling, at least she hadn't betrayed her oath to the Constitution like Garvey had by following Bent.

Kansas looked at her hand holding the gun behind Fang's back. It was rock steady.

"So whaddya say, Traine? Come along quietly? Or do you want to—"

Kansas stepped out with her pistol raised, gripped in both hands. "I want to."

"Whoa, whoa, whoa..." Garvey said, looking not at all flustered as he walked forward, pistol aimed way to the side. As he drew up behind Wenling, he suddenly stepped right against her, gripped her around the throat, and pointed the barrel of his pistol at her temple.

"What are you doing?" Wenling grunted, saving Kansas the trouble. Which was good because her heart had involuntarily leaped into her throat again.

"Tactical advantage," Garvey said. "You know why we figured you'd track down Ms. Zhou?"

Kansas shook her head. She still had her gun up and aimed at Garvey's face. Fang, she noted had walked away from her, through the door and down the hallway toward Garvey and Wenling.

Kansas hurried into the hallway after him. She didn't want him to jump the gun on this. Garvey would kill Wenling without a thought if it would even get him a moment's hesitation from anyone coming against him.

"Surveillance," Garvey said. "On you. On all our employees, actually. We recorded you and this little piece every time you got together and frantically bumped uglies. We scanned the love notes you sent her. Shocked the hell out of our surveillance team. Shocked the hell out of me. All those mopey days you had after she left? I was laughing my ass off. Could have gotten you fired for fraternizing with someone with ties to the Chinese government."

Wenling protested, "I don't have—"

Garvey ground the barrel into her temple to shut her up. "So we knew you'd figure out she was still alive and track her down. Not just for intel, but because dikes'll do that, right?"

Forcing herself to breathe evenly, Kansas lowered her gun just a little and pulled the trigger.

THACKK!

Garvey's lower right shin exploded.

He howled in pain and almost pulled Wenling down on top of him before he caught himself and threw his left shoulder against the wall, braced hard on his right leg, still clutching Wenling around her neck, gun still jammed to her temple.

"God*damn* you, bitch!" he screamed at her. "Fucking could have hit your lover here!"

"Yes, you could!" Wenling agreed. "Colonel Jian...?"

Kansas had the gun fully raised again and spoke first. "I don't like guns, but you saw my gun range scores last time I did them, Garvey. I don't miss. Your head's next."

Garvey ducked his head behind Wenling's. "Fuck you!"

"Blood on your leg says I hit your tibial artery. You're going to lose consciousness soon unless you get a tourniquet on that. Then you'll fully bleed out and die."

Halfway to where Wenling was held, Fang said, "I know how to do this."

Kansas shook her head at him. "What do you say, Garvey? Peek out to shoot me and you die. Or you throw down your gun, pay me with intel, and I save your life."

"Fuck you, stupid dyke! Whore!"

"My arms are getting tired, boss. I might have to step forward and shoot you now, while I still can."

Garvey's breath had turned to great sucking whoops, like some kind of distressed bird. Finally, he threw his gun away, let go of Wenling, and slid down to sit with his back against the wall, grunting and swearing in pain.

Fang walked forward and offered Wenling assistance, but she shook him off and stood by herself, white faced with anger.

Fang turned back to Kansas. "Now?"

Kansas shook her head and walked forward, keeping the Sig aimed down at Garvey with just one hand now. "He still needs to give me intel."

Garvey didn't look at her. His eyes were closed, and his body had started to shudder. "What kind?"

"Names. A list of all the SCATTER True Believers you know. If it's less than fifty and doesn't include a bunch of military and congressional personnel, I'll assume you're lying and let you bleed out."

"I...don't have...your fucking...memory."

"Wenling, please get him a laptop computer."

Wenling looked at her stonily. "I don't think you—"

THACKK!

This hollow point struck the floor less than a foot from where she stood, exploding into the wood and rocketing shards hard into the boots covering her lower legs.

Wenling's mouth dropped open. Then she turned and hurried out, returning with a laptop computer that she unceremoniously dumped into Garvey's lap.

"Turn it on for him," Kansas said. "Log in. Make sure it's connected to the internet."

While Garvey went through his own online security, Kansas collected the gun he'd thrown down and removed its clip. Less than a minute after that, Garvey handed her the laptop. She scanned the file he'd brought up, suppressed her shock at how many of the names she recognized, saved it as an encrypted PDF, and sent it to Lena's mailbox. Then she wiped it and handed the computer back to Wenling.

"Now?" Fang asked.

Kansas nodded and Fang trotted past Garvey and Wenling to turn into a side room. He returned with medical supplies and attended to Garvey's wound.

"Tie his hands behind his back when you're done," Kansas said.

Suddenly exhausted, she walked past all of them to check out the rest of the house.

Later, she stood in some kind of sitting room, shaking her head at how the delicate furniture defined the lower space, while cowboy gear and Western artwork covered the walls.

She heard booted footsteps and turned to see Wenling enter the room behind her.

"You fit this place," the shorter woman said.

"Why did you bring Garvey here?"

Wenling gave her enigmatic smile.

"That's not cute anymore. Was it to tell him about Poussaint?"

Wenling mouth twitched in surprise, but she brushed her ponytail back with a sniff. "I wanted him distracted. You see, I monitor important people. I stitched a tracking device into Jackson's belly. I put tracking devices in many pieces of clothing and personal items my loyal Colonel Jian uses. Uwe Bent found Jackson's tracking device and cut it out of him, but Jian was on hand to see Andre Poussaint's jets bomb that building."

She stopped as if done and smiled enigmatically again. Kansas waited her out.

"Jian saw both your brothers come down to the lobby as the building crumbled. They went into a door that led to an underground escape tunnel. Colonel Jian followed them through it and out of it to a town in Massachusetts before losing them. I sent other people. They confirmed that most of SCATTER has regrouped there. Including my brother."

"Xiaobo."

"Yes." For a second, it looked like an actual tear had appeared in the corner of one of Wenling's eyes. "Yesterday I gave the coordinates to one of Andre Poussaint's lieutenants, paying them quite a bit of money to do whatever they like to SCATTER as long as they return Xiaobo, Jackson, and Kentucky safely to me. It's 1:30. They should be approaching the location within the next half hour and will let me know once they've retrieved our siblings. Will you come to my day room and wait with me?"

Kansas stared at her. Could it really be that easy?

She nodded.

54

The incredible journey – Part One

I CHECKED THE MISSION watch Bent had given me. At 1:30 p.m., April 27, 2022, Xiaobo, I, and our handlers, Thing One and Thing Two, had passports, COVID vaccination documents, backstories, and encrypted mission files ready.

At 1:40, Bent, still in his Eurotrash velvet, Océane in a slinky white dress, walked us back down to the basement. We passed the operations room and an experimental laboratory that I suspect was the source of the late-night screamers I'd heard. At the end of the hall, we turned right into a shorter one. Near the end of it, Bent stopped us all in front of a door on the left marked *Keep Out. Hazardous Chemicals. Only Authorized Personnel.*

He looked intensely into my eyes.

"You and Xiaobo may well be the most talented time travelers in the world," he said. "I would ask that you not take any imprudent risks with your lives. Of course, should you try something stupid, I'll still have Kentucky. Don't do anything stupid."

"Please," added Océane behind him.

I stared back and nodded, feeling pity for both Bent's and Océane's weakness. They still didn't trust me. They felt they had to repeat the hold they had on me through my brother or, in Océane's case, my...loyalty? The irony was that I was totally aligned with their goals at that moment, at least as far as stopping this bioweapon was concerned. True, it was a mostly-intellectual-moral choice, since these two had stripped away my emotional attachments, but it was solid. The free world needed saving. I was going to save it.

Or was I really doing this to figure out what time traveler or group of time travelers was out there messing with me?

Or to clean up enough of the mess that Bent had made that I could finally leave SCATTER and walk away with Kenny?

The fact I wasn't sure of my motivations stuck in the back of my brain like a troubling itch or a tumor of doubt that was sure to expand and explode. It made this mission as much about figuring out myself and how to navigate this newly expansive, meaningless world as anything else.

I pushed that all away with a deliberate glance down at the mission watch Bent had given me. 1:45 p.m. "Time," I said.

Bent nodded and unlocked the Hazardous Materials door with a *ker-thunk*.

Xiaobo, the Things, and I walked through.

It was an underground tunnel. I guessed correctly that it led to an older building on the McLean Hospital campus. A safe exit if anyone was surveilling Bent's building.

That and the next part of our trip was long, but easy. We drove to Boston Logan Airport and flew Japan Airlines to Tokyo. It was business class, so a shell of boxy privacy wrapped around each set of two airline seats. They also threw in a pair of slippers, blanket, headphones, shelf table, and a twenty-three-inch fixed monitor for each passenger. Not too shabby.

Xiaobo sat by the port-side window. I sat beside him. In the boxed-in pair of seats across the aisle to my right sat Things One and Two, watching our every move for the first hour or two.

Once that might have scared or angered me, but it didn't. I didn't care. Even as I didn't really care about finally knowing the exact date again. I'd lost track amidst all the torture and running and buildings blowing up over and over again, but did knowing it now matter? We were flying west. That meant that April 27 would stretch out longer and longer as we chased the sun. But when we crossed the international dateline somewhere past Nome, Alaska, our evening of the 27th would suddenly be our evening of the 28th.

Magic!

Not.

It meant nothing to me.

Was I even human anymore?

Xiaobo went straight to sleep, but I wasn't ready yet. I pulled out my mission phone and reviewed the encrypted files Bent had loaded onto it.

The file on the layout of the virology lab was a waste because Kenny and I had virtually raided that lab with the strike team three times. I knew it better than the file or the waiting strike team.

The waiting strike team...

Now the file on them was more interesting. It gave me the names and headshots of all nine team members and something of their backgrounds. Former Rangers, SEALs, and a couple defectors from the Chinese PLA.

The team leader, Captain Harlan Bannerman, was a surprisingly round-faced man whose glare still looked like they could kill from twenty paces. He'd served in both Iraq and Afghanistan. Fifty-two years old. Heavily decorated, most notably with the Distinguished Service Cross and the Medal of Honor. He'd left the Army after his second tour in Iraq, gone private, and ended up working for SCATTER.

So, veteran to mercenary. Same with all the other team members. Given how Bent had recruited followers from a wide range of places and professions, I wondered how many of these men were motivated mostly by money, how many by ideology, how many by the adrenaline and comradery of battle.

Finally, there was the intelligence on the bioweapon itself. I read it carefully and learned more about the collection, handling, and disposal of virus samples than I'd ever wanted to know. Like, autoclaving, the way to kill them for disposal, usually involved super-heated steam. Okay. Also, how it was actually spies from South Korea who'd found out about the bioweapon first. Again, more than I'd ever wanted to know, but maybe important to the mission?

I finally switched from this review to absorbing what news of the world I could get from the in-flight selections. Then to a spy thriller, which seemed appropriate. Then, because it was now past midnight in Boston, I slept.

When I woke, it was to see Xiaobo awake and staring out the dark window with a slack jaw.

I wondered for a moment if he'd left us completely. What was he now? Twenty-five? Twenty-six? He still had the acne-scarred face of our earlier meetings, but he'd lost the spiky hair and wild attitude. Now he had a short flattop and a wan complexion. Disconnected. Not surprising for a guy who, Océane had said, had been close to abandoning this world altogether.

"Can you see anything?" I asked from the middle seat beside him. I assumed we'd still be over the Pacific Ocean. There might be moonlight on the clouds or water.

"You showed me stuff, yo," he murmured back.

I glanced back to my right. Thing One, whose name, I'd finally learned, was Micah Rowan—blond hair, slab face, big bones, mean as bent nails—looked to be sleeping right now. Good. To his right was Thing Two. Her real name was Britney Chandra. Her face was rounder than her partner's, her skin dark brown, but she was almost Rowan's height. And I remembered how good she was with a truncheon.

Right now, she seemed plugged into the onboard movie system. Earbuds in her ears. Eyes transfixed by some kind of bright romantic comedy.

I turned back to Xiaobo and spoke as softly as him. "What did I show you?"

"I got the power. 'Cause they can't do shit we do."

"That's right."

"But...it's not... I can't do big stuff."

"Like what?"

He screwed up his brow like his brain hurt. "Real stuff. Save the world shit."

"Isn't that what we're doing now?" My voice was barely a murmur. This was getting way too revealing for a public conversation. For all I knew, the Japanese woman sitting directly in front of Xiaobo was pressing her ear into her back seat cushion and listening for all she was worth.

Xiaobo shook his head at me and looked like a lost teenager. "You're doing it, yo. I'm just, like, a ticket guy. You missed your shot? Here's another ticket! I got stock market tickets. I got bullet-in-the-head tickets. I got, 'Fuck, they got away,' tickets."

It brought back Wenling's obsession with the heartache of *In the Mood for Love*. I blurted its key line, "'If there's an extra ticket, would you go with me?'"

Xiaobo frowned and muttered the line in Mandarin, then said, "Stupid fuckin' movie. She's more *Crazy Rich Asians*."

"Michelle Yeoh?"

"Awkwafina."

We looked at each other and both cracked up at the same time. I think it shocked both of us.

Then Xiaobo told me how, when he was little boy, Wenling would play with him, sing him to sleep, and protect him from their father. He got tears in his eyes telling it and had to blow his nose with one of the napkins that had come with the ginger ale. "But after we ran away?" he said. "She found out what I could do, and I became this *thing*. Money money money."

"Which she used to feed both of you and get you to America," I said.

He looked at me with a sneer. "She tell you that? We lived on nothing, yo. Rice bowls and a dirty room where I got lice and had to shave my head. All that money just got saved to pay off the big boys, yeh?"

"That got you to America."

"Where you think it's gotta be better, right, homie?" He shook his head and waved both hands back and forth. "Not 'til I met Doc."

"Dr. Bent?"

"Said he didn't need no money. He wanted me to help save the world."

"Yes."

"We doing that?"

"Might not be a one-and-done job," I said. "But I think so. Yeah."

"Okay." He sat back, and we rode in silence awhile, until he asked, "You ever think about marrying my sister?"

I snorted without thinking, then shook my head. "No."

He nodded. "She'd ruin you."

Thing One, Micah Rowan, woke up, and we talked little after that. When we touched down in Tokyo, it was the middle of the night. This was where the trip got crazy.

55

Lena

THE TRUE BELIEVERS LIST.

Lena had been tossing and turning in the lower bunk of the Wang children's bunk beds in Harbin, China on the last night of the "home stay" part of her post-flight quarantine when the message arrived on her phone with a spy movie, cool saxophone theme she'd assigned to Kansas' messages.

It woke her up.

She groggily read the list.

So many names she recognized. Politicians and titans of business, entertainers, influencers... This was a nightmare! How could she ever sleep now?

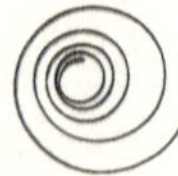

When her phone alarm went off at 6:30 a.m., April 28, local—that was 6:30 p.m., April 27 back in Virginia where Kansas was—Lena blinked awake again, looked around the room, and remembered what day it was. She barely remembered the list.

At first.

But as she struggled her way out of bed and set about tidying the room she'd been loaned by Dr. Wang Shěn, it came back to her, and she rechecked it on her phone numerous times. Why had Kansas sent it to her? Just to keep her in the loop? Something more? Would it somehow help her when she met Salim Noor al-Rashid face to face? Was there some other way she could use it now to help Jackson?

She finished the room, wishing there was a window to open to clear the air. It had to smell a bit funky after her continuous presence here.

The best she could do was at least make sure she herself smelled clean, so she temporarily archived the obsessive mental questions rolling around in her head, then dressed in a maroon cotton blouse, black slacks, and running shoes.

She carefully creaked open the door of the room.

"Ah, there you are!" the professor's light voice called happily the second she stepped out into the apartment's narrow hallway.

Wang was almost exactly Lena's height, though with a much slighter bone structure. But he had such a charismatic good nature that she guessed his students at the Normal University of Harbin would absorb their physics without ever noticing the passage of time. It came through even with the blue medical mask covering the bottom half of his face. His dark eyes twinkled at her. They'd drawn her to befriend him after they'd both presented papers on quantum replication a few years ago. And, of course, it was Lena's new findings on the attraction of replicated particles that had justified Wang supporting her visa to enter the country.

Lena hurriedly pulled on her own mask and bobbed her head at him. "Good morning, Dr. Wang."

Wang giggled and pulled off his mask. "I'm kidding, Dr. Cortland!" he sang out, losing the R in her name both because his native Mandarin didn't have the English "r" sound and because he'd learned his English with a British teacher. He did manage to hammer the "l" sound, though, which was impressive since Mandarin didn't use that either. "You are family now. We don't wear masks in the house."

"Phew," Lena said and pulled hers off, struggling a little as it got stuck in her currently-very-wild dark brown hair.

"Out there, though..."

"I get it."

He waved her into their small living room and their two kids, five-year-old Biyo and her younger brother Qian, looked up with fascination. Lena had actually said a masked hello the day she'd arrived and seen the children once or twice on her brief forays to the bathroom. Their parents had obviously told them to keep their distance, though, until she'd been there a full three days. So now...

Biyo jumped to her feet, stuck out both her hands and said in her very best English, "Weh-come!"

"Thank you, Biyo." She glanced at Wang, who smiled and nodded, so she stepped forward and crouched in front of the girl. She accepted a quick hug that smelled like peppermint. Then she took the girl's small hands and said, "Your English is so good."

The little girl beamed, and Lena found her long-held assumption she could never be a mother crumble into a little puddle in her chest.

Her brother was on his feet now, too, crowing, "Weh-come! Weh-come!"

Lena took one of his pudgy hands and said, "Your English is good, too," helplessly mimicking the boy's nodding and grinning.

With both kids happily returning to their play, Lena stood and turned to Wang. "Where's Yǔxī?"

Yǔxī was Wang's wife, as quietly gracious as Wang was outgoing. Her conversations with Lena through the door had said she taught elementary school, grades one to three. Presumably she'd be seeing Biyo in her classes next year.

"Early morning school meeting," Wang answered her and sighed. "They are changing the COVID safety protocols again. Now come and let me give you a real Harbin breakfast!"

He turned around and was basically in the small kitchen, but he walked in deeper to pull out bowls and ingredients. There was flour and...another type of flour? No, she could smell the chicken in the powder. Scallions. Eggs. Peeled tomatoes. Green leaves that might have been parsley or mint, for all Lena knew. She usually stuck to simple fare and delivery when she ate alone. When she'd been with Jackson, he'd done most of the cooking. That thought and this cozy family setting gave her a pang of longing for Jackson, for what she'd thrown away, maybe forever.

She pulled herself out of it as she watched Wang's fine-fingered hands deftly crack and mix eggs in one bowl with his chopsticks, then sprinkle water into flour in another. "I thought you said those burritos you've been feeding me were the northeastern Chinese breakfast."

"*Jiānbing guǒzi.* Yes. Very popular. Our kids love it." He called out to Biyo and Qian in Chinese with the word *jiānbing* as part of it, and they choroused back what sounded like "she" and "how."

"That's not what you're making now," Lena said.

"No," said Wang as the rich smell of frying scallions filled the air. A moment later he removed them from their silver bowl on the burner, and added the peeled, chopped tomatoes. "This is even better. It is *gē da tang*, dough drop soup. The perfect way to start a day."

The tomatoes released their juice. In went the mixed dough, then the mixed eggs, and eventually the fried scallions. He served it into four bowls and added a sprinkling of the green chopped leaves on top.

"Coriander," Wang said as he brought bowls to the small square table between the galley kitchen and the living room. The kids were in the chairs before the bowls touched down.

Lena and Wang joined them. They ate. It was warm, melted butter and salt in the nose, just a hint of tart in the smoothness. Heavenly. And such a perfect little world in the food and family around her. So perfect, in fact, that she wished it could last longer than it did.

If she ever found Jackson, she wanted him to meet this family.

She wanted to *be* this family. With Jackson. Free of SCATTER. Free of the list.

Would that it were so simple.

"Dr. Wang?"

"Please call me Shĕn," Wang said with a smile and lifted his bowl to his mouth to finish his soup.

"Shĕn," Lena said. "I have an address I need to get to..."

Wang had looked at a map on his computer. It showed Harbin addresses that Google Maps was apparently not allowed to. One of them was the address Salim Noor al-Rashid's cousin had given Lena. Wang told her how to catch the bus south past the medical university, then get off and walk a few blocks west. He drew the Chinese character.

"Many scientific buildings in that area," Wang said. "Is this person you're visiting also a scientist?"

"I don't think so."

Wang looked at her expectantly for more. When none came, he nodded his understanding. He rightly guessed her meeting had political, scientific, or personal implications. Right on all counts. And maybe more. Salim Noor al-Rashid had apparently told his cousin he was going to Harbin to "fix" things. If Al-Rashid could time travel, who knew what that fix entailed?

She finally set off in her navy-blue trench coat for warmth, her COVID mask over her nose and mouth, and her black shoulder bag slung crosswise over her front. She called back a promise to Wang that she'd share some of her most recent research soon. Beyond his curiosity, he'd need something to justify his support of her visa if Chinese authorities ever questioned him.

Thirty minutes later she was pressing a button marked simply "26" on an apartment building's entry plate that showed thirty-eight such buzzers. Thirty-eight homes. It was already 8:20 a.m. All the Chinese children were in school, and many Chinese adults had gone out, too. She hoped Al-Rashid wasn't one of them.

Assuming he actually *had* come here. And this was the right address.

She hit the buzzer again.

Lena looked up at the icy blue sky. Salim's building rose up ten stories against it, matching a dozen similar buildings to its right and left, all dwarves compared to the many high-rises she'd seen on her trip down here, morning frost still on the ground in the shadows they cast.

She startled as the speaker on the entry plate crackled.

A man's gentle voice asked something that sounded like, "Nee sheng yaow shenma?" When Lena didn't answer immediately, the voice asked again, this time in only-slightly-accented English, "Hello? Who are you looking for?"

"Salim Noor al-Rashid," Lena said quickly. "My name is Lena Cortland. I'm an American scientist who studies time travel. Your cousin Wissam Saleh told me where to find you."

There was a pause, then the voice said, "*Salaam aleikum.* Please wait. I shall come down to you."

Lena was about to protest, but the *Salaam* stopped her. Because unlike the Mandarin she'd been struggling to absorb with a lessons and translations program on her phone, *Salaam aleikum* brought back her mother. It was her mother greeting her own parents when they visited. It was how she'd trained Lena to greet Muslim friends or Muslim colleagues at conferences. Greet but not shake hands or touch. Use only your right hand when offering or receiving foods or gifts. Be modest in word and action.

Not because Allah or God demanded it, she'd been told, but because social etiquette and a respect for others' beliefs did.

Little of the Arabic and Persian her mother had taught her had stuck, but the greetings and customs—they'd been imprinted early and came rushing back now.

The one that applied here, that was strong for some conservative Muslims, was that a man must never be alone with a non-*mahram* woman, one who was not his wife or close relative.

Hence, the, *Please wait. I shall come down to you.*

"Should've worn a damn burka," she muttered. Or at least a scarf to cover her head. And baggier clothes. And a different personality. But for a time traveler who'd survived Abu Ghraib and traveled all the way to China to "fix" things? Come on.

Then suddenly he was there, walking through the lobby toward her.

Clearly him because he was about the right age—mid-forties—and the first Middle Eastern male Lena had seen since entering China. His gaze was softly appraising as he approached the glass entry doors. He wore his dark hair and beard neatly trimmed. The uneven wrinkles on his face and hands looked like old, long-healed scars. But he wasn't wearing a caftan and head cloth. His outfit was brown corduroy pants and a green flannel shirt under a gray sweater vest. And running shoes!

He turned the lock on the door and came out to face her. "Lena Cortland?"

"Yes. Wa alaikum assalaam." And upon you be peace. Her delayed response to his Salaam.

He blinked, then smiled widely enough to show white, well-cared for teeth. He pulled from his pants pocket a disposable mask that he fitted over the lower half of his face and said, "Walk with me."

And without waiting, he set off down the sidewalk at a fast enough clip she had to jog to catch up.

When she did, she noted they weren't exactly surrounded by hordes of people. They passed cars and people walking, but nobody came close to her and Al-Rashid.

"Does this count as not being alone with a non-mahram woman?" Lena asked. "The walking fast?"

He slowed and looked at her, confused, then smiled again behind his mask, still walking. "That is a fatwa issued by those who stretch the words of the Qur'an for their own ends. No, we walk because the Chinese do not put listening devices on the street here."

Lena felt her mouth drop open involuntarily, and she looked around. "Cameras?"

"Yes. The building with the red door. The lamp post across the street. Don't look directly at it."

She studied him as he spoke and saw she'd been right about the healed scars. They were all over his face, his neck, his hands. Maybe his whole body? So many that none stood out more than the others, the horrors running together to give him a mottled look. He'd been badly beaten or tortured once upon a time. In the Abu Ghraib prison, of course. It corroborated what Megan had found and fit the story Hazel had come up with.

"So, you escaped Abu Ghraib," Lena said.

That made him hitch his step just a little, and he pointed to a line of trees and grass coming up to their right. "We will talk in there."

The small park smelled like spring—clover and fresh grass. Mothers sat and gossiped while their small children chattered and played on the swings and teeter-totters. The ever-present apartment buildings looked down from above, but the trees made them seem temporarily unreal. Even the rumbling drone of the constant traffic along one side of the park couldn't break the spell.

The bench on which Al-Rashid and Lena sat was off in one corner, in the shadow of a large apple tree. Lena had drawn her trench coat tightly around her for warmth and told Al-Rashid her story, Jackson's story, and what they'd found about SCATTER.

He seemed remarkably unsurprised. "Allah has blessed the world with many strange things. I am one of them. Your Jackson Traine and the other people on this 'list' you spoke of, are others."

"Can you tell me how to find and rescue them? How you got out?"

He shook his head sadly. "I escaped with luck and circumstance. These are not transferable gifts."

"You switched places with translator Benny Barzani," she said, offering Hazel's theory. "And just walked out."

Al-Rashid closed his eyes and his skin colored. "Yes. It is my shame."

"It was survival."

"Benny. Did he...?"

"He died. I think the experiments they did..."

Al-Rashid nodded. He opened his eyes but did not meet Lena's gaze. "I warned him of this. He said it could not happen in America."

Lena pressed him awhile on what he knew about Dr. Uwe Bent and how Al-Rashid had fooled him. But other than Al-Rashid's last jump taking him back to before Bent had ever met him, he shared nothing that Lena hadn't already guessed. Bent was a narcissistic psychopath. Highly intelligent. Amoral. Capable of great cruelty in pursuit of scientific discovery.

And hadn't Lena herself been that, too? At least the great cruelty part.

She felt compelled to share this with Al-Rashid, explaining how she'd restrained and tried to suffocate Jackson when first trying to establish how he time traveled. The shame of that had stayed with her and joined with her later mistreatment of him when she was mourning her parents. It made her understand she might love him but could never be with him. He needed and deserved someone more fundamentally good.

Al-Rashid fully turned his scar-mottled face back to her and fully met her gaze. Lena could see in him the same guilt and sorrow that she carried within her always.

"I understand this," he said, and touched her hand gently. "Our greatest good is found in others. For me, after I escaped, I traveled north like a lost refugee, separated from my nafs, my soul, to find the woman I had wanted to marry. It was she who brought me back to myself."

Lena blinked the tears from her eyes. What was he telling her? That Jackson could save her? That she could save him? "Did you keep time traveling?"

"Only when absolutely necessary."

"Like here in Harbin?"

"Yes."

"You traveled all the way here to change...what?"

He looked at Lena for a long beat before he answered. Even then, Lena could hear how carefully he chose his words.

"There is...a plague, a great sickness, that was made in a laboratory here and used to kill millions of people in less than a week."

"Not COVID?"

"It was faster, deadlier. Medical scientists said it was a new form of Ebola."

Lena felt her heartbeat elevating and slowed her breathing to bring it down. "You're speaking like it was already done."

"It was. I traveled back in time to come here and stop it from happening."

Lena furiously searched the memory of her conversation with Al-Rashid's cousin. Had he said when his cousin Salim had come here? No. "How far back in time did you jump?"

"Three weeks."

Three weeks. So, the amount of time a person could jump, some time travelers could jump, was not limited to ten minutes. All right. Noted. Filed for future exploration. "When did you arrive here?"

"Sixteen days ago. It took time to arrange my visa and flight."

"I bet. The...event, the release or shipping of this virus, when did that happen, relative to today?"

"Yesterday. 10:20 at night here."

Lena swallowed with difficulty. She wiped away the sweat that had beaded suddenly up along her hairline. "Did you stop it?"

Al-Rashid nodded. "Three times. The last time, there was no virus to find. I believe they gave up."

"Yes!" Lena restrained her desire to punch a fist into the air in relief.

Which was good, because she saw Al-Rashid physically shudder and blink repeatedly.

It was likely fatigue, mixed in with the guilt and sorrow, hiding under a carefully cultivated calm. Much like Jackson had tried to hide from her all the horrible realities he'd been through with the Demon Monks. But that effort had made Jackson fall apart in the ensuing months. And Lena hadn't been able to help because she'd been struggling with the recent loss of her mother.

Then the full import of what Al-Rashid was saying hit. Three times. They gave up. No virus to find.

She asked, "Someone other than the Chinese caused this? They tried to steal the virus? To take where? And they kept trying each time you changed their success to failure? Over what time period?"

"That is...a complicated story. It will not help you."

"Or it may." Lena thrust her chin at him. "Just as what I have found out about time traveling may help you. I know something about it that you don't. How many people have you met who can say that?"

"What do you know?"

"You first. Tell me what happened."

The older man regarded her with fascination, doubt, then a kind of longing and a wry recognition that she had hooked him. He nodded. "My first attempt to stop them was weak, but I believe it worked. That is why they went back in time to try again."

"And you know this because..."

"They pulled me back with them somehow. It is strange. It is like they know I am changing things, and they also change me. I try a different tactic. They try a different tactic."

Other time travelers. Lena swore under her breath. She recalled wondering, the first time she'd learned about SCATTER finding multiple time travelers, how one person's time jump would affect another's. Remembering the way things had been, like Jackson and Kansas had done, was one thing. What Al-Rashid was describing sounded like a whole new level of quantum entanglement.

She felt Al-Rashid's light touch on the back of her hand again and jerked her eyes up to see his. Those eyes were tired, yes. Filled with guilt and sorrow and all the scars of yesteryear, yes. But calm. Concerned for her.

"I'm fine," she blurted and pulled her hand away. "How were you finally able to convince them there was no virus to find?"

"I made it that way. They still pulled me back but did not attack again."

"Wait. Unpack that. You 'made it that way.' And they're now not 'attacking' the lab. Start with number two. What kind of attack. One man? An army? What country?" Did other countries have their own versions of SCATTER?

Al-Rashid sighed, but Lena thought she also detected the pleasure of unburdening. For who else could he tell this to who would believe and appreciate it? Maybe his wife. Assuming she even knew he could time travel. "It was a small team of soldiers," he said. "Nine men. Very well trained. Dressed in black. I could not hear their speech."

He watched them. He saw them.

A sudden horrible thought swept through Lena, and she pulled out her phone, brought up and scrolled through her photos, stopping on a serious one of Jackson. Though most pictures she had of Jackson were serious, weren't they? At least the ones she took when he wasn't looking. He carried the same haunted look in his eyes that Al-Rashid did, though his was more weighted with fear than guilt.

She showed the picture to Al-Rashid. "Was this guy one of them?"

The man looked carefully at the picture, stroking his short beard slowly. "I do not think so, but they wore helmets and moved quickly. I was not that close."

She slipped her phone back into her trench coat pocket. "How close?"

"The window of my apartment. Nine floors up. With binoculars. But it was still hard to follow everything at night, you understand?"

"The backside of your apartment building—that's where the virology lab is?"

Al-Rashid nodded.

"That's why you rented in that building, that apartment?"

Another nod.

"And how you 'made it that way.' 'No virus to find.' What does that mean?"

Al-Rashid hesitated only a moment, then launched into a story of arriving in Harbin and trying to find who, in the Harbin virology lab, would have the authority to call for police or military backup. Or to remove the virus from Harbin completely by destroying it.

It had taken extensive research and persistent and dangerous questions that had required time traveling more than once to avoid death.

When he'd identified the scientist appointed by the Party to manage this especially dangerous project, Al-Rashid surveilled her, made contact, and gradually, in many park lunches, with many time-traveling restarts, won her belief in his ability to see the coming attack. Enough that she tightened security to prepare for it. And when this was not enough, Salim jumped back again, this time persuading her to bring serious military help. When the bloodbath that followed was still not enough, he jumped back and finally convinced her that she must destroy the virus completely or the attackers would never stop.

She did. The attackers believed this. They stopped attacking.

"They gave up?"

Al-Rashid nodded. "Or perhaps they now look elsewhere."

Lena sat back on the bench and regarded him with awe. "Just how long," she asked him, "do you think you've spent on this project? If you count all the repeated times you lived through? If you laid them all out, end to end?"

Al-Rashid looked thoughtful, dropping his chin so that his beard bunched up and out, and the scarred lines of his face squeezed and folded over one another.

"Two months?" he offered at last.

"Okay, that's...impressive and frightening." Lena sat back on her bench. The smell of grass and—was that lilac?—still filled the air. Some mothers and children had left, she noticed. Others had arrived. The squeals of laughter and unfamiliar babbling must have been going on throughout her discussion with Al-Rashid, but she'd been so focused it was like the rest of the world had ceased to exist.

In this timeframe. My god, what was she supposed to do with this? How had Jackson handled it?

"It is your turn," said Al-Rashid beside her.

"Right, the thing I promised to tell you about time travel that you don't know."

"First, the serious man in the picture. Is that the man you love? Jackson?"

"It is," she said, amazed how just thinking about him in the context of Al-Rashid's question spread feelings of warmth through her that physically pulled her back from the edge.

"Tell me about him. Is he a good man? Smart? Funny?"

"Yes, yes, and yes. You'd like him, but..."

"You hesitate."

"He's so...vulnerable. Emotionally. But so stubborn that he'll keep after something he believes in even if it might kill him."

Al-Rashid nodded. "I can see why this kind of man would appeal to you."

"God help me, he does."

"And the thing about time travel you know that I do not?"

Lena nodded and braced herself. "I have irrefutable proof that when you jump back in time to change things, you don't erase anything that's happened. You just start a new timestream, a new reality, in which different things happen."

She waited for the emotional destruction this had caused in Jackson.

Instead, she got Al-Rashid's familiar gentle smile and a nod. "I have read about this possibility."

"Not just a possibility. It's what happens."

"I will consider this. Thank you."

"You say that like we're done here."

"This meeting has been a blessing of Allah." Al-Rashid leaned forward and popped to his feet, looking less like a haunted, exhausted time traveler trying to save the world and more like a hip Muslim gym teacher. "Professor Lena Cortland, we have met and become friends who share a knowledge of how strange the world is. Yet I must go. I have important errands to run before I return to my wife in Baghdad."

Lena got hurriedly to her feet, fumbling in her shoulder bag for a paper and pen. She scrawled Wang Shĕn's address and phone number on it and handed it to Al-Rashid. "I'm staying with a Chinese couple, the Wangs."

He accepted it and nodded. "They are very fortunate."

"Will I see you again?"

He gave her a sweet smile. "If Allah wills, perhaps. Hello, hello, hello, as they say in my country."

"They say hello when saying goodbye? I wasn't taught that one."

"And we say, Wadaa'an!"

"And *Allah ma'ak*," Lena remembered.

"Yes. Hello, goodbye. May Allah bless you. Hello, hello, goodbye."

As he clasped her hands, then turned and walked away, Lena figured the smile he left her with would have to make up for her getting no leads on Jackson and only a tantalizing glimpse of time travel possibilities. Because he'd just told her in the politest way he could, yet in a way that told her he would not change his mind, that there was no way in hell they were ever going to see each other again.

It was only after he had passed out of sight that Lena realized he hadn't told her where, in the first scenario that killed millions, the virus had been released.

56

Salim Noor al-Rashid

It was amazing, Salim thought as he hurried back toward his apartment building. He had traveled as far east as one could go to save millions from suffering and death, only to encounter a Western woman who spoke Arabic and was trying to save just one man from suffering and death. And that one man was a time traveler! A captive as Salim had once been. Perhaps connected somehow to the attacks on the virology laboratory regardless of what he had said to Dr. Lena Cortland.

Surely Allah wanted him to stay with her and help her in her quest.

But he could not. Not until his work here was done.

While it seemed as if he had won his battle to stop the nightmare made in Harbin, he needed to make sure the virus would remain destroyed, so the world was safe.

For now. In this timestream.

He tacked on the last qualifier reluctantly, knowing he would have to reconcile himself to this understanding Dr. Cortland had given him. For he believed her. It fit with so many feelings and thoughts he'd experienced since his time in Abu Ghraib.

He arrived at his building, keyed his way in, and took the squeaky elevator to the ninth floor. There he walked through his sparsely furnished bachelor apartment to its rear window, looking west. He slid open the window and looked down.

Squatting like a giant gray wild boar behind a forbidding concrete guard wall across the street, the five-story gray building that housed Harbin's BSL-4 virology laboratory stared up at him.

Inside the arms of the concrete guard wall were two other buildings and a small parking lot that currently held twenty cars. But three times, from this very window, Salim had watched all those cars leave. And at 10 p.m., the small team of black-suited soldiers had come. They had attacked from the front and back. Short and deadly attacks. Then their time traveler had jumped back in time, dragging Salim with him.

Until last night, the fourth time that night repeated, and the attackers did not come.

Salim had celebrated. He had kept the horror from happening!

Only now he knew that this was not true. The first attack and all the death it caused, the possible end of all human life, would continue on in its own timeline.

That knowledge sat like a stone weight in Salim's chest, but perhaps this was a good thing. It drove him now to ensure this particular horror would never happen again. He'd convinced Dr. Ying, the doctor who'd overseen the creation of the bioweapon here, to destroy her creation twice now. Once for the third night, when the soldiers found the virus they sought was not here. Then again after Salim's time-traveling adversary had jumped him back in time and he'd had to convince Dr. Ying all over again.

But now, for the Dr. Ying in this timeline, there had been no attack. She must be wondering what she had done. She had risked her career and perhaps her very life on the word of a man who said he saw the future, and that man had lied!

Her response, Salim worried, would be to recreate this horrible weapon as quickly as possible. And how could Salim, seemingly proved to be a liar, convince her not to?

Yet he must. Having seen what the bioweapon could do, Salim could not simply walk away, hoping that this time it would never be used. He must remind her of the threat it posed to all humanity. He must convince her.

If Allah willed it so.

Saying a fast niyyah to prepare his heart, he looked up and squinted to see the position of the sun. Dhuhr, he knew, was earlier in the day here than in Iraq. This gave him just enough time to deepen his connection to Allah before going out to meet Dr. Ying.

He pulled himself back into the apartment, went to the neatly folded pile of clothing and personal items he'd unpacked into the divided cubbies of the bookshelf beside his bed, and pulled out his travel sajjāda, the thinner, foldable version of his usual prayer mat. He unfolded it out on the carefully swept space between the kitchenette along the north wall and the small, square table and chair set nearer the bed. He adjusted the mat so that the elaborate

Mihrab where Salim would place his head in prostration was aligned south-west toward Mecca.

Then he went to the sink of the small kitchen, wetted the hand cloth he had brought with him on this trip, and methodically cleaned his hands, feet, arms, and legs, before rinsing and hanging up the cloth to dry. He returned to the sajjāda and stood at the bottom end of it, raised his open hands to shoulder level, and began his second salah of the day.

When he had gone through each step of devotion and reflection and felt thoroughly grounded and connected with Allah once more, he asked Allah for forgiveness and mercy and rose to his feet. He put away his mat and hurried back to the open window.

As if on cue, the front doors of the virology lab opened and five people walked out. One of them was Dr. Ying.

This was surely a sign from Allah.

As the group split, some likely heading to cars or a nearby restaurant, Ying walked toward the exit gate with the shoulder pack in which she usually carried her lunch and various notes she could review as she ate in the park one block to the north and east.

Without waiting to ensure that's where she was going, Salim ran from his apartment, barely taking time to lock the door behind him.

The elevator was not at his floor and was too slow anyway. Salim ran for the stairs, throwing himself down flight after flight, bumping elbows and knees, feet slipping on stairs as he neared the last second-last landing, tired and sloppy. He crashed onto his tailbone and bounced into the end wall, thumping his head hard enough to blur his vision.

Then he was up and throwing himself down the last flight of stairs and out the back door of the building.

He slowed to a fast walk as he headed north, then west for the park where they had shared so much more than Ying knew. Month of meetings and confidences. He caught up to her as she came out from a cross street.

"Dr. Ying!" he called as he approached.

She startled and turned. When she saw him, her small mouth frowned below her long flat nose, but she did not turn away. She stood and waited.

"*Gǎnxiè nín de lǐjiě,*" Salim said when he reached her. *Thank you for your understanding.* It was one of seven or eight phrases he had learned from his Chinese-phrases audiobook that he'd listened to on his flight to Harbin.

When spoken with humility, he'd found it highly effective in melting Dr. Ying's defenses.

It did not work this time.

The statuesque woman gave him a slight head nod, but her frown remained fixed on her face as she motioned for him to walk with her to the park where they had met previously.

When they arrived and sat in a stiff echo of the earlier meeting Salim had enjoyed with Dr. Cortland, he asked quietly, "Did the other workers find out?"

"Nothing find out," she said in her heavily accented, broken English, as she pulled out her metal box of fragrant beef noodles with slivered vegetables. For all her scientific brilliance and impressive ability to read and understand spoken English, she had told Salim that she'd been given few opportunities to travel and no other incentives to improve her ability to speak.

"The destruction of...what we talked about."

"There is no destroy. No attack. Good thing, I think?" She used her chopsticks to hoist a mess of noodles into her mouth and chewed.

Salim felt his blood run cold. "You promised me you were going to destroy it. You said the government was too interested in it. This scared you."

She shook her head and finished her mouthful. "Stupid fear. Like you stupid fear. Nothing happen."

"I know it seems like that."

"Nothing *happen*." She poked a chopstick into his chest. "Because you, we hide it. I change log. I get all worker agree. And nothing *happen*."

Ah. They must have hidden it in the last timeline, too, and lied so well the soldiers who attacked the lab believed it was not there. But would they be the only ones? And should one trust, as Dr. Ying said she now did, her own government's intentions?

If he didn't believe Dr. Lena Cortland's assertion that timelines could not be erased or changed, only new ones created, Salim would simply, as Americans liked to say, "take the win" and go home. He had stopped the human-extinction-level event he had seen. Three times. If the Ebola bioweapon was released in a different way, he could stop that, too.

Only...like he'd told Dr. Cortland, a part of him had always known his magic rewriting of history was too good to be true. It was why he was here now. If he just left, waited for another release of the bioweapon, and acted again to "fix" it, he would only create new timelines. He'd still have allowed untold suffering he might have prevented now.

And if Dr. Ying would not listen?

He could find a way into the laboratory to destroy the virus himself. Blow up the laboratory. He would have to kill Dr. Ying and any scientist who'd worked on this project. Then...

He felt a coldness grip him like it wanted to drag him into the past, into all the darkness he had left there.

How far must he go? If he took this path, would it ever stop? What did Allah ask of him? Must he become the untiring counter to every evil of the world? Was this the true purpose of his gift that he had so long denied?

A touch on his knee startled him out of his dark reverie. He turned to see Dr. Ying considering him with the furrowed brows and intense gaze he imagined she used to study viruses in her laboratory.

"You not a god," she said.

The insight of this comment so shook Salim that he could only gaze back at her in wonder. Allah had heard his anguish and through this woman had answered.

Dr. Ying pursed her lips tightly, like she was struggling with the considerations warring inside her. When she spoke again, it was with the most considered precision he had seen in her in all their months of meetings.

"I not give *any* mans Ebola..." She added a Chinese word to the end of Ebola that was clearly a scientific descriptor of the enhanced virus, but Salim had not been able to process it the few times she had said it, and Ying had refused to repeat, explain, or write it down for him.

Her hand, still on his knee, squeezed hard. "You come to lab. Four morning. I show how *no* man take."

With this promise, Salim felt the dry tumbleweed that had invaded his heart suddenly uncurl, take root, germinate, and bloom with small white flowers of undying hope like the Anastatica, the Rose of Jericho, that his wife grew in their small rooftop garden in Baghdad. Its sweet scent flowed up inside him and he smiled at Dr. Ying. "Tomorrow morning? Four o'clock? The front door?"

She nodded and gave his knee a final squeeze. "You. Me. I show you."

The next morning, April 29, Salim was on time. Dr. Ying was there already. But what she showed him was *not* what she had promised.

57

The incredible journey – Part Two

Our late-evening, April 28, touchdown in Tokyo turned into a black limo ride to the American Naval Air Facility Astsugi. There some naval guy who described himself as Petty Officer First Class Wynn gave us more battle-ready clothes to change into—thick-soled boots, black flexible tops with zips up the neck and pockets on the arms, ripstop black pants with pockets, zippers, and thickened knees. When we'd dressed, he led us to a hulking shadow on a dark airfield that smelled like exhaust and engine fuel. He ushered us up a grated metal ramp and into the belly of what I figured was a bomber aircraft. Mostly because there were no true seats to accommodate us. We were just a payload.

POFC Wynn clarified, as he strapped Xiaobo and me down on one side of this metal gut, Things One and Two on the other side, that we were now in one of the world's newest stealth jets.

"Where's the inflight TV?" I quipped.

"Short flight," said Wynn, which I took to mean, *Don't complain.* Then, "Quiet flight," which I took to mean, *Like really, shut up.*

Then he walked out of the aircraft and the ramp pulled away from the bomber doors. Those doors closed with a whining electric sound that ended with a deep thump. Followed shortly thereafter by whines and clicking, things spinning up, lights dimming. And finally...the takeoff.

It was a jawbone rattling hurricane that pressed us hard into our side straps and made my head jerk side-to-side at least twice as we raced for whatever level a plane like this flew at.

When we reached it, the rattling hurricane smoothed into a boring vibration that gradually became just how the world was.

It didn't last long enough.

About ninety minutes into our trip, a slim man who was probably my age but looked far more mature in his navy flight suit, clattered down a short ladder I hadn't noticed before. He briefed us on what was going to happen as we approached the shoreline boundary between North Korea and Russia. When he got to the part where we parachuted out of a set of the bomber bay doors, I began shaking my head.

Thing One, Micah Rowan, spoke up for the first time on this flight. "It's a tandem jump. You're with me, Traine. Zhou's with Britney. You two don't have to do shit except not scream when we jump. You scream, we maybe die. Got it?"

"You've been lead on a lot of tandem jumps?" I asked.

"Enough."

"Great. Can I scream now before we go?"

Thirty-five minutes later, we did the plunge-through-the-dark-sky thing. Xiaobo told me later that two seconds after he and Britney Chandra's joint parachute snapped them to a slow descent, he turned his head back toward her and projectile vomited at her face.

I figured that was good payback for Britney sending me face-first into what I thought at the time was Wenling's red gore in the Capitol basement SCIF.

Micah pulled our cord five seconds after Xiaobo and Britney's, so he and I touched down first into the freezing waters of the East Sea/Sea of Japan. We triggered our inflatable life vests. Less than a minute later, a nearly invisible riverboat approached and flashed a signal that Micah responded to with his own flashlight. The boat found us and hauled us out of the water.

Then it motored in a sloshing circle to go back the way it had come and picked up the now-in-the-water-and-shivering Xiaobo and Britney.

We mostly dried out on the slow trip up the Tumen River that defined the border between North Korea and Russia. Even though the sky was moonless, Things One and Two and our Korean boat operator made us sit on the cold floor of the boat and not talk. The North Koreans had apparently been forti-fying their security all along this river since COVID hit.

Puttering up a windy patch of the trip, Xiaobo finally snuggled up to me like he wanted me to wrap all of him inside my arms. He whispered about his vomiting on the parachute jump. Said he hated the water. The rain. Marshes. He broke down crying.

I held him and stroked his head through the roughest part. Told him I'd look after him.

Once the water calmed, he was fine, and we didn't speak of it again.

I remembered from a map I'd looked at four years ago, that the right bank of the Tumen River switched from being Russian to Chinese about ten miles in. But we kept traveling five times that again before our pilot dropped us off on Chinese soil.

There we were met by a creaky looking flatbed truck. We covered ourselves with blankets and lay among the vegetables and cans of milk as the truck drove us to a private airfield outside Wangjiatuozitun. A small prop plane lifted us into a final bone-rattling flight to a small airfield outside Harbin.

Micah, who I decided had definitely been special forces, led us on a stealthy ingress into the city itself.

Total travel time from Boston: twenty-five hours.

But because Harbin was twelve hours ahead of Boston, we arrived in a pre-dawn blackness two calendar days after we'd left. April 28 (afternoon) in Boston. April 29 here. It was so dark coming into the city, I figured we could have crept within yards of any Chinese troops guarding the laboratory and they'd have never known.

Even so, I almost stumbled out into some patrolling soldiers before Micah yanked me back.

I was shaken, dizzy. Something...not right about this.

I chalked it up to my overwhelming exhaustion, though, and followed our leader to the one-story house in Harbin was almost across the street from the laboratory compound.

Huge troop buildup happening there. Didn't seem right. Didn't...

"Move it," Micah hissed at me, and I hustled into our house with Xiaobo.

Inside, Micah and Britney took the single room with two beds, modern kitchenette, and television. Xiaobo and I got the hidey hole under the floorboards. It had a battery-operated lantern hanging from a hook on the wall and a battered old mattress on the floor.

Since it was only shortly after 3 a.m., I suggested to Xiaobo that he catch a half hour of sleep before he did whatever ritual he needed to do to set his day for a later jumpback. We had to strike before sunrise at 4:25 a.m.

He nodded and flopped down on the mattress with a sense of happy compliance that made me think I'd become his new, kinder Dr. Bent. Except I was also almost puking with feelings of dislocation and dizziness. Overwhelming fatigue. My mind racing under it all, trying so hard to tell me something...

Something like...

Oh shit. There they were. A second set of memories alongside my current ones.

I'VE BEEN HERE BEFORE.

The changes in my memories had only showed up at the point where we'd hit the dark outskirts of Harbin, and even then, not really until I almost stepped in front of that soldier patrol.

Because that soldier patrol *had not been there* the last time I was here.

The last time. Here. Physically here. Where my time-traveling nemesis had obviously jumped me back from.

I grunted and shut my eyes hard. Had to remember the future of that previous timeline. Get a sense of what had happened. What I'd learned.

But Jesus, I was tired. It was hard to concentrate. All I kept thinking about was that I didn't know how far the fucker had jumped me back in time. Was it just to the entry to Harbin? Or was it further back? My nemesis could have been shifting huge things in the world and I'd never know because I only saw the difference when I reached Harbin.

April 29, 2022, 3:08 a.m. here and now.

HOW FAR BACK DID I GO?

58

Kansas

April 27, 2022. Wenling's horse farm in Virginia. The imminent attack on SCATTER headquarters that Wenling had promised was underway.

At 2:00 p.m., Kansas had watched it live with Wenling on the latter's computer. It was being narrowcast from a concealed camera on Wenling's paid-off CIA man. A line of black sedans and two attack vehicles with conspicuous fake FBI badging had pulled to a stop on a quiet, treed road that ran through a research hospital campus in Belmont, Massachusetts.

They'd piled out the cars, spread out, and started advancing on the building.

Then the land mines and automatic gunfire had started shredding bodies. The footage got shaky as its cameraman took cover. At 2:05, Kansas shook her head in disgust at all the mess resulting from obviously poor intelligence. She excused herself from the day room to check on Garvey.

The treacherous CIA section head was still in the main hall, breathing but lapsed into unconsciousness. Col. Fang had assured her the man would survive.

Fine.

Kansas checked on him anyway, then walked to the front door and looked out, seeing the normalcy of the day. The unmoving nature of the clear blue sky. The smell of the peaceful green fields and paddocks. The distant whinny of horses.

While in Belmont...

She collected herself and returned to southwest day room.

While she'd been gone, Wenling had changed into a long white satin pantsuit with low decolletage and matching slippers and now stared stiffly out the twenty-foot windows of the day room at the same peaceful scene Kansas had breathed in. On the low table beside her, the booms and overlapping sound of automatic gunfire continued to sound from her laptop.

"Well?" Kansas asked. "Has anyone gotten inside yet? Other police arrived? News teams?"

Wenling spun around and her beautiful face flushed with rage and tears. "They're all going to die!" she said over the sounds of battle.

Kansas felt a seismic shift in her belly. Not just from Wenling's expression or words, but from...what? "Who?"

"All of them. The CIA. Jackson. Xiaobo." The words made the Chinese woman's face scrunch up tighter, eyes blinking hard.

No! Kansas' head swam. Her breath grew thin. *This isn't right. This isn't what* happened. "What's going on?"

"Bent called Poussaint somehow. My man listened in. Bent offered to stop killing Poussaint's men if they withdrew. He said 'Wenling's brat' and Jackson Traine were already dead. And since they were the only ones with any real power, why didn't Poussaint piss off?"

"A lie." More than just a lie, though...

"Probably. It was enough to send Jackson's fat Jew friend—but not so fat now—running forward like he could dodge bullets and landmines."

Kansas felt a chill go through her. "He couldn't."

"No."

Of course not. Because... "A lot of people are dying on both sides."

Wenling nodded once. "Many, many. I thought Bent would run. Why didn't he run?"

As Kansas' former lover turned from her to stare out the window, still not bothering to watch the smoky, jerky footage, Kansas broke out in a sweat and...

Things suddenly clicked together in her head.

I'VE BEEN HERE BEFORE.

Before Lena's newspaper experiment, she would have written it off as a waking dream or déjà vu. But if she accepted it as a memory she somehow shared with herself from a different timeline, she realized now she could remember what had to be a previous timeline precisely.

When she'd walked back into this room, Wenling had been almost gleeful as she watched the destruction. She'd told Kansas that Bent had called Poussaint to offer a ceasefire because Xiaobo and Jackson Traine were no longer in the country. But if Poussaint accepted a truce, Bent could tell Poussaint where they had gone.

Wenling had cheered and stabbed her finger at the screen to show how the CIA team was close to breaching the building's doors. She'd laughed at how either side could still kill off the other, but she'd find a way to use it whichever way it went.

Then she'd thrown her arms around Kansas and kissed her like she'd done when she'd called herself Elizabeth, passionate and exotic and impossible to deny even in all her narcissistic psychopathy. It had made Kansas shiver with an excitement and self-loathing so strong she'd almost collapsed on the floor. And still she'd run with Wenling to a bedroom where they tugged off their clothes in desperate abandon and...

Kansas shook her head, not wanting to keep sharing memories of that other timeline and the way she'd acted.

It cut the connection with that other timeline.

Good. *Good!*

She'd stick with this timeline. The one where Wenling was angry and un-available, and Kansas might have a great big aching hole in her heart that would never be filled but at least she had her dignity.

"Kansas!" Wenling snapped now, demanding she be paid the attention she assumed was her due. She pointed at her open laptop. "Look at what's happening here!"

But Kansas shook her head. Her phone was buzzing in her pocket.

She pulled it out, shocked to find it was a secure connection from an unidentified location. Her heart skipped a beat because the only person she'd given that protocol to was Lena. But the caller didn't have her signal ID.

She touched "Accept" and held it up to her ear. "Who is this?"

A dreamy voice she'd thought she'd never hear again came on the line. "Heyyy, sis."

"Kenny? How do you have this... How did you call me?"

There was a pause and she realized she heard the muted sounds of booms and gunfire on the line. He was somewhere near the action in Belmont. "Yeah, look. Okay?" he said. "Long, long story. Not important. Crazy stuff here, right? Gotta tell you something."

Nothing but heavy breathing. Kansas prompted him. "Kenny? Can you get away from the building? I'll come get you."

"Whah? No! No. Ungh. Look, you gotta stay where you are, okay? It's one of the best realities. A person should hang onto those."

"Like I have a choice?"

"You don't…? Right. Yeah. Baby brother, though…"

"Jackson."

"Yeah. It's all up to him now. Middle of a widening gyre. The center cannot hold, right? William Butler—"

"Yeats. *The Second Coming.* Yes. What's that got to do with…?"

"He needs to, you know, go through…*all* that shit so he can find it. The perfect…"

"What, Kenny? What's he trying to find?"

There was a tortured sigh on Kenny's end of the line. "He's just doing his *best.* Get Lena to tell him that, okay? Find a way. A time. Before we all forget? We're going to forget."

"How does Lena…? Kenny! Kentucky!"

The line went dead.

She lowered the phone to find Wenling standing directly in front of her. Intense. "Your other brother," she said. "The one who was a drug addict. You thought he was dead."

"Step back," Kansas said coldly, her mind whirling through all the implications of what Kenny had said. Considering hundreds of possible scenarios. Shaving it down to Kenny's one clear message. Jackson needed something from Kansas, but it had to come from Lena. Now. Did that mean…?

Wenling hadn't moved. "This is my house. You tell me what's happening!"

"Step back now or I will walk through you."

After a beat, the shorter woman stepped back and dropped her face into an admirable imitation of a hurt puppy. "What are you going to do?" she simpered.

Kansas decided to give her this much: "I'm going to find someplace quiet to dictate a long, careful letter, about you, me, Lena and her friends, and Jude. I will then send it to the one person I think might actually be able to share it with Jackson. Then I'm going to take Garvey back with me to Washington, DC, along with the list he gave me. I know a few people in the DOJ."

A series of micro-expressions flashed over Wenling's face and Kansas realized she'd have to watch her back with this letter. But the tack Wenling settled on seemed almost pleading. "What about me?"

Kansas snorted. "I don't know, Elizabeth. I guess you be you. But not near me."

She turned her back on Wenling and walked out.

59

Lena

THE SPY MOVIE SAXOPHONES on Lena's phone brought her struggling out of a dream of wandering lost through a confusing department store with no exits. She blinked at the unfamiliar bottom of an upper bunk bed, then the rest of the dark room before remembering the where and when. Harbin. Dr. Wang's condominium. The last night of the "home stay" portion of her post-flight quarantine. She'd called Kansas before going to sleep and then…

The phone?

Suddenly wide awake, she scooped it off the child-size table beside the small bed she lay on and saw it was 2:58 a.m. A little over an hour ago, after she'd been sound asleep, Kansas had sent her an encrypted email that had dinged just like this. Lena had opened it to find a mind-blowing list of SCATTER True Believers. Lena almost hadn't been able to fall back asleep after that, so if this was more…

Yes! From Kansas again. Another encrypted message.

She opened it and felt her heart speed up with the first sentence.

This document and the list of True Believers are to be shared with Jackson when you see him, along with a message from his brother: *You're doing your best.*

What?

She gave the new document a quick scan and found it contained a long, dry account of everything Kansas knew about what had been done, seen, and heard by all the people helping Lena look for Jackson since SCATTER had taken him.

It ended with the revelation that a CIA strike team was, as Kansas wrote this, attacking SCATTER headquarters in Belmont, Massachusetts. Jude had been part of the attacking force and died heroically. As had many CIA agents so far. It wasn't clear who was going to win this fight. It seemed likely, though, that Jackson was no longer in Belmont.

Which meant what? Jackson was free? That Lena should fly back to the States so he could contact her, and she could give him the list? Or did it just mean that Kansas was giving up or dying? Kansas didn't think she'd see Jackson again so...

In a sudden terror, Lena tried to contact Kansas using their special protocols but got nothing. No answer. That could mean anything. She was on the move again. Or not in a secure place to answer. Or dead.

Lena made herself turn her terror into frustration. These impossible-to-pin-down Traine siblings. They were smart and charismatic, but damn hard to have solid relationships with.

She breathed it out into the room's darkness, put her phone back on the table, lay back into her disturbed sheets, and tried to fall asleep again. Even if Jackson wasn't in Belmont, he might still be captive. And before Lena went running back home on a wild hope, she needed to tie up the lead she'd found here. Interview the first SCATTER subject and ask him how he escaped.

Which meant getting some sleep and being truly ready for tomorrow. Well, today, but after sunrise. Simple, right? Ha!

Yet amazingly, the stress of Kansas' communiques and the promise of the day to come actually seemed to cancel each other out and Lena was asleep in minutes.

At 7 a.m., she was up and dressed in a maroon top and black travel pants. She quietly opened the door of the kids' bedroom where Dr. Wang Shěn had and his wife and two kids had let her sleep, fed her, and entertained her with stories through the door.

"Ah, there you are!" the professor's light voice called happily as she stepped out. Wang hurried down the narrow hallway to greet her. He was almost exactly Lena's height, but as fine-boned as a bird. His outgoing good nature more than made up for any appearance of weakness or delicacy, though.

And made it understandable how he'd landed the beautiful, gracious schoolteacher, Wang Yǔxī, who'd caught up to him and now stood at his elbow to celebrate their guest's emergence.

Both were unmasked, so Lena discretely tossed the mask in her hand into the room behind her. She forced out the sudden flood of anxiety she'd felt last night when reading Kansas' messages, took a deep breath, and gave each of her hosts a little head bow. "Good morning, Dr. Wang. Ms. Wang."

Wang and his wife shared a smile, then shook their heads at her. "Please call me Yǔxī," said the latter. "You are family now." She spoke with the same British accent her husband had but hadn't mastered the "l" sounds like her husband.

"And please call me Shěn," her husband added. "We will call you Lena."

Then it was into their small living room where their two kids, five-year-old Biyo and her younger brother Qian, practiced their English greetings on her. Especially, Qian, with his enthusiastic, "Weh-come! Weh-come!"

Lena took one of his pudgy hands and said, "Your English is so good," she said and found herself helplessly mimicking the boy's nodding and grinning.

When both kids were back at their play, coloring and building houses from blocks, Lena asked Yǔxī, "They'll be going to school soon? Do you take them?"

Yǔxī and Shěn exchanged looks, then Shěn explained that school was canceled for the day.

"Because..." Lena asked.

"Something military. Truckloads of soldiers rolled into the city last night."

"You don't know what for?"

Shěn shrugged.

Yǔxī sighed and waved her toward the kitchen. "Come. I will make the *jiānbing guǒzi*."

Biyo and Qian in Chinese chorused what sounded like "she" and "how" from where they played with their coloring book and building blocks, respectively. These savory burrito-like breakfast meals were favorites of theirs. And Lena's.

But on this first non-quarantined morning she'd had to spend with the Wangs, a gentle, knock on the apartment door interrupted the proceedings.

It repeated.

Again, Yǔxī and Shěn exchanged looks. Shěn squared his shoulders and walked to the door. He peered through the door's peephole, drew back with confusion on his face, then opened the door.

Wenling understood Shěn's confusion when she saw the man in the doorway. He was neither White nor Chinese. Taller than Shěn, of average build, he looked Middle Eastern, the first she'd seen in China other than herself. And the man was a puzzle in other ways. He wore blue jeans and a peach-colored turtleneck sweater. Old scars crisscrossed his hands and face. But above all, he radiated an amazing calm, like some kind of holy man or mystic.

When his soft eyes looked past Shěn to Lena, though, it all came together, and she knew who he had to be. His cousin must have reached him somehow and warned him she was coming.

"Dr. Cortland," he said in a voice as gentle as his eyes. "I am—"

"Salim Noor al-Rashid," Lena said.

"Yes. Salaam alaikum."

"Wa alaikum assalaam," Lena replied automatically, surprised at how easily the habits her mother had drilled into her decades ago came back. "How did you find me here?"

"You gave me the address."

"I—"

"In a different timeline."

"A different..." Lena let it trail off and glanced at Yǔxī standing interested but clueless beside her. Then she looked at Shěn and saw his eyes sparking with curiosity. Forestalling his questions, she said, "Oh, of course. The email chain. We'd arranged for...breakfast?"

Al-Rashid ducked his head in acknowledgment.

With a flush of relief, Lena nodded too and turned to Shěn and Yǔxī to give her apologies. She collected her shoulder bag and trench coat from her room, made a quick pit stop in the bathroom, then followed Al-Rashid out the door.

She waited until they were down on the street and walking quickly south before asking, "We've met once before? More than that?"

"Only once," he said, quietly, pointing discretely around them and miming being listened to and watched. "It was a delightful meeting, a gift from Allah, but too short. I thought it would be our only one."

Lena lowered her volume to match his. Chinese military vehicles sat both north and south of her on the street, she noted. They weren't stopping the flow of morning traffic, but it had to slow to divert carefully around them on the two-lane street. "Was our meeting short because I am a non-*mahram* woman?"

Al-Rashid flashed a genuine smile, as if this were a marvelous joke. "I wonder at the Muslims you met as a child. Even in America."

"We took trips to Iran."

"Your mother's parents. Yes. The ayatollahs and imams all have their own interpretations of the Qur'an."

"I told you a lot."

"Many things and not enough."

"Which is why you came to collect me."

"And things have changed," he said. He glanced at her as they walked, and this time it was not amusement that showed through the deep serenity of his face but a deep concern that did not seem a usual part of his makeup.

"Are you going to tell me?" she asked. "Somewhere...quieter? A park?"

He shook his head. "The military watches these today."

"Because...?"

"When we reach our destination, I will tell you."

She nodded and marched in focused silence beside him, ignoring the cool, sunny spring weather. The main environment was the military crack-down. Was that the thing Al-Rashid was here to "fix?" His cousin didn't suggest Al-Rashid was a revolutionary, but maybe? The only other thing Lena knew was happening in China was COVID.

They'd turned a corner to walk east, then back to walking south again along a road with a broader, four-lane road. The sidewalk was clearer, but the military presence was still visible. Another few blocks on, they turned and walked west again. Al-Rashid finally led her to the door of an apartment building in what looked like almost the heart of the military build-up.

"Won't they...?" Lena began.

"They will assume we are man and wife. Similar skin and so different from them. What else could we be?"

Lena searched for a hint of humor or bitterness in Al-Rashid's voice but found neither. He was simply stating a perceived fact. And Lena, having never dated Middle Eastern males, could only assume he knew what he was talking about.

He keyed them into the building, and they took the elevator to the ninth floor. From there into a sparsely furnished bachelor apartment that smelled of spicy cooked chicken and onions from a covered pot on the small stovetop. It made Lena's stomach growl. The room looked out the back of the building. West, she calculated.

She was about to go to the window when Al-Rashid shook his head and stepped past her to close the cheap horizontal blinds.

"If you would be so kind, wash your hands in the sink, then sit," he said. He gestured first to the sink of the kitchenette, then to the small table with two chairs that sat halfway between the kitchenette and bed.

He waited while she washed her hands and dried them with a proffered towel. As she went to sit, he washed his hands before pulling down two bowls from the kitchenette's open shelves. He lined their bottoms and sides with what looked like torn pieces of pita bread and filled them with the soup she'd smelled entering the apartment. When he brought them over with spoons, she saw it was indeed chicken and large slices of onions, but even more chickpeas, in a dark spicy broth.

The moment he sat across from her and picked up his own spoon, Lena dove in with an ungracious speed that surprised her.

When their breakfast ended, the conversation began. Al-Rashid assured her he had carefully checked the apartment and disabled two listening devices and one overhead camera. "But still, quiet speech. The walls are not thick."

Then he told her of their former meeting and all she had shared with him about herself, Jackson, their adventure into time traveling, and how it had ended with Jackson being forced to surrender himself to Dr. Uwe Bent, the same monster who had helped to trigger Al-Rashid's own ability to time travel eighteen years ago.

Finally, he shared, in a carefully vague way, the virus doomsday event that had made him leave his peaceful, obscure existence as a happily married teacher in Baghdad. How it had made him jump back in time to before the doomsday event, and travel here to Harbin to stop it from happening.

By the time he finished describing how he'd identified and worked with the chief scientist in the Harbin virology laboratory to stop the theft of the virus, over and over, Lena was almost jumping out of her skin in scientific excitement.

"Wait. Two time travelers, then. One pulling the other back with them when they jump. How...?" she asked, then interrupted herself. "No, wait. Before that, let's start with this: Just how far back in time can you jump?"

"I think the longest was sixteen days."

"Because…? I mean, what's your anchor point? Jackson has this perfect memory, so his mind or soul or self jumps back to a time he remembers everything about. Like a superattraction. Is that…?"

Al-Rashid was nodding. "Yes. I have always *lived* certain smells, tastes, beauty, sensations more deeply than others. My mother thought it made me holy, that I should be an imam. I did not do this. But my memory of these sensations, I think they are so powerful sometimes that they may be the anchors you speak of."

"But not past sixteen days."

Al-Rashid gave a small smile. "Perhaps not. Perhaps they become buried under other wonderful sensations after that much time."

Lena was up and walking about the room, eager to look out the covered window but even more to explore what Al-Rashid was implying. "If someone had perfect memory, though, even back twenty years, say, and they knew how to reach this anchor point…"

"You are referring to your Jackson."

"Of course. Yes. But right now…"

"He only jumps back ten minutes at a time."

"Yes! I told you that? Of course I did. So why does he have that limit?"

"Perhaps it is the will of Allah."

"What?" Lena spun where she'd been pacing and stared at him. He sat relaxed and still in his chair as he had throughout her excited questions. "You're not serious?"

He gave her another small smile that this time looked incredibly sad. "I do not know exactly how Allah works in our lives, but it may be He is waiting for Jackson to find a balance between the distance and connection, nothingness and joy. How else to explain how someone you describe as so loving and so loved can be so lost?"

Lena stared at him, trying to process what he'd just told her. "How…do you know he's lost?"

"I saw him. Face to face. Tomorrow. Matching the picture you showed me in our first meeting. He is leading the attack to unleash this deadly virus on the world."

"No. You're saying Jackson…" Lena looked down, remembering the message from Kansas. Had she known? Lena's heart began racing in her chest. "Tell me what happened."

Salim nodded. "I will tell you, Dr. Lena Cortland."

60

Salim Noor al-Rashid

I WILL TELL YOU, Dr. Lena Cortland, so you will understand what must happen next and why I will ask you to do a difficult thing.

The chief scientist of the virology lab, Dr. Ying Fāng Lì—I told you I persuaded her to trust me and make preparations to stop the soldiers who wanted to steal the deadly virus from the laboratory.

What I did not say was that after the third timeline, when the soldiers believed the special virus was no longer in Harbin, they seemed to give up. Yet their time traveler still jumped back to the beginning of the raid, dragging me back as well.

Ten minutes back, to just before the raid began. As he had done *every other time.*

Yet in this fourth timeline, there was no attack.

Victory, yes?

But for the Dr. Ying who only lived in this fourth timeline, there had never been any attacks, and her trust in me was shaken. Yet when I asked her again to actually destroy the virus forever, she recalled the proofs I had given her of my powers to see things other men could not. So, she invited me to actually enter her virology laboratory the next morning and see the special virus was safe and would never leave the lab.

The time she chose was strange, 4 a.m., before sunrise, but I reasoned it was because no one else would be there, and my presence would not be recorded.

Indeed, the grounds of the virology lab, which sometimes bristled with guards, lay empty and silent. The spotlights that lit the front of the building shone no brighter than the cold dawn in which I saw my breath.

Yet at least one light was on inside the laboratory building, so I approached its front double doors and knocked.

At that moment, a dark delivery truck rumbled to a halt in the front gap between the virology lab and the south guard building.

As I turned around to see it, less than thirty yards from where I stood, its rear doors opened, and twelve soldiers came running out in familiar clothing. They had their guns up, scanning the guard buildings, then scanning me. This close, I could see they had binoculars which reached down from their helmets over their eyes. Maybe to see in the dark.

Behind them, last out of the truck, walked an odd pair of men. One was short and clearly Chinese. The other was tall, thin, and fit, with light hair. They did not wear uniforms or binoculars over their eyes, though the taller man wore a headset like the soldiers.

I recognized this taller man from the picture you showed me in our first meeting. He was your love, Jackson Traine.

He seemed alert and focused, but unnaturally calm. As some of the soldiers spread out around me and the front door, while some ran around either side of the building, Mr. Traine, with his left hand on his short companion's shoulder, walked toward me, eyes staring into my eyes.

Then, suddenly, the entire area flooded with light. The front doors opened behind me, and two men grabbed my arms and dragged me into the lab building as guns all around me opened fire. The men threw me to the floor behind an overturned desk where Dr. Ying also huddled, her hands over her ears. It was so loud—guns thudding, people screaming. The vinyl floor was cold and hard.

Soldiers fell beside us, gushing blood from bullet wounds.

I grabbed Dr. Ying's wrists to pull them from her ears so I could shout, "How did you know?"

She shook her head in fear.

I squeezed her wrists. "How did you know to bring the army?"

"They to catch you!" she screamed and pulled herself away from me.

Sadness rushed over me, and I muttered a prayer to Allah in my humiliation. I thought I had made Dr. Ying my ally, but I had not. I had just scared her enough to call for my capture. Also, I thought I had fooled the time traveler into leaving this place alone, but he had shown his horrible face in person and seen mine.

Was there any way to stop this man who could not be tricked and would not stop until he destroyed the world?

I peeked over the desk and witnessed carnage in the front doorway as bodies screamed and staggered, firing their guns even as they died.

Into the middle of it, Jackson Traine walked like the invulnerable Garta, the muncher. He walked with his hand on his shorter companion's shoulder. Both men were shot and bleeding badly. The companion, a mere boy he seemed, eyes streaming tears, begged his stone-faced master to leave, but your love did not seem to hear.

I raised myself up higher to entreat him. Caught his eyes.

A new string of bullets tore holes in his chest.

He stumbled.

Go! I urged him.

He squeezed his companion's shoulder, and I felt myself ripped from that timestream...

To this one.

Or perhaps not this one precisely because I found myself only back in my room, with the clock showing 3:40 a.m. Jackson and his companion had pulled me back more than ten minutes! But it was not enough. This man and his small army would come again and again unless I stopped him completely.

No, do not protest. It is not what you think. Hear me out.

I first created yet another timestream, traveling in time to the night when I thought the attacks were done for good. Surprising Dr. Ying as she left the laboratory, I told her what she did in the future, and what Jackson Traine and his team of soldiers were going to do.

I believe she will contact the military again, but not to capture me. I think it will be an overwhelming force to stop Jackson and his team. Perhaps China even has its own time travelers who are pushing their leaders to do this.

Yet even this will not be enough because it is only one timestream. Jackson Traine, like me, can keep creating new timestreams.

Unless he *chooses* to stop, I am sure he will find a way to doom us all.

This, Dr. Lena Cortland, is why I must ask you to do a difficult thing...

61

Been here, done that

At 3:40 a.m., Xiaobo awoke and did a smooth Tai-chi-type dance that he called *Qigong*. It involved lots of breathing, humming, and muttering Chinese phrases to himself with each movement. Total concentration. Total relaxation. Establishing a calm Xiaobo to whom he could time travel back later in the day if need be.

I chewed on a mealy chocolate energy bar as I watched him, appreciating the practiced way he established the destination he could jump back to. Hell of a lot nicer than most of the states *I'd* been forced to use over the past couple of years. Jump back to peace. Back to who you are. Unless you don't know who you are anymore.

But at least I now remembered everything I'd *done* the last time I was here.

Xiaobo had napped, woken, done this anchoring shit, and we'd called Strike Team Leader Captain Harlan Bannerman who'd advised his team was ready to go and the site looked quiet. I'd gone up the ladder with Xiaobo, said goodbye to Micah and Britney, and walked out to casually climb into the dark brown delivery truck that had pulled up outside our door with the strike team and a shitload of advanced electronic communications gear inside. They also had a headset for me so I could follow the fight by the chatter, even if I couldn't see it all.

I gave the order, and the driver rumbled us into the compound. Bannerman, as round-faced and glaring as his picture, threw open the back doors. He and his mighty eleven, an increase I'd suggested, streamed out in full combat gear. Most headed straight for the apparently unguarded front door of the lab where... Wait. What?

A lone man in jeans and a turtleneck sweater stood with his hands raised in total shock.

A Middle-Eastern man.

Shit. *Shit.*

I walked out of the van with my hand on Xiaobo's shoulder as my lifeline, sensing this could go bad fast.

It did.

The virology lab's front doors flew open to reveal a mini-army inside. They grabbed the Middle-Eastern man and dragged him inside even as they began firing. My team also began firing. I began walking, taking Xiaobo with me.

It made no operational or logical sense. But my gut told me instantly who this Middle-Eastern man was. Out here like this, waiting for us? It had to be my nemesis, the time traveler who was better than me, always a step ahead. Because he'd had almost as many years as Xiaobo to perfect his technique, hadn't he?

Salim Noor al-Rashid.

Somehow, he wasn't dead like Wenling wasn't dead. I didn't know how he'd done it, but he was a fucking time traveler, so...of course.

I had to reach him.

Xiaobo and I walked faster toward him, into the hail of bullets. But we were time travelers, and this was just one stupid timestream in a million. What happened to this set of bodies didn't matter. Getting to Al-Rashid did.

It hurt, though. Bullets cut into my leg and arm and gut like knives, so fast I couldn't tell if I'd been shot by the Chinese or my own guys.

And Xiaobo was screaming at me, I think. Wanted to jump. But I ignored him. I had to look into the eyes of my nemesis. Speak to him. To be sure...

I was in front of the door when Al-Rashid's bearded face shot up from behind an overturned desk and our eyes met.

He knew.

I knew.

Then a spray of bullets raked my chest. I squeezed Xiaobo's shoulder and...

Yeah. Back to this hidey hole. That was Xiaobo. But then we'd been jumped back even earlier, to before we'd made it to Harbin. That jump had to come from Salim Noor al-Rashid.

Had he been jerking me back more than ten minutes through all my remote sessions too? I didn't think so. I hadn't felt it even once. And it fit my earlier ocean theory of time travel. If you were far enough away from the timestream change, and nothing in your perceptual world changed because of it, you might become part of a new timestream, but you'd never know it.

But if it changed something immediately around you, and you had a memory like mine, you knew.

Only...with this last time Al-Rashid had jumped me back, I didn't know how far back I'd gone. Because whatever Al-Rashid had changed *here* wouldn't have changed anything in my travels to get here. So I could have gone all the way back to London or even Boston and not known I was in a new timeline, that things were changing in Harbin—more troop deployments, apparently. Maybe SCATTER HQ could have seen it in the war room, but they wouldn't necessarily tell me unless it was need to know.

There was an angry thumping sound from the floor above and I instinctively leaped to the electric lantern and switched it off.

I heard Xiaobo freeze in the darkness to my right.

Had that been people pounding on the door to the house? That hadn't happened the last time we'd been here.

Above us, heavy, fumbling footsteps told me maybe both Micah and Britney had slept like Xiaobo. Micah's heavier footsteps went to the door. I heard him fumble with the latch. Probably with a gun close to hand. Probably with Britney in position just out of sight with her assault rifle cocked and ready.

A smashing sound—the door shoved forcefully open. Loud shouting in Chinese. Micah's voice responding in Chinese—another surprise—to explain, calm things down. The shouters at the door were having none of it. Their voices climbed registers of anger and anxiety that said they *knew* something. And they knew it because...

Oh shit. Al-Rashid hadn't just convinced more troops to be in Harbin; he'd obviously convinced them to get proactive and hunt us down before we attacked.

A thudding of semi-automatic fire erupted in the room above.

No quick wins, though. The battle lasted a little over a minute, with bullets thudding and bodies stomping around and falling on the wooden floor above us. That floor rattled and squeaked and shook down choking clouds of dust, coating me and, I assumed, Xiaobo as we stood blind and tense, ready to attack anyone who found the covered trap door that led down here.

Then silence.

More thudding.

Chinese voices.

Okay, that told us who'd won this little skirmish.

As Xiaobo and I waited, hearing each other's breathing now—*In...hold. Out...hold.*—I felt something dripping onto my head and reached up to feel it.

Water? No. Thicker. Oil? I rubbed it between my fingers in the dark then brought it to my nose. The scent crawled into my throat and made me instinctively gag.

Blood. Soaking through the floor above me. Charming. I stepped to one side.

Another fifteen breaths.

There were sounds of crashing furniture overhead and boots dragging stuff out the door. Slamming it behind them as they went.

Ten breaths later, I turned on the lantern, checked my watch, and looked at Xiaobo. He was pale-faced but smiling a little maniacally.

"Did you get your anchor set?" I asked.

"Ready to rock and roll, yo!" he replied.

"Good."

I trotted to the bed Xiaobo had slept on. Picking up the blanket which he'd ignored, I wiped the blood from my head and hands.

Then I pulled my mission phone out of one of my sleeve pockets to call Bannerman, dialed, and held my breath.

62

D-Day

WE'D USED CELL PHONES with a VPN tunnel to link up in the last timeline, so I knew they worked. But in this timeline, the military *could* have disabled all the local cell towers and blocked all radio signals around the laboratory compound. I had a satellite phone as backup, but the soldier-to-soldier comms didn't have those.

I heard the connection and ringing from Bannerman's phone on the other end of my call.

Yes! I released my breath and nodded. If the Chinese only swept the nearby buildings within an hour of the attack, it didn't scream operational efficiency.

Bannerman answered. "Going to be noisy coming in the front."

"Alternatives?"

"Take out the north flank, blow a hole in the perimeter, swarm the back."

"That's not noisy?"

"Surprise noise is better."

"Okay. You go. I'll follow you in."

"Ready now. Attack?"

"Attack."

I hung up and looked at Xiaobo. "We gotta run."

He nodded, and we went up the ladder and out with barely a glance at the corpses of Micah and Britney. They lived on in other timelines. I didn't need them in this one.

The street was almost pitch dark. But the mission map and looming shape to my left gave me my bearings. We'd come out front of a row of older homes. The looming shape was a fifteen-story apartment building that was almost directly east of the Harbin laboratory complex. Which meant across the narrow street from us. And the north side of that complex where my strike team planned to enter was a forty-yard run diagonally to the right and around the corner. We'd be exposed as we ran, but I figured anyone who saw us might be distracted by—

Bah-DOOM! BOOM! BOOM!

The series of explosions, followed by rapid, shouts and screams, covered our run, the ground shaking under our booted feet, bits of concrete and maybe human debris spattering us as we went.

When we rounded the corner to the complex's north side and slowed, the scene was as chaotic as I expected. "Surprise noise" indeed.

The north wall that protected the rear of the five-story laboratory building had been breached in multiple places as if my strike team had launched all the rocket launchers or grenades from different points for maximum havoc. A fire burned just inside one of the breaches. That and flashes of gunfire from the strike team backlit the perimeter wall. The headlights of the brown mission truck backing up in our direction lit up the rubble and dust and scores of dead Chinese soldiers on this side. They looked so young, like kids who hadn't know what hit them.

I stopped for a second and stared. Unlike the cold acceptance of Micah and Britney's deaths, a part of me told me the slaughter here should have bothered me. Just like the chance of getting shot should have scared me, since a quick shot to my brain could snuff me out before my body had a chance to react. Then I'd be dead. Some other me in some other timeline I'd jumped from might continue on, but this me, this "I" would just...end.

Hunh.

Nope. I found no internal reaction to the dead Chinese kids or my possible death. Blame some of that on my extreme fatigue, maybe. The rest would have been from my changed understanding of the infinite timeline continuum.

Did it make me less human or just more effective?

Bad thing or good?

I made a note to track it as I went.

I started jogging forward again as the mission truck finished its two-point turn and roared out of there per standard operating procedure. Withdraw. Stay safe. Prepare for evac. Not that I'd ever stayed with one of these attacks long enough to see if that worked.

Where the strike team had to be advancing inside the perimeter wall, I now heard wild Chinese shouts over the gunfire. I figured they'd draw the attack as Xiaobo and I came in behind them. I put my hand on Xiaobo's shoulder in the new way we had of communicating in battle, and we turned to head toward the nearest breach.

But as we approached it, there was a distinct cracking sound like you might hear if you forcibly snapped a piece of fine china. And a *Pfft!* like rotten fruit splatting on a rock.

Xiaobo's shoulder shook under my hand and dropped.

I spun and dropped with him. He had a single dark hole in his upper chest, but his eyes were open wide and lifeless. His body made a sucking sound as I turned it, and I saw the sniper bullet had taken out half of his back on exit.

Why hadn't he jumped? There had to have been a second between his torso exploding and his mind dying for him to react. Where was his survival instinct?

Excuses. He was my responsibility. I had to jump back to save him.

Also, to save my extra escape hatch. I needed him.

But...ten minutes. Would I screw up the successful breach by something I did? And if Al-Rashid was watching me and in contact with the sniper, would he know my pattern and just have death waiting for Xiaobo ten minutes back? And why wasn't *I* dead? My thoughts raced through this, but surely the sniper could have re-aimed or even reloaded and re-aimed and shot me. Unless Al-Rashid wanted me alive. So they could capture me? Enslave and torture me? Or did they think Xiaobo was the only time traveler, and I was just a ride-along?

Didn't matter. Morality and need. Had to jump. But maybe, just maybe, I could confuse the sonofabitch by trying something new. Something I'd never tried before, but that fit with my new way of jumping.

I shut my eyes in a total release of connection and saw myself reversing back up to my feet, back from feeling Xiaobo fall. I heard the sound of the sniper shot. Went just five steps back and saw the delivery truck back up to roar off. Took in exactly what that looked, sounded, smelled, tasted, felt like in my body, and ordered myself to *go there...*

The delivery truck backed up. I blinked. Found my body.

I grabbed fully alive Xiaobo by the arm and yelled, "Run!" as I yanked him with me on a zigzagging run to the breach in the perimeter wall.

A hard sniper shot hit the ground to our left and in my emotionally disconnected state, I found that hilarious, but did not laugh or slow down. We leaped over stones at the easternmost breach to enter the perimeter wall. There we kept going until we hit the rear wall of the lab building itself. Harder for a sniper to shoot us at that angle if he was in the building.

I saw Bannerman and most of his team fifteen yards west, night vision down from their helmets and headphone mikes in place, mowing down the last of a small army of Chinese at the building's west corner. I caught his eye and gave him a thumbs up.

Only after he'd given me a nod in response did I see the open second-story window between me and him where Chinese soldiers were positioning a heavy machine gun. Two of them held the leg braces for it. One had the sight and trigger. One managed a box on the gun's left side as the long barrel swung down.

"No!" I yelled and slammed myself and Xiaobo flat against the wall as hellfire rained on Bannerman and the others, wiping out most of the team in a clattering stream of blood and guts.

More Chinese soldiers appeared at the west corner.

More behind Xiaobo and me at the east corner.

We were so fucked.

Xiaobo and I were going to be shot any second and Xiaobo was just looking at me, waiting for an order. No. I wasn't risking screwing up my team's successful breach by having Xiaobo jump us back to the beginning of the day.

I slammed my eyes shut.

Walk it back. The team getting shot.

A bit more. Chinese soldiers in the window.

"AHHHH!" screamed Xiaobo as the soldiers finally saw us pinned to the wall and raked us with bullets. I just bore down harder into my calm mental experience of Xiaobo and I hopping over the last stones and running to the wall. Feel the wall. Smell, taste, hear, see it.

Go there...

Dizzy, but whole and not bleeding.

I grabbed onto myself and Xiaobo, also okay.

Bannerman was shooting the Chinese soldiers running around the western corner.

I yelled at him.

He looked back at me, and I pointed emphatically at the second-story window on the wall. He saw the soldiers there and ordered the two soldiers beside him to take them out. They did, but I heard another distinctive crack and a bullet like the one that had targeted Xiaobo now took out Bannerman. Head shot. He tumbled backwards.

Then *Crack!* Xiaobo went down again.

Blank face. Wiped out. Me still alive.

Again.

And again, Xiaobo hadn't jumped, or I'd have been dragged back with him. Unless he *had* jumped and one me had been dragged back, leaving *this* me clueless...

THIS WAS NOT THE TIME FOR MINDFUCKS!

Focus. The other strike team members, off-balance from Bannerman's death, were going down now in the second and third wave of Chinese coming around the opposite corners of the building.

The mission was failing again.

I had to... What?

I closed my eyes and *ran* backwards in time, looking for the right moment...when...*there! Go!*

Minimal dizziness this time, but mental exhaustion setting in. I gritted my teeth and shifted my grip to grab a fully healthy Xiaobo by his upper arm and pull him into a run with me.

The mission truck was reversing in our direction, and I waved my arms madly to catch the driver's attention. He obviously saw me in his rearview mirror because he stopped and let us catch him. I grabbed the handle of the back door of the truck and yanked it open, climbed in. I pulled it shut behind us with a thumping sound of the latch catching.

"Hail Captain Bannerman and warn him of a submachine gun coming, second-story window behind him!" I ordered the driver. "Then get back here and find me something to take out a sniper!"

As the driver spoke into what must have been a comm piece directly in Bannerman's ear, I breathed hard but blanked mentally. The next move. What was the next move?

The driver, a short, friendly guy about my age, finished and worked his way between the seats and back to us. "You know where the sniper is?"

"He's shooting at us both outside the perimeter wall and inside. Up high. From the east."

"You want to take out all the buildings across the street? Or just the top east floors of the bio lab?"

I stared at his blank face.

It cracked. "Kidding, sir. I don't got the ordinance for that. Give me an exact location and I can maybe shoot him out. Otherwise, no, and I gotta go. You want to come with?"

"No." I stared hard at the floor. Then up at the driver. "You got a spare assault rifle and comm headset?"

Without hesitation, he went back to the front seats and returned with a set of headphones and mike plus one of the chunky rifles I'd seen Bannerman and his team carrying. "Mine," he said about the rifle. "Make it count. Want a helmet?"

I shook my head. I wanted the sniper to know it was me so that he or she *didn't* take a shot. The gun was lighter than it looked. "AR-15?"

The driver looked suddenly worried. "M4A1. Basically the same, but shorter with selectable full auto." He pointed to the S-1-F (I guessed Safety, 1 Round, Full Auto) switch. "Don't use it, though, unless you're carrying lots of backup ammo, which you don't have. You've fired an AR-15?"

I shook my head. "Pistols and knives. Basic rundown?"

The driver hissed through his teeth but showed me the basic grip position and how to use the thermal optics. "5.56 mil, so not a lot of kickback. Use the thermal optics if you have time, but closer is always better, right?"

"Got it." I turned to Xiaobo, who was almost hanging on my arm like a puppy dog at this point. Maybe because he'd already been shot dead twice, and I'd revived him. "You're staying with the truck."

"What? Yo..."

"Too much going on. Force is spread too thin. I can't cover everyone. So, you *use your ability to save yourself* if it comes to that, okay?"

I was out the door before he had time for another objection, and I ran with the M4 slung around my neck like I'd been in training for the past three months and not locked up by a crazy (however noble minded) doctor who liked to slice off parts of my body to terrify me into time traveling.

Distracted by the chatter I was picking up on my headset, it took me an extra second to hear the helicopter thudding overhead. I whipped my head up and around mid-stride and stumbled to a halt, breathing hard, awed by the closeness of the rushing back body with the red bar-and-star of China on its side.

Then I realized it was roaring, head down, towards the fleeing mission truck I'd just left. A missile shot out of the canons on either side of its body with horrible hisses of orange flame and an instant later the truck jumped off its wheels in an explosion of light and fire and the stink of gasoline.

The concussive force knocked me back on my heels and I swore hard at the chopper as it swung around and headed back over the compound, flying low for intimidation. I'd felt no time jump from Xiaobo. I shrugged off the mindfuck from earlier. I knew I'd feel it if a version of me jumped, and I was the version of me that continued on. My sensitivity to other people's jumps made me sure of it.

But the number of PLA troops, their chopper, and my missing wing man meant that now we were not only clearly outnumbered and outgunned, but I once again had lost my last-chance reset mechanism.

He was also a kid I'd promised to take care of.

And for just a second, that last part tugged at the little bit of humanity I had left. I should jump back and...do what? Sneak Xiaobo out a side door so he could slip under the truck and not be seen when the truck took off to get blown up?

It could work. I'd be out almost as fast, lose only a few minutes.

Then the urgent cries and shouts came stuttering into my headset from the rest of my team and I began running again. There were other timelines, dozens, hundreds, thousands, where a version of Xiaobo was living and out his life, working with SCATTER or not, but not dying on the battlefield here with me.

Yes, it was a rationalizing mindfuck, but it was all I had. It meant *I* would never see Xiaobo again. The kid who'd come with me on our epic journey here? I'd failed him.

That left my thoughts as I reached the breach in the wall and hopscotched through it, jumping over dead bodies and rubble, fighting smoke in my eyes, blood slick underfoot.

I saw my team had blown open a rear door. I heard the sound of their gun battle inside.

I plunged in after them.

63

Lena

She took the binoculars back from Salim, as she'd finally started calling him after pressing him for hours last night about his plans and intentions. Did he *really* want to save Jackson after all Jackson had done, or was this some kind of setup? Wasn't there another way? How did his plan guarantee there wouldn't be a biological holocaust if the virus still existed at the end of it?

Around and around.

Salim was infuriating to argue with because he never lost his calm. Even when Lena raised his wife and kids and questioned his character and honesty. Or when she'd called Dr. Wang Shěn and told him she wouldn't be coming back to his apartment this evening because she'd decided to spend the night with Salim. He'd even nodded in understanding when she'd shown him the encrypted list Kansas had sent to her mailbox and whispered harshly, *"That's where I should be right now. Back there, dealing with this!"*

Like her heart would let her leave with Jackson almost in reach.

And that note in the beginning of Kansas' second message to her, the summary document of all that had happened that Jackson hadn't seen.

This document and the list of True Believers are to be shared with Jackson when you see him, along with a message from his brother: *You're doing your best.*

Had Kansas known Jackson was here? Because if she *had,* it gave a whole new and very disturbing meaning to that instruction.

Lena focused the binoculars through the window, scanning all around the laboratory building that was lit with spotlights mounted on Chinese military vehicles. The Chinese troops had finally changed from an all-out assault to a human perimeter. Half the soldiers now faced outward from the building to stop any more incursions, while half turned in to stop anyone leaving the lab building. The attack helicopter that had flown over the building five or ten minutes ago and blown up what looked like a delivery truck fleeing the area, still flew wide circles around the neighborhood as if looking for any locals who might be rushing in to get killed.

Inside the lab building, despite the desperate odds in this battle, there continued to be flashes of light which Lena assumed was gunfire. But she didn't get it. Or didn't want to.

"What's their exit strategy?" she asked.

"Perhaps they do not have one."

The calm way he said it made Lena shudder to the core, finally acknowledging the stakes here. She asked the logical next question anyway. "What's *our* exit strategy if we go in?"

At first, she thought Salim was just going to stare at her. Instead, he answered her question with a question. "Do you truly believe that each time I or Jackson or another of us travels back in time, we create a new timeline? A whole new existence?"

Lena swallowed dryly and nodded. She'd been afraid he was going there. As Jackson would say when he thought she wasn't listening, *Oh shit.*

She was ashamed to note she'd broken out in a cold sweat. "You and Jackson, you know, if things go to hell, you guys...carry on in a new timeline. I don't."

"This you. This I. I once believed I was fighting the will of Allah to change things that had happened. Now I understand, thanks to you, that His plan is so much more complex and filled with wonder than I had ever imagined."

Lena nodded. "But I'm still going to die, aren't I?"

"This you. This I."

No, she mentally fact-checked him. *Just me.*

Half an hour later, all signs of fighting had stopped within the laboratory building.

"It is time," Salim said.

Lena nodded. Her mouth had gone sticky dry again. She carefully stuffed her phone into her brassiere before straightening her maroon blouse and pulling her navy trench coat over it. Her shoulder bag stayed where it was, over the back of one of the kitchen chairs. It held mostly personal grooming items, gum, and mints. No personal information. Her card holder and passport, she'd stuffed into a pocket of her trench.

"They will find your phone," Salim said.

"We'll see."

They left the apartment, took the elevator to the ground floor, and went out the rear exit. They encountered no one until they crossed the dark street to the front of the laboratory compound. It was now blockaded by parked, backlit Chinese military vehicles of various sizes, all dark and menacing.

"Climb under?" Lena whispered.

"No. This way," Salim said and led Lena to the right, where a cohort of four Chinese soldiers blocked the one opening to the compound on this street.

The soldiers, all in their early twenties, blocked their way with raised rifles. The oldest-looking one shouted at them in Chinese.

Salim answered back with one or two basic Chinese phrases that Lena doubted answered whatever it was the soldier had asked.

"You! Wait! Hee!" said the soldier. Then he muttered to one of the others, who turned and ran into the compound.

In what seemed like an eternity of heart-pounding agony, the young soldier returned with a short female soldier who also carried a rifle and looked all of eighteen. She was fierce, though, her chin jutting up as she marched to stand before Salim. Her eyes addressed his beard.

"Who are you? Why are you here?" Her English was good, if high voiced and sharp. It was obvious why her peers had summoned her.

"We need to enter," Salim said calmly. "We can negotiate with the Americans for you."

The female soldier slammed her rifle butt down on the pavement. "What do you *know?!*"

"I am friends with Dr. Ying Fāng Lì, chief scientist in the Harbin virology lab. I warned her about the attack this morning."

The woman shook her head impatiently. "I do not know this person!"

"Your commanders and your general will. They will be grateful if I can speak to the American soldiers and make them surrender."

"Exactly," Lena blurted, then wished she hadn't.

The female soldier's gaze shot to her, and Lena saw, in the light from the compound, that the girl's expression noticeably darkened. The young woman's eyes flashed as she shouted something in Chinese.

In response, her male cohorts suddenly swarmed around Lena and Salim, with one male squatting to pat his way up Salim's leg, his crotch, all around his torso, his underarms, his neck.

Another male pulled off Lena's trench coat and his buddy performed a similar search on Lena, but assiduously avoided her crotch and breasts.

The female Chinese soldier noted this, shouted at him, and dragged him aside. She handed him her gun as he staggered back. She then jabbed her small hands into Lena's groin area, pressing, poking, and squeezing through the black slacks to make sure there was nothing there.

Then she went for the breasts.

"Wait!" Lena called out and reached into pull out her cell phone. "I had nowhere else to carry this."

The female soldier sneered, made a gesture, and one of the male soldiers grabbed the phone. Then the woman soldier's fingers were roughly unbuttoning Lena's blouse and yanking it open. She paused and turned to the snickering soldiers. Shouted at them in Chinese.

They shut up and looked away.

The female soldier shot her small hands forward and ran them inside Lena's bra, running them fully around the inside pocket and out, up and down the straps, front and back. Lena blinked at her, stunned as much by the speed and deftness of the search as its invasiveness.

"Close up!" the female soldier said.

"I need my phone," Lena said.

"No," said the female soldier.

"I need it to negotiate with the Americans. There are pictures on it that will convince them to surrender."

The shorter woman stared at her, chin jutting out in doubt and aggression. She motioned the soldier holding the phone to bring it over. "Show me," she ordered.

Lena did. Pictures of her and Jackson together. He was smiling in few of them, but the way he looked at her in many made her knees go weak and tears come to her eyes.

"Only him?" said the woman, snatching the phone from her.

"He's the leader," Lena said. "They'll do what he says."

The woman looked at Salim, who nodded and said, "This is true. Ask whoever spoke with Dr. Ying and brought you here."

The female soldier—*so young!*—frowned in deep concentration and the other soldiers waited on her as if she were already an officer. Finally, she nodded curtly, handed Lena her phone, and shot out a series of directions in Chinese.

Without explanation, they marched Salim and Lena, her heart pounding a wild dance of fear and excitement, into the compound.

But not toward the virology laboratory building.

64

More dark corridors

It was a reflection of my inner nightmare, I think, that I always ended up chasing or being chased in dark hallways. But at least I knew these hallways. I'd watched three assaults on them from my computer screen back in the Bent Wing in Belmont.

In person, even with my emotional detachment, they felt tighter.

I ran, ducked, jumped over dead bodies, and slid around corners as drywall chunked and cracked near me, riddled with bullets that missed or went through their targets. The only lighting was from the Chinese Exit signs and the gunfire. I assumed my team and maybe the Chinese, too, were still wearing night vision because no one had felt the need to turn on the lights. The shouts in my headset about keeping "them" on the lower floors just reminded me our ultimate objective lay up on the fourth floor.

As I ran, ducking into various rooms to wait out active firefights, I tried to pick out the players. I assumed the ones opposing the Chinese soldiers were my guys, but all the sputtering lighting meant I hadn't yet clearly ID'd anyone. I also wasn't sure "my" guys would actually recognize me before they cut me down as a hostile.

Because of that, when I passed an elevator with a stairwell beside it, I decided to take the stairs solo.

Bad choice maybe.

The stairwell had dim emergency lighting, which meant I stuck out like the pasty-faced *gweilo* I was when I went around a corner at the second-floor landing and face two Chinese soldiers clattering down toward me at high speed. I shot them on full auto, short trigger squeeze. They tumbled down towards me, making me step back, then forward with a jump over their corpses to continue up.

Murder? Preemptive self-defense? A part of my brain said my actions would have shocked me a year ago, maybe even a month ago. But this just was what it—

I heard another set of Chinese soldiers, talking loudly to one another, also coming down fast. This time I detoured onto the second floor. There I did another set of fight-dodging runs until I spotted another exit sign, which meant another stairwell.

Before I could reach it, gunfire and sounds of a rocket launcher somewhere made me duck into a room on my right.

A hand shot out and grabbed my ankle.

I heard wheezing. Even in the dark, I could tell the downed soldier was one of ours. He had bullet holes all over. His body armor had stopped most of the torso shots, but there were huge dark stains down his right side and his neck felt slick as I kneeled to lift his head and help him breathe.

Matching the face in that dark room to pictures of the team I'd seen in my mission brief should have been impossible, but a mist of dawn light seeping through the windows gave me just enough for an ID.

Seaman Antonio Perez, Navy SEAL's bottom rank. Got in on a SEAL challenge contract straight out of high school. Earned a Silver Star fighting the Taliban in Afghanistan before being dishonorably discharged from the military for desertion from a mission he claimed was about money, not national interest. Went into private security for a couple of years, married, had a son, then got recruited by SCATTER to help save the world.

He was twenty-six years old. A husband and father, but really just a kid. Only a little older than most of the Chinese corpses I'd seen so far.

"Hey, Antonio," I whispered.

"W-win," he said and died.

Sure.

I pulled off just his helmet, closed his eyes, then wiped my hands clean and put his helmet on my own head, pulling down the night vision goggles and finding they were still switched on.

Excellent.

I crept back to the door and was about to peep out when I heard a bunch of rapidly spoken Chinese that was obviously coming from some kind of loudspeaker outside the building. Had to be orders because the rattling gunfire from everywhere suddenly stopped. I heard running boots, followed by random spurts of gunfire.

Then...nothing.

I waited another ten seconds, then left the room and ran straight for the stairwell. The corridor I ran through was empty.

Swearing under my breath, I yanked open the exit door and almost collided with the four Chinese soldiers who were rushing to get through it. I leaped back, and they tore past me, not even bothering to wave a gun in my direction. I swung back into the stairwell and started running up the stairs like I could hear incoming missiles. Not that the commanders of the army outside, however impatient, would be stupid enough...

I had to get up to the fourth floor and the main BSL-4 room *now*. Find out what the hell was happening.

Go.

Go.

Go.

All sounds of battle anywhere in the building were gone as I reached the fourth-floor landing. I still kept the barrel of the M4 raised as I kicked my way out the door and slammed myself against the far wall of the corridor, then lowered it, swinging it left and right like I knew what I was doing. The hallways lights blinded me with my night vision on so ripped it and the helmet off my head.

When my eyes adjusted, I looked down the hall to where I remembered the Bio Level 4 room was supposed to be. Its door sat wide open, covered with red biohazard symbols. It couldn't close because a leaking female body in blue scrubs, face mask, and latex gloves sat slumped against it, head lolling to one side.

Shit. She was probably the scientist we needed to identify the bioweapon. If it had been one of my team who'd killed her, that was stupid. If it had been a Chinese soldier or commander, that was diabolical.

Except there'd been *two* female scientists in raids I'd watched from my cozy basement command center in Belmont, hadn't there? Where was the other one?

I could have used my headset to ask if we now held the main biolab, but something stopped me. A bad presentiment. Maybe even worse than the idea we were about to be bombed out of existence.

I walked with the best cat-like silence I could muster up to the door, gun still at the ready.

Looked in.

The room, mostly white and gray, held a whole shitload of high-tech gear bolted to metal tables. Oxygen lines ran overhead that I remembered were used to fill the positive pressure safety suits that protected their wearers from an environment of deadly pathogens that could easily escape if not handled properly.

I smelled urine, feces, and blood from the dead woman near my feet. Vomit from somewhere deeper in the room.

I walked slowly past her body to assess the two conscious bodies quietly waiting for me there.

One was a scrawny, black man—Petty Officer Lukas Schmidt, former SEAL. The other, a buff redhead—Second Lieutenant John Cultus, former Ranger.

Schmidt leaned back against a worktable, his right arm draped over some kind of toaster-size box that was blurting occasional static. A radio? He also had a camera on his helmet. The camera guy. I grimaced at it for Bent's benefit. Though if there was a backup repeater and Bent was watching all this, he'd been remarkably quiet. Not a word from him in my headset. And I *would* have recognized his voice. I'd recognize it whispering if I was sound asleep.

Second Lieutenant Cultus stood relaxed. His M4 hung loose but ready around his neck.

I finally turned to the third, unconscious, body in the room. She was duct-taped to a rolling chair, banged up, barely breathing. My South Asian translator back in Belmont had heard her call herself Dr. Ying. The mission brief had expanded on that. Her full name was Dr. Ying Fāng Lì, forty-three years old, a celebrated scientist who was vocally loyal to the Chinese Communist Party, though that may have been a purely career-required alignment.

"I'm Alpha Two," I said to Schmidt and Cultus. "What happened?"

Cultus spoke up. "Us and the Captain got here fast and questioned the two scientists. They were non-cooperative. The Captain shot the one by the door and thereby secured the cooperation of this one in the chair."

"You found the bioweapon? You completed the mission?" I looked around to identify the autoclaving oven amongst all the other machines.

"Pretty much," Cultus said.

"Meaning?"

"The Captain will tell you. Said he'd be back by the half hour."

I glanced at my watch. That was only another five or six minutes, but I was shocked to find the raid had started almost forty minutes earlier. There'd be sunrise outside. Even in my emotionally detached state, there'd been enough adrenaline to distort my normal sense of time.

"Dr. Ying—is she alive?"

Schmidt took that one. "Just a little banged up."

Keeping Cultus and Schmidt in my peripherals, I walked over to Ying and squatted in front of her to examine her flopped-down hands, noting the blood under her nails. Then her arms and the bruises there. I felt around her ribcage and felt what had to be at least one broken rib. I felt around her jaw which seemed intact but swollen. Her breath was shallow and irregular. Maybe a concussion?

Without looking up, I asked, "What if I were to time travel back ten or twenty minutes and got up here quicker? Would that help?"

There was a fractional pause before Cultus said, "The Captain said you shouldn't travel back yet."

"Why?" I turned to see both men fully. Neither had moved.

"Said you wouldn't want to miss what he's bringing back for you. Any time now."

Did this relate to the announcement that made all the Chinese soldiers flee? Whatever it was, it wasn't in the mission brief and hadn't happened in any of the previous missions here I'd watched.

Of course, I'd never stayed this long in any of them.

Probably shouldn't be staying this time either.

Something was definitely—

A clomping, shuffling sound came from the hallway and I, Schmidt, and Cultus all snapped into ready mode, rifles ready.

But the sight that appeared at the door of the lab was *not* what I expected.

Bannerman and a red-faced, heavily sweating lieutenant, James Emmanuel, escorted two prisoners into the room with their hands bound tightly behind their backs, the bonds tied to a leash held by Emmanuel.

"Jackson!" cried out the first in a voice that I'd missed so much.

"*Salaam*," said the second.

65

How the world ends

"Alpha Two," said Bannerman in his no-nonsense greeting. If it hadn't been for his man holding Lena and the man I'd pegged as Salim Noor al-Rashid on a leash, he might have been just acknowledging my leadership and about to give me a report.

This clearly wasn't that.

"You found the bioweapon?" I asked.

Lena started to speak, but I gave her a look and she stopped. Waited along with me.

"We did." Bannerman strolled deeper into the room, not in my direction, but to the north end, where the freezers were. He rubbed his throat. "Not in with the regular samples, though." He stopped short of the first freezer and felt along the bare wall hung with racks of equipment, wires, and tubes running up to the ceiling.

His fingers found what they were looking for and he pressed.

A door whose seams had been hidden by the wall clutter swung inward with a hiss of decompression. Inside was a metal room maybe five feet wide with a set of empty storage racks. The walls ringed those with floor-to-ceiling nozzles that I presumed shot in coolant to freeze whatever was normally stored in there.

Bannerman massaged one of his hands now. "Secret door."

The sound of the door opening also seemed to rouse Dr. Ying from her unconscious state, and she groaned and fought to open her eyes.

"You know what it means," Bannerman continued. "They built this place *knowing* they were going to be working on stuff they wanted to hide. Isn't that right, doctor?" He threw the last question at Ying who was fully awake now and glaring with bloodshot eyes at the round-faced captain like she wanted to rip his face off and suck out his spine.

"We be *careful!*" she said. She coughed up a bit of blood. Spat it to the floor.

"So careful you'd already created and stored 1,841 little ampoules of it. Size of my pinky. Each one with a bit of your special Ebola in a solution of, what did you call it?"

"Glycerol," Cultus piped up.

"Right. To freeze them for transport."

"No transport!"

"At least not yet," Bannerman said, shaking one leg out like a dog that's just peed. "Which is why they weren't frozen when we found them."

I was more focused on the open fridge/freezer unit he'd just opened, though. It looked empty. "Where are those ampoules now?" I asked.

Bannerman rubbed his eyes, and I finally registered how red they were. "They're kind of all over."

"Meaning?"

"About five hundred of them are spread out in little pieces in a roughly four-block radius around this building. We only had 35 RPG warheads to pack them into. The ampoules are tiny, but we could still only fit about fifteen in each. Damn things kept breaking. The rest we just threw out the high windows. Crunched them underfoot. Used 'em for target practice."

He was breathing heavily and holding onto a table now. I suspected it was the longest speech this man had ever given in his life. His crowning achievement.

"You're insane!" Lena shouted, then grunted when Emmanuel hit her so hard with the butt of his rifle she fell to her knees. As she did, Emmanuel leaned over and vomited a green-and-brown noxious stream of bile. Staggered as he forced himself up again.

Lena tried to tear free, but I made a move with my hand, telling her to stay down.

Before I could say anything else, I was cut off by the screeching laugh of Dr. Ying. "You so stupid! You are dead now. We aw *dead!*"

I turned to her. "How long?"

She spat out more blood. "In the air. He breathe, you get it. Some fast. Forty minute it show. Fifty, sixty minute, you dead. Other slow. Carry it weeks. Kill everyone around. This strain not die. Take *hour* of super heat to kill. No bomb. No vaccine kill. You understand?"

I looked at Bannerman with his flushed face and trembling body. "Did this plan come from you or Dr. Bent?"

"I'll answer that," boomed out a precise, German-tinged voice from the box Schmidt was still carefully guarding with one arm as he aimed his helmet cam at all of us.

Fuck. Bent. Listening after all.

And no doubt watching everything through Schmidt's helmet cam.

Bent.

I didn't need to see his face in order to see his face. It was like he was standing right there in front of me in the Eurotrash midnight-blue velvet suit he'd worn in that basement ops room of the Bent Wing. Matching silk shirt. Sparkling red tie. Shoes the color of blood. Because he enjoyed wearing blood.

"Talk," I said.

"I must say, you've developed so much, Jackson," he replied. "So competent. So cool. Such a commanding presence. But you are geopolitically naïve. It's a shortcoming."

"Because I'd rather stop wars than destroy enemies?"

"Appeasement. Peace-making. Threats. Negotiation. It's no answer to a nation like Russia or China. Do you really think American big-stick waving deters them? It infuriates them! It's why they developed this weapon which they *were* going to use. 1,841 ampoules. Eighteen-forty-one. You know the date?"

I frowned, reviewing any articles or books I'd read on Chinese history.

Bent beat me to it. "The year China lost the opium wars to Britain and started a 'century of humiliation.' Of course, now America continues the humiliation, so the revenge had to include us. I suspect Japan was going to get its share as well. They were very cruel to China in World War Two. In Harbin particularly. Did you know that?"

"So, the solution is to hit them first," I said. "Wipe them out."

"I see the rifle you're carrying. Did you get up here without killing someone who wanted to kill you? If so, bravo. But why are you even carrying it? Survival, of course. It's not only right. It's a moral *imperative.* And here we're dealing with a country that wants to kill us. So, we're stopping them. We give them their own poison and quarantine the country so it doesn't spread. If Russia or another Chinese ally breaks the quarantine, we quarantine them, too. This will kill their economies and their peoples. It will let us save Ukraine. Then, after the virus has died out, we'll help rebuild Ukraine, and Russia, and China. Slowly like we did with Japan. In our own image. Reinforcing democracy and our place as the primary custodian of the world order. It's the American way."

"Well, hey," I said, pushing past the complicated feelings of guilt and anger that surprisingly coursed under my detachment. "When you put it like that, what's not to love? Except for one thing."

"What is that?"

I glanced over to see Salim Noor al-Rashid watching me closely. "Xiaobo and I will be dead. That means SCATTER loses its main power players, and you're back to being a fringe group that the FBI's going to hunt down and lock up one day."

Bent chuckled. It sounded odd coming out of the speaker resting under Schmidt's forearm. Especially with Bannerman now sweating profusely and curling over in pain. Emmanuel who'd already been struggling by the time he'd entered, was now rocking back and forth, red as a tomato, his face grimacing in pain.

And Bent was *chuckling?* "What's so funny?" I asked.

"You think I'd just leave you to die? I needed you to find the opposing time traveler, and you did. This Middle Eastern man in the room with you, obviously. The anomaly. I've reviewed the tapes. Saw your look of recognition. Now please get Xiaobo to jump you back to before this began. When you're back, you tell Bannerman about the Middle Eastern man, then leave the country. The plan was always to have the same people who brought you there take you back before the attack began."

"And let you go ahead and kill millions."

Bent shook his head impatiently. "Of course, you will. Once you think it through. Consider the alternatives. It's Hobson's Choice—meaning not a real choice at all. You stay here and you're dead. And Lena's dead. Is that what you want?"

I looked down at Lena, who was still on her knees, but shaking her head at me now. I could almost hear her telling me that *this* her would be dead anyway.

Yes! I wanted to shout back. *But so is every other version of you in every reality I can reach now!* We were past forty minutes from the time Bannerman took the bioweapon and started spreading it. More than that from the time he reached this room, with Lena and Al-Rashid already heading into this nightmare. And even though I'd learned to jump back without needing a trauma trigger, *and* I could now choose a specific jumpback point, the hard limit of each jumpback was still TEN MINUTES. And they still made me dizzy. Which meant the other hard limit—too many jumpbacks in a row close together would kill me—was also certainly still there too. So, jumping back now, over and over, even spacing them out as much as possible, would incapacitate or kill me before I got back far enough to stop Bannerman or save Lena. I couldn't even save myself.

Then what did Lena expect me to—

Oh. She'd heard Bent say *Xiaobo* would jump me back.

I looked back at the camera. "Xiaobo's dead," I said to Bent. "I'm stuck here. Dying. You're right that I've got no choice at all."

Silence. Bent and Lena taking in the situation.

Then Bannerman blarted another stream of vomit. He dropped to his knees, curled over in pain, and panted like a dying dog.

Al-Rashid, though, actually smiled at me. He reached down his hand toward Lena.

"What a shame," Bent finally said as Lena took Al-Rashid's hand. "Sergeant Emmanuel?"

Emmanuel, panting and clenching his teeth, did possibly the one thing in life he was good at. He swung the barrel of his M4 up behind Salim Noor al-Rashid's head so fast it barely registered and pulled the trigger.

The hard pop-spatter took out much of the time traveler's brain and most of the upper right side of his face. Al-Rashid's body fell forward, lifeless. There was no jump in time.

Lena screamed, covered in the gore of this man—her friend?—and let go of his hands, scrabbling away from him.

Without thinking, I lunged down to the ground beside her, holding her up as I'd done the one other time I'd seen her in this much existential pain, in a distant past when there was a future ahead of us to heal it.

"It's okay. It's okay," I said, holding her to me and stroking her hair.

Emmanuel had dropped to the ground finally, clutching his head and wailing, puking, crying out blindly. Bannerman now bled profusely from his eyes, ears, and mouth.

Schmidt and Cultus watched both of them with wide eyes, no doubt seeing what was coming for them.

I tuned everything out except for the one thing I actually cared about in this moment, however intellectually.

"Lena," I murmured into her hair, "I'm so sorry for everything. That it ends like this. I think I've loved you in a fundamental way from the first time you followed me to my campus office. When you were wet, and your hair frizzed out like..."

Her body shook in my arms, but it took me a second to realize it was laughter, not tears. Well, both tears *and* laughter in a kind of repeating cycle, I saw when she pulled back to look at me.

She brushed back her hair and the bits of gore still on her cheeks. "F-frizzy hair?"

Then she gasped and wiped her eyes and nose. Focused on me and frowned. She reached for the comm headset I still wore, pulled it off, and ripped the microphone from the receiver with so much force she cried out in pain. Then she leaned in close to me and whispered, "Get rid of every fucking way he can hear or see us."

I didn't get it, but okay? I rose and retrieved the assault rifle I'd fired once. It was still on full auto. I sprayed both Schmidt and Cultus with bullets before they understood what was happening. I went to both their bodies, removed and smashed their headsets with the butt of my rifle, then ground the pieces under my boot. Same for the camera and the separate radio Schmidt had been using.

I considered killing or at least knocking out the furiously squirming Dr. Ying but coldly decided it would be more just for her to die like Bannerman and Emmanuel. The duct tape holding her looked sound. She wasn't going anywhere.

Bannerman and Emmanuel, I noted, had stopped moving.

I walked back to Lena and sat down beside her, taking her hand. It was burning hot, and her face was flushed like Emmanuel's had been. Her breath sounded labored.

"Fever, sore joints, nausea," I said.

"No time for that. Reach into my bra." She grimaced at the look on my face. "My phone's there. The Chinese officers let me keep it because of the pictures of us. To help me get you to surrender."

I reached in and got it. She was like a furnace. Like her body was trying to make her explode from within.

"Oh my God," she grunted. She squeezed his hand and leaned forward with her eyes so tightly shut that tears flowed out. She took two deep breaths and forced herself to sit up again. "Give me the phone!"

He handed it to her, and she unlocked it with her thumbprint, then called up her downloaded documents and scrolled through them to what looked like a multi-page list of names, contact details, and descriptions. She handed him the phone.

"Two messages from Kansas," she said. "A list of the True Believers. A story of everything that's happened while you were captive. Read it all. Record it...in your head."

"But—"

"Please!"

I did. The list was extensive. Nine-hundred-twenty-one names. It included numerous military people from our own forces and those of several other countries, high-ranking people in each branch of our own and other governments, and both business and thought leaders worldwide. I'd only heard of maybe twenty percent of them, but they all took up permanent residence in my brain. Not that it meant much if that brain was about to expire.

And the "story." The terse prose stirred surprising feelings deep inside me. Pride. Gratitude. Love. A sense of the deep loss of these friends and, empathetically, the loss the survivors would feel for those of us who didn't made it. *Sorry, Jude.* I wasn't able to even *think* about losing Lena yet, even though she was right here in my arms.

Lena saw me nod, then grabbed the phone back from me, scrolled through the contacts, found one, and showed it to me. "Cousin of Salim," she said. "The man who..." She looked over at his body and couldn't continue. She leaned as far from me as she could and vomited, almost falling into it before I caught her.

"I know who he was. But I don't see the point of this." I could see the veins in her eyes almost rippling as I watched.

"It's this. You're going to jump back and create a timeline where Bent and his minions don't win."

"I can't," I said coldly. Logically. "It's too far. It's not just forty minutes back. It would have to be before Bannerman makes it up here and finds the bioweapon. But then what? Kill him and my entire team and let the Chinese rush the bioweapon out to all their enemy countries?"

"Destroy the Ebola!"

Dr. Ying heard that and broke into a sniggering laugh, still twisting back and forth to free herself for no good purpose. Both Bannerman and Emmanuel had stopped moving. Stopped breathing.

"It's not possible," I said evenly, letting my emotional detachment and intellect fully reassert itself. Knowing what was right and wrong and that I loved Lena with an essential core of my being did not change facts. This was the end.

Lena was blinking hard. She turned and spat out blood. She tried to look into my eyes, but apparently found it too hard to focus her own so just closed them and squeezed my hand hard and put all her energy into speaking. "S-S alim..."

"I know."

She shook her head and bore down. "Salim could jump back days, weeks, months, without any kind of strain. He said it was because...he found the middle way between distance and connection, nothingness and joy. But he didn't jump often. I think he thought if you jump too often or too far, you lose yourself. But maybe if you just start with smaller jumps, then..."

"With each one creating a new timeline where you and millions of Chinese innocents die."

"Christ, Jackson! Starfish! Make a difference!" She squeezed my hand hard, panting. A bloody tear slipped from her eyes. It jabbed something deep inside me. Not an intellectual knowledge of love and loss. Not a set of emotions that ran underneath my detachment like a vague reminder of my humanity. No, this was like a needle that jabbed through the outer layers of what I now saw wasn't a new true understanding, a cynical dismissal of meaning, but a carefully built mental wall between me and the current reality, me and emotion, me and caring about anything.

The needle stabbed in deeper. Harder.

It made me feel and *care*.

About Lena. This moment. Everything.

"Don't talk," I said. "Just let me tell you that I love you and—"

"Damn it, NO!" she croaked at the top of her lungs and forced her eyes open, fully bloodshot and horrible. "I die! You live! Go! GO!" Then she shook her head furiously and hid her face from me. "No, wait. One last thing. You have to know one thing. If...*when* you finally figure out how to go far enough back in time to fix this, you find me and tell me to get my head out of my ass. Because whatever else is true, every me, in every timeline, was made to love you and be with you. You make sure I understand that! *Now* go."

Then she cried out like she was the one going.

I held her hand until, finally, she did.

It almost blew apart the thick wall inside me.

Almost.

But necessity made me shake that off, close my eyes, and lower my heartrate to freezing to keep out the probing needle. Maybe it made me inhuman, but that's what I needed right now to honor Lena and Salim's sacrifice and do the right thing.

Dissociation fully reestablished, I jumped.

66
Race to the top

I GOT THE STARFISH reference. Old story of a man (or woman) walking on a beach, picking up stranded starfish and tossing them back into the water. Blah. Blah. Thousands of starfish. What does your teeny number of rescues matter? Man picks up another starfish and says, *It matters to this one,* and tosses it to the waves.

Multiple timelines. Make one better, it helps the people in *that* timeline. Sure.

But in my state of hard-won, heartless calm that I had just slammed back into place, I didn't really care. I was jumping because Lena told me to. I thought I'd see just how many sequential ten-minute jumps I could manage before my heart stopped. No targeting like the mini-jumps I'd learned to save Xiaobo a couple times, just jumping my max and letting my soul figure out where that got me.

One back and Bent was droning on in his supercilious way through the radio speaker under the still-alive Schmidt's left arm.

I flipped Bent a finger and jumped again.

Ten more minutes back and I was questioning Cultus about the mission. Hadn't yet felt Dr. Ying's broken rib. She'd certainly showed enormous toughness to keep fighting through that kind of pain when she finally woke up to yell at Bannerman.

I jumped again.

Now in a room with Antonio Perez's corpse behind me, his helmet and goggles on my head. The Chinese commanders outside the building were making the announcement that got all the Chinese in the building to evacuate. Something about the virus being loose, obviously. But Bannerman and Emmanuel would have already been rocketing ampoules of it out into the surrounding blocks of apartment buildings, parks, schools, and research centers by this point. Had they already collected Lena and Al-Rashid from the front door of the building, too?

I itched to find out but knew that wasn't far enough back. If Dr. Yee's count of forty minutes to first symptoms was accurate, I still had two jumps to go. So I jumped…

And suddenly had two bodies rolling down the stairs toward me!

I hopped over these two Chinese soldiers I'd shot and looked around. I was on the second-floor landing. No helmet. This was the moment before I'd decided to duck out here and creep through the hallways. Where I ended up in the room with Perez, holding him while he died. Taking his gear.

Interesting. Major time distortion. I recalled that whole process as taking like two minutes.

One more jump. Go!

Where? Right. Open hole in the wall behind me meant I'd just entered the hole my team had blown in the back of the building. I could hear the battle around me and he shouted orders in my headset.

More time distortion. I'd thought I was only a few minutes behind them. My time in the truck with Xiaobo, leaving him, seeing it get blown up. During that episode, Bannerman's team must have blown their way in and taken the lower floors while Bannerman and his closest had raced up to the fourth floor.

Which meant I had to run as fast as I could now to catch up to them before they pulled out all the ampoules and began rocketing and throwing and stomping on them all over the place.

I put caution aside and just ran.

Got shot.

Jumped back.

Ran.

Got up to the third floor on the central staircase before getting shot.

Jumped back.

Ran again.

More deaths and jumps.

But I wasn't losing myself like Lena had warned. Nor did my disorientation or blood pressure increase. There was no emotional fatigue or whatever weak-ass excuse my old self had used before to limit me. Not even a hint of trauma as I shot three Chinese soldiers in the back of their heads and one of our team in his face, then ran over their bodies without stopping.

I was cold and detached, inhuman, but *focused.*

And here my motivations were very clear. I needed to stop Lena's death or that of millions of Chinese, yes. But mostly I had to stop Bent from winning. He was...bad. His plan was bad. I was going to end it.

I reached the fourth-floor landing and stopped for a few seconds to let my current body recover from the climbing sprint. Then I eased open the door and looked left down the hall.

Not good.

The BSL-4 lab door was open like before with the corpse of the first Chinese scientist slumped against it, but Cultus was standing over the body, on guard duty.

Thankfully, the loud argument and rising female screams—Dr. Ying, I presumed—had him distracted.

I slipped out the doorway and ran as quietly as I could toward Cultus. The sound of yells and female screaming should have covered me, but when I was less than ten feet from him, he must have seen me out of the corner of his eye.

He turned, raised his rifle, and I slid under it, kicking out his legs as I grabbed his gun arm and twisted him down over me and to one side. I rolled on top of him and knocked him out with his own rifle butt.

I sprang up to my feet and looked into the lab room, only to find everyone in the room looking back at me. From a silent lab room. The vomit smell must have come from the dead scientist by the door. No one in here was sick yet.

They raised their rifles, and I raised mine, pointing it at Bannerman. He stood beside the open door of the secret chamber that was filled with what had to be exactly 1,841 ampoules of a modified Ebola nightmare in a glycerol suspension. Dr. Ying, who'd been screaming only moments ago, slumped, unconscious in her chair. She must have finally given up the location of the secret room and gotten hammered as a thank you.

"Who the hell are you?" Bannerman snapped.

A crackle in all our ears announced Bent's presence in this little scenario. "Calm down everyone. Jackson, introduce yourself."

I momentarily considered shooting the helmet cam on the top of Schmidt's head to blind Bent, but Schmidt was a good five paces to Bannerman's right, over by the unconscious Dr. Ying. Emmanuel was another four paces past him. If I shot Schmidt, Bannerman and/or Emmanuel would take me out immediately.

I lowered my rifle.

"I'm Alpha Two," I said to Bannerman. "Sorry about Cultus. Battle instinct. I assume that's the bioweapon you've found?"

Bent sighed. "Film it, Captain Bannerman."

"Yes, sir."

Bannerman lowered his gun and nodded to Emmanuel and Schmidt to do the same. Then he motioned for Schmidt to join him and take in the sight of all the ampoules and the markings on the shelves with his helmet cam.

While he was doing this, I said, "Then you'll close it up, activate the auto-claving, and destroy all the research that went into it."

"Pardon me?" Bent's voice sounded truly puzzled.

"I heard her screaming about the dual function of that room. Freeze them for transport or superheat them to kill them all. Autoclaving."

"Ah, yes," Bent said. "We're not going to do that."

"I know," I said. I'd flipped my M4 to full auto and was pressing the trigger even as I raised it to mow down Bannerman and Schmidt. Then I dropped and rolled over twice to get in a position to take out Emmanuel who was firing madly at where I'd been.

I might not have come into this mission with awesome gun skills, but my practice in the many jumpbacks it had taken me to get up here certainly helped. And dead cold focus. And the element of surprise.

None of the men I'd just shot were fully dead, so I had to walk around and finished them off. Also Cultus.

I dragged in the bodies of Cultus and the first dead scientist and shut and locked the airtight door of the laboratory. My initial gunfire had broken a number of the ampoules. I had to assume the virus had become aerosolized and was already in my lungs. Hopefully, shutting things up tight now would contain whatever had gotten out. And obviously the body I was in now would not be leaving this room ever.

Then the loudspeaker announcement I thought had been triggered by Bannerman's ampoule rocket launches sounded from outside the building.

I heard a tut-tutting from my headset. Bent's voice.

"How many times have you been up here, Jackson?"

"Enough."

"With Lena and the Persian man? I'm assuming he's the opposing time traveler I sent you here to find?"

"Don't know what you're talking about." More precisely, I couldn't figure out how he knew.

"You forget I have your very talented brother at my drugged-up disposal."

"Is he watching now? Kenny, you need to stop helping him. Do you understand?"

"I cut him out of this particular conversation. Not that it matters. Both I and Dr. Sauveterre believe his addictions and dissociative state are stronger than his loyalty to you. He also told me that Xiaobo's dead, so you have no way back."

That wasn't strictly true. If I just jumped back over and over and over and—

"Nor do you have a way to beat Captain Bannerman to this room or stop the explosives his team planted all over this building as a fallback in case you betrayed us as you're obviously intent on doing."

Curious, I said, "I can go back far enough to tell him to delay his attack."

"I did give you the *illusion* of command, didn't I. Told you only what you needed to know. For instance, your one-time best friend, Dr. Jude Spiegelman. You know what he got up to right after you left here? Wait... Never mind. The Chinese have just offered us Lena and her friend as negotiators and... Oh, my. She made the mistake of calling him by name. Salim. You don't think... Hm. That would explain so much. Kenny, I want you to remind me to have my people do a deep dive on someone named Salim Noor al-Rashid. Got that? Good. And, Jackson, I've just had the strike team members who received Lena and Salim from the Chinese to put your lover on the microphone."

This was not good. Just the idea of it actually caused a tremor in my psyche. I thought I'd gotten beyond that. Had to *shut that down.*

"Jackson?" Lena's voice said in my ear. I could hear the excited mix of tension and fear.

Coolly, I said, "Tell Salim to—"

There was a loud pop-spatter sound. Lena screamed and shouted, "No, no, *no!*"

It was like that earlier needle that had pierced my armor had become an ice pick now, shoving its way in with a rough intensity. I fought it. Mentally slowed it down. Lena was just a woman. One woman. And she was alive in so many timestreams. A different her in every timestream I'd created with my jumps.

Unless...every single one of those somehow led here?

"Th-they just shot him," Lena sobbed in my ear.

"Run, Lena," I said quietly. "If you can, run before the building blows up."

Another loud pop-spatter sound.

I waited. There was no more Lena.

Bent laughed. "I'll always be a step ahead of you, Jackson. Five. Four..."

No.

More.

Lena.

The ice pick reached my heart, and I jumped.

67

Uwe Bent

April 27, 2022, 1:45 p.m.

Fly, my pretties, thought Bent as he watched Jackson, Xiaobo, Micah Rowan, and Britney Chandra disappear into the long underground tunnel to Proctor House and out. They'd soon be flying to Tokyo. Then Harbin! And oh, the devastation they would wreak.

As he swung the tunnel door closed, it released a cool backdraft against his face, and he added his own sigh of satisfaction.

Not that Bent trusted Jackson to stay ignorant or compliant. It wasn't in his nature. But Bent had twenty years of experience herding time travelers. You just had to find the limits of their power. Then you predicted their deviations from orders, used compliant spies like Xiaobo and Kentucky to provide intel, and finally constructed boxes within boxes that would keep even strong subjects like Jackson Traine in line.

"Uwe," said Sauveterre.

He turned from the *Keep Out. Hazardous Chemicals* door to see she was looking from her phone to the ceiling. Distressed. Then he realized his own phone was buzzing and pulled it from his pocket. Held it up before him. Kgabu Zungu, SCATTER's operation and security chief appeared, his shaved black head and face looking shiny and intense.

"There has been a stealth breach of our exterior. Cameras track forty-two bodies approaching with weapons and body armor. FBI markings. Four tactical vehicles parked on Mill Street. Weapons range."

"Show me the cameras," Bent said.

His phone screen changed to images at various ranges of FBI in full brown battle dress, advancing with helmets, communication gear, and guns up like real soldiers. Among them, he picked out three of particular interest. In the rear was a slow-moving old man in civilian clothes and his own personal escort. That would be Andre Poussaint. What an utterly obsessive *futze* that man was. With no qualms about borrowing his rival agency's badging for an illegal raid.

In the middle of the pack, Bent saw the rangy, hard-looking man Bent had run into a few times when SCATTER had still been part of the CIA. He seemed to be riding control over the slimmed down, but still soft-looking figure of Dr. Jude Spiegelman. Bent had received reports that Spiegelman had been in the fizzled CIA raid on Bent's *alma mater* a couple of weeks back, too. Bent could picture the little simp jumping with delight that he'd remembered where Bent had studied, thinking he was so brilliant. Bent had no idea how they'd tracked him here, though.

He looked forward to finding out.

"Initiate evac, sir?" asked Zungu.

This SCATTER setup certainly had the ability to lock things down, feign innocence, evacuate all its personnel through the same tunnel he'd just sent Jackson and Xiaobo out of. But that could hamper Bent's guidance of the Harbin mission. Maybe even delay it. That was unacceptable.

And this raid on Bent's command center?

It was almost certainly a solo shot by a Poussaint. Bent's True Believers in the CIA had said Poussaint was already under investigation for the jet bombing of the SCATTER Site 2. And he'd been sanctioned over the Johns Hopkins debacle. Now he was pretending to be FBI and raiding a hospital campus, guns hot?

This had to be a rogue mission. Which meant no backup.

Bent could put him down here and it might be days before anyone in the CIA even noticed he was gone.

"No," he told Zungu. "Bring all the patients into the basement and fortify the access behind them. Activate all our automatic defenses. Blow these attackers up. Shoot them down. But if any of them get through to the building itself, let them come in. I want to meet them. Please get me some suitable armor and weaponry. I'm coming to the ops room."

He signed off and looked up to see Sauveterre's stricken face.

"Now, Oshee. What good is power if you can't wreak a little destruction on your enemies? And a couple of days from now, nobody will give a rat's fart about what happened in this little part of the world. Coming?"

68

What the—?

"H-GAH!" I STUMBLED AND felt my head swim as badly as the first time I'd ever jumped. Where the hell was I? Or...when?

"Hey! What're you doing?"

I blinked at the speaker. It was Thing Two, Britney Chandra. Brown skin. Thick biceps for a woman. The last time I'd seen her, she'd been riddled with bullets, dead on the floor of the small house we'd stayed in before "saving the world" became mass genocide.

Genocide. Lena shot.

Britney's death was at least seven jumps back from that.

This was...further.

The tunnel walls lit with LED lights. The stone stairs up ahead that led to a door covered by, of all things, a tapestry. Dusty. Rarely moved. And past it, outside, had been the rented van and driver who took us to the Boston airport so we could fly to Japan and onward to China.

"Okay," I mumbled, blinking hard to see if this impossibility dissolved as dreams do. It didn't. I'd jumped back in time more than twenty-seven hours. A rumbling feeling that had been thrown off kilter by the massiveness of my jumpback came surging up again. Rage, I think. Pouring out of my heart through the hole made by Lena's death.

Rage that had brought me here.

To make Uwe Bent pay. Maybe to save Jude, too, I thought as I remembered the story Kansas had sent about what had happened around the time I'd walked out of SCATTER HQ with this little group.

"Let's move, Traine," growled Thing One, Micah Rowen. "We've got a long trip ahead of us."

"I've already done it," I said.

He frowned. "Say what?"

"You and Britney die an hour after we get to Harbin. They know we're coming. They do a house-to-house. I'm under the floorboards with Xiaobo when you shoot it out with them. They win." I turned to Xiaobo. "You die three times as we try to join the assault on the lab. Twice by sniper. Once by helicopter rocket. You stay dead after the last one."

"What about you?" Britney asked.

"Many, many deaths. But I'm here now. And I need to talk to your boss. Give me your guns."

The Things looked at each other, then at me. Micah cleared his throat and said, "We can't let you do that."

I might have been smiling a little as I said, "You want to try to stop me?"

It took me a good eight or nine minutes to jog the long tunnel back to the door. Alone. Carrying Micah's Glock 19 in my right hand and Britney's slightly smaller Glock 43X in my left. Far behind me, the Things and Xiaobo were likely trying to figure how they'd explain why they'd given me their guns, instructed me how to use them properly, then looked the other way as I left.

I was prepared to jump back further in time to be on the other side of the door Bent sent us through, but the rage leaking out of my heart didn't want any detours, so I was glad to find the door didn't lock from this side.

Stuffing the Glock 43X into the back waistband of my pants, I yanked it open and did a quick fade to the far wall, ready to fight anyone still in that corridor.

No one. But a lot of pounding music and noise from around the corner to my left where the experiments and op center rooms were.

I ran toward it and rounded the corner.

Stopped.

What the hell?

It was like all of SCATTER was having a Mardi Gras in the middle of the basement hallway. People thronged in uniforms and combat gear, gas masks dangling around their necks, talking loudly and gesticulating to one another. Upbeat Latin music played over the sounds of what I now realized was banging, gunfire, and explosives coming from somewhere up above. The thick, moving air smelled sharp with sweaty anticipation.

Along the right side of the hallway, being guided like cattle into two side rooms, shuffled familiar faces I hadn't seen in months. There was Norman Daknworth, hunched over and wiping his large nose as he moved. Danny Reet, trying hard to look the nonchalant gambler, but his sweaty face gave him away. Zura, shuffling with wide eyes, looking very lost for someone who'd once been the hero of her people in Crimea.

The final two walkers who did *not* look cowed. Señor Cruz Condore Quispe walked with insolent dignity, looking about him with eyes that said all the lackeys who worked for SCATTER were no better than the drug traffickers he'd put in prison back in the day. Behind him walked Sunday Salisu, the youngest of the Pit prisoners but the only one with her eyes fully up so that she saw me and locked eyes with surprise and what might have been hope before she was pushed into her room.

The gap that had been held open for them along that wall filled with Quispe's despised SCATTER personnel, including the ones who'd been herding the Pit prisoners. They all looked armed with some sort of firepower. Most held assault rifles, but one was positioning an anti-tank rocket launcher on his shoulder.

Finally, in the middle of the swarming, busy throng who all seemed to be jockeying for the best view of the stairs down from the ground level above, I caught glimpses of the peacock in the center of it all.

Bent. Still in the midnight-blue velvet because it was only what? Fifteen or twenty minutes since I'd left him in that other timeline. Now *this* timeline.

What was happening? Could I just shoot him and end Harbin? Avenge Lena and end SCATTER?

He had lackeys all around him, blocking any easy shots, but I could still run in.

Would it cause the nuclear holocaust Kenny had seen when I'd killed Bent before? Could I kill him and still stop that now that I knew what I knew?

A string of five lackeys were holding up a line of opaque riot shields between Bent and the staircase at the end of the hallway everyone was clearly afraid of. The shields were a wall of defense, but a short wall, shorter than Bent. I guessed he planned to crouch and rise to shoot? I could see the oversized M4 in his right hand. He did not have a gas mask around his neck, but there was one on a rolling steel table beside him. The table also held what looked like multiple ammunition clips, rows of neatly cupped hand grenades, a few knives, and, on its lower shelf, a flame thrower. I was surprised he hadn't lined up a bullwhip and some ninja throwing stars.

Then one lackey beside him turned in a vague, distracted way, and I realized it was Kenny. Even just a glimpse of him in Bent's crowd of sycophants told me he was high on something. Barely there.

"Hey, Uwe!" I shouted over the music.

No response.

"*Asshole!*"

He finally recognized his name and turned his head back. Registered my presence. The two guns I held in my hands. "Changed your mind about going?" he asked.

He said something to his front shield bearers and the two outside ones peeled off to run around behind him, holding the heavy shields up to protect his ass from me. The other SCATTER personnel who'd been hiding behind Bent quickly moved to the walls. Except Kenny, of course. I wasn't sure he even registered my presence.

"Oh, I went," I said. I started walking toward him and Kenny. The rest of the mob faded out for me. Whatever the longer-term consequences, it was time to at least avenge Lena, end Harbin, and save Kenny.

"Not possible!" Bent called out without looking back.

"It is!" gushed Dr. Océane Sauveterre's voice from somewhere, and she finally separated herself from the crowd packed around Bent and rushed part of way toward me. Put herself directly between me and my targets. "Multiple jumps or..."

"One," I said. "Uncontrolled." I raised the Glock 19 and fired past her at one of the riot shields protecting Bent's rear. It thudded and presumably rebounded, but nobody screamed out in pain.

Sauveterre shuddered and took a deep breath. It made her chest swell toward me under her sweater top. And even with everything else happening, that motion finally told me, in my newly clear-eyed state, that the dreams I'd had about making love to an overripe Lena in between my counseling sessions with Sauveterre, especially that first dream that came when I'd been drugged—they hadn't been dreams. And they hadn't been Lena.

"You raped me," I said, turning the gun on her.

Her face went instantly scarlet, and her arms instinctively crossed over her chest. "I was..."

"Trying to form a closer bond? Sexual transference?"

Behind her, Bent swiveled fully back to face us, laughing. Kenny turned with him automatically. "Is that what you meant, Oshee?" Bent asked. "He couldn't jump more than ten minutes because he might lose you. Hence your 'extreme' solution. You kill yourself in front of him and hope he'll eventually jump back and save you?"

Still scarlet, Sauveterre shot back, "After he saved the world."

"Except he's not going to do that, are you, Jackson? You said you went there, came back. Because you didn't like what I'm *going* to do there, correct?"

"It's evil," I said. "And without identifying the other time traveler—"

"What's evil?" Sauveterre interrupted.

"Shut up, Oshee!" Bent snapped. "Jackson, if you—"

"What are you going to *do*, Uwe?" Sauveterre's face had gone from red confusion to pale terror, and her heaving breaths threatened to drown out the intellect she had projected into the world, her empathy and creative work with Xiaobo, with Kenny, with me...

"It is irrelevant to you! Irrelevant to everyone here, other than to know it will secure all our futures and the future good of the world."

"He made his men spread the live virus as far as they could," I said, speaking loudly enough for everyone to hear over the music. "Kill millions."

"No, Uwe," Sauveterre cried, walking back toward him but stopped by the riot shields. I was surprised to see Kenny listening closely. "We discussed this! There's another way. There's always another way."

"Just one solution," Uwe said, holding up a finger like Dr. Strange explaining things to Iron Man.

"You're insufferably, egotistically, fatally *stupid!*" she shrieked at him over the shields.

"And you're dead," he replied as he raised his rifle and shot her with unexpected accuracy right between her eyes.

I was surprised that when she crumpled down dead, it was...reminiscent of the spike Lena's death had pounded into me. But to Kenny, it was bigger. Because while my brother might have been barely conscious of *my* presence, he'd obviously been highly conscious of Sauveterre's. He started to shriek like a crazed animal, his gas mask swinging wildly around his neck, drugged eyes blinking fast. Then he began climbing over the people holding up the rear line of riot shields.

"Kentucky, no!" Bent shouted and leaped at him, only to have Kenny throw him back.

Still shrieking, Kenny fought his way around the two riot shields and kneeled by Sauveterre's dead body. He scooped her up, surprisingly strong given the wasting of his limbs from all the drugs Bent and Sauveterre had kept him on.

"Put her down," Bent ordered.

Kenny ignored him and staggered toward me like he was offering me a gift, like he actually *did* know I was there.

He was still maybe twenty feet from me when bullets thudded into his back and he went down with Sauveterre in his arms. He thumped down sideways on top of her like a perversion of Michelangelo's Pietà, a dead Christ holding a dead Mary.

I blinked at them, then raised my eyes and my pistols only to see Bent's rifle was still up to his shoulder, aimed at me now.

"Rifles are far more accurate than a Glock at thirty feet," he said. "Look around."

I did and saw there were at least six more assault rifles aimed at me by Bent's acolytes, employees, lapdogs.

He lowered his rifle again. "I don't want to shoot you. Any more than I wanted to shoot Dr. Sauveterre or Kenny. But sometimes even the most valuable resources become liabilities if they *fuck with my schedule!* You, more than anyone, know this is true. Schedules and time. I will let you fix this, but only if you first see the absolute mess that I'm facing here so you understand why certain actions can only be handled by people with clear vision! Now why don't you go sit down somewhere. It sounds like the show is about to begin."

Which is when I noticed the pounding that had been going on upstairs had stopped and changed to the sound of many boots coming down the stairs. Bent reached for his gas mask and pulled it on. Other than four acolytes who kept their guns aimed at me, his assembled army followed suit. Then Bent gestured and the Latin music doubled in volume, turning the dance that followed into a kind of grotesque movie montage.

First came the gas grenades, tossed down the basement hallway toward the waiting SCATTER mob. Then the gun-toting men and women in FBI-branded attack gear came storming down after them into the basement, guns blazing.

And were met with even more guns blazing back.

Plus, explosive grenades from Uwe.

A rocket from the bazooka guy I'd seen earlier.

Plaster, wood, and huge chunks of concrete spattered down, mostly in the area where the "FBI" members fought. It added to the chaos of screams, gunfire, smoke, explosions, and a wild Latin beat that made you really want to move your body.

I grabbed the gas mask off one SCATTER soldier who staggered back my way, bleeding profusely from too many spots to count and soiling himself as he went.

With the mask on, I picked my way forward to find Kenny's and Sauveterre's bodies. Kenny never knew just how powerful he was or how loved and so just…died. And Océane Sauveterre? Ocean save the Earth? She tried.

Like Lena.

Like me.

I thought this double insult to justice would draw out more of the rage Lena's death had blessed me with, and it did. But not in the way I expected. Because it drew with it a darker strain of anger, a wild nihilism, a conviction that this world *deserved* its tragedies because it was inherently flawed. What had Sauveterre said about Xiaobo? That his power came from believing this shitty existence didn't deserve to be held on to.

Bent's maniacal laughter caught my attention and drew me forward. A pistol still gripped in each hand, I pushed my way through his distracted followers who'd totally forgotten about me as they fought for their lives. Bloody heads to my left and right, alive or not. Blood underfoot. More vomit, piss, and feces in the air like my new theme scent. And a blazing heat that must have come from so much gunfire and so many expiring lives. It was thick like molasses, swirling and pushing at me.

When I reached Bent, he was crouched behind the two shield serfs he still had standing. Glancing my way, he jumped up and fired a string of bullets at the few attackers still firing back.

Then he dropped down and grinned at me. "Three more. Maybe four. I think I'm over fifteen! I finally get the attraction! Did you see who was in that crowd? Lost so much weight, he was hard to hit, all bouncing and running and screaming out for Yahweh."

And even as a horrible guess ran through my bones, all sounds in the basement suddenly stopped.

All I could hear now was heavy breathing on either side of me. A few sobs. People falling to their knees, guns thunking softly beside them.

No sound from the attackers' side of the divide.

"Ha. Sixteen then," said Bent. He pulled off his gas mask and sniffed the air. "*Good* ventilation system. Come with me, Jackson. Let's find him."

Dropping his mask and slinging his rifle over his neck, he pushed aside his remaining shield bearers and walked through the hallway of dead bodies, almost slipping once on the blood and chuckling over that.

I pulled off my own mask and walked behind him, thinking, *This shitty existence. This place in time and space.*

Then Bent called out, "Here!" He rolled over a short, slender body with the toe of his pointy oxblood dress shoe.

For a second, I didn't recognize the face even after I'd pulled of his helmet and gas mask. Jude had lost so much weight. And they'd given him a helmet, mask, and gun. Why had they done that? Who had done that?

"He no doubt thought he was coming to rescue you," Bent said with his uncanny, if erratic, ability to read my thoughts. "Did you know he's been held under lock and key for a few months now? By Andre Poussaint. Because you sent him to the *man* and the *man* locked him up. Poussaint's dead outside, though. Don't worry. Now can we finally talk realpolitik? How the world is and what has to be done to set things right? Are you finally mature enough to handle it?"

I looked at Bent, at his long face with his high forehead, his startling blue eyes. "The world," I said, "is shit. You killed Lena."

"Will I do that? Because I haven't yet, obviously."

"You did. But I don't think you will." The nihilistic rage inside me had become a smooth river of fire now. I could feel it eating up every last connection I had with this place, this time, or any place and time. It told me I was in this world, but not *of* it. That this version of my body was just a tool to pick up and use.

"And why do you think..." Bent began.

I whipped my right-hand pistol into Bent's temple.

It drew blood and staggered him but didn't knock him down. He grabbed his dangling rifle and tried to raise it but was having trouble telling right from left, up from down.

I stepped closer and whipped my left-hand pistol against his other temple.

He went down and lay unmoving. I shot him three times in the head to be sure.

When I looked back at the SCATTER members still standing, including the imposingly hulking form of the ops chief Bent had called Mr. Zungu, none of them raised their guns at me. In fact, the ones along the left wall from where I stood now, the wall I'd seen them shepherd in the prisoners of the Pit into two rooms, walked carefully away from the doors to them. They silently stepped over dead bodies as they went.

I approached that wall, the room where I'd seen Señor Quispe and Sunday Salisu go in. The door stood open. As did the door beyond it. Had the Pit crew had used this nightmare for one final escape attempt?

Then I picked out Sunday's dead body. And Norman's, holding her hand. It took maybe five minutes to find all their corpses. Danny Reet had gotten the furthest. He'd grabbed someone's gas mask and made it halfway to the corner that led to the way out through the secret tunnel. Had he known somehow?

But the last body I found was actually Zura's. She'd saved her people in Crimea when she was fifteen. She'd been captured and held by SCATTER and held for eight years. Abused by Quispe and Bent, she'd still had the spirit to attempt multiple escapes and knock one of Bent's cameras off the wall to stomp on it, crying out, *We is people.*

Only to be shot here because of Bent's woeful overestimation of SCATTER's physical power in the world.

The river of fire in me ate the last tiny connection between me and this world. And I suddenly knew I could go to any *when* in my life that I remembered with clarity.

As Lena had predicted.

And what else had she said? Jump too often or too far and I'd lose myself. Too late for that one, but also…throw a starfish. Make a difference.

I knew where to start.

I saw it in my mind, just like when I'd done my mini-jumps and…

69
Starfish

THE PIT

I landed in the Pit the day in the week after I'd made my Hell bargain with Bent. In the time when the Pit crew had opened up to me. When Sunday and Zura had opened up to everyone about what Bent did to them on a regular basis. When Zura got *mad.*

I arrived right after she smashed the camera off the wall of our common room and ground it under her foot.

But in our new timeline, I didn't answer the scared call for me to come for my first session and stop inciting the inmates. I stayed and told them just how they were going to escape. With my help. With me jumping back over and over until they all got out.

Did I lie to them by omitting how each failed attempt might leave a set of themselves worse off? Yes.

But would some group of them eventually get out? I thought so. At least one of the me's I left behind in all the new timelines I created would get them out.

I had to leave before I became the successful one.

Time might be endlessly repeatable, but my focus was not. I had other appointments.

THE TAYCAN

The human heart I took control of in the passenger seat of the pink Porsche Taycan EV, being driven by a still-wild Zhou Xiaobo, was squealing as hard as the car's tires as we drifted hard through the six-way crossing of New Jersey SE, North Carolina SE, and E Street E, through red lights and rushing, honking cars.

I calmed the heart and turned to Xiaobo with a bemused grin, seeing how hard he was pushing this through a world and timeline that meant nothing to him. And though it meant little to me, too, I told him what he needed to hear to reconnect. I told him about his coming decompensation and rescue by Dr.

Sauveterre. About our mission to Harbin, China and what its true intent was. I invited him to consider leaving Uwe Bent to his twisted schemes that I was already unravelling.

We were slowing to an almost sane speed by the time I jumped, leaving a newly empowered-by-nothingness me in to finish the job.

JUDE'S TOWNHOUSE

I felt the relief in the body I slipped into on one of Jude's living room couches. That body had just been through the wringer of interviewing with the supposedly low-level Wilson and Dadashev in the CIA building, then with a mysterious but very hard-assed old man I only learned later was Andre Poussaint, obsessive SCATTER hater. I'd fought, got Jude shot dead in an escape attempt, and finally managed to jump far enough back to bail on the whole process before Poussaint got involved.

Now we were chatting amongst comfy knitted afghans and pillows. We'd eaten chicken, drunk tea, and Jude was cluelessly pushing me to give the CIA another chance.

The more-informed me from the future held up my hand.

"What?" Jude said, stopping himself mid-wheedle.

"Here's the thing, dude," I said, very much acting a kind of casual friendship that I mostly remembered rather than felt. "I get the sense the CIA has some very intense people dealing with a lot of really serious stuff on a daily basis and they're doing their best to keep the country safe. But it's also gotten into some ethically messed up shit over the years."

Jude broke in. "You're talking MK Ultra stuff, right? That was dealt with. Cleaned up."

"No, dude. I'm talking about Dr. Uwe Bent and his SCATTER program."

Jude blanched. "I've heard of it. Crazy stuff. Psychiatrist looking for time travelers. Got kicked out."

"But you're still working for him."

And you can imagine where the conversation went from there. My revelations knocked the wind out of him. Especially when I told him I was a time traveler and gave him a simple proof by having him tell me a story of something that just happened, then jumping back. Etc.

I was giving him a chance to find his best self, do the right thing. And the me that stayed with this timeline would help him with advice and foreknowledge to hopefully come out of this tangle as the good man I knew he yearned to be.

Incidentally, I made sure he shared with me exactly where SCATTER was based before it relocated to Baltimore. And the organization of its rooms, where Kenny was kept, etc. Maybe the me who stayed in that timestream could use it to free Kenny. And if that me didn't, this me certainly would.

Because I was finally ready to jump back to a time I'd thought long and hard about. Not so far that I destroyed my younger self, but the exact point where I needed to fix my biggest mistake.

If I did it right, I hoped I'd never have to do a *big* jump ever again.

70

The thing about love

I CAME INTO MY body gasping for cold air from around the plastic saliva monitor that filled my mouth. Wires sprang out from the pads taped to my shaved chest. The smell of rubbing alcohol. The stink of terror. Mine. In my peripheral vision, I saw the wires coming out of the EEG cap strapped to my head, holding down gooped-on tiny electrodes. Monitors beeping. White walls. Br face—Dr. Irene Gopal! Olive face—Lena Cortland! Alive! Younger! Meaner!

My heart thumped was thumping out of control. My head swam. This disorientation, good God, how had I lived through it so often?

Bring it down. Steady. Just a body. Just a shitty world and Lena's shitty choice.

Okay. Right. Building #4, the industrial park in Redmond. Lena's sub-ground particle accelerator laboratory was below us. But this room was up on the fourth floor. Medical.

Pre-SCATTER. Pre-Wenling. Pre-Demon Monks.

Be calm and focused. Calm and...

No. Lena's oh-so-scientific tone as she sat in the plastic chair facing me, looking down at her hands. "From what you told me about what happened two days ago downstairs..."

I yanked the saliva monitor out of my mouth and jumped up from my chair. "Get this stupid garbage off me." I ripped off my EEG cap and electrodes, yelling at the pain caused by some of them yanking at my skin.

While the traitorous Dr. Gopal called out, "That was an event!"

"No shit!" I snapped at her while Lena knocked over her chair, she stood up so fast. I looked around wildly for my shirt.

"Jackson? Jackson, please. What is it?" Her eyes were scared. Her voice, tight. "You jumped, right?" She'd scooted to the monitors. "I can see it here. Your brain activity. Your heart rate. It's proof! It's... This is fantastic!"

I whirled on her with my teeth bared. I remembered what I'd thought when this happened to my inexperienced self. That she was fucking *evil* because another timeline, eight minutes from now, she'd shackled me to that chair *without my consent,* toyed with me sexually, then tried to fucking suffocate me!

And…and…why the fuck was I feeling like this now? Why was I attached to this world? To this woman? To caring whether she was good or bad? Whether she'd been moral or foolish in her brutal form of testing my power?

"It is *not* fantastic," I said as I found my flannel shirt, pulled it on, and did up the buttons. From one of the rolling carts, I grabbed some paper towels to wipe the EEG goop from my forehead and hair. "I was right the first time when I said you could have caused a psychotic episode."

"What do you mean, the first time?" Lena said, frowning hard. "You jumped twice?"

I shook it off. "The way you made me jump was…" I just shook my head again. But why the hell was I so caught up in this? It happened. I forgave her for it…eventually. Because I understood why she did it—her passionate pursuit of knowledge, which I *loved* her for. As I loved her for so many things. So why the fuck…?

"Oh, my God." Lena's face collapsed. "I followed the plan. I actually went through with it, didn't I? The shackles and… I told Irene I needed to make you believe you'd die, but I didn't think you'd actually… My God, your face. How far did I go? Did I actually…"

Her face blanched, and she sank to the floor.

As I leaped to catch her, I finally remembered why I'd chosen *this* moment in time to jump to. It wasn't my indignities and suffering that mattered here. It was how it had rebounded onto Lena. One mistake in judgment and I and the shitty world had jammed it down her throat so deep it festered and metastasized into a belief she was fundamentally flawed and could never be the woman I needed.

Which ultimately TOOK HER AWAY FROM ME.

That was not acceptable.

Because while her two deaths in Harbin were the scalding fire that pushed me away from the world, the chance of having her alive and in love with me again was something some deep part of me insisted on.

It wanted me back.

I wanted me back.

But only if I could figure out how to do it right this time. It had to start here.

She was sobbing now, falling apart in my arms. Not even bothering with the speech she'd made the first time about being raised with privilege, blind-ed by science, ends justifying the means, being like Hitler.

Just as well. I didn't think the anger flowing through me now could have properly delivered the story I'd used back then about her not being allowed to buy a puppy and what that meant.

This me was rougher. More direct.

I said, "You *should* feel horrible. It was a horrible thing you did. But it doesn't mean *you* are horrible. Objectively examining the larger sum of your achievements, words, and actions, you are brilliant, moral, and caring. You taught me things."

My awful delivery served as a thought-cycle interrupt. Her sobbing quiet-ed.

I could smell the floral scent of her shampoo. And the soft warmth of her body against me. It brought back our first ever lovemaking session—last night in this timeline. More connection, but it was so wrapped up with the knowledge of her rejecting me, shutting me out, then finding me only to die in my arms. This world. This shitty fucking world.

She spoke into my chest. "What did you learn from me?"

"Saving starfish."

"What?"

"You told me, will tell me, that I can't save everyone or fix every timeline. But the ones I do, they matter for the people in them."

She pushed herself out of my arms and sat up straighter and pushed back her hair from her face. She wiped her eyes and nose. Then her objectively beautiful brown eyes firmed up and bored into mine exactly like I'd intended. "'Will' tell you. You're not talking about this...torture session you just jumped back from."

I shook my head. *Tell her.*

"Of course not," she said. "Because I'd have no reason to share that story or sentiment. And you talk about timelines like... I thought you could only jump back ten minutes in time."

"I could. Until recently. My recently." *Just* tell *her.*

She frowned and shook her head. "You're giving off crazy-man vibes now. And I'm suddenly thinking everything you've told me..." She waved her hand at all the equipment still around us. "I don't know how you would have pulled off knowing all about my experiments, how you made all these sensors jump so dramatically. And your story of how you jump, using my theory of superattraction. That's good. That's deviously good. So, you read up on me, found out what I've been researching, how much it means to me. And you romance me with your social anxiety thing. 'Cause I'm a sucker for vulnerable, compassionate men, right? Is that it? Was it all an act?"

Before I could answer that, I had to deal with what I'd seen when she'd waved at the equipment. Dr. Irene Gopal was standing only feet away, listening to every word. I stood up.

"Dr. Gopal, I think we're finished here for the day. No need to stick around. We'll clean up."

Gopal looked at Lena, who considered, then nodded, and stood up herself to escort the Indian doctor out.

When Lena returned, I said, "It was not an act, and this is not a con. But I am different than the man you knew this morning. That me, in that timeline, is just starting an awesomely painful series of adventures that make him love you, lose you, and deal with shit you cannot imagine. If he repeats all of what I did, he'll go through a hell that ends with you dying in his arms less than two years from now. That will both give him enormous power and strip away his humanity. Which is why he may do what I did and come back here, to this moment, in a bid to reclaim it. And you. To...make things work out better this time. In this timeline."

This was the full-on crazy my earlier words had only hinted at, but I saw Lena considering it. Maybe because I wasn't hinting or dodging around it; I was giving it to her straight. I think she could hear that.

"Prove it," she said.

I nodded. "Irene Gopal is a spy for your boss, Zhou Wenling, who also goes by the name Elizabeth Chan. Ms. Zhou does not work for or with Amazon. She goes by many names and backgrounds to keep the size of her business empire private so she can use her billions to do things like fund your research and, eventually, kidnap me to become her..." What had I been? "Her private time-traveling weapon against an organization called SCATTER."

It got Lena nodding quietly. Maybe because she'd already sensed something off about Irene Gopal and Elizabeth Chan. And with the sort of intellectual courage and keen focus that had always taken my breath away, she said, "Tell me everything. The key events. Start from how we finished this day in the other timeline and go from there."

She picked up the chair she'd knocked over earlier, fished a tissue out of a pocket, and blew. Then she sat down and nodded at me. "Go."

So, I did, walking around as I spoke to keep focused. I omitted her mother's death, Lena's rejection of me, the timeline where a Demon Monk raped her, her ex-boyfriend's attempts to kill me, and my sleeping with both Wenling and Océane. But I covered most of the other key events that took place over the fourteen months she and I experienced in the earlier timelines. It took some time, but Lena wisely said little that would stop me. When I finally got to the part where she died, I stopped short of her final words. My voice was hoarse. It was way past dinnertime.

I stopped speaking. I was beside the chair where I'd been shackled. My legs were tired, but I refused to sit.

She stared at me for a few beats, then asked, "What am I going to say next?"

"I don't know. It's a new timeline. I told you what we did in that one—worked on my very limited ability to jump all afternoon, so I turned down your dinner invite. You said you had to write a progress report on your experiments that you said would take all weekend."

She nodded. "Then you went out and took on all of Seattle's street gangs."

"Not this night. Tomorrow." I smiled crookedly, surprising myself that I still had a small sense of humor. She'd liked my humor once. I recalled that.

"You said I discovered proof that time travel creates new timelines rather than destroying old ones? How?"

"Something about establishing two nearly identical states of the same photon existing simultaneously. With people, unless you're directly affected by the change, things would still unravel as they did in the original timeline."

"The butterfly effect?"

"Is not as strong as people imagine."

Lena's brows knitted in deep concentration, her earlier emotional turmoil forgotten. It made my hopes, despite all the roaring disgust it was fighting, flutter up like doves inside me. I wondered if this hyper-intellectual part of her was the main thing connecting us. That even if I no longer had true emotions, she could still love me.

"You realize," she said at last, "that I don't know this you at all. I was attracted to that compassion and vulnerability you 'grew past.' This you is... I don't know."

The rage inside me roared hot. "You do. I am a heartless freak of nature who's trying to fix things that should be left alone."

Lena raised her eyebrows in surprise, and the beauty of them clawed furrows of pain into my soul. *In every timeline,* her ghost whispered. *I was born to love you and be with you. Tell me to get my head out of my ass.* But that ghost, hadn't truly known *this* me. This monster.

Lena shook her head. "I never said you shouldn't fix things. With the power you have? If you truly have that, you need to fix things."

I nodded. "I'm...trying."

"Give me the list. What you're going to fix."

I gave her the list. I told her what I'd done already in this timeline and what I still planned to do.

She fed my still-to-do's back to me. "One, meet with a patrol officer named Bryan Miller and give him information about the organization and plans of a street gang named the Demon Monks. Good. Two, kick your best friend out of the double-agent mess in this timeline as well. Three, contact Zhou Wenling and promise to take her to where her brother is if she can put together an army big enough and if she lets you lead the raid of this time traveler organizatio n..."

"SCATTER."

"Right. I assume that's so you can save your brother? Kentucky, right?"

"Yes."

"I want to meet him sometime. Four, release to the press the full story about SCATTER, including its CIA beginnings and its current followers who exist in all levels of power around the world. You're certain *I* gave you the list of followers?"

"The you in the other timeline, fourteen months from now, yes. You got it from my sister, Kansas. I will need to speak to her before I release the names."

"And tell her about the Chinese developing a bioweapon."

I frowned over that one. I'd been torn about how to handle that knowledge and Lena had instantly given me the perfect person to alert. "Yes," I said.

She nodded and chewed her lips absorbing it all. "So, we'll make it five things. You also said there's one last thing to be shared later. Why later?"

"It can only come after I manage the first four things, and you do two things in your own life."

Again, the raised eyebrows. "Do tell."

"You need to visit your parents tomorrow," I said. "Tonight, if possible. You need to convince your mother to get vaccinated, wear masks, and take serious precautions. I know she doesn't 'believe in it' or whatever. But as things stand right now, she's going to be in the hospital with COVID in five days. Dead in seven." *And you start falling away from me in eight or nine.*

Lena's jaw dropped. "How do you...? What if she's already...?"

"Get her checked. They have drugs that work better if you catch it early. Do something."

She froze for a second, then nodded.

"Number two, start looking for alternative funding for your research. If I'm successful with Wenling, I doubt she's going to feel the need to keep backing it, and it's important work. Go government, if you have to, but insist on unfettered publication. I bet Jude could get you some introductions."

Lena nodded. She again regarded me long and hard, her mouth twitched, then she stood and walked to me. She wrapped her arms around my neck, pulling her body in tight to mine so I could feel every soft shape of her, the heat of her, the perfume. It made me *want* to tremble. Even more when she reached her nose into my neck and nuzzled it, smelling me, then tasting me. She took my hand with one of hers and put it to her breast, while her other hand went down to my crotch and massaged it. Squeezed. Held it.

"Okay, that's different," she said to my total lack of response. "You still smell like the man I had sex with last night. Who blew my mind and pretty much stole my heart. I know how *that* man responded. And that mind. Different. But I confess I still get a sense, somehow, that he's still in there. In you. You still want to do what's right for people."

"I do."

She released me but not to step back. She reached up and cupped my face with both her hands. "Come to where I'm staying. Have dinner with me. Maybe I want to see if I can fix this new you."

I wanted to say yes again, but my tongue froze. If I went, my penis would still sleep. My heart would be unyielding. Because the only fire I had inside was a barely contained contempt for the world, for love, even for Lena. Even as my memories told me this was not right. Not healthy. Not who I wanted to be.

It meant I had to handle everything so carefully. If I did not, I could lose it all for good.

I dropped my head. "After," I said quietly. "Put your work on hold and go see your mother. Take your time with it. You know what I'll be doing."

So, she did. And I did.

I connected with Bryan at Ziggy's like we had the first time. Like it was meant to be. Like both those guys also somehow saw through my cold nihilism to something deeper. Or I like to think they did.

Bryan took what I said about Undercover Detective James "Dead Eyes" Gillespie to heart when I talked about how he needed saving. And he knew where to pass the information about the Demon Monks and their plans.

From there, I decided a phone call to Wenling wouldn't do, so I took a chance and drove all the way out to her house near Davenport where she'd first wooed and abused me. She was there, surprised I had come to her uninvited. Then not surprised at all when I told her what we were going to do together. Raising a time traveler brother had obviously made her open to such ideas.

She'd always been smart. Like Bent.

During the few days it took her to organize her army, I taught my final classes of 2021 at UW, prepped the exams, and graciously turned down the offers to take an extended two-year teaching contract. I was keeping options open for the me I hoped to recover, especially since I didn't know how long that recovery would take.

I also had a video call with Jude which was a little trickier than the in-person meeting I'd had with him in his apartment because I didn't know if his line was tapped. On the video call, I told him in code that he had to end his work for the evil empire immediately, and I'd follow up later. I didn't want him to be visiting SCATTER when I showed up there with Wenling's army.

That army, I discovered, was peppered with active federal officers. Wenling still let me lead them, in full battle gear with an assault rifle and battle coms. We hit the 22nd, 23rd, and 24th floors of the Ganouche Building on North Arlington Ridge Road on a Friday afternoon, taking it with little struggle. We escorted all the Pit prisoners out to supervised care where they would be providing statements before any release. Our federal officers arrested twenty-three SCATTER personnel, including Uwe Bent and Gordon Trench.

Wenling took Xiaobo into her personal custody.

I took Kenny into mine.

He just smiled when I brought him out and drove him to our family home in Renton. There, Carmelita crowed with happiness to see us both and to care for him until I had a proper detox center lined up. This version of him hadn't been through the bombing of Site 2, but he'd seen a version of me order the raid on Chinese laboratories. He'd lived through a nuclear holocaust.

Some part of him wanted to survive enough that I hoped this time he was going to finally get clean.

And the love I felt for him through all my coldness, the strange feeling that resembled happiness at bringing my lost brother home? Like my love for Lena, it gave me hope I was not completely lost to the world. Not yet.

This helped when I called my sister and insisted on a secure video protocol before giving her a version of the last fourteen months suited to her understanding. She told me they were already working on bioweapon chatter, but this would focus things considerably. When I gave her the list of True Believers, it might have been the first time I'd ever heard her swear out loud in a way that would have left the old me speechless.

"You're giving it to the media tomorrow?" she asked.

"Anonymously. Yes."

"Delay it a few days? I can at least make sure the heads of the intel agencies who aren't on this list are prepped. We're going to need a clean house to handle all the rest of it."

"I'll give you a week."

"Thank you. And Jackson?

There was something strange in her voice. "Yes?"

"Halfway through this conversation, I...started having flashes of huge pieces of it, like a dream. Is that something?"

"We need a longer conversation to get into that. Simple answer? It's not time travel, but it's linked to the Traine memory. You told me all about it in an email Lena showed me. In the future. A different timeline."

"I think I remember a bit of that. About Lena. And...oh, my God. Elizabeth?"

The shakiness in her voice unnerved me. I'd never heard her this uncertain about anything.

"Stop frowning," she said. "It's a lot to take in all at once. Even for me. And I'm glad you made it back, Jacky. I love you."

"And I, you," I said tonelessly, then hung up.

But while my earlier self might have been blown away by my big sister's declaration of both uncertainty and love, this me was...intrigued. Because the love I felt for her, like the love I felt for my brother, was like a strong buzz that ran below my disconnected emotions. Not as disconcerting and urgent as my need to fix the world and connect with Lena, but powerful. I was sure it would be a part of the last puzzle piece, the fifth thing on my list I needed to put in place to make everything work.

To find that piece, I used the contact information which the Lena in my Harbin timeline gave me to track down a charming young man named Wissam Saleh. Like Bryan and Ziggy, he, too, seemed to hear something in me that I struggled to. Enough to trust me with the address and contact information of his mother's sister's son, Salim Noor al-Rashid. Wissam told me his cousin did not have a phone or internet, though. So, I wrote Salim a long letter, knowing that if it ever fell in the wrong hands, it could get me arrested or involuntarily committed.

I estimate it took six days for the letter to reach him. On the morning of that sixth day, I received a phone call and spoke to the man whose face I had seen up close, but whose voice I had only ever heard say, Salaam.

We talked. Reached an agreement. I hung up and called Lena.

This time, she and I met in my apartment.

It was the day after I'd released the story of SCATTER and the list of True Believers. The newspapers were full of it and of the crackdowns that had already been going on behind the scenes.

That may have been one reason Lena's face was so flushed when she arrived, radiating even more inner peace and excitement than the first time we'd gone out to dinner together. Her trip to see her parents had gone amazingly well, marking a difficult but positive shift in their relationship. Her mother was still alive. And I was her (mostly anonymous) hero.

"The funding for your research?" I asked.

I hadn't hugged her or commented on the figure-hugging dress she wore and the way its forest green made her skin glow in the candles I'd set on the coffee table. I saw it. I knew what it said. What it should have done to me. But my insides, for all their sense of having righted wrongs and saved people in *this* timeline, were still barren.

My discussion with Salim had made it clear to me what I had lost, just as he had once lost it. For good reason. For survival. Because, like me, he had been too much in the world, too hurt by it. And so had separated himself from all attachment to it. Yet he had known, as I did now, that he could not stay cut off from life or he would perish.

"Well?" Lena asked.

I realized I'd completely missed her answer to my question. My ear had heard it though, so I could review it. Wenling wanted to continue funding her research. "Why?" I asked.

"Personal interest? You said her brother's a time traveler. Isn't that enough?"

"Maybe."

She smiled. "So, are we going to eat some good food or eat something more interesting?"

I must have looked stricken because she quickly backtracked.

"I mean, um, dinner, of course. I don't... I'm sorry. It's just...I *see* you now. Like you're hiding, but trying to get out, and a part of me really wants to help that happen."

I held out my hand. "Lena, come over here and sit down."

Suddenly nervous, she hesitated. "The fifth thing on your list?"

"Yes."

She took my hand and let me lead her to my couch. The sun had just set to the west. I remembered thinking shortly after I'd rented this apartment that when the lights over the east Capitol Hill and Arboretum started coming on, it was as if they were wiping out the struggles of the day with fairy dust and magic.

When we sat, though, it wasn't about magic. It was about hard truths and promises.

Now holding both her hands, I closed my eyes for a moment to find a place to begin. And I saw her face, her eyes bleeding, dying before me. I said, "A party trick I used to play when I was young and stupid? I'd repeat things someone had said, word for word. I never realized that if no one had a recording to fact-check you, it meant nothing."

"Whose words do you want me to hear?" she asked, squeezing my hands.

I opened my eyes and looked into hers. "Yours. The ones you said in a different timeline as you were..."

"Dying."

"Yes."

"Tell me."

"I can't. As you. Because they're not *your* words and might never be. But they are, I realize, mine. So…this." I found myself oddly calm and sure. "Every me, in every timeline was made to love you and be with you. But I need to get my head out of my ass so I can do that properly."

Lena had sucked in her lips. "Nice. Either by you or me. What will it take for you to get your head out of your ass?"

"A future friend of yours, a man named Salim, spent five difficult years working through the same thing that's happened to me. But he believes that what he learned, and what he knows of me, may help me get through it faster. As little as five months."

Lena blinked and pulled her hands from mine. "Seriously?"

"Of course, I *could* time travel back at the end of it. Show up here, tonight. Then the you in that new timeline would have an improved me almost immediately. But there would also be another you who waited five months, maybe only communicating with me infrequently. I'd know that person as well or better than I'd know the you I came back to see here, this night. Would you be comfortable with that?"

Lena sucked in her lips. "Hm. How many versions of me, in how many timelines, have we been together? One for every time you jumped?"

"Every time I jumped and saw you in that new timeline. Yes."

She nodded then sat back with her legs long and together, one arm up on the back of the couch and the other on her leg. "Do you know how much this dress cost?"

I shook my head.

"Enough that I want at least one version of me to get full value out of it tonight."

"It's a nice dress."

71

And balance

I'D LIKE TO TELL you exactly what happened when I healed myself and jumped back to that time in my apartment, but I'm still in Baghdad as I write this. What Salim's cousin said about him not having a phone or internet was simply family guarding family. In fact, Salim, as a teacher, husband, and father of three young girls, has a broadband internet setup that's fast for Iraq.

It's been enough that I've been able to exchange emails and make video calls to all the people in my life, keeping in touch and getting to know them well enough to imagine all the pieces of the story I just told that weren't in the Kansas-dictated version I read in Harbin.

The Lena in this timeline, before I jump back, is making new breakthroughs weekly in her understanding of the quantum dynamics of time travel. In between our love talks, we try together to understand how her discoveries might apply to human time travel. Salim and his family sometimes join these discussions.

As a consequence, I think Salim, his wife, Nazya, and his girls, Sama, Shada, and Shaheen have all fallen a bit in love with Lena. Especially after Lena brought her multilingual mother in on one of our calls to regale these Iraqi kids with Iranian folk tales from her childhood, all relayed in an Arabic that was so expressive I almost thought I could follow the plot without understanding a word.

My heart, in the midst of all this love, is expanding daily. I learned from Bryan and Kansas that the Pit time travelers, Bent, Trench, and most of the captured SCATTER personnel were never booked or registered anywhere official, so they're still out there. But I'm at peace with that. There are always terrors in the background. It only adds to the great balance I'm exploring, the middle way between distance and connection, nothingness and joy. In my conversations with Kenny, I share what I can, reassuring him I will be there for him always and will help him find his own way to handle his immense gift.

And while I am not religious, I appreciate the faiths of Salim, of Jude, of the Christians and Buddhists and other folk I seem to meet daily. There is meaning everywhere, lessons in every stumble and success. I used to see this in some of my clients. I hope when I return to my practice, I'll see it in all of them.

Because somehow, even though life can keep splitting into endlessly multiplying timelines, it has a pattern, rhythm, and beauty that make it a seamless whole.

Live.

A promise

Jackson Traine will return.

If you want to be informed when that's happening and about other things I'm writing, you can sign up for my email newsletter at www.terryhayman.com. You can also scan this QR code to take you there:

All the best.
Stay in touch.
Leave a book review on Goodreads.com or where you got this book.
Tell your friends.
Throw a starfish.

About the Author

Terry Hayman is a former lawyer who grew up in a military family with a father who was a general and a mother who was a beloved psychologist. He's a husband, father, and the author of many novels and short stories under various names.

Also by Terry Hayman

Novels & Novellas

Jumpback
Scatter
Unglued
Chasing the Minotaur
Jessica Falls
Shelter
Bone Dance
Raised by a Vampire

Acknowledgements

Last but not least, I want to express my endless thanks to my wife and soulmate, Faith, for her unwavering support through long process that produced this story. She was a sounding board, shoulder to cry on, and cheering section as I wrestled the more difficult parts of the structure into their proper place.

Thanks are also due my first readers, Rob Donovan, Adrian Chaster, and John MacMillan, who each provided useful feedback about where things were working and where I needed to do a bit (or a lot) of tinkering.

Also, um, thank you, internet? I know we're an off and on couple, I don't thank you enough, and you have many many more faithful lovers than I, but I couldn't have traveled the world like this without you. Please don't let AI (or trolls, bots, and conspiracy theorists) ravage you and distort all your wisdom. Even writers of fiction need the truth as a solid foundation for our stories. Stay strong.